D0369916

Also by Tiffany Reisz

THE SIREN

Watch for the next book in The Original Sinners series

THE PRINCE

coming soon from Harlequin MIRA

TIFFANY REISZ

THE
ANGEL

Recycling programs
for this product may
not exist in your area.

ISBN-13: 978-0-7783-1399-1

THE ANGEL

Copyright © 2012 by Tiffany Reisz

For questions and comments about the quality of this book, please contact us at
CustomerService@Harlequin.com.

www.Harlequin.com

Printed in U.S.A.

To Gina Scalera, my Angel. I miss you.

To Eve, the original Original Sinner.

And to Andrew Shaffer, *many waters...*

Part I

1

"Fudge."

Mostly upside down with her head hanging off the bed, Nora saw the ominous slant of sunlight sliding through the window and across the floor. Søren pushed into her again, and she flinched with pleasure.

"Eleanor, are you thinking about food at a time like this?" Søren thrust hard once more and came with a controlled shudder.

Laughing from her recent orgasm and the absurdity of having this conversation in her current position, Nora finished her thought. "You're the one who told me I wasn't allowed to swear on Sundays anymore. So, fudge, I'm going to be late for Mass, sir."

Søren dipped his head and kissed her neck.

"I have it on good authority that your priest would be quite displeased if you were late," he whispered into her ear.

"Then my priest needs to untie my leg from his bedpost."

Søren raised up and glared down at her; she innocently batted her eyelashes at him.

"Beg," he ordered, and Nora started to growl. Arrogant son of a bitch.

He never said anything about not swearing in her mind. Just that she could never curse out loud.

Søren put a finger over her lips.

"No growling. Begging."

Clenching and unclenching her jaw, Nora took a deep breath.

"Please, sir, will you let me go so I can drive my as— *bottom* home, take a shower, eat breakfast for once this week, throw on some clothes and drive back to church so I can sit in my pew looking prim and proper all the while imagining you naked as you're giving some homily on sin and how, shockingly, God's against it? Pretty please with you on top?"

Søren slapped the back of her thigh hard enough she yelped. But still he reached up and unknotted the black silk rope from her ankle. With obvious reluctance, he withdrew from her and rolled onto his side.

Now free, Nora started to crawl out of his bed.

Søren propped his head on his hand and stretched languidly across his white sheets. She wasn't going to look at him. If she looked at Søren, she'd crawl right back to him.

"In a hurry, little one?"

"To leave you? No. To not be late for Mass and earn yet another beating this week? Yes." Søren caressed the back of her calf and Nora turned back to stare daggers at him. "Are you trying to make me late…sir?"

Sighing, Søren pulled his hand away from her. It wasn't fair. The rectory stood all of two minutes' walk from the church; being male and not having to worry about what outfit to wear, Søren could get ready in ten minutes.

"A vicious accusation, Eleanor. Of course I would never try to make you late. You are a role model for the young people in the church after all."

Snorting a laugh, Nora started picking up her clothes. She pulled her shirt off the top of the bedpost she been tied to last night while Søren had flogged her senseless. Her skirt lay in a crumpled heap on the floor where it had landed after Søren unzipped it and let it fall before bending her over his bed and strapping her ankles to a spreader bar. Somewhere under his bed she found her bra, and her underwear was at home in a drawer. She rarely bothered with underwear around Søren—counterproductive really.

"A role model? Nora Sutherlin—erotica writer, ex-dominatrix. It's a pleasure to meet you." She held out her hand to shake. Søren only looked at it and raised his eyebrow at her.

"You're a role model to Michael. He adores you."

"But Michael's one of us, sir." She smiled at the memory of Søren's anniversary gift to her last year: the virginity of possibly the prettiest teenage boy in the known world. Pretty, kinky and unfortunately deeply troubled. "Of course he's got a soft spot for me. Or a wet spot. Anyway, none of those vanilla twerps at church need to look up to me."

Nora shoved her feet into her shoes as Søren got out of bed. Her heart pounded at the sight of all six feet four inches of his perfectly sculpted, unashamedly naked body coming toward her. No one watching him now would ever believe Søren was forty-seven years old. And no one seeing them last night and this morning as he beat her and fucked her repeatedly in a variety of delightfully degrading positions would have dreamed he was one of the most respected Catholic priests in all of New England.

"You give them hope that one can be an adult Catholic without being conventional or condescending."

"You're trying to say the kids think I'm cool, aren't you?"

"My sentiments exactly."

She turned her face up to him for a quick goodbye kiss. Instead he bent down and kissed her long and slow…deeply, possessively. No one had ever kissed her the way Søren did, as though he was inside her body even when he was only inside her mouth. After nearly five minutes of pure passionate kissing, Søren finally pulled back.

"Eleanor, you really should stop dawdling." His steel-gray eyes glinted wickedly.

Nora glared at him. "You bas—" Nora began, and Søren glared at her. This "no swearing on Sundays" thing was going to kill her. But she would do it come heck or high water. "Bastion of evil intentions. You just stole five minutes by kissing me. God Almighty."

"Young lady, if you don't stop using the Lord's name in vain, I'm going to reintroduce caning into our relationship. Are you really complaining that I kissed you?"

"Yes. You're cheating. You want me to be late so you'll have an excuse to beat me."

"As if I need an excuse." Søren smiled at her, and she was torn between the twin impulses to either slap him or kiss him again.

"I'm gone. Goodbye. I love you, I hate you, I love you. I'll see you at eleven, and I'll try very hard to listen to your homily this morning instead of having flashbacks from last night. But no promises."

Nora headed for the door.

"Eleanor…forgetting something?"

Nora spun on her heel and came back to him. Reaching up she wrapped her arms around his neck.

"Am I, sir?"

He bent to kiss her again.

"The bed."

Nora rolled her eyes. She pulled away from him and quickly made his bed, fluffing his pillows with near-hurricane force.

"There, sir. Happy now?"

Søren pulled her to him and ran his fingers over her cheek.

"You're here. Of course I am."

Nora sighed at his words and his touch. In the years she and Søren had spent together—those ten beautiful years in his collar before the incident, until she'd left him—they usually spent two or three nights a week together at the most. Then, after five years apart, she'd come back to him, and since returning, she spent nearly every free moment she could with him—at the rectory, at their friend Kingsley's Manhattan town house or at The 8th Circle, the infamous underground S&M club where Søren was practically worshipped. She hated being at home alone these days. The house seemed too big, too empty, too quiet.

Søren's hands left her face and reached around her neck. She heard a click, felt something give way, and Søren removed her white leather collar. As always, the moment her collar came off her neck, she felt something tighten around her heart. Søren opened the rosewood box that sat on his bedside table, took out his Roman collar and replaced it with Nora's collar.

"Jeg elsker dig. Du er mit hjerte."

I love you. You are my heart.

With a dramatic moan Nora collapsed against his chest.

"Do you know how much it turns me on when you speak Danish?"

"Yes. Now go. You're running late, and I believe you recall what happened the last time you were late for Mass."

"I do. But I sort of enjoyed it, so that's not much of a threat."

"I could threaten you with a week of celibacy, but as *I'm*

not going to be late, I see no reason to punish myself. Eleanor, you could always move closer. Have you considered that?"

She had considered that. For about five seconds before deciding she'd rather cut off her arm than sell her house.

"I love my house. I want to keep it."

"Is it the house or the memories you love and want to keep?"

Nora stared at the floor.

"Please don't make me move."

Søren had asked her over a year ago to move closer to him and the church. She'd said no then and she was saying no now. She knew he could order her to move closer, and she would if he made her. But so far it hadn't come to that. Søren nodded and Nora pulled away from him.

"We're scening after church again, right?" Nora asked from the bedroom doorway. Sunday afternoons belonged to them. Søren's parishioners always left him alone on Sunday afternoons. They assumed he was busy praying. Not quite.

"Barring divine intervention."

"Divine intervention, Father Stearns?" Nora tossed her hair with arrogant playfulness. "God oughta know better by now."

Throwing a smile over her shoulder, Nora gave Søren one last long look. He had, without a doubt, the most handsome face of any man she'd ever known. The most handsome face, the keenest mind, the wickedest libido, the sexiest body and the most devoted heart.... For the five years she'd lived apart from him, four had been agony. And now they'd been back together for over a year and everything was perfect.

Well, almost perfect.

As usual, Michael woke up long before his alarm. He lay in bed with his hand down his boxer shorts and contemplated finding a tie to make this process more enjoyable. But he'd promised Father S that he wouldn't hurt himself anymore. Father S had no objections to erotic asphyxiation but he forbade Michael from doing it alone. "We almost lost you once, Michael. I'd rather not repeat that experience," Father S had told him, and Michael knew he would never forgive himself if he put his priest—the man who'd saved his life—through that nightmare again.

So instead, Michael merely closed his eyes and conjured the memory of Nora Sutherlin tying him down, guiding him inside her and clenching so tightly around him he'd flinched. That one sensory memory worked as usual, and Michael came hard on his hand.

Forgoing a tissue, Michael got up and headed straight to the shower. He spent a long time in the shower, longer than most guys his age probably did. Of course, most guys his age didn't have hair that fell to their shoulders and a predilection for self-abuse in the literal sense. Scalding water wasn't quite as much fun as scalding candle wax, but it was the best he had.

After his shower Michael toweled off and dressed. He dried his long hair and pulled it into a low ponytail. He ironed his white button-down and his black cargo pants and even put on a tie. But not for erotic reasons…unless he counted trying to impress Nora Sutherlin as an erotic reason.

As usual, before leaving his bedroom, Michael rolled up his sleeves and rubbed liquid vitamin E onto the white scars on both of his wrists. The vitamin E supposedly helped scars heal and fade, but so far the effect had been minimal. He strapped his wide leather watchband on his right wrist and pulled a black wristband on his left before heading to his mom's room.

Michael tapped on her bedroom door.

"Go without me," she called out, as he knew she would. Still, he always had to ask. "Leave the car. I have to run errands this morning."

Leave the car...great. Good thing Sacred Heart was only a few blocks away.

He pushed on his sunglasses, grabbed his skateboard and his backpack on the way out the door, and hit the street. Skating straight up to the front steps of Sacred Heart, he flipped his board up and tucked it under his arm. Before entering the sanctuary, he went to the church secretary's office, dug something out of his backpack and sent a quick fax.

Michael headed to the sanctuary and saw Nora hadn't arrived yet. He sat in the tenth pew from the back, two rows behind Nora's usual spot. Her little shadow, seven-year-old Owen Perry, already waited for his Miss Ellie to show up. Owen adored Nora—Miss Ellie—and did nothing to hide that fact. He sat next to her during Mass and sometimes even curled up on her lap. Once Michael walked past them and saw Owen lying half-asleep on her knee as Nora mindlessly ran her fingers over his tiny forehead. Both of them had wavy black hair. Anyone seeing them for the first time would think Nora was the kid's mom.

It bugged him seeing Owen cuddling up to Nora. He envied that little kid for so fearlessly showering Nora with affection and attention. Michael would kiss her feet if she'd let him. But then again, he also envied Nora. She at least had someone who wasn't afraid to touch her in public. Michael couldn't even remember the last time anyone had touched him. Even his own mother had stopped hugging him after his father moved out.

Nora didn't just have people who would touch her in public. She had Father S, who touched her in private. Michael secretly worried someone would find out about Father S and Nora. Everybody knew Nora wrote erotica, and the church secretly loved having a mini-celebrity in their midst. And everybody at church worshipped Father S. But Nora and Father S had fallen in love when she was only fifteen. If their past, and even worse, their present, came out… Michael didn't even want to think how bad it would get.

Checking his watch, Michael saw he had just enough time to run for a drink of water. He stood up quickly and headed to the door. As he exited the sanctuary Nora breezed in through the front doors wearing a tight white skirt and a tailored black blouse. Her long hair was swept up in a loose knot and she wore a little smile at the corner of her full pale red lips. He could only imagine what Father S had been doing to her that morning to put that grin on her face—could imagine and often did imagine.

Nora came toward him and Michael froze. They never talked to each other—not in words anyway, not since that one night together. But as usual he gave her a little wave. Instead of waving back, Nora reached out and took his hand in hers for the whisper of a second. She squeezed his fingers and let him go, walking off as if nothing at all had passed between them.

Michael gazed down at his hand. She'd touched him.

When Michael looked up, one of the married men in the congregation who had a bad habit of flirting with Nora sat staring at him. Staring at him with a look Michael recognized as envy. Michael stood a little straighter and walked back to his pew. He paused a moment before changing his mind, taking two steps forward and dropping down right next to Nora. She didn't look at him, just chatted with Owen about a drawing he'd done for her. But Nora snuck her hand out again and pinched Michael hard enough on the thigh he knew he'd have a bruise tomorrow.

Michael smiled. God, he loved Sundays.

Suzanne woke up to find Patrick's arm across her bare stomach and his mouth on the back of her neck.

"Patrick, seriously. I'm sleeping." She pushed his arm off her. "I still have jet lag."

Laughing, Patrick nipped at her shoulder. She responded by turning onto her side, her back away from him.

"Sex is a homeopathic cure for jet lag. I read that somewhere."

Suzanne closed her eyes, pulled the sheets up to her chin and tried to remember exactly when last night she decided sleeping with an ex-boyfriend was a good idea—probably somewhere between the fourth and sixth rum and Coke.

"Last night wasn't enough for you?" Suzanne vaguely recalled at least two but possibly three encounters—once in the living room and twice in her bed. The third one may not have counted.

"I don't remember much of last night. Impressive 'welcome home' party." Patrick nuzzled into her neck.

"Patrick, seriously," Suzanne said when she felt his erection pressing into her lower back. Patrick could be insatiable sometimes—one of his better qualities in her estimation. Not that she ever told him that.

"It's Sunday morning. Let's fuck while all the Goody Two-shoes are at church."

"Mentioning church is not going to get you on my good side, Patrick. Or on whatever side you're interested in."

Suzanne felt the bed shift as Patrick rolled up. Turning over onto her back, she made herself meet his eyes. An IED had exploded not far from a convoy she'd been riding in right outside of Kabul two weeks ago. It wasn't her life but Patrick's face—his shaggy brown hair, soulful eyes and playful smile—that had flashed before her eyes. He was an ex-boyfriend for a reason, she told herself. Sometimes, though, she had trouble remembering what that reason was. This morning, she remembered.

"Shit, Suz. I'm an idiot. I didn't mean… God, I was so glad you were coming back, and I've fucked it up already."

"Shut up," she said, but not unkindly. "I think I heard my fax machine."

She grabbed Patrick's shirt off the floor and pulled it on as she left the bedroom. In the corner of her living room sat her small home office. She dumped books and notepads onto the floor. Readers lauded her newspaper and magazine articles for their clarity and organization. Those same readers might be amused to see how much chaos it took to create such organized, erudite stories.

Behind the second pile of books and notes she found her dust-covered fax machine. A single piece of paper lay on the Out tray. Her eyes widened as she took in the logo and the letterhead at the top.

"Patrick?"

"What's up?" he asked, buttoning his jeans as he entered the living room.

"Read this." She thrust the paper into Patrick's hands.

"Anonymous tip?"

"I think so. No cover sheet. No fax number imprint at the bottom. Bizarre."

Suzanne watched Patrick's eyes scan the page. He shook his head in either shock or confusion.

"Is this what I think it is?"

Suzanne took the sheet of paper back from him and read it again. "Wakefield Diocese—what do you know about it?" she asked.

Patrick ran his hands through his hair and looked straight up. She knew he always did that when thinking deeply, as if God or the ceiling would tell him all the answers. "Wakefield…Wakefield…small diocese in Connecticut. Safe, clean, suburban. Fairly liberal, pretty boring."

Suzanne heard the hesitation in Patrick's voice.

"Just spill it, Patrick. I can take it."

"Fine," he said, sighing. "One of their guys, Father Landon, was supposed to take over for Bishop Leo Salter. Last minute, he gets nailed on a thirty-year-old abuse accusation. So instead of becoming bishop, he's getting sent to wherever they send the sex offenders."

"They send the sex offenders to another church full of children usually." Suzanne's hands nearly shook with barely restrained anger.

Patrick shrugged and took the fax back from her. An investigative reporter, Patrick acted as a walking encyclopedia of every scandal in the tristate area. They'd met two years ago when they were both working for the same paper.

"Suzanne," Patrick said in a warning tone, "don't do this, please. Let it go."

Suzanne didn't answer. Sitting in her swivel chair, she curled her legs to her chest and reached for the framed photograph that sat on the corner of her desk. Her older brother Adam smiled at her from inside the frame. He was twenty-eight in the picture. Now she was twenty-eight and Adam was gone.

"Suzanne," Patrick said with quiet solemnity. For a moment she heard the echo of her father in Patrick's concerned tone. "This is the Catholic Church. They are their own country with their own army and that army is mostly lawyers. I know you hate the Church. I would too if I were you. But you need to think about this before you dive in blindly."

"I'm not blind. I know exactly what I'm looking at. An anonymous tip that says something's rotten in the state of Wakefield. And I'm going to find what it is."

Patrick exhaled heavily. "Okay," he said. "But you're going to let me help. Right?"

Suzanne rolled her eyes and tried not to smile.

"Right. Fine. If you insist."

"So where do we start?" he asked her.

Suzanne pointed to the one name on the fax that interested her.

Father Marcus Stearns, Sacred Heart, Wakefield, Connecticut.

"We start with him."

Patrick grabbed his laptop out of his messenger bag that he'd left on her sofa last night.

"Easy enough," Patrick said, booting up his Mac. "What do you want to know about him?"

Suzanne stared at the picture of Adam again. Had Adam not died, he would have turned thirty-four this month.

"Everything."

Nora bit back a grin as Michael, for the first time ever, sat next to her. Poor kid—for a year now she'd been waiting for him to work up the courage to talk to her. As young and fragile as he was, she didn't want to push him. Michael might be the name of God's archangel and chief warrior, but the Michael next to her easily qualified as the meekest young man she'd ever encountered. Out of a mix of affection and plain heathen mischief Nora gave Michael a quick, viciously hard pinch on the leg as Owen bestowed another one of his drawings on her—this one a seven-armed amputee octopus. She declared it worthy of George Condo himself as she carefully folded it and slipped it in her purse. A good morning so far— she'd been fucked by her favorite man, hugged by her favorite boy and silently adored by her favorite angel. But her happiness faded when she noticed a priest she'd never seen before taking his seat in the front pew. He glanced back at her with a disapproving glare. That didn't shock or surprise her. She'd received her fair share of disapproving glares in her day from the clergy, Søren especially. But then the glare passed from her to Michael. The mysterious priest looked at Michael with a mix of pity and disgust. Michael noticed the look and the color drained from his already pale complexion.

Nora's heart pounded. Did the priest know something about her? About how she and Søren had "helped" Michael recover from his suicide attempt?

Before Nora could descend into a full-blown panic attack, the bells rang, the processional music began and Søren entered behind the crucifer and took his place at the altar.

"The grace of our Lord Jesus Christ and the love of God and the fellowship of the Holy Spirit be with you all," Søren said. The visiting priest remained in his seat. Bad sign. A visiting priest almost always shared Mass duties. That he simply sat and watched meant something. Something bad.

"And also with you," Nora recited with the rest of the congregation. Søren seemed calm and unperturbed as usual. The visiting priest didn't bother him at all. Seeing Søren so calm did little to comfort her. Søren could be calm in the middle of a blitzkrieg.

Nora watched as Søren slid his fingers up the side of his podium and tapped the corner three times. To anyone else it would have been a mindless gesture, but Nora knew it was a signal to her. He wanted her to come to his office after the service instead of heading straight for his bed. Something was going on. Barring divine intervention, Søren had said. Nora hated divine intervention.

Nora turned to Michael and she saw her own fear reflected in his strange silver eyes. She looked up at Søren and whispered one terrified word to herself.

"Fuck."

2

Returning Owen to his bemused parents delayed Nora in the sanctuary a few minutes after Mass. By the time she made it to Søren's office, Michael already stood outside the door, leaning against the wall with his arms crossed.

"He summoned you too?" she asked, sitting across from him on the bench opposite Søren's door.

Michael nodded.

"Kind of feels like we're sitting outside the principal's office," Nora said. "I hear you're valedictorian this year, so you probably never had to sit outside the principal's office, did you?"

Nora waited and still got no reply from Michael. He smiled but didn't speak.

"Michael? Pussy got your tongue?"

He laughed...audibly.

"Finally," Nora breathed, relieved to hear something from him. "You have any idea why we're here?"

Michael shrugged. "None. I don't think it's good though."

"Michael, you didn't talk to anyone, you know, about us, did you?"

The look Michael gave her abounded with so much hurt that she realized immediately she'd been an idiot to even consider that Michael would say a word to anyone about her or Søren.

"Nora," he said, his voice barely a whisper, "I don't even talk to myself."

Now it was her turn to laugh.

"I'm sorry, Angel. I'm just being paranoid."

"It's okay. I didn't say anything, promise. I never talk."

Nora stood up and walked over to Michael. She sat beside him and stared full-on. He started to look away, but she snapped her fingers in front of his face and pointed right at her eyes. Immediately his silver eyes met her green ones.

"You talked to me that night," she breathed into his ear.

His pale face flushing, Michael whispered, "That was just a dream."

Nora blew air over his neck under his ear.

"We had the same dream then."

Michael's pupils went wide and she knew he was remembering the night Søren had given him to her—as a gift and a test. She'd enjoyed the gift. She'd failed the test.

"Are you doing okay?" she asked, taking a step back to give him some breathing room.

Michael nervously rubbed his arms.

"Okay, I guess."

"Did Søren give you that book?"

"Yeah. It helped. Thank you," Michael said. She'd passed on her old beat-up copy of *The Other Secret Garden* to him, a classic work on the psychology of sexual submission.

"You're welcome. Is our priest on the phone?"

Michael nodded.

"What language?"

"French first." Michael leaned closer to the door. "Now Danish."

"Hmm…that's good news and bad news."

"How?"

Nora returned to the bench and crossed her legs, a move that caught Michael's attention.

"French is bad. French means Kingsley."

"Who's Kingsley?"

Nora grinned. Who was Kingsley? Kingsley Edge, the King of Kink in New York City. Half-French, all pervert. Her occasional lover and Søren's best friend. Well, best friend on those occasions Søren wasn't threatening to kill him.

"French is bad since Kingsley gets called when anything disreputable needs doing. But Danish is good. Søren always calls his niece in Copenhagen on Sundays after Mass so whatever's going on isn't so bad it's upsetting the routine yet."

"Father S has a niece?" Michael looked incredulous at the idea.

Nora grinned at him. Søren did have an aura of having been sprung full-formed from the head of Zeus about him. One could hardly imagine him as a little boy or having parents, going to school and doing homework. But she knew all about his family—the good and the evil.

"Two nieces, one nephew. And—" she held up three fingers "—three sisters. Two American sisters, one in Denmark."

Michael looked up at the ceiling.

"Wow."

"Can you imagine having him—" she pointed at the closed door, behind which stood one of the more intimidating men alive "—as your brother? Terrifying, right?"

"I don't envy the boyfriends."

They laughed together even though Nora knew Søren hadn't gotten a chance to have any of the normal brotherly experiences with his sisters. He and Freja had grown up in separate countries and Claire was fifteen years younger than him. And Elizabeth…well, Elizabeth was another story.

"Come here and let me look at you," Nora said, tearing herself away from the dark trajectory of her thoughts. "How tall are you now?"

Just thirteen months ago he'd been only a few inches taller than her.

"Five-ten." Michael obediently moved to stand closer to her.

"I knew you weren't done growing," she said, remembering how she'd studied him as he slept that night. "You grew into your hands. Haven't put on much weight though."

He grimaced. "Don't remind me."

"None of that teen angst now, Angel. You're tall, thin, have perfect porcelain skin and supermodel cheekbones. And unlike mine, your long black hair behaves itself. You, young man, are prettier than any guy I've ever seen."

Nora studied him. Poor kid probably got ostracized at his school for his looks. He wasn't at all effeminate, but he had passed pretty boy miles ago and landed straight in the middle of beautiful. The girls no doubt envied him for waking up looking lovelier than they could after an hour of primping, and the boys probably hated him for inspiring homoerotic thoughts in their fevered teenage brains.

"If you say so."

"I do say so. And I'm always right about these things. Aren't you legal yet, jailbait?" she teased.

"Turned seventeen last month," he said, blushing.

"That's legal in this state," she said and winked at him. The blush deepened and Michael started to say something. But before he could speak, the door to Søren's office opened. Without a word, Søren crooked his finger at both of them before disappearing back inside.

Nora took a deep breath.

"That's our cue." Standing up, she held out her hand. Michael hesitated only a second before slipping his trembling fingers into her grasp.

Hand in hand they entered Søren's office. Despite knowing Søren for almost twenty years, she'd spent relatively little time in his office. Every member of Sacred Heart knew "Father Stearns's Rules"—no children under sixteen were allowed in his office without a parent present, no one was allowed alone in his office without the door being left open, private conversations were for the confessional alone, and no one, absolutely no one, was ever allowed at the rectory. Ever.

Except Nora, of course.

The rules were stringent but necessary in the controversy-wary Catholic Church. And in all his years at Sacred Heart, Søren hadn't caused even the barest whisper of scandal.

Nora and Michael sat in front of Søren's desk. Glancing around, Nora noted little had changed in the office since he took over Sacred Heart nearly twenty years ago. His neat and elegant office was replete with books and Bibles in nearly two dozen languages. On his huge oak desk sat a framed photo of his beautiful niece, Laila. Laila must be Michael's age by now. Nora hadn't seen her since their last trip to Denmark. Nora loved their rare excursions out of the country together—only on another continent could she and Søren walk down the street holding hands. But he was a priest when she gave herself to him, and he'd warned her before she made her commitment that theirs would never be a normal relationship. At eighteen it was nothing to promise him she didn't care about the sacrifices she'd have to make. At thirty-four she would still make the same decision she had back then, but maybe she wouldn't make it quite that easily.

Nora turned her eyes to Søren. She still held Michael's hand for comfort. But whether he was comforting her or she him, she couldn't say.

"Eleanor, Michael," Søren began. "We have a situation."

"Fuck, I knew it," Nora swore and didn't even receive the slightest scolding from Søren. Now she knew it was bad, very bad, for Søren to lift the "no swearing on Sundays" edict. "Someone rat us out? I swear to God, I'll kill them—"

"Eleanor, calm down. I said we had a situation, not a crisis. The priest visiting today—"

"The one who gave me and Michael the stink eye?"

"That one," Søren said with barely concealed amusement. At least one of them could find this whole nightmare funny. "That was Father Karl Werner—"

"God, I hate German Catholics," Nora, born Eleanor Schreiber and possessing not one but two German Catholic grandparents, said with venom.

"Father Karl," Søren continued, pretending not to hear her, "is rather conservative. If he gave you a dark look, Eleanor, it was only because your reputation precedes you."

"And Michael?" she asked. Michael was only seventeen and apart from scandalously choosing public over Catholic school, he was a model teenager at Sacred Heart: quiet, hardworking and about to graduate at the top of his class.

Michael sighed, flipped his palms upward and thrust his wrists out meaningfully. She didn't need to see his scars to know that's what he meant.

"Yes," Søren said with sympathy. "Father Karl is not pleased that we are home to—"

"A walking mortal sin?" Michael completed for Søren. Nora wrapped her fingers around Michael's wrist. She slipped her index finger under his wristband and lightly stroked the raised white scar she knew lurked underneath. A little over two years ago, when Michael was only fourteen, his conservative father had found out that Michael had a real and burgeoning interest in BDSM. Much like her when she was a teenager, Michael often hurt himself simply for the sexual thrill of it. Unlike her, it was his own judgmental father, not his empathetic priest, who caught him at it. Michael's father had laid such shame and guilt on him that Michael had slit his wrists one day and nearly died. Some Catholics, especially of the older generation, considered suicide the most dire of all sins. No doubt Father Karl thought Michael should attend another church. Preferably one that didn't still sport Michael's bloodstains on the hardwood.

"Father Karl's opinion of you both has nothing to do with his visit today," Søren continued, making it clear in his tone he couldn't care less about Father Karl's opinion on anything. "The reason for his visit today had only to do with me. As you both may know, Bishop Leo has colon cancer and will soon retire."

"And Father Landon is replacing him, right?" Nora asked.

"Father Landon *was* replacing him. Until three days ago when certain allegations came to the fore."

"Jesus H. Christ," Nora groaned. "Why priests can't keep their holy cocks inside their goddamn pants is beyond me."

Michael inhaled sharply and Nora grimaced. She looked at Søren and smiled apologetically. Søren arched his eyebrow at her.

"Present company excepted, of course," she said.

"Of course."

Søren stood up and came around the desk. Nora looked up at him and stared at his face. Everything about him was so aristocratic and aquiline. Even in Denmark, where pale blond hair and blue eyes were the rule and not the exception like here in America, Søren still stood out for his height and his undeniable male beauty.

"With Father Landon's transfer there remains the question of who will replace Bishop Leo." Søren paused. The implication of his words hit Nora harder than a rattan cane across the thighs.

"Oh, shit. Søren." Nora covered her mouth with her hand.

"Well put," he said, nodding.

"What's going on?" Michael asked. "This is bad, right?"

"Very bad." Nora turned to Michael. "Our Father Stearns might be the next bishop of the diocese."

Michael looked up sharply at Søren.

"Oh, shit," he said.

"I'm afraid I can't disagree. That Father Karl came here in person means I'm at the very least on the short list of candidates."

Nora closed her eyes. Bishop…if Søren became the bishop he'd be the priest to all the priests in the diocese. He'd have to leave the Sacred Heart rectory where a few hundred trees gave him near-total privacy and move to a home he'd have to share with other priests. His already busy schedule would turn hectic and she would rarely if ever get to see him. And that's if he got the job. Which he would, unless they found out about her and Søren's extracurricular activities.

"Can't you just tell them no?"

"Not without raising both ire and suspicion. This is supposed to be a great honor."

"Honor my ass," Nora said and saw Michael suppress a laugh. "I don't mean that literally," she said to him and noticed again what a gorgeous young man he was turning into. "Okay, maybe I do."

"Eleanor, five minutes of decorum is all I ask," Søren said.

"I'm sorry," she said and meant it. "I'm just a little bit terrified. What's the plan?"

She knew Søren. He wouldn't be freaking her out with something like this unless he already had a plan.

"Usually the vetting process for a new bishop is one to two years. With the bishop growing weaker every day, they will attempt to have a new bishop installed by August at the latest."

Today was May 16th.

"So what do we do for the next two and a half months?" she asked.

"You two will do nothing." Søren eyed her and Michael. "I will handle this. The diocese will investigate me, of course. This is not a concern. Even if they do discover something about our personal life, Eleanor, the Church will do what it always does when faced with imminent scandal."

"Hush it up," Nora supplied, and Søren didn't disagree. "But?"

"But tomorrow morning an article will appear in the *Times* about Father Landon. The press will likely descend on the diocese and involve themselves thoroughly in the investigation."

"The press, huh? Explains why you were on the phone with Kingsley already today."

Kingsley had a fascinating relationship with the press— fascinating in the way the sack of Rome by invading Barbarian hordes was fascinating. A reporter once threatened to run a story exposing one of Kingsley's clients—an internationally renowned human-rights attorney—as a transvestite with multiple sexual fetishes. Two nights before the story ran, a sex tape that the reporter and her husband had made played in an endless loop on every computer in their six-year-old's exclusive private school. The video was unremovable. All two hundred computers had to be scrapped and replaced.

The story never ran.

"I'd rather not resort to any of Kingsley's methods to keep our private life private," Søren said. Søren might be a sadist but he only hurt people consensually. "But his information is often invaluable. Rest assured, Eleanor, I will find a way to avoid becoming the next bishop. That is not why I called you both here."

"I'm already dying not to know why you called us here," Nora said. Something in Søren's gray eyes warned her that whatever he was about to say, she wasn't going to like it.

"You and Michael are the only two members of Sacred Heart who know who and what I am. The press will come, and they will ask questions. I cannot ask either of you to lie for me. And as I know neither of you will tell the truth when asked—"

"Damn straight," Michael said under his breath, and Nora said a prayer of thanks for Michael's loyalty. She knew Michael credited Søren with saving his life. She'd never heard the whole story, but she knew Søren had risked his career by telling Michael the truth about himself and his relationship with Nora. The night she and Michael spent together over a year ago was Søren's reward to Michael for going an entire year without harming himself again. Although an unusually wise and mature teenager then and now, Michael had been fifteen the night she'd taken his virginity. Sixteen, not fifteen, was legal age in Connecticut and New York, and that made their night together a crime. She'd done the deed not knowing his age, but Søren had made the introductions.

"Okay. So Michael and I aren't allowed to lie about you? Vow of silence then?"

Søren smiled. "You taking a vow of silence, Eleanor, is as likely as you taking a vow of celibacy. No, I think it's best that you both leave town while this is going on. Together."

Silence descended on the room like a shroud.

"Can I talk to you alone for one minute please, sir?" Nora asked, and Søren released a much put-upon sigh.

"Michael, would you mind?"

Michael stood up and left the office.

"Are you insane?"

"Little one, who owns you?"

Nora sunk back into her chair.

"You, sir. But you really want—"

"Eleanor, if a reporter asked you if we were lovers what would you do?"

"I'd tell him to mind his own goddamn business. Then I'd have Kingsley freeze his credit cards and bank accounts for the week just for fun."

Søren raised his eyebrow.

"Okay. Point taken," she said.

"I need to able to deal with this situation without worrying about you. But the most important reason is Michael. He needs you."

"Needs me for what?"

"What you are best at," Søren said simply.

"You expect me to *train* Michael?" Nora asked, aghast. "I was a pay-for-play dominatrix, remember? Training wasn't my area. Surely there's someone else—"

"There's no one else I trust. And no one else Michael trusts. He starts college in the fall. This summer is our last chance to help him."

Nora heard something underneath Søren's words, and a shiver of worry rippled through her. She hadn't really talked to Michael since their one night together, but she still cared about the kid.

"Help him? The last time I helped him it was because you were afraid he was going to try to kill himself again. What's wrong with Michael?"

"Nothing I can tell you, I'm afraid."

Sighing, Nora stood up and wandered over to the stained-glass window that adorned the back wall of Søren's office. Unlike the stained-glass windows in the sanctuary, this window depicted no saints or biblical scenes but instead a bursting bloodred rose. Nora traced one of the cool metal spokes of the beautiful window with the tip of her finger.

"Søren, we've only been back together for a year," she reminded him, reluctant to leave him for a day much less the entire summer.

"I know, Eleanor." Søren stepped behind her and wrapped his arms around her stomach. "But you have to trust me, trust that I know what I'm doing. I need you to help Michael. I need you to help me."

I need you.... The infamous underground community they belonged to universally considered Søren its top dominant. Søren had even earned the nickname the Alpha and Omega Male. But those words—*I need you*—had escaped his lips more times than most who thought they knew him would believe. During their five years apart, Nora would sometimes be awoken early in the morning by a phone call and those three words from Søren. Although she had left him, she never told him no on those rare occasions that he called. Sometimes even he could not rein in his own dark desires. *I need you,* he would say, and Nora would leave her bed and answer simply, *Okay. Tell me where and when.*

"Okay." She answered that need now. "Where and when?"

"As soon as possible, I'm afraid. And I'll leave the where to you. I would only suggest you go far enough away that no one would attempt to follow you."

"England?" she asked. "Zach and Grace are trying to get pregnant. This is something I can help them with. Or at least, you know, watch."

"Out of the question," Søren said. "I know how you behave in other countries. That you still are allowed a passport is one of the universe's great mysteries."

"That was not my fault," she reminded him. "The consulate cleared me."

"Eleanor…"

"Fine. We'll go to Griffin's," she said. "He inherited his grandparents' old horse farm, and he's been bugging me for months to visit. How's that?"

Søren heaved a labored sigh. "Griffin…"

Nora bit back a laugh. "Come on, Griffin's okay. He's one of my best friends."

"He's spoiled, juvenile and a coward."

He was also rich, gorgeous and great in bed, but she decided not to remind Søren of those facts.

"You always call him a coward. Care to tell me why?" She turned around in his arms.

"No. But I suppose even Griffin deserves a second chance."

Although curious what Søren meant by a second chance, Nora knew better than to ask. For a moment Søren stood in silence. He tapped his chin as he always did when plotting something.

"I'll allow you to spend the summer with Griffin," Søren finally said. "But he is not to touch Michael, or I will revoke both his key to The 8th Circle and you from his life completely. Understood?"

Nora blanched. Serious threats indeed. "Yes, sir."

"Where is his grandparents' farm?"

"Way upstate," she said. "Near Guilford."

Søren looked at her sharply and his mouth twitched in suppressed mirth.

"That area is rather close to where your mother is, isn't it?" he asked. "Perhaps you could take a day and visit her."

"Don't even think about it," she said, horrified by the prospect of Søren ordering her to visit her mother. "I'd rather go jogging in hell. Wearing stilettos on a hot day in Aug—"

"Eleanor."

"Yes, sir?"

"Your cleavage is chirping."

Nora swallowed and pulled her cell phone from her bra where she'd tucked it before Mass.

"Sorry. Forgot to turn it off." Nora silenced the ringer.

Søren stared at her. Nora stared back. As usual, Søren won the staring contest.

"It's Wes," she confessed, not even having to look at the number. Sunday afternoon—always Wesley.

Søren studied her. This time she couldn't meet his eyes.

"Does Wesley call you often?"

Nora nodded. "Once a week," she admitted. "Every Sunday after church."

"And why is this the first time I've heard about this?"

"Doesn't matter. I never answer."

"Why don't you answer the phone when Wesley calls?" Søren asked her in the same tone he used in the confessional booth—lightly curious, not at all condemning, and completely and utterly infuriating.

"Because you haven't given me permission to."

"You've never asked permission. Were you afraid I would tell you no?"

Nora bit her bottom lip, a nervous habit Søren had been trying to break her of since she was fifteen. Søren reached out and brushed his thumb over her mouth. Nora looked up at him.

"I was afraid you'd tell me yes."

Søren slowly nodded.

"I love you," she said, standing up straight. "And I'll leave you this summer, but only because you're making me go. But if they pick you to be bishop, I'm going to move to L.A. and convert to Scientology. Fair warning."

Relief washed through her at the sight of Søren's smile. But she knew they weren't done talking about Wesley.

"Michael's waiting for you outside. I think he would appreciate an explanation and a ride home."

"I can do both," she said and started for the door. She paused before leaving and turned around. "Can't believe I have to spend the whole summer without you just because of this stupid promotion."

Søren said nothing but Nora saw something flicker across his eyes.

"It's just the promotion, right?" she asked. "There isn't anything else, is there?" A sudden fear gripped Nora, a fear that Søren didn't want her around for some other reason.

"Kingsley called. Last night, someone broke into his town house."

Nora's eyes widened.

"Is he okay? Was Juliette there? What happened?" Her heart raced; Nora's mind immediately flew to the worst-case scenario—that Kingsley and his beautiful Haitian secretary were hurt.

"He and Juliette are both fine. They were…distracted last night. Someone drugged the dogs and stole a file from Kingsley's private office."

Nora collapsed into a chair. Whoever the thief was must have balls of steel. Kingsley's name alone usually scared off anyone who lusted after a piece of the reams of blackmail material he had on nearly every cop, judge, politician and lawyer in the tristate area. If his name didn't scare off thieves, then his well-trained rottweiler pack usually did.

"Just one file? That's good at least."

"Eleanor—it was your file."

"Mine? Why mine? I'm not even a dominatrix anymore." The words hurt coming out, more than she expected. While she'd been a dominatrix in Kingsley's employ, she bitched about it constantly. Now that she'd quit, she found she sort of missed it. Just another thing to add to her "miss every day" list, a list that was growing dangerously long.

"I wish I knew, little one. Kingsley believes an old client might be attempting to dispose of any evidence concerning him."

"Makes sense, I guess." Back in her dominatrix days, Nora's client roster read like a Who's Who of the rich, famous and kinky; Fortune 500 CEOs, high-level politicians and rock stars had paid through the nose to kiss the toe of her boot. "Doesn't matter anyway. Whoever he is won't be able to read what's in the file."

Kingsley and Juliette were the perfect team. Kingsley's files were notorious for two reasons—first, they contained the secrets of an entire city, and second, they were utterly unintelligible to anyone but Kingsley and Juliette. Only they could read the pages written in encoded Haitian Creole.

"It's the motivation, not the crime, that concerns me," Søren said. "Still, simply one more reason why you should spend some time away from the city while Kingsley and I sort this out."

"I could help sort things out if you'd let me. I'm not fifteen anymore, remember?"

Søren stood up and came to her. He held out his hand and she took it. Gently he pulled her to her feet and stared down into her eyes.

"You are my heart," he said. He'd said those very words to her that morning. But that morning they'd sounded affectionate and playful. Now he said them as if he were stating a fact of anatomy. "I will not lose you. I'm sending you away to keep you safe. Do you understand that? Say 'Yes, sir.'"

Nora nodded and swallowed a sudden lump in her throat. "Yes, sir."

Søren bent his head and kissed her long and slow before pulling back. Relaxing against him she put her ear to his chest. She loved hearing the steady beat of his heart. She'd called Søren dangerous, and to those who crossed him, he certainly was. Whoever it was who stole her file…she didn't envy him. But Søren was not evil. He had the best heart of any man she'd ever known. A strong and good heart.

"My heart," she whispered and gazed up at Søren.

"Rest assured, little one," Søren said as he ran his hands possessively from her neck down her back, "I may send you away, but I will give you a goodbye that will hold you all summer."

Michael waited outside of Father S's office hoping that was what he was supposed to be doing. He sat on the bench with his skateboard under his feet and rolled it mindlessly back and forth while recalling every word Nora and Father S had said. The priest who was going to be the next bishop was being transferred. Father S was on the short list of candidates to be the next bishop. Father S wanted him and Nora to go away for the summer. He was supposed to spend the entire summer away with Nora Sutherlin.

The entire summer…with Nora Sutherlin…

Michael had dreams like that. Just last night he'd had a dream like that.

Nora emerged from Father S's office and smiled at him.

"Good, I'm glad you waited. Want a ride home?"

Michael shrugged and stood up. He couldn't believe this—over a year without saying a word to each other and now she was offering to drive him home?

"Sure. Thanks."

The parking lot sat deserted but for a shiny two-seater silver convertible.

"Like it?" Nora clicked the button on her keys to unlock the car.

"Yeah. Awesome," Michael said, walking around the car. He bit his lip with suppressed laughter when he saw Nora's vanity license plate: it read NC-17.

Nora stood in front of her car and studied it.

"Decided to treat myself last month. Not as nice as my Aston Martin, but a BMW Z4 Roadster is nothing to sneeze at. I'm a fan of fine German engineering."

Michael looked her trim but curvaceous body up and down—talk about fine German engineering. He started to say that out loud, knowing she'd laugh at the compliment and the reference to her German background. But as usual he couldn't get the words out.

"Here, you drive." She tossed him the keys.

Michael reached out and caught the keys with his fingertips.

"You want me to drive your brand-new BMW?"

"You're old enough to drive, right?" She opened the passenger-side door and looked over the top of the car at him. "And considering I've let you inside my body, it's not that big of a stretch to let you drive my car, right?"

She dropped into the seat and closed the door.

Michael's knees buckled at her words. Taking a deep breath, he opened the driver-side door. He slid his skateboard behind the seat and sat down slowly behind the wheel.

"Let's talk," Nora began as he started the ignition and started to drive. "Well, you don't talk so you can listen while I talk."

"Just, please don't—"

"Don't what?"

"Don't say stuff like that again or I'll get us into a wreck." Nora laughed and squeezed his knee.

"All right, Angel. I promise I won't talk about the night I tied you down and took your virginity. If you insist."

"Nora, please," he begged. He loved that she still called him Angel. No one ever called him that except for Nora.

"Fine, I'll behave. For now. Anyway, here's the deal. Søren wants us gone for the summer so he can handle things in his own way. I think he knows that if someone started sniffing around me, I'd probably kick their ass, which, admittedly, might not help the situation."

"Probably not."

"And considering I sort of kind of committed statutory rape the night you and I were together, well, I think he's trying to keep me out of this whole mess as much as possible. And you too."

Michael put on the turn signal at a four-way stop. No cars were coming from any direction. As nervous as he was, he hoped they didn't encounter another car the entire trip home.

"You didn't rape me, Nora. I wanted it. I was fifteen, almost sixteen, not five."

He couldn't believe he was finally getting to talk to her about that night. He knew Nora and Father S were upset about this whole thing. But today might be the best day of his life.

"The courts have a funny way of not caring about the legal age of consent when underage boys and famous writers are involved. But hey, you aren't jailbait anymore."

"So what are we supposed to do?" Michael sent up a quick prayer that he hadn't been hallucinating when Father S had said he and Nora needed to get out of town together.

"I have a friend named Griffin Fiske. He's got a farm in upstate New York. I think we should go wait this catastrophe out with him this summer."

"Griffin Fiske?"

"Yeah. He's the son of John Fiske, Chairman of the Stock Exchange. Wall Street type. Griffin's a trust fund baby. But he's a sweetheart. Søren can't stand him, but Søren has terrible taste obviously," she said, pointing at herself.

"Is he—" Michael paused and tried to force the words out. "You know, one of us?"

Nora grinned. "Let's just say that in the Underground, his nickname is Griffin Fist."

Michael's stomach clenched.

"Oh, God."

"Tell me about it." Nora patted his knee again. She really needed to stop touching his knee. "So the plan—we'll go hide out at Griffin's place for the summer."

"Hide and do what?"

Michael pulled into the driveway of the small bungalow he lived in with his mother. Thank God his mom didn't seem to be home.

"This is where you live?" Nora asked with nothing but curiosity in her voice.

"I know it's not great. But it's a nice neighborhood."

"It's a palace compared to the house I grew up in. Do you like it here?"

Michael shrugged. "Things aren't great with Mom," he said. "She'll probably be glad when I start college."

"Where are you going?"

"Yorke. Got a full ride. Faxed in my scholarship acceptance letter this morning."

"Yorke? Good school. My old roommate used to go there. Anyway," she said and seemed to brush off a sudden sadness, "Søren said this summer might be our last chance to help you. Help you—what did he mean by that?"

Michael didn't answer at first. But everything within him

told him Nora could be trusted. That not only could he trust her but he should trust her.

He leaned back in the seat and shut the car off.

"Two weeks ago…I almost hooked up with someone I met on the web."

"A dominatrix?" Nora asked.

Michael nodded and said nothing.

"Michael, do you have any idea how dangerous that was?"

"I know, I know. Father S gave me hell for it too. I was just…"

"What, Angel?"

"Lonely. For you."

Nora reached out and touched his face. His heart fluttered in his chest as her gentle fingers traced the line of his lips, the curve of his jaw.

"Now you don't have to be lonely anymore. You'll get me the whole summer. Søren thinks you're ready to be trained. I think so too."

"Trained?"

"To be a submissive." Nora let her hand drop from his face. She got out of the car and Michael followed suit.

"I thought I was…" Michael glanced around to make sure none of his neighbors were out. He'd die if anybody found out what he was. "I thought I was a submissive."

Nora leaned back against her car and crossed her shapely legs at the ankles.

"Søren trained me for two years before he ever hit me or fucked me the first time, kid. Subs have to be as well trained as dominants if you're going to do it right and not get hurt."

"I want to get hurt."

"Different kind of hurt."

Michael hazarded a smile.

"Michael," Nora began and all the mirth had left her voice,

"being a sub is hard. Being a male sub is even harder. A woman says she wants to be tied up, everybody thinks it's sexy. A man says that and everybody thinks—"

"He's a fag," Michael finished for her. "At least that's what my dad thinks. Says I need therapy for my fetish."

"Forget what your dad thinks. I'll teach you how to be the best damn sub in the Underground. And to quote the wise and powerful Kingsley on the subject of fetishes," Nora began and then slipped into an exaggerated but sexy French accent, "'Fetishes…they're the pet you feed or the beast that eats you. We'll feed your beast until it's tamed. *Oui?*'"

Michael laughed. Feeding that beast sounded like a great idea to him.

"*Oui.*"

"Good. So you're in?"

"I've been dreaming about this for…ever. If you and Father S think I'm ready—"

"That doesn't matter. Do you think you're ready?"

Was he ready? God, for Nora Sutherlin he'd been born ready. Michael nodded. "I'm in."

"Great. Now how do we get you out of Dodge without your mom calling the cops?"

Michael scoffed. "You don't know my mom. She'll be relieved if I disappeared for a few months. Or forever."

Nora pushed her sunglasses on top of her head. Empathy shone in her green eyes.

"I'm sure she loves you, Angel. If she doesn't come around, you've always got us. I got in trouble when I was fifteen— big trouble. My mom totally washed her hands of me. Our priest practically raised me after that. How do you think I turned out?"

"Amazing," he said, and Nora curtsied.

"Your mom will come around, maybe. Hell, maybe my mom will eventually come around."

Michael hoped it was true. He missed his mom. They lived under the same roof but they existed in two different worlds.

"I'll just tell her I got a summer job upstate. I was gone most of last summer working as a camp counselor."

Nora mulled it over.

"When's graduation?" she asked. "You have to be there if you're valedictorian, right?"

"It's Wednesday night. I can skip though. I'm not valedictorian. I flunked AP physics."

"Oh, I'm sorry, Michael."

"I'm not. I flunked it on purpose."

"Why?"

"Didn't want to give the speech."

He expected Nora to chew him out for his willful stupidity. Instead she just laughed.

"I like your style. Look, don't skip graduation. Even I went to mine. I'll send a car for you Thursday morning." She pulled a pen and notebook from her purse. "Here. This is my email address. Keep in touch, okay? Ask me anything."

Michael took the sheet of paper with subtly trembling fingers.

She traded the sheet of paper for her keys.

"Nora?" Michael said as she opened her car door.

"What, Angel?"

Michael looked down at the paper in his hands.

"Thank you."

She smiled at him. "You're welcome."

"Father S…it's going to be okay with him? He's going to fix it, right?"

"He has his ways of getting anyone to bend to his will. If he doesn't want to be bishop, he'll find a way out of it."

Michael nodded, wanting to believe her. He hated the thought that Nora and Father S would get in trouble just for being in love with each other.

"You really think he's going to have to deal with the press?"

"The media is all over sex scandals in the Church these days. Probably so."

"What's he going to do?" Michael's stomach formed a tight knot of worry. But Nora only smiled at him.

"He'll probably do what I do when I talk to reporters— charm the pants off of them."

"Anything?" Suzanne asked and stretched out her aching arms.

"Not much. Every time I click on a link to a Marcus Stearns, all I get is an essay on the expulsion of the French Huguenots."

"Me too," Suzanne said and closed her laptop. She looked down at her notes. In four hours of searching online she and Patrick had found out nothing about Father Stearns. Nothing useful anyway. The anonymous fax she'd received hadn't merely been a list of names. At the bottom of the page the asterisk had been explained within four ominous words— "possible conflict of interest." That list of names told her two vital truths—Father Marcus Stearns was on the short list to be the next bishop of the diocese, and Father Marcus Stearns had something to hide.

"Dug around on Facebook, et cetera. A few parishioners mention him," Patrick said, flipping through his notes. "'Father Stearns performed a wonderful wedding homily from the Book of Sirach,'" Patrick quoted. "'I can't believe Matthew didn't howl when Father Stearns poured the water on his head.' Nothing exciting. Going from all this, we're looking at a perfect priest who's adored by his church."

"I don't buy it. Nobody's that perfect. And I've got an asterisk that says differently," Suzanne said, holding up the fax again. All day she'd been picking up the fax again and staring at the asterisk by Father Stearns's name.

"Suzanne," Patrick said, giving her a level stare, "the phrase *conflict of interest* could mean anything. You know that, right? He might have donated money to some political candidate the church doesn't like. It doesn't automatically mean he's a child molester."

Suzanne shook her head. "If it were that innocuous, no one would have gone to the trouble to send me the fax. We've got to keep digging."

"Fine. So what now?" Patrick asked, dragging Suzanne into his lap. She knew he hoped the answer would be *Give up and get over it*. But she'd only just begun to fight.

"You're the investigative reporter. What would you do?" she asked.

"Start making phone calls. Get the gossip from the locals."

Suzanne pulled away from Patrick and found her cell phone.

"You're the pro," she said, giving her phone to Patrick. "I'm just a war correspondent. Show me how it's done."

Patrick sighed heavily and flipped his laptop back open. Peering over his shoulder, Suzanne watched as he looked up the phone number for the chief editor of the Wakefield newspaper. Patrick dialed the number and talked his way past a few peons.

"Patrick Thompson for the *Evening Sun*," he said, and Suzanne was impressed he was using his own name and newspaper. "I'm looking into an incident that happened at Sacred Heart Catholic Church a few years ago. I'm sure you know what I'm referring to."

Suzanne covered her mouth to stifle a laugh. What a bullshitter. She and Patrick knew absolutely nothing about anything that happened at Sacred Heart in its entire history.

Patrick had been smiling when he called but the smile

faded as he listened to whatever the voice on the other end was saying.

"Two years ago," Patrick repeated and scribbled something down on the notepad next to his knee. As she read the words, the blood drained from her face and hands.

Patrick hung up and looked at Suzanne. Suzanne tore her eyes from the page and looked back at Patrick.

"Now you know why I'm going after this," she said, and Patrick nodded. "It's not just about Adam. Not anymore." She gazed down at the words again.

Michael Dimir, age fourteen, attempted suicide in Sacred Heart sanctuary.

One witness—Father Marcus Stearns.

3

Nora waited until after dark and drove to Sacred Heart. She parked her car in the shade of the densely wooded copse that shielded the rectory on all sides. As she walked the short path from her car to the back door of Søren's home, she smiled up at the trees. She remembered sneaking out to the rectory one Friday when she was sixteen, when she was still Eleanor Schreiber and Nora Sutherlin didn't even exist yet. She'd skipped school that day for no reason in particular other than the sunshine called to her, and she'd had a hunch that if she had to sit through chemistry, she'd end up chugging the acetone in the supply closet. Strolling through the woods behind her church, she'd come upon Søren in his backyard. Never before had she seen him wearing anything other than his vestments or clericals. But that day he wore jeans and a white T-shirt. Even in his clericals she could tell he was well muscled but now she could see his sinewy arms, taut biceps and strong neck without his Roman collar for once. His hands were covered in dirt as he dug holes with impressive strength and efficiency and put three- and four-foot saplings into the ground. In his secular clothes and sunglasses, the April sunlight reflecting off his blond hair, her priest appeared a being of ungodly beauty. The deep muscles in her hips tightened just at the sight of him.

"Eleanor, you're supposed to be in school." He didn't even look up at her from his work as he squatted on the ground and covered the roots of the sapling in black earth.

"It was a life-or-death situation. If I stayed in school, I would have killed myself."

"As suicide is a mortal sin, I'll absolve you for cutting class. But you know you are also not supposed to be at the rectory." He didn't sound at all angry or disappointed, only amused by her as usual.

"I'm outside the fence. I'm not at the rectory—I'm just near it. What are you doing anyway?"

"Planting trees."

"Obviously, but why? Are the two million trees around us not enough for you?"

"Not quite. You can still see the rectory from the church."

"Is that a bad thing?"

Søren stood up and walked over to the fence. Nora remembered how her heart had hammered at that moment. She thought for certain he could hear it beating through her chest.

Face-to-face with only the fence and a fourteen-year age difference between them, Søren pulled off his sunglasses and met her eyes.

"I like my privacy." He gave her a conspiratorial smile.

"It'll take years before you get any." Søren arched an eyebrow at her, and she'd blushed. "Privacy, I mean. Trees take forever to grow."

"Not these. Empress trees and this particular species of willow are some of the fastest growing."

"In a hurry for your privacy?"

"I can wait."

Something in his eyes and his voice told her that they weren't talking about the trees anymore. *I can wait,* he'd said and looked at her with a gaze so intimate she felt as if it was his hand on her face and not just his eyes.

She summoned her courage and returned the gaze.

"So can I."

Nora shook off the memory and entered the rectory through the back door. In the nighttime quiet, the only sound came from the creaking hardwood. She would miss that sound this summer, miss this house and the priest who presided here. Tonight would be their last night together until the end of summer and the bustle about a replacement for Bishop Leo had died down. Then she and Søren would be able to return to their own unusual version of normal life.

But only if he wasn't chosen to replace the bishop. *Please, God,* she prayed, *please don't pick him.*

Passing through the kitchen, Nora saw a single candle alight on the center of the table. Next to the candle sat a small white card, and written on it in Søren's elegant handwriting were instructions: *Bathe first. Then come to me.*

Holding the card by the corner, she dipped it into the candle flame and let the fire eat Søren's words. She blew out the flame just as it touched her fingers, and she rinsed the ashes down the sink. Like almost all parish priests, Søren had a housekeeper who handled all his household needs. Nora was grateful for Mrs. Scalera—a woman formidable enough that she could force even Søren to sit down and eat something on occasion—but Nora knew all it would take would be for his housekeeper to find a stray note from him to her, a single long black hair or hairpin, or any other telltale sign that a woman had spent the night to endanger Søren's career.

Nora started undressing even as she took the narrow stairway to the second floor. She loved the rectory. For seventeen years it had been her secret second home. A small Gothic two-story cottage, Nora knew it was a far cry from the sprawling mansion where Søren had been born and had lived until he was eleven. But that house had never been a home to him. For all its exterior beauty it had been a house of horrors. This place, however, had captured his heart just as she had all those years ago.

Breathing in the steam from the warm water, Nora let the heat seep into her skin. Søren often bathed her before their sessions. It was an act of dominance, the act of a parent with a small child, but more importantly, it relaxed her muscles so that his beatings would only hurt, not injure her.

Nora did not linger in the bath. Nor did she bother washing her hair. She wanted him, needed him. Tonight was their last night together for two or three months. Five years, she reminded herself, as tears welled up in her eyes. Five years they'd lived apart. Two months should feel like nothing.

But what if she left him and this time she couldn't come back?

She pulled herself out of the water and dried off. Wearing nothing but a white towel, she walked down the hallway to his bedroom. At first glance Søren's bedroom seemed an appropriate reflection of what he appeared to be. The dark wood of the two-hundred-year-old four-poster bed perfectly matched the wood of the floor. The ceiling arched like a church nave. The oriel window broke apart the moonlight that intruded into the room. All was neat, spare, humble, elegant and pious. Unsullied by modern technology, uncluttered by superfluous decoration, it was the bedroom of a man who had nothing to prove.

Still…a trained eye that knew what to look for would see

marks on the bedposts that were not the natural byproducts of time. The lock on the heirloom chest under the window seemed unnecessarily heavy for simply guarding linens. And the rosewood box on the bedside table didn't just hold his white collar—it held hers.

Nora's eyes scanned the candlelit room trying to locate Søren. She didn't see him. Instead she saw the bed... He'd changed the sheets. The white sheets were gone and in their place rich black sheets graced the bed. Black sheets meant only one thing. Nora inhaled sharply and forgot to exhale again.

"Breathe, little one," Søren instructed as he came up behind her and wrapped his arms around her.

"Yes, sir." In and out she breathed, dragging air into her stomach and pushing it out through her nose. Nora closed her eyes as he brought her collar around her neck; she shivered as he raised her hair to buckle and lock it closed.

"Down," he ordered.

Nora stepped away from him; her feet trembled beneath her. As she walked to the bed, Søren took the towel from her. Naked, she lay across the sheets, the black sheets, and forced herself to keep breathing.

Søren stood next to the bed looking down at her. He reached up to his neck and removed his own white collar. He unbuttoned his shirt and slowly pulled it off. Nora had never seen a man with a more beautiful body than Søren's. His morning runs and the five hundred push-ups and sit-ups he did every day kept him in immaculate shape. Lean, taut muscle wrapped every inch of his tall frame. Sometimes she could simply not keep her hands off him. But tonight she feared his touch as much as she craved it.

Søren let his shirt fall to the floor. Barefoot and wearing only his black pants, he crawled onto the bed, crawled over her. He bent his head and kissed her. She loved how he kissed her, like he owned, as he owned her. Sometimes Nora marveled at the thought that while she'd had more lovers than she could count, Søren had shared his body with only three people in his entire life. His devotion to her humbled her, and Nora wrapped her arms around him to pull him even closer. Rarely, if ever, could she touch him when they made love. Søren was a sadist and a dominant. When he took her she was almost always tied down, bound to the bed, the floor or the St. Andrew's Cross. Only on nights like this did he leave her arms and legs free. The act he was about to perform was sadistic enough no bondage was necessary to satisfy him.

Søren pulled up from her and reached to the bedside table. Nora's hands dug into the sheets, the black sheets.

Nora looked up and into his eyes—gray eyes the color of a rising storm.

When he brought his hand back she saw the small curved blade shining in his hand.

Michael paced his room while trying to decide exactly how to tell his mom he planned to leave town for the summer. He hated to lie to her. But he couldn't just come out and tell her that he was running off with Nora Sutherlin. He knew his mom knew what he was. Or at least she knew that he wasn't like other kids. The boys at his school got in trouble for *Playboy* magazines stashed under their mattresses or for knocking up the cheerleaders. But when Michael got in trouble it was for burning and cutting himself, for downloading pictures of men being tied up and beaten by women and even other men. And when in trouble, he didn't get grounded. He got slapped and thrown against the wall by his dad with enough force to leave bruises—the bad kind—all over him.

Sicko…pervert…freak… His father had said them all. When his mother tried to defend him against his father, saying Michael was just young and confused, his father had hit her too. The fighting had become an everyday thing, until his dad finally just up and moved out. Michael's mom had gone into shell shock and still hadn't completely recovered from it. The night Michael slashed his wrists it was with one thought in mind: maybe if he died his parents wouldn't have anything to fight about anymore.

Michael took a deep breath and left his bedroom. He found his mom in the kitchen putting away groceries.

"Hey," he said, rubbing his arms as if he was cold. He wasn't, but he had goose bumps anyway.

"Hey, you," she answered as she balled up a plastic bag and threw it under the kitchen sink. His mom was still pretty even after two kids and a marriage that had fallen apart around her. From her, Michael had inherited his straight dark hair, thin frame and pale complexion. From his dad he'd gotten nothing as far as he could tell. Sometimes he wondered if his father wasn't his real dad. No one on either side of the family had his color eyes. But he knew it was wishful thinking. He looked a lot like his father's youngest sister, so he knew there was no loving, forgiving real father out there waiting to be found.

"Can I help?" Michael had learned to ask before he helped with anything involving the kitchen. No matter where he put things away, his mom always came back and moved them to their mythical "right" place.

"Almost done. How was your day?" His mom opened the cabinet over the stove and rearranged the pitchers and jars on the shelf to make more room.

"Good. Glad to be out of school. I took your books back to the library. You were done, right?"

"I was. Thank you."

Michael shifted from one foot to the other. His mother's stiff posture and her refusal to make eye contact with him did not portend anything good. He wasn't sure what he'd done this time, but he decided now might not be the best time to tell her he was leaving for the summer.

"Okay, I'm going to go read, I guess."

"Michael, are you missing something?" his mother asked before he could leave the kitchen.

"What? No, I don't think so."

His mother gave him a long, searching look, a familiar look, a look he'd been getting from her for the past three years. He'd even named the look—he called it the *Who are you and what have you done with my son?* look. The long hair, the incident over the websites and the burns, the night he'd tried to kill himself... Michael knew his mother was convinced he'd lost his mind a few years ago and she'd given up all hope he'd ever get it back.

She shook her head and walked to the back door. She pulled his skateboard out from behind the open door and handed it to him.

"Thanks. I left this somewhere."

"You left it in the backseat of Nora Sutherlin's car."

Shit. Michael took a breath, decided to try a little deflection on his mom, a survival strategy Father S had taught him during their counseling sessions.

"It's a BMW Z4 Roadster. It doesn't have a backseat."

Her eyes flashed with anger.

"What were you doing in Nora Sutherlin's BMW Z4 Roadster that doesn't have a backseat, Michael?"

"Nothing. She gave me a ride home from church."

Michael's mother continued to stare at him.

"You know she's old enough to be your mother, right? I know she doesn't look like it and God knows she doesn't act like it, but she is."

"It was just a ride home, Mom. She's nice. She's not like you think she is."

"I think she's a very dangerous woman. And I think you could get hurt if you spend any more time with her."

Michael thought about Nora, how she lived so brazenly. Would he ever be as fearless as her? Michael remembered a few months ago he'd been lurking around the hallways after church, eavesdropping on Nora's conversations. One of the resident old bats had been going on about the abomination of sodomy. Nora had patted the woman on the back and said, "If it's an abomination, it's because you're doing it wrong. Bear down hard, then relax. It'll fit better." Then she'd breezed off, leaving the old ladies blushing and huffing. Michael had run into the bathroom and laughed his ass off in one of the stalls.

Fearless. He could do that.

"I like getting hurt," he said.

His mother shook her head. "Don't remind me."

Michael started to turn and walk away. He felt as though he'd spent most of the past two years turning and walking away from his mom. He'd much rather run up to her and hug her than walk away from her yet again. But that didn't seem to be an option anymore.

"I'm going to be gone this summer. I leave on Thursday. That's okay, right?"

"Fine," his mom said. He thought he heard a note of relief in her voice. "If that's what you need to do. You're going to be a camp counselor again?"

"Something like that," he said. "I'm good on money and stuff. So you don't have to worry about me."

"I've been worried about you since the day you were born. Won't stop now."

Michael tried to laugh but the sound didn't come out quite right. He started to leave.

"Michael?"

Slowly Michael turned around and faced his mother.

"You aren't really going to camp, are you?"

"Mom, I—" Michael said and stopped.

"I don't think I want to know what you're doing this summer, do I?"

Michael weighed his words.

"No, probably not."

Søren placed the first cut on her hip.

A shallow cut only an inch long, it bled out slowly. Nora's blood welled up and slid in a thin line over her hip, drying on her skin before it reached the black sheets.

Second, Søren cut her stomach right at the edge of her rib cage.

"Talk to me, Eleanor," Søren ordered as he made a third cut, only a half inch long, on her chest.

"Ow." Nora laughed a little. Søren looked down at her, love and desire burned in his eyes.

"It will hurt less if you talk to me. What are you thinking?"

"I'm thinking we haven't done this in a long time, sir."

The last time they'd done blood-play was over a year ago, just two weeks after she'd returned to him. That night they'd recommitted themselves to each other—Nora pledging to belong to him again, and him promising that he would do everything in his power to make her happy and keep her safe. Like their first night as lovers fourteen years ago, blood was spilled that night, her blood. Their very first night together, the blood of her torn hymen had stained his sheets; the night one year ago, the blood came from eighteen cuts all over her body. Eighteen…one cut for each year he'd known her, one cut for each year he'd loved her.

"It's for the best we do this rarely," he said, gently caressing the side of her face with the back of his hand. Søren seemed perfectly calm right now, his face a mask of utter serenity. But she knew him like no one else did. Under the surface of his placid demeanor rippled dark, dangerous and barely restrained desires.

Nora looked down as Søren brought the blade just underneath her right breast and made a deliberate cut.

"You love this," she said and Søren solemnly nodded. "We could do this more often if you wanted, sir."

"Of course we could," he said simply, and Nora smiled even as the eye-watering pain from the stinging, burning cuts bit into her. They could and would engage in blood-play every day if he decreed it so. "But we both do have to work."

Søren smiled down at her and she grinned through her tears.

"Work? What is that again?" Since quitting her other job as a dominatrix, Nora worked only as a writer these days. A job that required little more than drinking coffee and tea and wearing pajamas until four in the afternoon didn't really qualify as work to her. Søren, on the other hand, gave his life to the church. Up nearly every morning at five to run, he was in his office at Sacred Heart by seven at the latest. He heard confessions, visited the sick and dying, counseled married couples, performed weddings, christenings, baptisms, funerals and celebrated Mass four to eight times a week.... Nora knew if it came out that she and Søren were lovers, it wouldn't be the sex that caused the greatest scandal. Søren was himself nearly an object of worship at Sacred Heart and within the diocese. If the Church discovered he was a sadist who beat women, even consensually, he would be expelled from the priesthood. Søren would not give her up, would not repent and would never agree that their relationship was a sin. And so the Church would excommunicate him. Few outside the Catholic Church understood what excommunication meant.

It wasn't just being fired or kicked out of the church. Søren would be denied the sacraments, shunned and condemned.

"I'm scared, sir," she finally admitted.

"Do we need to stop?"

She shook her head. "Not of this. Of what might happen. What about Michael? What if it gets out what he is? What if they learn about The 8th Circle?" Nora didn't even want to think about how bad it could get if the press found out about them. Kingsley Edge guarded the members of their underground community with terrifying tenacity. But not even he could stop the sharks once the blood was in the water. A Catholic priest and an erotica writer who'd belonged to him in one way or another since she was fifteen…a teenage boy who'd attempted suicide over his sexual orientation and who had lost his virginity to Nora during a ritualized S&M scene…and The 8th Circle, where everyone from a high-level FBI agent to the governor's stepdaughter were key-carrying members. If the world found out about her and Søren, there would be no end to the digging. The 8th Circle, named for the level of Dante's *Inferno* where dwelled those who abused their power, would become a real hell for those who thought they had found the one safe place where they could be themselves.

"Eleanor, what did I promise you the last time we did this?"

Nora inhaled and bit her bottom lip.

"You promised you would keep me safe."

"I meant it. I will handle this, and nothing bad will happen to you or Michael."

The fifth cut was short and sharp and fell along the edge of her collarbone.

Søren set the knife aside and spread her legs. He kissed her inner thigh; the kiss moved higher until he touched her clitoris with his lips and opened her with his tongue. Blood-play made Søren even more amorous than usual. As blood welled up and dried on her skin, Nora felt her climax building hard and deep within her. Søren knew her body like no lover ever had or ever would.

"Permission to come?" she asked and knew Søren wouldn't deny her, not tonight. The orgasm, like the hot bath, had a utilitarian purpose. The more endorphins flooding her system, the more pain she could take.

"Come," Søren ordered as he slid a finger into her and pushed into the front wall of her vagina. As Nora's orgasm waxed, Søren picked up the small knife again and made a quick slash to her thigh. She flinched but only a little. The pleasure and pain danced together without touching.

Nora panted as Søren brushed her hair off her forehead.

"Can you take more?" he asked.

She wanted to say no and end it. The pain was almost too much even for her. But the intensity of it was heady, intoxicating. The intimacy of it greater than even sex. Only with Søren would she ever submit to this act. Søren did not demand sexual fidelity from her. She continued to see Sheridan, the favorite of all her old clients, and Søren still shared her with Kingsley on occasion. But when it came to pain, only he was allowed to hurt her.

"Yes, sir."

Søren pushed her over onto her stomach.

The sixth cut sliced open her shoulder.

Nora bit into the sheets trying to stifle her cry of pain. Turning her head to the side she swallowed hard and braced herself.

The seventh cut didn't come at all.

"Look at me, little one."

Nora turned over again, wincing as her raw and bleeding shoulder made contact with the sheets.

"You will come back to me. You believe that, don't you?"

"Yes, sir," she said, nodding. Søren had never failed her before. When she'd been arrested at fifteen, it was Søren who'd kept her from going to juvie. When her fuckup of a father had tried to take her away, Søren had stopped him. When she'd gotten into trouble at school over a story she'd written, it was he who'd come and pulled her ass out of the fire yet again. He'd helped her get into college, helped her graduate, kept her safe, kept her close, kept her happy, and shown her a world that few even knew existed and then had made her queen of it…and all he'd ever asked in return was that she give herself to him, heart, body and soul.

It seemed such a small price to pay.

"How many cuts tonight?" she asked as Søren studied her bleeding body with reverent eyes. She saw his chest heave; his eyes had turned black from desire. Blood-play aroused him like nothing else. And nothing aroused her more than seeing him like this…so desperate for her it made even him almost weak.

"Seven," he answered, his voice low and breathy. She'd already survived the first six.

"A good biblical number," she noted.

"Five for the years we were apart. And one for the year you've been back with me. And one for the rest of our lives."

The final one was always the worst. And she didn't have to ask where it would be. Søren waited and Nora worked up her courage. This was Søren, she reminded herself. The man she'd loved for nearly twenty years. She'd only ever loved one person other than him, and for Søren she'd given him up. If she could give up Wesley for Søren, she could do this.

Nora spread her legs wide-open. Søren positioned himself between her thighs and with shockingly steady hands, spread her wide.

Nora closed her eyes tight and breathed through her nose as Søren ran the flat of the blade along the seam of her vagina and left a small cut on her labia. She refused to flinch as she knew her bravery would be rewarded.

The pain had already faded even as Søren took her hand and laid the knife in her palm. Nora steeled herself as she raised her hand. With one swift and sure motion, she cut his chest over his heart. She lowered her hand and sat the knife aside. Lifting herself up, Nora brought her mouth to his skin and licked his bleeding wound. The act severed the last thread of Søren's restraint. He shoved her onto her back and opened his pants. When he pushed into her bleeding body, she felt a pain so acute it threatened to overwhelm her. Her safe word sat poised on the edge of her tongue. But she breathed in and swallowed it whole as Søren began to move in her.

She wrapped her arms and legs around him, dug her fingernails into his back and scored his skin. He bit at her neck and breasts, dug his fingers into her skin. Her body came alive with pain, pain that turned to pleasure as he continued his assault on her. She pressed her heels into the bed and arched back into his hips. When she came, she came hard. The orgasm racked her back. The pleasure spiked through her, clawed at her and cut into her like the sharpest of knives.

Søren kept thrusting and she clung to him in love and desperation. At moments like this, he was lost to himself, lost in the shadows that hid beneath his heart. Rarely did he let himself go, and when he did it was only with her. Nora lay beneath him and let him use her body as a vessel for his need. When he came at last, it was with a final thrust so fierce Nora knew she would be bruised inside from the force of it. He gasped her name as his whole body shuddered in her arms.

Nora held Søren as they lay intertwined, his body still embedded in hers. For a long time they said nothing, merely lying together content in their silence and their nearness to each other.

"You're shaking, Eleanor," Søren finally said, touching her cheek with his lips.

"A little. I'm just cold," she admitted. Nora ran her hands through Søren's hair and kissed his forehead.

"You're shaking too." His arms, his back trembled beneath her hands.

"Not from cold," he confessed. She knew why, and he needed to say no more. "You belong to me…always."

"Always," she repeated.

"I will do whatever I must so you can come back to me."

"I know you will, sir."

"And we will keep our promise to each other."

Nora reached up and touched his face.

"I will die in my collar." She repeated her part of the pledge.

Søren turned his head and kissed the inside of her palm.

"And I will die in mine."

Suzanne sat cross-legged on her sofa with her laptop open on her legs. She'd started a file on her computer called Asterisk and in it she was putting all the information she could dig up on Sacred Heart and Father Marcus Stearns. So far, it was a very small file. Patrick had gotten almost no additional information on the boy who'd attempted suicide in the sanctuary. No charges had been filed and the boy apparently still attended church there. What sort of kid would keep going back to the same church that had inspired him to kill himself? she wondered. Who was this priest who had that sort of pull on him? It turned her stomach just to imagine it.

She was dangerously close to thinking about her brother Adam when her cell phone rang. She checked the number. Patrick, of course.

"Any luck?" he asked as soon as she answered.

"Not much. This guy is a ghost. What about you?"

She heard a laugh on the other end of the line.

"What?" she demanded.

"I'm about to go into a dinner meeting so I can't really talk. But you'll never guess who goes to Sacred Heart. Not just goes but apparently never misses Sunday Mass."

Suzanne exhaled noisily. She didn't have time for games.

"I don't know. The Dalai Lama?"

"Even better—Nora Sutherlin."

Suzanne's eyes widened and her stomach did a small flip.

"You've got to be kidding me."

"I've gotta run. I'll call you back tomorrow. But no, I'm not kidding you."

Hanging up, Suzanne simply stared out at her living room for a long time. She closed her computer and headed over to her bookcase. Scanning the titles, she finally found what she was looking for—a book entitled *The Red*. On the cover was a picture of a woman's beautiful pale hands tied with a bloodred silk ribbon. The author? Nora Sutherlin. It was the story of a woman who owned a failing art gallery called The Red and the mysterious man who shows up and offers to save it in return for her submitting to him in every possible way for one year. Lurid and graphic with some of the most explicit sex scenes she'd ever read, *The Red* was possibly one of Suzanne's favorite novels. Not that she ever told anyone that.

A fourteen-year-old boy attempting suicide in the middle of the sanctuary...the world's most infamous erotica author attending Mass with the constancy of a nun...and that mysterious asterisk by the name of its priest.

"Jesus," she breathed. "What kind of church is this?"

4

Søren made love to Nora twice more that night. He pulled her to the edge of the bed and took her while she lay on her stomach and he stood behind her. And after that they lay side by side, her back to his chest while he moved slowly and gently in her. As he thrust into her, he whispered how deeply he loved her, how much he would miss her and what he would do to her when she came back to him again. When Nora came the final time, she did so through tears.

"Hush, little one…it's only for two months," he promised her as he kissed the tears off her face.

She clung to him and cried even harder. "But I miss you already."

Her tears dried, Nora lounged before the fireplace in the living room—Søren had built a low fire to warm her up again—and smiled at the sight before her. As if Søren hadn't tortured her enough already tonight….

Studying the board on the floor before her, peering at it

first through her left eye and then her right, Nora reached out and moved a pawn two spaces forward.

"Little one," Søren said with thinly disguised disgust. "That was pointless."

"Well, it wasn't a step backward so we'll consider it a step forward. Besides, I'm only playing chess with you to keep you awake longer," she admitted. "I'm terrible at this game and you know it."

"I do indeed." Søren moved his queen. Checkmate.

"Fine. You win," Nora conceded. "I'd kick your ass if we were playing Battleship though. That's my game."

"Battleship?"

Nora smiled. Søren had had such an unusual childhood that things she took for granted—silly board games, Saturday morning cartoons—Søren had no experience with. At age five he'd been sent to England to attend school. An unpleasant incident with a fellow student forced him back to America at age ten. A far more unpleasant incident at his home ended with him being shipped off to a Jesuit boarding school in rural Maine when he was only eleven. But it was there among the priests and monks that Søren found not only his salvation, but his calling. That and he met a certain young half-blood Frenchman who would change the course of his life forever.

"Battleship. It's this stupid game Wes and I played when we were procrastinating from doing our work."

"You so rarely speak of Wesley, Eleanor. And yet so many memories you have of him make you smile. Why don't you talk about him more?"

Why didn't she talk about him more? Nora shook her head and stared at the chessboard. Looking back she still wasn't sure why she'd asked Wesley to move in with her, other than he'd intimated that he might have to move back home to Kentucky as Yorke was a prohibitively expensive liberal-arts college. But as soon as Wesley was in her home, she'd begun to wonder how she'd ever lived without him. Before Wesley, she'd practically lived at Kingsley's Manhattan town house. She worked in the city so much that several days would pass before she'd return to her home in Connecticut. Once Wesley was there, however, she'd find herself racing back to her house after a job, throwing on normal clothes and curling up on the couch with him.

Nora would never forget the day she got tired of writing in her office and had taken her laptop to the kitchen just for a change of scenery. Wesley joined her in the kitchen and sat opposite her at the table. He opened his laptop and started working on a paper due in his European History class that week. Nora remembered casting furtive glances over the top of her computer at him. He had brown eyes with little flecks of gold in them and dark blond hair that fell over his forehead. Only eighteen then, he was utterly adorable, and sometimes she had to practically sit on her hands to keep from reaching out and grabbing him when he walked past her. They were just roommates, just friends, she always had to remind herself. And Wesley was a good Christian kid and a virgin. One night with her wouldn't just take his virginity, it would steal his innocence too. But that day all she felt for him was affection. Affection and amusement.

"Wes, I'm going to say it," she said, glancing at their back-to-back open laptops.

"Don't say it, Nora," Wesley said as he kept typing.

"I have to say it."

"Do. Not. Say. It," Wesley ordered, trying and failing to sound intimidating. His sexy hybrid Kentucky-Georgia accent made her toes curl but it did not lend itself to intimidation. "If you say it, I'm leaving."

"Wesley…"

"Nora…"

Nora took a deep breath, pretended to type something and whispered, "Wes?"

"What?"

"You sunk my Battleship!"

At that Wesley stood up and left the kitchen. Nora dissolved into giggles as Wesley threw on his coat, grabbed his car keys and walked out of the house. She was still laughing half an hour later when Wesley returned carrying a just-purchased Battleship game with him. Nora closed their computers and they set up the game on the kitchen table. She beat him soundly, two to one. After that, every time one or both of them needed a break from work, they'd sneak up behind the other, yell, "You sunk my Battleship," and the game would be on.

"Eleanor?" Søren's voice pulled her out of the memory and back to the present.

Nora touched her face and held out her hand. In the light of the fireplace, the tears shimmered on the tips of her fingers.

"This is why I don't talk about Wes," she said, and Søren reached for her and pulled her into his arms.

He bent his head and kissed her as his hand crept under the shirt she wore—his shirt—and slipped two fingers into her. She wanted him to make love to her again, but the moment had passed. A true sadist, Søren could only become aroused by inflicting pain and humiliation. So instead it was his prob-ing fingers that penetrated her. He spread his fingers wide within her, slipped in a third and pushed hard up against her pubic bone. Nora's hips lifted as her inner muscles gripped him. She grew wet at his touch even as the cut on her labia still ached and burned.

"Come for me," Søren ordered, "and then we're sleeping."

"I can hold off having an orgasm for a long time," she teased. "Anything to keep you awake."

Søren, as she knew he would, took that as a challenge. He pressed his thumb into her clitoris and made precision circles that left her panting. Still she breathed through the pleasure.

With his free hand, Søren unbuttoned her shirt and bared her breasts. He kissed her nipples and they hardened in his warm mouth. As his lips and tongue made languid circles on her breasts, his fingers continued their gentle onslaught inside her. Nora flinched and clutched at the rug beneath her. Still she didn't let herself come.

Søren slid his hand behind her neck and forced her to meet his eyes.

"The day we met, you were wearing a black pleated skirt and combat boots," he said, and Nora knew no matter how hard she fought him, he would win. "You had scrapes on your knees and wore too much eye makeup. And I would have laid you out on the altar, beaten you and taken your virginity in front of God, Christ, all his saints and angels, and the entire church that very day had I one ounce less of self-control. I would have drunk the blood off your thighs, turned you onto your stomach and taken you again, fucking you until you begged me to stop. And do you know what I would have done had you begged me to stop?"

"No, sir," she breathed, her heart pounding so hard she thought it would burst from her chest.

"I wouldn't have stopped," he said and shoved his hand hard into her. Nora cried out; the climax ripped through her stomach and hips as her inner muscles contracted wildly around Søren's fingers.

She lay underneath him gasping through the orgasm that was so intense her lower back spasmed. After a few minutes her heart slowed and her eyes were able to focus again.

"You cheated."

"I can't imagine what you're referring to," Søren said, carefully pulling his hand out of her sore opening.

"You brought up the day we met. That's cheating."

Søren rolled onto his back and Nora crawled on top of his chest and collapsed against him.

"You're the one who is going to be sleeping with two young men who are not me this summer, and you accuse me of cheating?"

Nora grinned up at him.

"Jealous?"

"Not even remotely," he said and she knew it was true. Søren's certainty in her love for him precluded even the slightest hint of jealousy. He couldn't care less who she had sex with as long as he owned her. More than not caring, Søren was aroused by the sight and thought of her with other men. He didn't even mind if she did kink with others as long as no one hurt her—that was his job alone.

"Speaking of jealous, Simone and Robin said they'd happily take my place on the rack this summer while I'm gone."

"Lovely girls, both of them," Søren said, smiling. If Nora was going to spend the summer in bed with two other guys, the least she could do for Søren was arrange for him to have access to two of the most beautiful, well-trained and discreet submissives in the Underground. She knew he wouldn't have sex with them. Sadism was sex for him. So Søren going two months without beating someone would be akin to her going two months without sex—horrifying thought.

"Now I'm afraid this nonsense will have to end. I'm hearing confessions in—" Søren paused and glanced at the clock on the fireplace mantel "—four hours."

Nora winced.

"Shit, I knew there was something I was supposed to do before I left. Will you have time for me before I leave tomorrow morning?" she asked. She'd meant to go to confession during the past week but had completely forgotten. Wasn't her fault. She blamed her editor Zach—the other sadist in her life—for sending her fifty pages to revise in two days.

"I can hear it now if you like."

Sitting up, Nora buttoned Søren's shirt over her breasts. Søren rolled up and faced her. And although he too wore his black pants and nothing else, the minute he met her eyes, she knew her lover had gone, and she now sat in the presence of her priest alone.

Nora took a deep breath and began.

"God have mercy on me, a sinner."

"'Are not five sparrows sold for two pennies? Yet not one of them is forgotten in God's sight. But even the hairs on your head are all counted. Do not be afraid; you are of more value than many sparrows.'"

Nora smiled. Luke chapter twelve, verses six and seven—one of her favorite passages.

"Bless me, Father, for I have sinned. It has been…"

"Eight days," Søren supplied.

"Eight days since my last confession. Let's see…where to start?"

"Pace yourself, Eleanor. If you forget something, I will remind you."

"Oh, thank you very much, Father. You are too kind. I have done some serious lusting this week."

"Per usual."

"I lied in a phone interview. Not the first time for that, either. They wanted to know summer plans and I said I'd probably be overseas working on a new book. Let's see…what else? Oh, I got a big fat royalty check and I didn't give a damn bit of it to charity."

"To whom much is given, much is required," Søren reminded her. God knew he certainly had room to talk.

"I know," Nora said and sighed. She did know. She just needed a refresher of that every now and then. "Does the church need anything?"

"Owen's parents have suffered financially this year. Not terribly but they may have to put him into public school."

"Public school? That little guy will get eaten alive in public school. He loves St. Xavier."

"St. Xavier is not inexpensive."

"Will five cover it?"

"Yes, and then some."

Nora nodded. Not that long ago she could make 5K in a few hours topping someone. Surely Owen deserved as much kindness as her clients received of her cruelty.

"I'll leave a check on the kitchen table tomorrow morning. Don't tell them it's from me."

"Of course not. Anything else?"

"Well, I did do blood-play with a priest this evening, after which came much fucking."

"Those were good works."

"I'll say."

"Eleanor, what else?"

She heard in Søren's voice an expectation. He knew she had more to confess.

"I lied about something else," she finally whispered.

"You never have to be afraid to tell me anything," Søren said, in that priestly tone that coaxed confessions like scared shadows from the darkest corners of hearts.

"You asked me today why I don't answer the phone when Wes calls. I said it was because you hadn't given me permission. That wasn't the truth."

Nora stared at the floor, unwilling and unable to meet Søren's eyes.

"What is the truth?"

Swallowing, Nora forced herself to meet his eyes.

"I think," she began and took a hard breath, "it wouldn't be good for us if I did."

Søren seemed to study her through the low and dying light of the fireplace. Her heart ached at the thought of hurting Søren. But he wanted the truth from her no matter what.

"Your penance," he began and she braced herself.

"Yes, Father?"

"Make your peace with Wesley this summer while you're away from me. Make your peace and do not return to me until you do."

Nora's stomach clenched. Make her peace with Wesley? What did that even mean? Just get over him? Or would she have to talk to him? She didn't know. She didn't want to know.

"Yes, Father" was all she could answer.

She bent her head.

"Through the ministry of the Church may God give you pardon and peace, and I absolve you from your sins in the name of the Father, and of the Son, and of the Holy Spirit."

Nora crossed herself.

"Amen."

Nora stood up with a heavy heart. She hated that on their last night together before she left, she'd had to confess something so hurtful. But suddenly she was off her feet and in Søren's arms. Without a word, he carried her upstairs to his bedroom.

"You aren't angry?" she asked as he stripped her of his shirt and laid her in the bed. He slipped out of his pants and pressed his naked body into hers.

"Eleanor, will you ever learn that when I say 'I love you' I mean it?"

"Eventually maybe," she said and smiled at him through the dark. "I'll miss you so much this summer. Are you sure I have to go? Running away really isn't my thing. Not anymore anyway."

"I'm afraid in this scenario, discretion will be the better part of valor. Eleanor, this isn't simply about the Church or the public finding out about us. There is more to fear than someone simply discovering that we're together."

"You don't agree with Kingsley, do you? You don't think it was just an old client of mine who stole my file, right?"

"I'm truly in the dark on this matter." Søren gazed toward the shadows that lurked outside of the lamplight. "Whoever it is, and for whatever reason…I will not let them harm you. I'd let them cut out my heart first."

Nora reached out and touched the wound over Søren's heart. A superficial cut, it would heal in just days. The wounds underneath, however, were old and scarified and likely would never completely heal. Scar tissue, she'd once read, was the strongest of all tissues. Maybe Søren's heart was so strong because it was so scarred.

"Eleanor? Do you remember my father's funeral?"

Nora closed her eyes and became suddenly seventeen years old again. She'd faked a good excuse for her mother and accompanied Søren to his father's funeral. She was there for Claire, his sixteen-year-old sister. Or at least, that was the cover story.

The night after the visitation she'd found Søren sitting in a large armchair in his childhood bedroom—a bedroom that held only the memories of nightmares for him. She remembered walking in and seeing him sitting, praying silently in a pool of moonlight. The white light had illuminated his face, his pale hair. On silent feet she came to him, and he'd taken her in his arms and held her. It had been the first time he'd admitted that he loved her, had loved her from the moment he saw her when she was only fifteen years old. His sadness and grief for the father who'd tried to destroy him came out that night as he told her the horror story that was his childhood. She'd only meant to comfort him. She'd made it to the next morning still a virgin, but just barely.

Nora giggled. "Oh, no. As long as I live I will never forget that night."

Søren caressed her lips with his fingertips. "I know what you overheard, little one."

Another memory came to her. This time it wasn't nearly so pleasant. After leaving Søren that night, she'd headed for the room she and Claire were sharing. The house had over a dozen bedrooms but Søren insisted that neither she nor Claire sleep alone. The minute they'd arrived at the house, Søren changed. He'd always been highly protective of her, but suddenly he'd turned almost paranoid with both her and Claire. He acted as if there was a dangerous ghost haunting his childhood home. And in Søren's arms that night she learned that wasn't far from the truth. On her way to the guest room she saw the outline of a woman standing by an open window. She stood with her arms crossed over her chest and her head bowed. Next to her stood Søren, and they whispered back and forth to each other. Nora had slipped into a shadow and hidden herself there. Closer she crept and heard the woman say to Søren three words—*I'm not sorry.* And she heard Søren's three-word reply. *Neither am I.*

At that moment Nora knew she'd heard something she shouldn't. She disappeared into the room she shared with Claire and stared wide-awake at the ceiling until dawn—her body burning from where Søren had touched her, her mind reeling with what she thought she'd heard.

At the funeral she'd come face-to-face with the woman Søren had been speaking to the night before. Tall and elegant with auburn hair and violet eyes, the woman had terrified her with both her beauty and the despair that seemed to surround her like a dark halo. Søren introduced her as Elizabeth, his elder sister, and introduced Nora as a friend of Claire's. Nora remembered studying Elizabeth and realizing that she was looking not at a person, but at a ghost. A living, breathing ghost, but a ghost all the same. Even in the dark, Nora saw that ghost flicker across Søren's gray eyes.

"I promised I would protect you, little one. That is the only reason I'm sending you away," Søren said and pulled Nora into his viselike arms.

"Your sister... You're afraid they'll find out about what Elizabeth did, aren't you?"

Søren pushed a strand of hair behind her ear.

"My fear of Elizabeth is the same as it has always been. I'm afraid she'll find out about you."

5

On Monday morning, Suzanne woke up with the dawn and didn't even bother turning on her computer. She'd never been stymied like this before. It was as if some sort of presence sat on the other end of the internet purposely thwarting her every attempt to find out anything of substance about Father Marcus Stearns. But today she was going to pull out all the stops. Desperate times called for desperate research.

She was going offline.

The library opened early but she arrived even before the doors unlocked. As soon as they let her in, Suzanne rushed the research desk with pencils and notepaper. She hadn't done hardcopy research in years. Probably not since middle school when her entire class had taken a field trip to the library and learned how to dig through the fat green tomes and write down the name, date and issue of the periodical they were looking for. Suzanne didn't have much to go on. All she'd gleaned from her online research was that Father Marcus Stearns had been at Sacred Heart for nearly twenty years and had presided at no other parishes. Apparently Father Stearns also acted as confessor to a nearby order of Benedictine sisters. One of them had a blog and mentioned that their Father Stearns, like her, had been born in New Hampshire. Guessing he graduated seminary at age twenty-eight, that meant he would be forty-seven or forty-eight. So she knew his name, approximate age and state of birth. A place to start at least.

By noon, Suzanne decided to give up again. There was simply nothing on Marcus Stearns out there. But she took one more dive into the stacks and came up with a Marcus Stearns who'd been in his early forties in 1963 and lived in New Hampshire. At least it was the same name if not the right age. Possibly a relative, she decided, and kept digging.

By one o'clock, Suzanne knew she was onto something.

Marcus Augustus Stearns, born in England in 1920, was the heir to a small barony. He'd come to New England in his late thirties and used his title to marry into a spectacularly wealthy family. The mother, Daisy, had realized her Edith Wharton fantasy and married the baron despite the fact that his only asset was his title. After just one year of marriage, Daisy had given birth to a daughter, Elizabeth Bennett Stearns. Not just an Edith Wharton fan but a Jane Austen fan as well, Suzanne noted. And then barely one year after, Suzanne was thrilled to discover, a son, Marcus Lennox Stearns, was born. Beyond that, the trail went cold. Marcus the Younger seemingly disappeared. No school records, no college records, no mentions of him at all.

Suzanne leaned back in the chair in her cramped library study carrel and closed her eyes.

Catholic priests made almost no money. No one became a Catholic priest to get rich. And yet, if this was the same Marcus Stearns, he'd given up a huge inheritance and a title, albeit a minor one, in the British peerage to become a priest. She had trouble believing it was possible. Still, a tantalizing possibility.

"Father Stearns," she whispered to herself, "who the hell are you?"

When Nora awoke the next morning, she found her neck bare of her collar and the bed empty but for her. She disposed of all evidence of her presence—she replaced the white sheets on the bed, put the candles away and made a sweep for any stray female flotsam—before dressing in Søren's bathroom and heading down to the kitchen. Nora got out her purse and wrote a check for Owen Perry's school fund. She knew Søren would find a way to get the money to the Perry family without them learning it was from her. Her small shadow at church, Owen's sweet, innocent company during Mass was always welcome. But still…she had a very bad reputation to uphold.

Leaving the check on Søren's table, Nora groaned when she saw he'd left her another note. This time the note was in a sealed envelope and on the outside were the words *Do not open until instructed.*

"Sadist," Nora growled and stuffed the envelope into her purse. She dug out her keys and checked the time on her cell phone. She had one new text message.

Hurry up, it read. My cock can't wait to see you. Love, The Griffin.

Nora wrote back, Just for that, I'm taking the scenic route.

With a hint of heaviness in her heart, Nora left Søren's house and headed to her car. She threw her stuff and herself inside and started the engine.

Griffin… It had been over a year and a half since they'd slept together. The last time had probably been in Miami at his father's beach house. She'd lied to Wesley and said she'd had a book-signing at an alternative bookstore down there when all she really wanted to do was get away from her slightly dis-approving roommate for a few days and have uninterrupted kinky sex. She'd gotten her wish. She probably would have continued to see Griffin even after going back to Søren, but even Søren's patience could be tested by the young and often obnoxious Griffin Fiske. For Søren, S&M was like air or water—he needed it to function. For Griffin, S&M was a game that he played to get laid as often as humanly possible.

Nora remembered her last night with Griffin at the beach house. They'd gone out to a club and brought home some in-sanely hot Portuguese kid named Mateo or Mateus…some-thing like that. Bi-curious and barely twenty-one, he'd never been with another guy before or done kink. Nora had taken her turn first, Griffin second. Then they'd tackled him at the same time. The next morning the kid dropped to his knees begging them to take him back to New York with them.

Suddenly Nora found herself grinning like an idiot. She and Griffin did make a good team.

Nora revved up her engine, put on some Beastie Boys, headed for the parkway and hit the gas.

Fuck the scenic route.

It didn't matter where he'd fallen asleep the night before—the couch in the living room, his tiny twin bed at his grand-mother's house, his own bed under his mother's roof—no matter what bed he fell asleep in, he was always back in the hospital bed when he woke up.

Michael remembered the dryness in his mouth when he'd finally woken up, how his lips felt like torn paper. He remem-bered the tubing around his nose and the wires running in and out of his arms. He'd been afraid to move his hands, afraid if he tried they wouldn't be there to move.

He'd opened his eyes and blinked painfully. A man in black

stood at the window in the hospital room staring out onto the helicopter pad. Deepest night, the only light in the room came from the life-support equipment that beeped and breathed in the dark.

"Father S?" It took everything Michael had to croak out those words.

His priest turned from the window and walked to his bed. Looking down on Michael, he smiled and Michael saw nothing in the smile but forgiveness.

"Your mother is here, Michael," his priest said in a voice quiet as the night that surrounded them. "She's with your father and the doctor right now. Should I find her for you?"

Michael shook his head. He wasn't ready for his family yet, wasn't sure he'd ever be ready to face them again.

"Am I," he began and coughed a little. "Am I going to hell?"

Father S reached out and briefly placed a hand on Michael's forehead.

"No," he said simply and with such conviction that Michael immediately believed him.

Michael looked up into his priest's face. He'd admired Father S from the moment his family started going to Sacred Heart. What he wouldn't give to have Father S's peace and certainty.

"Am I going to live?" Michael barely heard his own voice.

"You are, yes. Thank God." Michael heard the shadow of fear lurking behind the relief in his priest's voice. He never imagined he'd ever see Father S afraid of anything. Even in the dark he could see a smudge of red on Father S's white collar. Michael's own blood, he realized. "Your hands will have some numbness, but all feeling should return eventually. You lost a great deal of blood, and will be fatigued for a few weeks as you recover. I'm afraid you'll be in counseling for some time.

I've asked your family if they'll allow me to counsel you instead of sending you to a secular psychiatrist. They're discussing it with your doctor right now."

"I don't think even you can help me."

Father S had looked down at him and exhaled slowly.

"Your mother told me about the pictures your father found you looking at a few months ago, and the cuts and burns."

Only the severe blood loss kept Michael from blushing.

"Dad thinks I'm sick. He left Mom because they keep fighting over me. I think I'm sick too. I want bad things. I don't know why." He paused to cough again. "I don't know what I am."

Father S looked at him for a minute and Michael felt himself being weighed in his priest's mind. He must have passed the test because Father S sat on the side of Michael's bed and began to speak words Michael never even dreamed he would hear from the sainted Father Marcus Stearns.

"Michael, as a priest I hear a hundred confessions every week. But now if you'll allow me, I'm going to let you hear my confession. And be warned, it is a long confession and will certainly shock you."

"Your confession?" Michael swallowed the sandpaper in his throat.

Father S crossed his arms over his chest and met Michael's eyes. Michael studied his priest's profile. Even now he seemed the epitome of piety and tranquility, his handsome face unlined and serene, his eyes as strong and gray as steel.

"Michael," Father S said, his voice low but steady, "I know what you are."

"You do?"

"Yes. You are something different—something some people find strange and fearful—but what you are is as natural as being male or female or awake or asleep. The things you desire, you long for, I understand them. You belong in a different world from the one you now live in."

"What world? What am I?" Michael asked, wanting to sit up but finding his body would not work with him yet.

Father S had met his eyes and Michael saw the hint of a smile in them, a secret smile and the passing shadow of a green-eyed girl who could make any man lose his religion.

"My confession begins," Father S said, "as the confessions of many men begin—with three words."

"Father, forgive me?" Michael hazarded a guess.

Father S sighed.

"I met Eleanor."

Michael opened his eyes and saw, as he knew he would, that he lay in his own small, neat room at his mother's house. Rolling out of bed, he threw on clothes and booted up his computer. His hands shivered with excitement when he saw he had an email from Nora.

Michael—A car will pick you up Thursday morning at ten. Pack whatever you want, but I'll make sure you get everything you need. It's a long drive so bring something to read and eat. Can't have you wasting away. God knows you'll need your strength this summer. Oh, don't bother packing your halo, Angel. You're not going to need it.

This message, and your pants, will self-destruct in five minutes.

Covering his mouth as he laughed, Michael leaned back in his desk chair.

Michael knew enough about dominants and submissives to know that the relationship between them wasn't always sexual. He'd happily live as Nora's personal slave whether she fucked him or not. Dominants got off on dominating, and submissives got off on submitting, and if Nora wanted him to mop his floor with his hair, he'd do it with bliss. Finally his long

hair would come in handy. But something about that line—
Don't bother packing your halo—made him think that Nora in-
tended to use him for something other than janitorial services.
Awesome.

You took my halo over a year ago, he wrote and hit Send
with a smile.

Making a quick mental calculation he realized he had forty-
nine hours until the car came for him. Forty-nine hours…
He'd pack tomorrow, leave the next day, and today he'd be
lazy and read.

Digging behind his headboard, he found his copy of Nora's
newest novel. He hadn't read this one yet. He'd been forcing
himself to wait until school was out so he could properly enjoy
it. Propping himself up on his pillows, Michael started to flip
through to the first page. On the way he stopped at the dedication and looked for Nora's usual secret message to Father S.

Michael's eyes widened a little when he saw the dedication page.

To W.R. Many waters…

Michael furrowed his brow at the message.

Who the hell was W.R.?

It took a lot of money to impress Nora Sutherlin. She had
enough money of her own to not think very highly of it.
And she'd had enough wealthy clients, very wealthy clients
and stratospherically wealthy clients and acquaintances, and
seen their homes, at least their bedrooms, to know there was
more elegance and beauty in Søren's rectory than in all their
mansions combined.

But at her first glimpse of Griffin's house, farm, estate…
dukedom, she couldn't hold back a flabbergasted, "Holy shit,
Griff…"

Nora double-checked her GPS to make sure she hadn't

ended up in Scotland by mistake. Soft rolling hills lay back under sheets of softest green. A white fence ran the length of the fore and back land. And the house—Greek Revival with a touch of medieval castle—rose up proudly, straining across her field of vision. No wonder Griffin had been haunting The 8th Circle less these days. Now that he had installed himself in this secluded Wonderland, he had a private playground of his very own.

She drove up to the massive gate—wrought iron and guarded by two stone griffins on either side. It seemed Griffin had been named for the family avatar.

Nora pressed the call button on the intercom. She'd expected to hear the voice of a servant or security guard.

"Hey, bad girl," came the deep, sexy voice of The Griffin himself. "Can't believe the Pope let you out of the Vatican."

"Call it an indulgence. Now are you going to let me in, Griff?"

"Say please and call me sir."

"Did you forget who you're dealing with?" Nora raised her eyebrow and directed a stern stare at the security camera.

"Never, babe. Come on in. Let's get this orgy started."

The iron gate screeched open and Nora pulled up to the house—even more impressive up close than from a distance—and turned off the car. The door yawned open as she neared it. Stepping into the cathedral-like foyer, she gazed around her with unabashed awe at the interior; it might be a farm in name but it was a castle in spirit. And coming down the main spiral staircase taking two steps at a time and wearing nothing but a black kilt and Doc Marten boots was the lunatic laird of the manor himself.

Griffin Fiske… He was one of Kingsley's finds seven years ago. Griffin had been only twenty-two then but he was damaged, dangerous and dead sexy—Kingsley's favorite combination. Apparently one night Griffin had been partying at the Möbius, Kingsley's infamous strip club, and Kingsley watched Griffin beat the hell out of a guy who'd crossed the line with one of the strippers. Six feet tall, bronzed skin and with the broad chest and shoulders of a heavyweight boxer, there wasn't much in the world more fun to stare at than Griffin Fiske. He had elaborate armband tattoos around both biceps, dark hair that spiked up just too perfectly, and the dirtiest smile she'd ever seen on anyone besides her. The house might be Greek Revival but the master was Greek warrior.

"Fiske isn't a Scottish name, Griff," Nora reminded him as he skipped the last four steps to land right in front of her.

"But the house is from Mom's side. And she was a Raeburn. Anyway, I heard you had a weakness." He grinned at her before pulling her into a bear hug.

"Two words—easy access," she said, giving him a sharp swat on the kilt.

"Topping me already? Can't have that."

Nora squealed as Griffin picked her up, slung her over his shoulder and started up the stairs.

"Sir?" came a low, well-modulated English accent from the bottom of the stairs. At the landing Griffin turned around before Nora could glimpse the source of the voice.

"Alfred, are you looking up my skirt?" Griffin demanded as Nora squirmed on his shoulder.

"Master Griffin, I would marry my own mother for the excuse to stab my eyes out with her brooches rather than see anything under your kilt," the man's voice said with elegant aplomb. "Where would you like your guest's things, sir?"

"That's an *Oedipus Rex* reference," Nora, the eternal English major, supplied. The voice clearly came from Griffin's butler, who sounded utterly unperturbed by the sight of his employer strolling around in nothing but a kilt and boots wit[1]

a woman over his shoulder. Nora guessed this was not an un-
common occurrence.

"Stick them in the Blue Room. And no interruptions for
the next couple of hours, please. My guest and I will be fucking. Two hours, Nora?"

"At least," she agreed.

"Better make it three, Alfred." Griffin shifted Nora higher
on his shoulder and continued up the stairs.

"This is going to be a long summer, isn't it?" she asked.

"Eight and a half inches long, if you'll recall."

Griffin kicked open the door to the master bedroom. He
threw her unceremoniously across the monstrous bed draped
in mountains of black pillows and luxurious white-and-black-
striped sheets. Nora's heart raced as Griffin climbed on top of
her. She playfully put up a struggle but only for the pleasure
of having Griffin capture her wrists and push them over her
head. If she had to choose only one man to be with the rest
of her life, it would be Søren, hands down and for all eternity. But as Griffin held her down with one hand while digging under her skirt with the other, she couldn't deny Griffin
had his own charms.

"Left boot or right?" he asked, teasing her clitoral piercing
through her lace panties.

"Right."

He dug around her right boot and pulled out a condom.

"Griffin, before you fuck me, I have to tell you something."

Griffin paused after ripping the condom wrapper open with
his teeth. He leaned close and put his mouth at her ear.

"Tell me anything…." He kissed her from her ear to her neck.

"   " she panted as he started to slip a finger into her

    "I need to pee."

    groaned and rolled off her. "There," he said and

    door.

"Thank you, darling. That was one helluva drive, you know? You get sick of the city?" Nora stood up and walked into the bathroom.

"Parents are in the city. Parents who want grandchildren. I am here so I won't be forced to give them any."

"Understandable," Nora called out. "My mom stopped asking about grandchildren ten years ago. Just start fucking a priest and they'll back off."

"Your priest doesn't put out for me."

"True. But he'll beat the hell out of you if you ask nicely though. Jesus, Griffin, your bathroom is bigger than my basement. Spoiled much?"

"Not nearly enough. You done yet?"

"Yes and no."

"I don't want to know what that means, do I?"

Nora washed and dried her hands. Pausing in the bathroom doorway, Nora looked at Griffin, who sat on the bed with his legs open wide enough she could see he wore his kilt in true Scottish fashion. She approved of this.

"You know, I should probably take a shower before we fuck. Søren gave me a very intense goodbye last night, and I haven't washed it off yet."

"You know I don't mind sloppy seconds. And knowing Pope Whatadick, he probably blesses his cum before he blows it."

"I promise you he does not," Nora said as she strolled slowly back to the bed. "Why do you and Søren loathe each other so much?"

"Ask him," Griffin said, reaching out to unbutton her shirt.

"I did. He won't tell me."

"Let's just say we have an ongoing difference of opinion. My opinion is that he's a pretentious arrogant prick, and he disagrees with that."

Nora stared Griffin down. He couldn't quite meet her eyes.

"I know that's not true. I tell him he's a pretentious arrogant prick all the time and he's in full agreement. I could beat it out of you."

"Not a chance. You don't get to top me anymore. This summer you're my bitch, switch."

"You used to let me top you all the time." Nora recalled the dozens of time she'd tied Griffin down and used and abused his poor willing self.

"Only because it was the only way you'd let me fuck you. And even then you never got to beat me."

"Too bad. I think a good hard beating would be good for your soul. Fine, you can top me. But no beating me, either. Only dominance and bondage, alas. Søren's rules."

"I know. He called and read me the riot act yesterday," Griffin said as he unbuttoned her top button with a deft flick of his fingers.

"He's very protective of his property."

"I can't say I blame him." Griffin leaned back on the bed and stared her up and down. "Strip for me, beautiful."

At thirty-four, Nora would take all the erotic appreciation she could get from younger men. She let her shirt drop to the floor and peeled slowly out of her camisole.

"Jesus," Griffin said and took her by the arm; gently he pulled her to him. The grin vanished as he stared at her stomach and chest. "He did give you one helluva goodbye, didn't he?"

"Oops. Sorry. Should have warned you."

"You two did blood-play?" Griffin asked in horrified awe. Nora shrugged.

"A little. Just seven cuts. Speaking of, we should probably stick to anal for the next couple of days. The last cut was in a pretty sensitive area."

She expected Griffin to laugh—if they weren't fucking, they were laughing. But Griffin only stared at her a moment while he studied her skin. He gently ran a finger around her wounds—the cut on her collarbone, on her rib cage, under her breast.

"We don't have to play if you aren't up for it," he said.

"Griff, I've had papercuts worse than this. And also on my crotch. This is what happens when you fall asleep while working on your edits naked. I'm up for it. Seriously."

"Okay. We'll fuck if you make me," he said, smiling at her again. "We'll just go vanilla until you're healed."

Vehemently Nora shook her head. "Not a chance. No vanilla. The one time I even attempted vanilla sex I nearly passed out."

"Nora Sutherlin tried vanilla sex? This I have to hear about." Griffin stretched out on his side and playfully patted the bed next to him. Rolling her eyes Nora crawled onto his sheets.

"It's not a big deal. Tried it. Didn't like it. Stopped."

"Why'd you stop? Vanilla sex is boring but it's not hard. You're the chick. You just lie there and pretend to like it."

Pretend to like it…that was the problem. She didn't have to pretend…. Nora closed her eyes. For a second she wasn't in Griffin's bed anymore…she was on her bed back home with Wesley on top of her. They were kissing, their bare chests pressed to each other's. Wesley's hands stroked her hair and caressed her arms. She kissed his neck and muscular shoulders. He was so young, only nineteen then, and still a virgin. And there he was, as brave as he was beautiful, ready and willing to give her his virginity. And she wanted it, wanted him…and not for his body and not for the pleasure and not for the sex. For something else so much deeper and scarier that instead of letting him make love to her, she let him go.

"It's hard to explain," she said, opening her eyes. "Vanilla just doesn't work for me."

"Not that hard to explain—vanilla blows," Griffin said. "So what? Celibacy?"

"Don't even joke about that. Just tie me down, fuck me up the ass, call me a slut and just watch the cuts."

Griffin grinned at her. "Yes, ma'am."

"Ha," she said. "I'm still the top."

Griffin raised his eyebrow at her and she knew she was in trouble—the good kind.

In a second she found herself flat on her stomach with Griffin peeling her clothes off. From behind the corner of his bed, Griffin pulled out a leather strap. He grabbed two sets of bondage cuffs from the bedside table. With practiced expertise, Griffin buckled the cuffs around her wrists and ankles, bound her hands to the bedpost and strapped her legs wide-open to a spreader bar.

Nora groaned with pleasure as Griffin prepared her body for him—she was going to have to ask him what kind of lube he was using because it felt amazing—and then pushed carefully inside her. She felt the brush of wool as his kilt rubbed against her naked skin. Nora decided there and then to take her next vacation in Scotland.

This is who she was, she reminded herself. She was a switch. All summer long Griffin would top her. All summer long, she would top Michael. She'd have the best of both worlds and no vanilla sex at all. No staring into big brown eyes with flecks of gold in them and saying "Wesley" instead of "sir." No holding each other while they made love with only sweat wet between them and not blood. Sex was sex. Pain was pain. And Wesley and that part of her was in the past.

Griffin continued to move inside her. Nora buried her head against her arm and whispered Wesley's name into the sheets.

6

Michael sat on the porch outside his house waiting for the ride Nora promised. He still couldn't quite believe that in a few minutes, he'd be whisked away to a farm in upstate New York to hang out with Nora Sutherlin and her kinky friend Griffin all summer. The Griffin part of the equation worried him. Nora he'd known for over a year now, even known her in the biblical sense. They hadn't talked much since the night they spent together, but he still felt comfortable around her. Well, as comfortable as he felt around anyone. This Griffin guy might hate him. After all, Nora was supposed to train him this summer. Griffin might not like sharing her with somebody else, especially not a teenage boy with no money, from nowhere. Michael still couldn't believe Father S would share Nora with any guy. But then again, Father S was an unusual man. He had a very literal concept of ownership where Nora was concerned. Since he owned her, he could lend her out and she'd still be his. Michael wondered how Nora felt about being treated like a library book. Michael kind of liked the idea himself. The thought of being owned by someone he was in love with got him so turned on he could barely breathe. He felt disowned these days. His mom didn't really want him anymore. And God, his dad...his dad?

"Michael? What are you doing?"

Michael froze. Slowly he turned his head to the side and saw his father in his usual blue business suit stalking toward him. So engrossed in thoughts of Nora, Michael hadn't even noticed his father had parked across the street.

"Nothing," Michael said, crossing his arms over his chest. "Waiting on a ride."

His dad stopped and looked down at him. Even if Michael hadn't been sitting and his rather tall, stocky father standing, his dad would still be looking down at him.

"A ride to where?" his father demanded.

Michael decided to try a little deflection again.

"It's Thursday morning."

"I took the morning off. Your mother said you were going to be gone the whole summer. I thought I should see what was going on with my son."

"I'm your son again?"

"Michael, I thought we put that behind us," his father said in his most ingratiating voice. Michael liked the yelling better than the sucking up. At least the anger seemed genuine. His father's friendly voice only meant he wanted something. Answers obviously. And Michael wasn't about to give him any.

Yeah, I'm totally over that whole you wailing on me and Mom thing. We're best buds again, Dad, Michael thought but didn't say out loud. His father could turn anything against him, so Michael wore his silence as a shield.

His father's eyes turned cold and menacing.

"Young man, tell me what you're doing this summer, or I'll make very sure whatever it is doesn't happen."

"I'm staying with some friends this summer. That's all."

Michael's father stared at him without speaking. Bad sign. His dad talked. Constantly talked. He spouted off about sports teams, about the assholes at work, about the president, the job market, the world's problems that would go away if everyone were just more like him.

"Didn't know you had any friends, Michael," his father said with cold suspicion.

Michael clenched his jaw and didn't answer.

"What friends are these?" his father asked in a neutral tone Michael didn't trust for one second.

Pulling his knees even tighter to his chest, Michael concentrated on the cold concrete underneath him. He always played this game when his father was angry. Michael would disappear, pull into himself, let his body become a hard outer shell that protected that part of him only Nora and Father S understood.

"Answer me, Michael."

At times like these Michael wished he could talk like Nora did, wished he could say everything he thought. What he wanted to say right now was, *You asshole*.

"You as—" Michael began, but stopped when a shiny silver car, a Rolls Royce maybe, turned the corner of his street.

"What the hell?" his father asked, his angry dark eyes narrowing at the car.

Michael stood up, grabbed his duffel bag and head toward the car.

"Michael, get back here," his father yelled after him. Whoever was driving the Rolls Royce slowed in front of Michael's house, and the door opened for him. Michael threw himself and his duffel bag into the backseat and the car started off again. Glancing out the window, Michael saw his father glaring at him with unstrained fury. There'd be hell to pay when he came back at the end of the summer. But at least now he was free.

Suddenly Michael realized he wasn't alone in the back of the lavish car. First he saw riding boots, black riding boots, and dark gray trousers. The trousers belonged to a rather old-fashioned but dashing-looking suit worn by a crazy-good-looking dark-haired man who studied him with a little smile on his sculpted lips. Michael had no idea who the man was, but he had no doubt in his mind that he sat in the presence of a dominant friend of Nora's, and probably a very important one.

Michael hazarded a timid, "Hello, sir."

"Bonjour, Michael," the man said with a French accent, pronouncing his name like *Michelle*. French? So this was Kingsley, Father S's necessary evil. The man looked Michael up and down once more before reclining back and throwing his riding boots on the seat opposite him and crossing them at the ankles. "*Mon Dieu, chérie* does have good taste in her pets, doesn't she?"

"Pets?" Michael repeated, in some distress.

The man leaned forward and Michael nervously studied his handsome face—the dark umber eyes, strong European nose, the sensual tilt to his mouth.

"Tell me, Michael, have you ever had sex in the back of a Rolls Royce?"

Nora arched her back and tilted her hips high. Finally she found the right angle of penetration. Admittedly, it had been her idea for she and Griffin to fuck on top of her Aston Martin, but once he tunneled inside her, she realized that car hoods and sex didn't always mix. Not that Griffin seemed to mind. While she lay on her stomach across the car hood, her hands tied behind her neck, Griffin thrust blithely into her. Once she raised her hips, he slipped his hand under her and found her clitoris. Now equally blithe, Nora turned her head to the side and smiled.

"When did you get a Ducati?" Nora asked, noticing for the first time the motorcycle sitting in the corner of Griffin's garage stocked with Ferraris, Porsches and one hardcore Shelby Mustang.

"I'm fucking you and you're asking me about my motorcycle?" Griffin gasped through gritted teeth.

"Sorry, sir," she said without any actual contrition. "A Ducati is the reason Søren and I are together."

"Dammit, I hate that he has one too."

"I don't…"

Nora closed her eyes as a memory floated up out of the mists of the past.

"Eleanor Louise Schreiber! Get out of bed this instant," her mother shouted at her. Nora remembered throwing the covers over her head in her determination that this would be the day she broke her mother's spirit. This would be the day she would defeat the tyranny of organized religion. She'd skip Mass today and never, ever, go back.

"I'm a Buddhist," she shouted back from under the sheets.

"Eleanor, get out of bed this instant and get ready for Mass."

Nora remembered hearing real anger in her mother's tone. Good. Anger made her erratic. She'd either kill her or storm out. Either way, it meant no church today. If Eleanor could just fight her way out of Mass, she'd be free…unchained, unfettered, unbound by the Catholic Church forever.

"I'm an atheist." She flipped over onto her stomach. "I'll incinerate the second I walk into church. It's for everyone's good that I stay away from that place."

Her mother had growled under her breath. So that's where Nora got that habit from?

"Eleanor," her mother said, sighing. Damn. Sighing wasn't

good. Sighing meant her mother was going to try to either reason with her or bribe her.

"What?"

"Father Greg is retiring soon. Today is the day the new priest is starting at Sacred Heart. If the new priest hires someone else to do the church's books, you don't get free tuition to St. Xavier anymore."

"Don't care. Send me to public school. No more uniforms."

Nora remembered the sharp breath her mother took. That her mother hadn't just beat the shit out of her yet was one of life's great mysteries.

"Eleanor," her mother began, her voice dripping with saccharine. "Mary Rose told me the new priest is supposed to be very handsome."

Rolling her eyes, Nora had flipped back over and glared at her mother.

"Mom, he's a priest. That's gross."

But her mother continued.

"And he rides a motorcycle."

That got her attention.

"What kind? Not some no-thrust piece of crap from Japan, is it?" Her father hadn't taught her much but he had taught her cars and motorcycles.

Shaking her head, her mother tapped her chin. "I can't remember what it was called. Something Italian sounding. Du-something."

"A Ducati?"

"That was it."

Nora remembered her heart racing a little right then. A handsome Catholic priest who rode the finest, fastest, most wicked motorcycle money could buy? She'd have to see it to believe it.

"Fine," she'd said, throwing off the covers. "I'm coming."

Nora came hard and relaxed against the hood of her Aston Martin as Griffin made a few more spiraling thrusts inside her before pulling out of her and untying her hands.

"Good idea," he said, dragging her back to him. With her hands now free, Nora tugged down her skirt and leaned back against Griffin. "Never fucked on an Aston Martin before. Something for the scrapbook," he said.

"Neither have I. Or in it. Came close with Zach though. He had a major hard-on for this car."

"Zach?" Griffin asked, peeling off the condom and zipping his pants up.

"Blue Eyes, remember? My insanely hot Jewish editor who left me for his wife?"

"Right. That guy. I think he had a hard-on for you. The car was just a bonus."

"She is a very nice car," Nora said, running her hands over the hood. The Aston Martin had been a gift from a lover three years ago—a member of a Middle Eastern dynasty who came to the States every few months to indulge his very top-secret obsession with female dominants. Gorgeous man. He loved painting Arabic poetry on her naked body after sex. After their first week together she'd found the Aston Martin in her garage as a thank-you. "She's my baby."

"Why did you have me drive her up here and put her on blocks then?" Griffin asked, making a circuit around the car.

Nora kissed her fingers and touched the hood in a little benediction. Noticing the smears on the paint, she grabbed a chamois. With care and elbow grease she buffed the Nora/Griffin smudges off the inferno-red finish.

"I was going to give it to Wes, my old roommate."

"You had a roommate?"

"Live-in intern. Never told you. Gorgeous kid. You would have tried to fuck him."

"That's probably true. What happened to this gorgeous intern?"

Nora sighed heavily. "He fell in love with me. Bad situation. Had to let him go." She tried to sound cold but she could tell Griffin wasn't buying it.

"Sounds like he wasn't the only one in love." Griffin eyed her meaningfully.

"Griff, you're too pretty to also be smart."

Nora deserved the glower he leveled at her.

"Do you still talk to him?"

"He calls, but I don't answer. All I know is that he withdrew from Yorke and went back to Kentucky."

"You ever Google-stalk him? See what he's up to on Facebook or Twitter?"

Nora shook her head. "I've been tempted, but I don't know. What if he was still sad and lonely? It would break my heart."

Griffin came around the car and stood in front of her. He cupped her chin and forced her to meet his eyes.

"What if he was happy? Dating somebody even?"

Nora exhaled heavily.

"It would break my heart."

"Nora," Griffin sighed. "You really need to—"

"Master Griffin? Mistress?" came an English-accented voice from the door to the garage.

"God, it turns me on when he calls me Master Griffin," Griffin groaned as Nora laughed and straightened his clothes. He'd actually put on pants today—khakis with a white T-shirt that stretched across his powerful tattooed biceps. Pants and a shirt but no shoes or socks. Still, they were making progress.

"Your other guest has arrived," Griffin's stately white-haired butler said.

A grin spread across Nora's face. "Junior kinkster's here. Let's go."

Nora grabbed Griffin's hand and raced past his butler.

"So tell me about this kid," Griffin said. "You said he's a seventeen-year-old submissive from your church. Anything else I need to know about him?"

"Like what? Food allergies?"

"Let's just say I barely remember being seventeen. I think I spent half the year drunk and the other half of the year high."

"You don't have to worry about Michael. He's very straight edge. Søren said he doesn't even drink. But there's three things you probably should know about him."

"I'm ready," Griffin said, opening the front door just as Kingsley's silver Rolls Royce pulled up in front of the house. "Hit me."

Nora slapped his arm.

"First, Michael doesn't talk."

"Is he a mute?" Griffin asked, sounding slightly horrified. Griffin only shut up when you put something in his mouth— preferably a body part.

"No, just really quiet. Nervous type. Quiet."

"Submissive?"

"That," Nora said as the door to the Rolls opened and Michael stepped out. He pushed his sunglasses onto his head and smiled up at her. Raising his hand, he gave her a nervous wave.

"Holy shit," Griffin breathed, his dark eyes widening at the sight of Michael.

"Yeah," Nora said, smiling back at Michael. "Number two—Michael is absolutely, completely, ridiculously beautiful."

"Nora…" Griffin said in a distressed voice. "I think I'm in love."

"You're in heat, Griff. Big difference. Oh, and number three…Søren says you can't fuck him."

Skipping down the steps, Nora left a speechless Griffin behind her. She grabbed Michael and pulled him into her arms.

"Hey, Angel," she said, kissing him on the lips. "How was the trip?"

"Bizarre," Michael whispered. "There was a guy in the backseat. In riding boots. We dropped him off at Father S's."

"Oh, that was just Kingsley. He likes to inspect the new recruits. Did he hit on you? Ask you if you've ever had sex in the back of a Rolls Royce?"

"Um, yeah," Michael confessed, blushing. "But I didn't—"

"Good," Nora said. "You passed inspection. Go say hello to Griffin while I make out with your driver."

Nora bodily spun Michael, aimed him toward the steps and slapped him on his jeans-clad bottom. Robin, one of her and Søren's favorite submissives from The 8th Circle, stepped out of the driver's seat in her chic gray chauffeur's costume complete with driving hat and leather gloves.

"I love a woman in uniform," Nora said, giving Robin a long, thorough kiss. From the top of the steps, Nora heard applause. She pulled back from the pretty submissive and saw Griffin clapping and Michael gaping. Michael looked at Griffin, who looked at Michael. Michael looked at her. Griffin kept looking at Michael.

Nora groaned. "Robin, take me back to the city with you."

"I'm sorry, mistress. Mr. King said I wasn't allowed. Oh, and Mr. S has a message for you."

"What, pray tell, is Mr. S's message?" Nora asked, already dreading whatever message Søren decided to pass on to her through an underling.

"He wanted me to ask you if you still had that note he left for you? The one that said 'Do not open until instructed'?"

"Yes. I still have it. What about it?"

"He said you still can't open it."

THE ANGEL   103

Nora nodded. "Fine. Great. Wonderful. You can tell Mr. S that he can take his note and shove it up—"

"Nora?" Griffin called down to her. "Kiss Robin again. I want to get a pic."

Nora rubbed her forehead. Long summer ahead. Too long.

Nora shook Robin's hand goodbye, a move that led to boo-ing from the peanut gallery at the top of the steps. Robin got into the Rolls and drove off, leaving Nora alone with a timid teenage boy and a horny Griffin.

Looking up at the blue sky above her, Nora sent up a quick prayer to St. Mary Magdalen, patron saint of ex-prostitutes, and St. Jude, patron saint of lost causes. Her prayer consisted of one word.

"Help."

Suzanne took a deep breath and whispered one word to herself—"Afghanistan."

An odd mantra, but it worked for her. She'd been in Afghanistan for the past three months, and in that desolate, broken country, she'd eaten fear and slept with courage. Lieutenant Hatton, the handsome Texan who always called her Red—IED took his right arm. Staff Sergeant Zimmerman, the New York Jew who couldn't stop flirting with her—a bullet to the sternum. And Private First Class Goran, the shy North Dakotan with a one-year-old daughter back home—a bullet to the brain. His own.

She'd seen all of it. Witnessed horrors she could barely recall because her mind had done such a good job of burying the visuals so deep even she couldn't find them. No one really understood why she did what she did, not even her really. In college when she decided to major in journalism, her advisor told her she had the looks to be a top-notch weathergirl. Her impressive intelligence could get her far, he'd said. But a face and body as choice as hers could take her anywhere she wanted to go. And he'd grabbed her ass and told her exactly where he wanted her to take it. Instead she took it to the dean and got the tenured, award-winning professor canned. As he cleaned out his office, she knocked on his door, smiled at him and said, "Cloudy with a chance of fired," before walking off. Weathergirl her ass. A man who couldn't keep his hands to himself had been the death of her brother Adam. Her advisor had been the first abusive man with too much power she'd taken out. Father Stearns might be next.

"Afghanistan," she repeated. She'd been in war zones. She could do this. Suzanne changed into a reasonably nondescript black dress and pulled her long red hair back into a knot. Earlier that day when she'd hit yet another brick wall attempting to dig up anything on Father Stearns, she'd decided she had no choice but to meet the man. Scanning Sacred Heart's website she found that Father Stearns presided over Thursday evening mass. Purposefully she hadn't told Patrick about her trip to Wakefield. He worried about her, worried she'd get hurt. "Afghanistan," she told him every time he started to patronize her. He chased cheating politicians around the Upper East Side. She covered war zones. That usually shut him up.

Before leaving, Suzanne slipped into a pair of plain black flats. At five-nine in bare feet, Suzanne stood as tall as most men she knew. The priests of her childhood were all small men, old and weak. She wanted this priest to feel comfortable around her, comfortable enough to talk. Intimidating him with her height wouldn't help the situation.

Being a city girl to the core, Suzanne didn't own a car. Luckily Patrick did, and he trusted her just enough to let her borrow it. Either that or he really did want her back and would use any means to get in her good graces. Using Google Maps she found Sacred Heart Catholic Church a scant five minutes before Thursday evening Mass was due to start. She raced from the car and into the sanctuary, taking a seat near the back where she could lurk unnoticed. Once inside and seated, Suzanne took the opportunity to look around and get her bearings. Digging in her bag, she pulled out her little steno pad and flipped it open.

Beautiful sanctuary, she wrote. *Stained-glass windows depicting Christ's miracles, traditional architecture—Richardsonian Romanesque maybe? Choir loft above me, seats about 300 people. Truly gorgeous church. I fucking hate it here.*

She hadn't sat in a Catholic Church in years, not since Adam died. Even before that she'd given up on the church, on her childhood faith, on prayer. Any God who could let the sort of evil she'd witnessed happen on His watch wasn't a God she wanted any part of. And since there didn't seem to be any other gods out there doing any better, she'd just given up on the concept altogether. She didn't miss Him or It one bit.

Suzanne stiffened with nervousness as a hymn she hadn't heard in a million years began and filled the sanctuary. For a 5:30 p.m. evening mass, an impressive number of people were in attendance, almost a hundred by her estimate. Well, if Father Stearns had made the short list to be a bishop so comparatively young, he must have something going for him. Maybe he was one of those liberal theologians who did a lot of social work. Or maybe the church had a fairly active youth group or music ministry. Or maybe…

Suzanne's body rose from her pew as her heart plummeted through the floor. Shock came first and gave way to disbelief. Disbelief lasted but a moment before suspicion reared its head.

Never before in her life had Suzanne seen a man more strikingly, viscerally handsome. Blond, incredibly blond, and so tall she could have worn five-inch stilettos on her feet without fear of even meeting him eye to eye.

The vestments, the white collar…it had to be him. But how could a Catholic priest be so… She couldn't even find the right word. Attractive? Beautiful? Desirable?

Still staring, Suzanne nearly forgot to sit down with the rest of the congregation. She'd chosen her seat carefully hoping to go unnoticed in the crowded middle of the sanctuary. But as Father Stearns came up to the altar he cast his eyes across his people and let them rest on her for a long, deliberate moment.

As his gaze touched her, Suzanne felt something stirring in the recesses of her stomach, something that formed a tight knot and sunk in deep and hard. Her hands went numb. Her skin flushed. Even her toes tingled in her plain black flats. For the first time in over a decade, for the first time since Adam died, she felt compelled to release one tiny desperate prayer under her breath.

"Oh…my…God."

7

If Michael didn't worship the ground Nora walked on, he'd probably kill her. From what he could tell, Griffin's horse-house-mansion-farm, as Nora called it, had about a billion rooms. And of all those one billion rooms, she was forcing Michael to sleep here. She'd left Griffin in the grand foyer while she'd escorted him to his room. His room in the—

"The nursery?" Michael asked in horror.

"Isn't it cute? Griffin said he spent half of his childhood up here. This is his old room. There's no crib anymore. It's been redecorated."

"It's the nursery," Michael reiterated, feeling about five years old. Nora merely batted her eyelashes at him and kissed his cheek.

"Get settled in. I'll be back for you later so we can start training."

With that she flounced out of the room—an impressive feat considering her tight skirt and low-cut shirt weren't even remotely flouncy—and left him alone.

Michael stood in the middle of the nursery and decided it wasn't as bad as the name implied. In fact, the room, suite actually, was pretty impressive. In an arched alcove sat a sumptuous-looking full-size bed. A big bay window looked out onto a huge inground swimming pool. The pool…perfect, Michael thought, mentally draining it. Deep with perfectly sloped sides. He dreamed of skateboarding in swimming pools like that.

"She's fucking with your head."

Michael turned toward the voice and saw Nora's friend Griffin standing in the doorway. Never before had Michael seen anyone quite like Griffin. Really tall and handsome and obviously all muscle, Griffin had hair that was kind of long but still spiked up in a way he'd only seen on male models with their own hair stylists. He had a slight crook in his nose as though it had been broken once and not fixed right. Instead of marring his appearance, it made him look more interesting, as if he'd really lived. He seemed young though. Too young to own a house this big and old. Michael guessed he was in his late twenties, if that.

"Nora is," Griffin continued when Michael didn't answer. "With the nursery thing."

Michael nodded and stuffed his hands into his pockets.

"So she wasn't kidding about you not talking," Griffin said, coming into the room with Michael's big army-green duffel bag over his shoulder. Michael nearly buckled under the weight of it but Griffin carried it like a backpack.

"Sorry," Michael said. Earlier he'd been able to squeak out a hello to Griffin before they both got distracted at the sight of Nora kissing his driver.

"Better." Griffin nodded his approval. "One word is better than no words."

Michael tried to think of something to say, something a

rich, handsome guy like Griffin would want to hear from him. He came up blank.

"Where do you want your stuff?" Griffin asked.

"Anywhere," Michael said. Griffin gave him a stern look.

"You give me more than one word or I'm keeping your stuff," Griffin warned.

"On the bed?" Michael offered.

Griffin held up one hand and ticked off something on his finger. "That's five words total. Fabulous."

Michael laughed and blushed a little. He held up his own hand and ticked off two fingers.

"Thank you."

"You're welcome," Griffin said.

Pausing, Michael counted again on his fingers. He held up both hands.

"Ten words?" Griffin guessed and Michael nodded.

"Thanks for letting me stay here. Your house is awesome."

"You're welcome. The mistress and her friends, Søren excluded, are always welcome here."

Michael smiled.

"Do you like the room?" Griffin asked.

"It's really nice. For a nursery."

"It's an English nursery, not an American nursery. Suite of rooms in a big damn house to hide the kids. No Winnie-the-Pooh anywhere, I promise. Actually," Griffin said, looking around his old room, "I think it was Noah's ark when I was a baby. I've never gotten that, you know?"

"Gotten what?" Michael asked, unable to stop following Griffin with his eyes. Griffin was twice his size. Usually big muscular guys intimidated him. His father certainly used his large size to make everyone around him feel scared and small. For a dominant into kink, Griffin actually seemed really safe and friendly.

"Noah's ark nursery decor. I'm not religious like you and the mistress, but if I'm not mistaken Noah's ark was about the destruction of the entire world, right?"

"Right," Michael agreed.

"Might as well decorate with the Four Horsemen of the Apocalypse."

Shrugging, Michael looked at the walls now painted an elegant light blue.

"Kids like ponies."

Griffin turned around and stared at him before bursting into laughter.

"She didn't tell me you were funny," Griffin said, smiling at him. Michael blinked. Griffin had the kind of smile that shone so bright and white it made your eyes water.

"I didn't know I was."

"You are," Griffin said, still staring at him. Michael flushed a little under the scrutiny. Nora did the intense staring thing too; so did Father S. Must be a dominant thing. Only reason Michael could come up with why a guy like Griffin would look at him so keenly. "Anyway," Griffin continued as he seemed to remember something. "The mistress sent me to do your checklist. She thought you'd be more comfortable doing it with another guy. Your checklist, I mean."

"Checklist?"

"A lot of doms do checklists with their partners before doing kink. That way the dom knows beforehand what you want and what you don't. Helps prevent subby from having a freak-out in the middle of a scene. You know, don't want to accidentally do cage-play with an ex-POW."

"Whoops," Michael agreed.

"Exactly. So get comfortable. This thing is like ten fucking pages long," Griffin said, throwing himself into the bay window seat and crossing his legs. In his loose-fitting khakis and white shirt, he looked like a well-groomed beach bum. Michael looked around for a chair. Not seeing any he decided to behave like the submissive he was and just sit on the floor.

Once again Griffin stopped and stared at him. Michael hugged his knees to his chest and tucked his long hair behind his ears. It made him a little uncomfortable the way Griffin looked at him. But uncomfortable in a way he kind of liked.

"Right, okay," Griffin said, pulling a sheaf of papers and a pen out of his back pocket. "Easy enough. Everything's on a one-to-five scale—one meaning it turns you on as much as kissing your grandmother and five meaning it makes you spray your shorts just thinking about it. Doesn't matter if you've done it or not—just if you want to do it. First category—sex."

"Five," Michael answered.

Griffin grinned at him. "That was just the category. But I like your enthusiasm, Mick."

"Mick?"

"Can I call you Mick? Michael's too formal. I'm not formal. You're lucky I've even got pants on today."

Michael mulled it over. No one had ever called him anything other than Michael except for his father, who'd called him Mikey as a kid—a nickname Michael loathed. And Nora called him Angel. But she was Nora. She could call him anything.

"I like it," Michael decided and smiled.

While skimming the pages of the checklist, Griffin muttered something that sounded to Michael like "assassinate the Pope for this." Michael decided he must have misheard.

"Category one," Griffin continued, "on a scale of one to five...vaginal sex?"

"Five."

"Agreed. Oral sex?"

"Five."

Griffin looked at him before dropping his eyes to his notes
again.

"Even better. Anal sex?"

Michael coughed. "Five."

"Multiple partners?"

Michael looked down at his wrists and checked that his
watch and wristband completely covered his scars.

"Five."

"Threesomes?"

"Five."

Michael didn't look up but he could feel Griffin's curious
eyes on him.

"Two women and one man?"

"Five."

"Two men and one woman?"

Michael shifted on the floor and didn't look up at Griffin.
It took him a long time to answer.

Five minutes after Thursday evening Mass ended, Suzanne
stood outside of Sacred Heart in the shade of a willow tree
and watched Father Stearns.

Gorgeous. The priest, her target, was absolutely gorgeous.
The congregation filed out of the front doors and greeted their
priest in the warm evening air. With the men he exchanged
handshakes. From most of the women he received light, chaste
hugs. Every child received a touch on the top of the head like
a tiny blessing. Every child but one.

A young boy of about six or seven with unruly black hair
stormed up to Father Stearns and turned an angry face up to
the priest.

"Owen, I've already told you—" Father Stearns began but
the small boy wouldn't let him finish.

"It's not fair," he said, stamping his tiny foot. "I want to say thank-you. You have to tell me—"

"Owen," Father Stearns said, bending low to meet the boy eye to eye. "You know priests aren't allowed to tell secrets. The person who gave you your tuition money asked me not to tell you."

Suzanne stiffened at the sight of the little boy, Owen, and the priest standing so close together. At least the boy didn't seem intimidated by Father Stearns. She already was.

Owen raised his little fist, narrowed his eyes and growled.

"Young man, did you just growl at me?"

The boy looked immediately contrite.

"Maybe," he confessed, wrinkling his face up.

"Clearly you've been spending too much time with your Miss Ellie. She growls at me too."

At the mention of the mysterious Miss Ellie, Owen's anger fell from his face.

"When's she coming back?" Owen said. "I did a new painting for her."

"I can't say," Father Stearns said, standing back up to his full height again. "She may be gone for some time."

Owen nodded and stared down at his shoes.

"I miss her," the boy said, digging the toes of his sneakers into the grass.

Father Stearns sighed and tapped the boy on the top of his head.

"As do I."

Owen ran off at that, and Suzanne realized she finally had an opening. Nervously she strode up to Father Stearns and plastered on her best attempt at a weathergirl grin.

"Father Marcus Stearns?"

He turned to her with the slightest smile on the edge of his lips.

"Very nice to see a new face at Sacred Heart. How do you do, Miss…?" he began and extended his hand.

Suzanne froze momentarily before remembering she was undercover. She held out her hand and let him take it. He had perfect hands, sculpted like a statue's. Smooth, warm skin but strong, very strong, although he gripped her fingers lightly. He grasped her hand like a man who knew his own strength, knew how to command and control it.

"Kanter," she supplied. "Suzanne Kanter. I'm very well, thank you," she said, answering etiquette with etiquette as she pulled her hand back. "I enjoyed the Mass."

"I'm glad to hear it. What brings you to Sacred Heart?" he asked, his voice curious but not suspicious. Suzanne decided to press her luck a little and see if she could get a reaction out of him.

"Nothing very pious. You see, I heard a rumor that Nora Sutherlin attends church here. I'm a big fan so I thought I'd drop in. But I didn't see anyone who looked like a famous writer."

"She is difficult to miss," he said, his small smile widening just slightly. "Usually we are graced with her presence but she's on something of a sabbatical this summer."

"Too bad. I have to say I'm impressed your church would be so welcoming to her. I've read a few of her books. Sinful stuff."

Suzanne saw something flash in his eyes. Surprise maybe? Or was it mirth?

"It was Christ's way to welcome sinners and tax collectors and other nefarious characters into His company and His Kingdom. On His especially compassionate and generous days he would even speak to reporters."

His smile changed again. Now pure irony graced his lips.

"How did you—" she began, shocked into near speechlessness.

"You were taking notes during the Mass. Only an Evangelical Protestant or a reporter would bother taking notes during a homily or sermon, especially one of mine. And after twenty years in the priesthood, I can spot a lapsed Catholic at a thousand yards."

"Is that so?"

"You stand and sit at the appropriate times without looking lost. You called me Father comfortably, not Pastor or Reverend. And you have a distinctly Catholic look in your eyes."

"What Catholic look?"

"Guilt."

Suzanne stood up straighter, refusing to let him see he'd rattled her. After all, she didn't see one iota of guilt in his eyes.

"Okay, yes. Guilty. Reporter and ex-Catholic," she said, painting on an even wider fake smile.

"We do see the occasional lapsed Catholic here but not many reporters," he said, his tone conversational. "I assure you nothing noteworthy had happened lately. I haven't performed an exorcism in, well, weeks."

Suzanne looked at him a long, confused moment.

"You aren't what I expected," she said, dispensing with all pretense.

"Considering what the common perception of the clergy is these days, I shall take that as a compliment. You'll have to forgive me, Ms. Kanter. I have my people to attend to. But my office is always open. Something tells me you have some questions for me."

"Yes. A lot more of them than I originally thought."

"Then I shall see you again soon. Good day to you."

With a polite nod he left her to join a group of men who had apparently been waiting to speak to him as well. Suzanne followed him with her eyes as he walked away. That had not gone as planned. Not even close.

Trailing behind a boisterous family of five or six children arguing over where to eat dinner, Suzanne made her way to the parking lot. Once inside Patrick's car she pulled out her notepad again.

Extremely intelligent, she wrote. *And ridiculously handsome. He was expecting me.*

At the bottom of the page she scrawled, *I don't trust him,* and underlined it three times.

Nora sorted through her luggage, separating her clothes from her toys. At times like this she missed having her own dungeon. Back in her dominatrix days, she had a palatial dungeon, if such a thing could exist, in the VIP wing of The 8th Circle. Søren still had his own personal quarters there, of course. As did Kingsley and Griffin. But once she returned to Søren as his submissive, she'd had to give up her dungeon to her replacement—Mistress V. However, she'd kept most of her gear for those occasions when Søren gave her permission to top someone. Some of the kinksters in their community frowned on her playing switch while in the possession of their alpha dom. But Søren loved her and understood her. And he knew better than to put his foot down in this area. She loved topping women and even a certain secretly switch-hitting Frenchman of their acquaintance. The jealous haters could have her spreader bars and her signature red riding crop when they pried them out of her cold, dead hands.

Nora'd bought a collar for Michael, a black one to match his hair. She had no intention of collaring him permanently, but he needed to get used to wearing one if he planned on joining the Underground with her and Søren. She dug to the very bottom of her bag. Whips and chains, a Wartenberg wheel, two sets of handcuffs—rope and metal—bondage cuffs, snap hooks…all ended up in an impressive array on the floor.

Nora dove once more into her luggage and laughed at what she pulled out. How did her duckie pajamas get in with her kink gear? She remembered she'd been on the phone arguing with Zach, her editor, while packing. Obviously Zach had distracted her a little.

Nora stared at her pajamas, at the little baby ducks printed on the blue flannel. Pajamas had been the cause of her first fight with Wesley right after he moved in. No one would ever call her an exhibitionist—she knew too many real exhibitionists to even make a claim on that title—but she had a good body and didn't care who saw it. So the first morning after Wesley moved in she came down to the kitchen in her usual sleepwear—a little nearly transparent black camisole and panties. Half-asleep still, she'd entered the kitchen, patted Wesley on the top of his blond head, grabbed a croissant and a cup of coffee, and headed for her office. A few minutes later a visibly troubled Wesley came into her office and stood with his back to her.

"Yes, Wesley, those jeans do make your ass look fabulous," she'd said, glancing over at his tall, lean and way-too-sexy-to-belong-to-a-virgin body.

"That is not why I have my back to you. You have no clothes on, Nora," he'd said, sounding royally perturbed.

"I do have clothes on. I have on my pajamas."

"You're wearing saran wrap and nothing else."

"That is not true. I've worn saran wrap before and it looks nothing like this. This is La Perla."

"It's La Transparent. Pajamas have substance to them. They are made of cotton or equally opaque fabrics. If I'm going to live with you without losing my mind—"

"Or your virginity," she teased.

"You need to wear real pajamas around me. That's final."

He'd gone off to school in a huff that day. When he came

home she surprised him with a little pajama fashion show. First the sock monkeys, then the penguins, then the baby ducks wearing galoshes on their little feet.

"Better?" she'd asked.

Wesley had grinned at her as he reached out and buttoned the topmost button of her baby-duck pj's. She'd feigned choking although she felt quite comfortable with a tight collar around her neck. Wesley had undone the button again, and for a moment their eyes had met and she wanted nothing more in the world than for him to keep going. His fingers shook enough that she knew he'd been tempted to do just that.

Wesley had smiled at her and whispered, "Perfect."

"He's perfect, Nora."

The words pulled her out of the past. Turning around she saw Griffin coming into the guest bedroom he'd given her, the room right next to his, naturally, looking both annoyed and aroused.

"Nobody's perfect, Griffin," Nora said, throwing her duckies into a drawer. "Except Søren."

"Søren's not perfect."

Nora stared at Griffin. "Bastard priest lied to me."

Griffin rolled his eyes. "Michael's perfect. He's my dream man…boy. Whatever. Holy shit, Nora." Griffin threw himself across her bed. He picked up a pair of handcuffs and laid them on his face like a giant pair of glasses.

"Very fetching." Nora removed the handcuffs from Griffin's face and put them in her bondage-gear pile on the end of the bed. "Did you finish his checklist?"

"Yeah. Junior's a freak. I'm in love."

Nora threw her thigh-high boots in the closet.

"You aren't in love."

"Would you buy 'love with honorable intentions'?"

"Nope."

Griffin glared at her.

"Griffin Fiske, you know as well as I do you've never had a relationship that lasted longer than three weeks. And that was when you were cheating on your girlfriend with her step-brother. You just met Michael."

"Yeah, so? How long did it take for you to fall in love with the Pope?"

Nora smiled to herself. "Two to three seconds. But that lasted about one week before I decided I hated him."

"It is pretty impressive how long you two have lasted." She heard the grudging respect in Griffin's tone. Griffin had scores of lovers and approximately zero serious relationships under his belt. "What's your secret?"

"Well, Søren has great staying power. And it does help I'm still in love with him. Helps even more that I still hate him," she said, suddenly not wanting to talk about Søren. It hurt too much knowing it could be two months or more before she saw him again. "So what's up with Michael's checklist? Anything I need to know?"

Griffin flipped over and dug the papers out of his back pocket. Nora made the bad decision to join him on the bed. It took all of two seconds before she landed flat on her back with Griffin slapping the handcuffs from her bondage pile onto her wrists.

"That reminds me," Nora said, relaxing into the grip of the cuffs, "I need to call my editor."

"You can call him after I fuck you."

"Can you fuck me after we talk about Michael's checklist?"

Griffin collapsed next to her and left her lying on her stomach still cuffed. Groaning in frustration, Nora used her shoulder to flip herself onto her side.

"Checklist first, then fucking. What's up with junior?"

"Sex stuff? Fives across the board. Horny little twerp."

"He's seventeen."

"Point taken."

"What else?" Nora asked.

"No big fetishes. No watersports or anything."

"Good," Nora said, "I have a shy bladder."

"The usual kink works for him," Griffin continued. "Bondage is good, all kinds. Pain is good, all kinds. This was weird though," Griffin said as he flipped to the last page.

"What?"

"He wants pain and domination. All fours and fives in that area. But when I asked about cutting, he gave it a big number one. Weird, huh?"

Nora's mind immediately went to the scars on Michael's wrists. Didn't seem weird to her at all—he'd had more than enough cutting in his life already.

"I hate bastinado," Nora said, trying to deflect Griffin's attention. If Michael wanted Griffin to know about his suicide attempt, she'd let Michael tell him. "Do whatever you want to me but don't beat my feet. I'm ticklish."

Griffin raised an eyebrow at her. "Duly noted. Oh, he doesn't like yelling, either."

Nora sighed. That probably came from Michael's asshole father.

"I was never a fan of yelling at my clients. Hard on the throat. Plus a really good dominant can put the fear of God into a sub with a whisper. Søren certainly can."

"Søren can put the fear of God into a sub by just showing up," Griffin said with barely concealed envy.

"I know. I love that man," Nora said, smiling with pride. In their huge underground kinky community, no one commanded more respect or fear than Søren. Sometimes she thanked God Søren had gone into the church and not the military. He'd be a dictator for sure.

"One final thing about Mick," Griffin said, folding the checklist back up.

"Mick?"

"That's what I'm calling him. *Michael* has too many syllables."

"Okay, what's the final thing about Mick?"

Griffin rolled onto his side and met Nora eye to eye. He reached out and freed her hair from her black hair clip and caressed her face and neck. Bad, Nora thought. It had to be bad news if Griffin was buttering her up.

"It's just, and don't freak out," Griffin said, opening her shirt, pulling the strap of her bra down and taking one of her nipples into his warm mouth.

"Freaked out is not why I'm feeling now," she said, leaning back to give him better access to her breasts. "Tell me the freak-out part while I'm turned on."

Griffin slid his hand under her skirt between her thighs; he slipped a finger under her panties and inside her.

"It's just, the thing about Mick is," Griffin said as he pressed a second finger into her wet warmth, "he's bi."

8

Alone in the room Nora and Griffin had given him, Michael unpacked his duffel bag. His skateboard, wheels up, he'd packed on top of his things and that came out first. Now that he held it in his hands, he almost regretted bringing it. Nora knew he was a skater, but Griffin didn't. Surely someone like Griffin would find skateboarding childish. Michael sat the board on the floor and rolled it under the bed.

He unpacked his clothes—jeans and T-shirts, boxer shorts, socks, the usual—and tucked them in the empty dresser. Putting his rather ratty clothes inside furniture that probably cost more than his mom's car felt a little wrong. Digging once more in his bag, Michael found his most precious possession and pulled it out.

Right after he'd moved with his parents to Wakefield and started attending Sacred Heart, Michael heard rumors that the writer Nora Sutherlin attended that same church years before she'd become *the* Nora Sutherlin. One day at the mall he'd snuck off to the Borders store and found a copy of her book

The Red. The cover had a picture of a woman's wrists tied with a bloodred silk ribbon. He remembered staring at the picture for so long without blinking that his eyes had started to water. But there was no way they'd let a thirteen-year-old buy a book like that. He thought about stealing it, but even the idea of shoplifting made his stomach churn with guilt. He found a fantasy novel about kings and unicorns that was the same price and size as *The Red* and he switched the covers. He didn't need the cover. The image of the tied wrists had burned into his retinas. When he looked at it, looked at those tied wrists and pale hands, he couldn't help but imagine his own wrists and own hands. It spoke to him, that image. It whispered to him. Love, he thought, when he first gazed on the image, looked just like that.

He bought the book and took it home. After his parents had gone to bed he'd stayed up all night reading it. He stayed up all the next night reading it again.

When Father Stearns started counseling him after his suicide attempt, Michael finally worked up the courage to ask him about Nora, who Father S called Eleanor. For some reason the first question that came out was, "Is she pretty?"

Father Stearns answered, "Michael, Eleanor is without a doubt the most beautiful woman who has ever or will ever live. If you could take a nighttime thunderstorm and turn it into a woman, you would have a very good idea what she looks like. And a fairly good idea how she behaves as well," he'd said and smiled. Michael was quiet for a long time after that. He loved storms at night, how they made the whole house shiver with the force of the wind and the rain and how they broke the sky open with white light. After a long silence his priest had paused and turned to him. He looked at Michael for a long moment. "Would you like to meet her?"

Father S had made him a deal: if Michael could go one entire year without harming himself in any way—no burns, no bruises, no cuts, no suicides attempts—he would arrange for him and Nora Sutherlin to meet. Eleven months into their deal, Michael had been at Sacred Heart doing homework. His mom had gotten a new job after the divorce was finalized. It paid better than her old job but it meant she had to work until 11:30 p.m. some evenings. She didn't like leaving Michael home by himself. Father S had offered to stay late at church on those days so Michael wouldn't be alone.

A Monday night, a school night, he remembered. He was working on a Mendel chart due in biology the next day. He heard Father S on the phone with someone but couldn't make out what he was saying. It sounded as though he was speaking French. He did that sometimes on the phone. Sometimes French. Sometimes another language that sounded maybe like Swedish to Michael, but which he later learned was Danish. Michael heard Father S hang up the phone. When his priest emerged from his office, he wore that same sad smile again.

"She would do her homework out here too," he'd said without preamble. Michael didn't have to ask who "she" was. "You could always tell when she was working on her math homework."

"How could you tell?" Michael had asked.

"I, and anyone else in the church at the time, could hear the litany of profanities."

Michael had laughed then. "I can't wait to meet her."

"You don't have to wait anymore. Are you ready?"

Michael's hands had gone numb then for the first time since regaining all feeling a month after leaving the hospital. Her—Nora Sutherlin—the woman who'd stolen his deepest dreams and put them on paper. Michael took a scared, shallow breath and started putting his homework away.

Michael had nodded. "I'm ready."

He'd followed Father S out of the church and into a gray Rolls Royce that waited on the street. The car had pulled away from the curb and Father Stearns had stared out the window.

"What do I do when I meet her?" Michael asked.

"You will call her ma'am or mistress. And you will do anything she tells you to do."

Michael had shivered then like a house in a thunderstorm.

"Will we… I mean, what will—"

"She'll take your virginity, Michael. If that's what you want."

Michael nodded and stared out the window. It seemed as though the car was staying still and only the streets were moving.

"Yeah, that's what I want."

And now here he was in a freaking mansion in upstate New York with Nora Sutherlin herself. God, it was surreal. *What the hell am I doing here?* Michael asked himself as he put the book into the bedside-table drawer. This house reeked of wealth and power and old money. He was just a seventeen-year-old nobody with nothing going for him.

"If I ordered you to smile, would you?" came a voice from his doorway.

Michael looked up and found Nora watching him with her arms crossed and her usual little grin on her face.

"Yes, ma'am," he said, trying to smile for her. She entered his room and came to him. Taking both of his hands in hers, she lifted his wrists to her lips and gently kissed his scars.

The real smile finally came.

"He saved my life, you know?" Michael said. "Father S did."

Nora pulled away and sat on the bench in the big bay window.

"Did he?"

Michael nodded. "Not just that night when he found me.

Telling me about himself, about you…that helped more than anything."

"Did he ever tell you how he saved my ass?" Nora asked, crossing her lithe legs.

"No."

"Well, he does try to keep my reputation as sterling as possible. One of the labors of Hercules obviously. Right after I met Søren, I got into some trouble. Almost went to juvie."

Michael boggled at this news. "For what?"

"My mom thought she'd married a mechanic." Nora leaned back against the wall. "Nice blue-collar husband for a girl from a big, poor German Catholic family. Not really a mechanic it turned out. More like he ran a chop shop with mob connections."

"Holy shit. Your dad was in the mob?"

Nora shrugged. "Not in it really. Just of it. He was in and out of jail. Always owed some dangerous somebody money. Mom tried to keep me away from him but it's hard for a Daddy's girl to tell her father no when he calls and says he needs her help. Let's just say I was a little too good at the family business."

"You got arrested stealing a car?"

Nora held up one hand and spread out her fingers.

"Five cars?" Michael asked, aghast.

"They caught me on the fifth one. I was on quite a roll that night. Nobody suspected the fifteen-year-old girl skulking around Manhattan in her Catholic school uniform was out for their Porsche. I looked so innocent. It was the perfect disguise."

"Innocent? You?"

Nora stared at him a moment before composing her face into a blank expression. She widened her eyes, fluttered her eyelashes and bit her bottom lip like a nervous child. She suddenly looked fifteen, sweet and scared.

"Damn," Michael breathed.

"Oh, yeah," she said, her face returning to normal. "I can do innocent. That look worked on everybody—Mom, Dad, cops…everybody except Søren. He saw right through it. He sees right through everything."

"I've noticed."

"I was sitting in the police station in an interrogation room. Fifteen years old, and the priest I've met all of twice before comes in and unlocks my handcuffs…with his own personal handcuff key, I found out later. He sat down across from me and waited, not saying a word, until I met his eyes. He said he could get me out of this but I would have to do everything he told me to do."

"For how long?"

"That's what I asked him. He said, 'Forever.'"

"What did you say?" Michael asked, fascinated by the image of a fifteen-year-old Nora trying to save herself from juvie by making a desperate deal with the mysterious priest.

"You've met him. What do you think I said?" she asked and winked at him. "But enough about me and ancient history. How are you?"

"I'm okay. Griffin's nice," he said and immediately regretted it. Where the hell had that come from?

"He is. Very," Nora said, staring at him long and hard. Michael looked at the floor and studied the scuff marks on the white tips of his Chuck Taylors. "I'm glad you like him. He and Søren do not get along."

"How come?"

"Neither of them will tell me. If you can find out from either of them, I'll give you anything you want."

Michael smiled and shook his head. "Nora, I'm here with you. What else could I ask for?"

Nora stood up and walked over to him. Standing in front of him she looked him up and down.

"How about this?" Nora asked as she opened his pants.

"Okay," Michael agreed. "Maybe that."

When Suzanne arrived at her apartment, she found a folder on her desktop Patrick had labeled Nora Sutherlin, Fine Writer. She thought that a rather odd name for the folder until she noticed the capitalized initials: NSFW, internet slang for Not Safe For Work. That she believed.

Still shaken from her meeting with the ungodly handsome priest, Suzanne poured a glass of wine to calm her nerves. She sat at her computer and opened the file.

Hey Beautiful, read a note from Patrick when she clicked the folder. I scoured the interwebs for you and dug up everything I could on one Ms. Nora Sutherlin. You'll be shocked to learn I didn't find out as much about her as I thought I would. She, like your priest, seems to have some sort of internet force field around her. Writing career stuff? Tons. Personal life? Not so much. But I made some calls and got the scoop. Read file #1 first. Then read file #69. Then call me and let me take you out to dinner, you beautiful obsessed woman. I'm sexier than any priest, right?

Suzanne gave a little rueful laugh. Any priest but Father Stearns. She still couldn't believe he was so… *No*, Suzanne told herself. She was not going to let herself get blinded by the man's appearance. Something bad had to be up with this priest for someone to anonymously fax her about him. As good-looking as he was, it wasn't hard to imagine him having a sexual-predator side to him. Even if he wasn't going after kids, he could be preying on the women in his congregation.

She opened the file marked #1 and found a list of quotes from Nora Sutherlin in various interviews.

From *Writers' Weekly.*

Interviewer: Where do you get your ideas?

N.S.: I have my best plot ideas in the same place I have my best orgasms.

Interviewer: In bed?

N.S.: At church.

Suzanne snickered out loud at that.

From *Literary Friction,* the largest erotica blog on the web.

Interviewer: Do you rely on personal experiences when writing your sex scenes?

N.S.: No.

Interviewer: Secretly vanilla?

N.S.: Legal advice. I don't want anything out there that can be used against me in a court of law.

Suzanne read through a few more of the quotes Patrick had compiled. Nora Sutherlin certainly talked a good game. But she'd met a few too many novelists to believe that any writer lived as wildly as his or her characters. The days of crazy Kerouac and Hemingway types of writers was long over. Nora Sutherlin could easily be an overweight fifty-year-old housewife who'd only had missionary-position sex all her life and even that with just her husband. That was Suzanne's theory on what most romance writers were like anyway.

She closed out file #1 and saw a file marked Pics. She clicked on the folder and her eyes went wide.

"Wow," Suzanne said out loud to the empty room. Patrick apparently put a great deal of time and effort into finding photographs of Nora Sutherlin. Poor thing. What a chore. Nora Sutherlin could have been Rachel Weisz's sister—wavy black hair, big green eyes, full pouty lips, pale skin and curves that wouldn't quit. In one photograph Nora Sutherlin sat at a table signing books with a red Sharpie. The corset she wore did magnificent things to her cleavage. In another photo she stood on the top of a spiral staircase in a short red skirt with an extremely handsome man with a dark Brutus haircut. *Writer Nora Sutherlin with Royal House Editor Zachary Easton,* read the photo caption. Something about the way they looked at each other in the photo made Suzanne wonder if Mr. Easton did a little more than just edit her books. Not that she would blame him. So much for her theory on romance writers. The last photo appeared to have been taken at some sort of party or fund-raiser. She wore a gorgeous bloodred satin gown. Next to her stood a man, no, a boy really. Although significantly taller than she was, the boy looked considerably younger. He couldn't have been a day over eighteen or nineteen at the most. In his tuxedo he looked like a teenager playing dress-up. He, like Zachary Easton in the other photo, gazed at Nora Sutherlin with equal parts longing and adoration. She seemed to be something of a man-collector. Suzanne had to wonder if Nora ever "collected" Father Stearns.

Okay, Suzanne thought, so Nora Sutherlin was a babe. Interesting. And she wrote erotica. And in interviews she acted as though her books were pale shadows compared to her real life. Suzanne had read a few of the books. Hard to believe Nora Sutherlin could be living wilder than her characters. That would take a lot of effort. Suzanne remembered Patrick's instructions—read file #1 first and then file #69. *Classy, Patrick,* she thought. *Very classy.*

She double-clicked on file #69. The document inside contained only two sentences.

If you want to know more, you have to have dinner with me, read sentence number one. But it was sentence number two that got Suzanne's attention.

Nora Sutherlin is a world-famous dominatrix.

★ ★ ★

Michael groaned in ecstasy as Nora rubbed the backs of his legs with her incredibly talented hands. He'd been a little disappointed when Nora said they weren't going to scene together or have sex yet. But a full-body massage from the one and only Nora Sutherlin? He couldn't find much cause to complain.

"I'm the sub," Michael said when Nora moved up to his back. "Shouldn't I be giving you the massage?"

"You are the most stressed-out, tightly wound sub on the face of the earth," Nora said, digging her strong fingers into the knot that was his back. "I can't beat you up until you relax a little or you'll pull every muscle in your body in our first session. Relax. That's an order."

"Yes, ma'am," Michael said, tensing when she slid her hands into his boxers.

"Michael," Nora said with obvious exasperation, "you just clenched your ass tighter than the second pair of Spanx on a drag queen. Did I forget to mention *relax* was an order?"

"I'm sorry, I'm sorry," Michael said, laughing.

"What has gotten you so tense, Angel?" Nora pulled her hands away and stretched out on her side next to him.

Michael turned his head to face her.

"You're my priest's girlfriend. I'm in a stranger's house. Both of my parents would freak out if they knew I was here."

Nora reached out and caressed the arch of his cheek.

"Tell me the truth. Why are you really so stressed out?"

Swallowing hard, he rolled up and pulled his T-shirt back on.

He turned his face from her and stared out the window.

"There's a huge swimming pool right out that window," Michael said.

Nora smiled. "I know. You want to drain it and skate it, don't you?"

"How did you know?" he asked, grinning sheepishly.

"I'm old. I've seen *Gleaming the Cube* about a million times. Christian Slater as a blond punk skateboarder? The movie's probably the reason I'm so attracted to blond men."

"Never seen it."

"We'll rent it. Now answer the question. Why are you so stressed?"

Sighing, Michael pulled his legs to his chest and rested his chin on his knees.

"I don't belong here, Nora. With you, with Griffin, in this house…this is crazy."

Nora said nothing at first. She stood up and switched on the small bedside lamp. When he was a kid he had an ugly plastic Power Rangers lamp. Young Griffin had a Tiffany lamp.

"Get into bed," Nora ordered.

"It's only 10:30 p.m.," Michael protested.

"I'm getting in with you."

Michael couldn't scramble under the covers fast enough. In the low light he watched Nora strip out of her shoes, skirt and blouse. Wearing only her black bra and barely there panties, she slid into bed next to him.

"Clothes off," she said and Michael awkwardly stripped out of his shirt and boxers. "Good boy. Spoon with me—your back to my chest."

Nervously Michael pressed into Nora, nearly groaning aloud as his skin met hers. He did groan aloud when she reached down and wrapped her hand around him.

"You're not just taller," she said into his ear. "You've gained a couple inches in another area too, I see."

Michael blushed and said nothing.

"Now I'm going to do two things," Nora said. "I'm going to give you an orgasm and tell you a bedtime story. Which do you want first?"

"Ah…orgasm?" Michael answered tentatively. If he didn't come first, he probably wouldn't be able to concentrate on a word Nora said.

"Understandable." Nora tightened her grip on him, bit his shoulder and gently stroked upward. His body tensed hard at Nora's touch and he released with a silent shiver. "Feel better?"

Michael nodded. "And wetter."

"Leave it," Nora said. "This is Griffin's old bed. Trust me. Yours is not the first cum to hit these sheets. Bedtime story now. Ready? Say 'Yes, ma'am.'"

His own personal bedtime story by Nora Sutherlin?

"Yes, ma'am," Michael said with the closest thing he had in his verbal repertoire to gusto.

"Once upon a time," Nora said, as she fluttered a series of kisses over his shoulders that sent every nerve in his body reeling, "a very poor girl from a fucked-up family became a famous writer with a wicked pen and an even more wicked tongue who made seven figures a year. And she went everywhere she wanted to and did everything she wanted to. And nobody ever tried to stop her. And she had her own pet Angel who needed to learn how to talk. So guess what she did?"

"What?" Michael asked. He laughed in surprise as Nora slammed him down onto his back and slid on top of him.

She brought her mouth onto his and forced his lips apart.

"She gave him her tongue."

9

A gentle hand on her shoulder roused Nora from sleep. She turned over and saw Griffin standing next to Michael's bed holding out her cell phone.

The Pope, he mouthed.

Nora nodded and took the phone. She turned and saw Michael curled up in the fetal position with his long lush eyelashes resting on his cheeks. For nearly an hour after sticking her tongue down his throat to make him laugh, they'd lain in his bed and talked. Well, she'd done most of the talking. But he'd listened and asked a few nervous questions about what would happen with them this summer, what she expected from him, what he needed. Finally he'd relaxed enough to fall asleep.

Carefully Nora slid out from under the covers. Griffin stood staring, obviously transfixed by the curve of Michael's pale bare shoulder peeking out from under the sheets and glowing in the moonlight. Nora grabbed Griffin by the shirt and dragged him into the hall. She closed the door behind her and gave Griffin a stern stare.

"Yes, sir?" she said when Michael lay safely out of earshot.

"How are you, little one?" came Søren's voice over the line.

"Lonely for a certain six-foot-four blond Scandinavian guy I know."

Griffin started to go back into Michael's room and Nora barred the closed door with her body.

"Anyone I know?" Søren asked.

"Alexander Skarsgård." Griffin feinted to the right before attempting to duck under her arm. She raised her leg and braced it on the door frame to block him.

"I'm afraid I'm not familiar with the gentleman."

"He's a Swedish vampire. Anyway, how are you, sir?"

She heard Søren's quiet laugh on the other end of the line.

"Intrigued."

Nora's blood momentarily turned to ice at the utterance of that word. Intrigued. Søren intrigued? This could not even begin to be a good thing.

"Intrigued by what? Or by whom, should I ask?"

"By a certain reporter who appeared at Mass this evening. Suzanne Kanter."

Nora groaned and not just with worry but reluctant plea-sure. Griffin had taken a different tack and now kissed the sensitive tendon where her neck met shoulder. As he kissed her, he unbuttoned his shirt to reveal the expanse of his mus-cled chest and stomach.

"Oh, God, she's pretty, isn't she?" she asked, not feeling the slightest shard of jealousy, but only fear. An intrigued Søren was a distracted Søren. She needed him cold, calculating and detached so he could deal with the mess swirling around him in Wakefield. Not intrigued.

"Yes, she's lovely. Dark red hair, dark eyes, quite tall," he said and she heard the slightest amorous tinge in his voice.

Griffin unhooked her bra and started sliding it down her arms. "She would look exquisite on my St. Andrew's Cross."

Suddenly visions of newspaper headlines danced through her head.

Respected Catholic Priest Exposed as S&M Lord
Catholic Priest's Erotic Dungeon Found
Accused S&M Priest Defrocked and Excommunicated
Bestselling Erotica Writer Linked to Excommunicated Priest
Bestselling Erotica Writer Found Guilty of Statutory Rape

"We're all going to jail," she sighed.

"Eleanor, calm down," Søren said, his voice now stern and commanding, just the way she liked it. "All will be well. I will handle Ms. Kanter. She came out of suspicion, not simple curiosity, and that is what intrigues me more than anything. For all of her smiles and polite posturing, she appeared to be absolutely terrified of me."

"Terrified?" Nora repeated as Griffin nibbled at her hips while attempting to remove her underwear. Søren, unlike her, never exaggerated. She knew most people found Søren intimidating at first, what with his height, extraordinary handsomeness, his priest's collar and his remote demeanor. And he could certainly scare the shit out of people when in the right mood. Zach Easton could testify to that. But terrified seemed uncalled-for unless this reporter had some sort of priest-phobia. She knew a few traumatized Catholic school graduates who nearly wet themselves around nuns and sisters.

"She must be Catholic," Nora concluded.

"Lapsed," Søren said. "Also, she's a fan of yours. Or claims to be. Somehow she learned you attend Sacred Heart."

"If she's a fan then I have to like her," Nora said, hating this reporter who'd come sniffing around Søren. Bad sign that the reporter already linked her with Søren. Things were getting sticky already.

Nora glanced down and discovered Griffin had succeeded in getting her completely naked and himself half-naked in the hallway. He brought his hand between her legs and lightly toyed with the tiny silver hoop that pierced her clitoral hood. She attempted to slap his hand away but he carried on, impervious to her defenses.

"What are you going to do?" she asked as Griffin slipped a finger into her while his other hand expertly teased her nipple. Michael being denied to him, Griffin had clearly decided to take his frustrated lust out on her. Against her will, her body started to respond to his gentle assault. At least a couple hours of kinky fucking would distract her from Søren worries.

"Anything I have to," he said simply, the threat of Søren's deep darkness in his words. "Take care of Michael. Keep Griffin away from him. You will be home with me where you belong soon enough."

"Yes, sir," she said, her stomach tightening both with both nervousness and arousal. "I love you." Tears pricked at her eyes as she said the words. Not good. Just a few days apart and she already missed him enough to get weepy.

"I love you too, little one. Nothing and no one will keep us apart. Know that and believe it."

"Trying," she said and took a ragged breath.

Griffin took her bra and panties and his shirt and started heading down the hall toward the east wing. He turned back around and beckoned her with the condom package between his index and middle fingers. Which reminded her…

"Søren?" Nora asked sweetly. "Beloved priest of my heart? Can I ask a little favor?"

Dinner with Patrick always started out with dinner but never ended with dinner. Suzanne lay underneath him as he pulled her panties down her legs. Bad idea, sleeping with an

ex-boyfriend, even if he was helping her with her investigation. But she couldn't deny she wanted this, wanted his warm
mouth on her breasts and his fingers on her clitoris and…

"I want your cock in me, Patrick," she gasped as he covered her naked body with his.

Patrick laughed softly and Suzanne's body temperature
kicked up a couple more degrees as his strong bare chest vibrated against her taut nipples.

"I'll happily put my cock in you. Where did that come
from?" he asked as he slipped on a condom. Reaching between her thighs, he caressed her wet folds with fingers that
knew exactly where she liked being touched.

"Your fault," she said as he traced leisurely circles into her
with one and then two fingers. "You're the one who told me
Nora Sutherlin went to Sacred Heart. I've been reading her
books…for research."

"One-handed research?" Patrick kissed his way across her
shoulders and neck and up to her mouth.

"Wouldn't you like to know," she teased.

"Wouldn't I love to watch," he said, pushing gently into
her. She spread her legs and took him deeper.

She groaned in the back of her throat as Patrick started his
slow forceful thrusts. Rocking her hips into Patrick's, she tried
to keep from dwelling on all the reasons she shouldn't be—
again—having sex with her ex. They weren't getting back together. With her work, her traveling, she couldn't have a real
relationship. He wanted so much from her—commitment,
promises, love—that she didn't have to give. But at dinner
they'd talked about Nora Sutherlin, how she had appeared almost out of nowhere six years ago and become the most celebrated dominatrix in the Underground. Patrick didn't know
too many specifics. Specifics were hard to come by where
Nora Sutherlin was concerned. Still, that didn't stop Suzanne

and Patrick from wildly speculating about her personal life—who she slept with, who her clients were, what kinky people did behind closed doors. By the time they stumbled into Suzanne's apartment after dinner, they were both flushed and breathy and ready to fall into bed together.

Closing her eyes, Suzanne felt the tension in her thighs that signaled she was close to coming. Patrick's hands groped at her back as his mouth sought hers again and again. She pressed into the bed as she felt the familiar tightening. For one brief moment a vision of someone other than Patrick flashed across her mind's eye—a vision of a man, taller than Patrick, more viscerally handsome, older, far more intimidating and significantly blonder. Suddenly she orgasmed, the vaginal spasms fluttering through her stomach. For another few seconds Patrick kept thrusting. He pushed one final time, gathered her to him and came hard. At the back of her mind she heard him whisper something into her ear. But shocked by the vision she'd just had, she didn't understand the words.

"You're not going to say anything?" Patrick said, kissing her cheek, her neck.

"Sorry," she said, panicking a moment. Had she said something when she came, said another name? "I just—"

"I said I love you, Suzanne." Slowly Patrick pulled out of her and lay on his side. "No comment?"

"Oh, God," she said, gathering the sheets to her chest. "I'm sorry. Good orgasm—I think it killed some brain cells."

Patrick rolled onto his back. "I killed some brain cells. Nice. Well, not quite what I was hoping for but better than 'I hate you. Get out.'"

Suzanne heard the hurt in his voice, the hurt she knew he desperately wanted to hide from her. Reluctantly she turned to face him.

"Patrick, we've had this conversation. Nothing's changed since the last time we had it."

"Right," he said, dragging his lean, toned body out of her bed. Why did he always have to make sex about something more than sex?

He grabbed his jeans off the floor and pulled them on. "Work is your life. In Iran one month. In Cambodia the next. Can't settle down. Unfair to me. Just won't work. I've heard it all. What I haven't heard is you looking me in the eyes and saying, 'Patrick, I don't love you.'"

He threw on his shirt and brusquely buttoned it.

"Waiting," he said. "Can you say it?"

Suzanne rolled her eyes. "Yeah, I always make my declarations of love during post-sex fights. Maybe we should talk about this another time. When I have clothes on."

"Yeah, that'll make a difference. I'll just go now so I can let you get back to work. Call me when you need more help digging up dirt on this priest of yours. Or when you want my cock in you again, as you so delicately put it."

He slammed his feet into his shoes, grabbed his jacket and stormed out of the bedroom. Groaning, Suzanne yanked the sheet free from the bed and wrapped it around her.

"Patrick, please don't leave. We were having such a good evening. Why do you always have to ruin it by starting a fight?" Patrick paused at her front door and turned around.

"You're beautiful," he said. "And you're brilliant. And you drive me insane. And I've been in love with you for a year. I didn't sleep with a single person after you dumped me and ran off to Afghanistan—"

"I didn't run off," she countered angrily. "I'm a war correspondent. It was my job."

"And I didn't start a fight. I told you I loved you. Only you would hear 'I love you' and think I'm starting a fight.

I'm leaving now before I say something really horrible, like 'I love you' again."

Suzanne exhaled and ran her fingers through her hair.

"Patrick…" she began and could think of nothing else to say.

He stared at her a long time and shook his head.

"She left," Patrick said as he turned the doorknob.

"What?"

"Nora Sutherlin. Her real name's Eleanor Schreiber, you know."

"Yeah, I know. Nora Sutherlin's just a pen name."

"Anyway, Sacred Heart keeps meticulous membership rolls. She left the church seven years ago, came back last year. Doubt it means anything. Meant to tell you that at dinner."

Suzanne nodded. Patrick waited.

"Thank you," she said, drawing the sheet tighter around herself.

Patrick only looked at her. He opened the door and walked out, leaving her alone in her apartment.

Frustrated and hurt, Suzanne headed back for the bedroom. On her way she paused by her bookcase and stared at her copy of Nora Sutherlin's book *The Red* sitting on her shelf.

"All your fault, you slut," Suzanne said, trying to make herself feel better. It didn't work. She took the book off the shelf and leafed through it, hoping to distract herself from the fact that during sex with Patrick, she'd pictured the face of Father Stearns, the target of her investigation—the enemy. She stiffened her spine and pushed her shame aside. Father Stearns had shocked her by being so breathtakingly handsome. That was the only reason his face came to her while Patrick was inside her. That's all.

Suzanne nearly shut the book and put it back on the shelf. The last thing she needed was to think about sex or men anymore today. But as the pages fanned closed her eyes fell onto the book's dedication.

As Always, Beloved, Your Eleanor

She read it again. An odd phrase, oddly worded. It seemed to say more than it actually said. Nora was short for Eleanor. That part she understood.

But who was her beloved?

Michael woke up alone. The moon rested high in the corner of his window. Still night. He rolled onto his back and stared up at the ceiling. Part of him still couldn't believe he was here spending the summer in a mansion and learning kink from *the* Nora Sutherlin. Before he'd fallen asleep, she'd interrogated him about his fantasy life, what he wanted to try, what he wanted to learn. Having a beautiful domme gently scouring his naked skin with her fingernails while telling him stories about her life as a submissive might have been one of the most erotic moments of his life. Unfortunately when she'd tried asking him specific questions about what he wanted to do, to try with her, he clammed up, too embarrassed to answer. He'd apologized for his inability to articulate his sexual needs to her. But she'd just kissed him gently and whispered, "We'll get there."

One thing they had been able to talk about was safety. Tomorrow he'd start taking the sub-cocktail, as Nora called it. vitamin K and zinc, to help his bruises heal faster. During their scenes he was to use the green/yellow/red light system to let her know how he was faring. And, of course, his safe word would still be what she'd given him their one night they spent together: wings.

Michael remembered that night, that moment when he'd told her his name. Nora had smiled and reminded him that Michael was the name of God's chief archangel, God's fiercest warrior. A fierce warrior? Whatever. His father had named him and obviously expected a different sort of son. His dad would have been much happier with a masculine, athletic son. Not the pale, thin, almost feminine-looking kid he'd ended up with. A guy like Griffin, that's what his dad would have wanted in a son. With his sinewed muscles and powerful build, his strong nose and jaw, Griffin was the sort of man anyone would want—men, women, everybody. He'd said as much to Nora when she asked him about his parents.

"Your father would find as much fault with Griffin as he does with you," she'd said, caressing his forehead with the loving touch of a mother checking for a fever. God, when was the last time his mom had even touched him? "Griffin was a hell-raiser of the highest order when he was your age, and didn't even begin to settle down until his twenties. Plus he's crazy kinky and bisexual."

"Griffin's bisexual?" Michael had asked, a strange thrill running through his body.

"He is. So, you know, watch your back, beautiful," she said, winking down at him.

Michael had groaned. "Guys aren't supposed to be beautiful," he'd protested as Nora stroked the high arch of his cheekbone.

"But angels are," she said and gave him another soft kiss. And then she'd brought her lips to his ear and whispered, "Saturday night."

"What's Saturday night?" he'd asked.

"That's when I'm going to beat you and fuck you again. If you're ready. Ready?"

"Very ready, ma'am."

Michael exhaled loudly, irritated at himself. He'd grown hard again just thinking about Saturday night, which fell an agonizing two days from now. And Nora had already warned him he couldn't come without her permission. Apparently Father S imposed the same rule on her during the two years he'd trained her before they became lovers. She said that being a madly-in-love eighteen-year-old virgin with a raging libido who had to get permission from her priest before she could even masturbate might have been the worst torture Søren had ever inflicted on her. Caning was a breeze in comparison.

Slowly Michael crawled out of bed, pulled on his boxers and T-shirt, and walked to his bathroom. No, he corrected himself. Griffin's bathroom. Everything belonged to Griffin, and Michael was merely a guest in this house. He couldn't, wouldn't, get used to this luxury. At the end of the summer, he'd move from his mother's small house to an even smaller dorm room where he'd go back to being alone. If he got used to this house and the people in it, it would hurt so much worse when he left it in August.

Leaning over the sink, Michael splashed cold water on his flushed face. He brushed his teeth and combed out his hair with his fingers—routine actions that helped his arousal die down a little. His stomach rumbled. How long had it been since he'd eaten? Yesterday maybe? Griffin had told him where to find the kitchen and that anything in it was fair game. Food. Food was good. Food would distract him.

He crept out of the room in the nursery wing and headed for the main stairs. He remembered Griffin's rather idiomatic instructions—down the fuck-off big stairs in the middle, left at that stupid marble whatever that I want to get rid of but Mom would kill me if I did, past the dining room with the anal table, and the kitchen's on the right.

"The anal table?" Michael had asked.

"Perfect height for anal sex," Griffin explained.

So Michael descended the fuck-off big stairs in the middle of the hall and turned left at the marble statue, which was some

kind of horse, he guessed. A door on the left side of the hall
stood slightly ajar. From inside escaped soft sounds of pleasure.

Quietly he crept to the door. Inside the expansive, opulent
dining room Michael saw Nora and Griffin. Nora lay naked on
the center of the enormous table. Long cords of red silk bound
her wrists to the table legs while her own legs lay splayed
open at the edge. Griffin, wearing nothing but leather pants
that rested low on his trim hips, stood between her knees as
he worked his hand into her. Carefully he pushed first three,
then four and finally all five of his fingers inside her straining body. Michael winced but Nora seemed to enjoy it. Her
back arched and her hips rose off the table as Griffin's entire
hand disappeared inside her.

If a cannon had gone off behind Michael, he still wouldn't
have been able to look away. Nora had such beautiful breasts,
and they rose and fell with her every ragged breath. The
sight of Griffin's muscled, tattooed arm wrist-deep in Nora
brought Michael nearly to orgasm from watching alone. He
never thought he had a leather fetish or anything, but for some
reason the sight of Griffin in leather pants, looking like some
kind of rock star bathed in sweat and candlelight, brought
every part of Michael's body to full attention.

He heard Griffin whispering carnal encouragements to
Nora, who rode his hand with hungry undulations of her
pelvis as she pulled at the scarlet scarves. Her breathing grew
harsh and labored. Griffin's fingers massaged her swollen clitoris until her entire body went rigid for what seemed like an
eternity before she released an exalted cry.

Her orgasm over, Nora lay still for a minute panting and
laughing a little as Griffin gingerly worked his way out of
her. He untied her wrists from the table and used the scarf to
clean his hand. Reaching out, he grabbed Nora's spent body
and lifted her off the table with a casual display of strength. A

small puddle of fluid glimmered on the table's polished surface right where Nora's hips had rested.

Pulling Nora to him, Griffin hissed a harsh command into her ear as he took the silk scarf and tied her wrists behind her back. Nora protested, pouted, begged a little. But Griffin only took her by the neck and pushed her onto the floor. He leaned against the table as Nora sunk to her knees in front of him. Michael nearly moaned out loud as Griffin freed his erection from the confines of his leather pants. Good God, Griffin was seriously well hung. Michael couldn't tear his eyes away as Griffin grabbed the back of Nora's head and forced her to take his impressive girth into her mouth. Griffin braced himself on the table with one hand as he moved in and out slowly.

Michael knew he shouldn't be watching this. Griffin and Nora were having sex. No way would they want him gaping at them the whole time. But he couldn't leave, couldn't look away, couldn't stop staring at the line at the center of Griffin's chest, the line that started at his strong neck, trailed down his broad chest, divided his ridged stomach and led down all the way into Nora's mouth. Griffin's stomach tightened further as a little grunt of pleasure passed his lips.

The hand in Nora's hair now caressed her face, her cheek, and Griffin stared down at her with hooded, lust-filled eyes. He playfully tapped her on the chin and winked. Winked? At the wink, Nora's rather occupied mouth twitched with a little smile. Until now Michael had always thought of kink as something dark and dangerous, something for fetishists and freaks like him. Now it suddenly dawned on him. BDSM was a game—a game where both players won.

Griffin returned Nora's smile before another desperate breath escaped his lips. Michael's heart clenched at the obvious affection Griffin felt for Nora. Would someone ever do that to him—smile at him like that, touch him like that, with affection, with love during sex? He worried constantly he would never find anyone to love him. Finding someone who understood his sexuality and didn't judge him for it seemed a near-impossible dream. Nora had Father S, and surely Griffin had tons of lovers who satisfied all his wants and desires. Would Michael ever have that? Surely most girls would make a run for it the second he told them he needed to be dominated in the bedroom. And Nora sort of seemed like one of a kind.

With a heavy heart, Michael finally pulled away from the cracked-open door and headed back to his room. Once again the demon of envy danced in his chest. He stopped and rested his head against the wall to breathe for a few seconds.

The scene he'd just witnessed flashed in front of his mind's eye again, but this time it was him in the dining room. He could feel the plush Persian rug soft but prickly under his knees, the cord taut around his wrists. In shock, Michael's eyes flew open as he realized for one second he didn't envy Griffin because he got to be with Nora.

He envied Nora.

10

Nora checked the time on the clock in her bedroom and made a quick mental calculation. Sunset hit at about nine o'clock and it was just six. She still had three hours to kill before Michael's first session. She didn't want to have sex with Griffin first. Knowing him, he'd wear her out and she wouldn't have as much to give Michael. Too wound up to write, she decided to do the next best thing.

Digging into her purse, she found her cell phone and hit number three on her speed dial. A slightly groggy voice answered after three rings.

"Nora, do I need to remind you that it's midnight in England?" came Zach Easton's sexy British accent over the line.

"Were you dreaming about me again?" she teased as she sat on the floor and stretched her legs out in a V.

"God, I'm never going to hear the end of that, am I?"

"Your fault for telling me you had a sex dream about me," she said, leaning over to stretch her back. A few weeks ago, Zach had sounded a little odd on the phone when she'd called him one morning. He'd confessed he'd just woken up from an intensely sexual dream about her. They'd been back at her S&M club, The 8th Circle, and playing in her old dungeon. She never got it out of him exactly what they'd been doing, but it must have been pretty steamy for him to tell her he needed a good five minutes alone before they could finish their conversation.

"I shall never do it again, I assure you," Zach groused but Nora heard the smile in his voice.

Nora flipped over and raised her hips off the ground.

"I had this dream the other night that I was eating oysters at Sacred Heart, and Søren rode in on a unicorn. I thought it meant something, but when I told him about it, he said I wasn't allowed to eat Cajun food before bed anymore. That man has no respect for Jungian archetypes."

Zach sighed. "Yes, well, Gracie and I have the same problem."

"Speaking of your wife, where is she? I want to ask her how to say 'Roughly from behind' in Welsh."

"Gracie's in the bathroom taking her temperature."

"She has to do that in the bathroom?"

Zach coughed. Nora understood.

"Oh...I see. Also, now I'm wondering if they make butt plugs with built-in thermometers. You know, for when you might have a slight fever and the urge for anal penetration."

"Your mind is both fascinating and repulsive," Zach said.

"Thank you. I try. I'm guessing you two are still attempting to conceive?"

"Hence the constant temperature taking."

"Try dominating Grace in bed." Nora lowered her hips to the floor and twisted her knees to the side.

"Is kink your answer for everything, Eleanor?"

Nora winced at the use of her birth name. Retaliation was in order.

"No, Zechariah. It's just the answer for everything sexual. For male dominants, kink causes a testosterone surge. That can up your sperm count. For female submissives, kink can cause the body to release opiate-like hormones. She relaxes deeply. Makes conceiving easier when you're less stressed. There is a method to my madness. Tie her up. Knock her up. Doctor's orders."

"You may very well be my new favorite doctor."

"You're welcome. You can borrow my speculum. Borrow only. You have to give it back." Nora twisted her legs to the other side and let out a small grunt of pain-pleasure as her back loudly popped.

"Are you having sex right now?" he asked in response to the sound.

"Nope. Just doing some pre-sex stretching," she said, turning over into a yoga downward-dog position. "I'm fucking a teenager tonight. Gotta be prepared."

"Fucking a teenager?" Zach asked, laughing. "Good to hear both you and Wesley have moved on."

At the mention of Wesley's name, Nora dropped the phone and collapsed onto her side.

She heard Zach saying her name and she grabbed the phone off the floor.

"Nora? Everything all right?" Zach asked.

"What did you say about Wesley?" she asked, her hands almost shaking. "Do you talk to him?"

She heard Zach exhale heavily. "I'm sorry. I'm still half-asleep. I shouldn't have said anything. Yes, Wesley and I exchange emails on occasion. He said you won't answer his calls so he emails me to check on you."

Nora pulled herself off the floor and sat on the edge of her bed.

"You still talk to Wesley," she repeated, stunned by the news. It never once occurred to her that Zach and Wesley would stay in touch.

"Just an email every few weeks," Zach said. "He worries about you."

"Why?" she asked, her heart pounding against her rib cage.

"Why? Oh, I don't know. You're sleeping with a sadist?"

"Søren's the best man on the face of the earth," Nora said sharply.

"You say that and I want to believe you," Zach said. "And if any woman on the face of the earth can handle being with such a man, it's you. But Wesley's a teenage boy and rather romantically inclined. He simply sees Søren as dangerous and violent."

Closing her eyes, Nora pictured Wesley's face the last time she saw it. His beautiful golden-brown eyes had turned bloodred with unshed tears. His lips that she'd kissed too few times had gone bloodless. Her handsome, sweet-faced boy disappeared and was replaced by a broken man.

"He's not a teenager anymore," Nora said, her voice soft and hollow. "He turned twenty on September 9th. Did you know I'd already decided on his birthday present?"

"No, I didn't," Zach said, his voice flush with sympathy.

"I was going to surprise him with a trip to the Virgin Islands. Just me and him. I planned on teasing him that while we were there, we could change the island's name."

Zach laughed. "Why am I not surprised?"

"You said he moved on," Nora said, suddenly remembering Zach's words.

"Nora, let's not talk about this."

"What did you mean, 'Glad to hear both you and Wesley

have moved on'?" Nora demanded, putting her dangerously good memory to use.

"You're sleeping with a teenager tonight. Yes? Or was that a joke? I can never tell with you," Zach teased awkwardly.

"I am. I'm training a new submissive. The training will be rather thorough," she said, matching false levity with false levity.

"Well," Zach began and paused. And in that pause Nora's stomach clenched into a knot so tight it formed a tiny diamond that shone bright with agony. "Wesley has a girlfriend. She's a little older than he."

Nora swallowed.

"Who is she?" Nora asked, trying not to let the sorrow and anger she felt with unreasonable force seep into her voice.

"I believe he said her name is Bridget. She's his father's secretary, apparently."

"Bridget?" Nora repeated, snorting a little in disgust. "Sounds like a high-functioning moron. I've yet to meet a woman named Bridget who could read."

"This isn't some latent jealousy talking, is it?" Zach asked. Nora heard something in the background, the sound of a woman's voice. She heard the soft sound of a mattress sighing and knew Zach's wife, Grace, had gotten back into bed with him.

"No," Nora said. "Of course not. Are they sleeping together?"

"I'm afraid you'll have to ask him that. Have you considered answering the phone the next time he calls?"

Nora nodded and then remembered she and Zach were on the phone.

"I'll think about it. Søren wants me to. He thinks I need to make peace with my past."

"Then I'll say something I never thought I'd ever say in my life—I agree with Søren."

Nora gave a little rueful laugh.

"Here, Grace wants to speak with you," Zach said and she heard him whisper something and pass the phone.

"Nora? Are you all right?" came Grace's lilting Welsh-accented voice over the line.

"I'm fabulous. I was just flirting with your husband while you were out of the room."

"I don't blame you. He's looking quite nice tonight. I can't tell you what he's wearing because he's not wearing anything," Grace teased and Nora smiled finally, a real genuine smile.

"You're torturing me, Grace," Nora said, impressed. She still couldn't believe how cool Grace was with her continued friendship with Zach. The ocean between them probably helped. "I think you might be a sadist. I approve of this."

"I really do want to meet this mysterious priest of yours."

"We'll have a foursome next time you and Zach come to the States."

"Capital idea," Grace said before bidding her good-night. Nora hung up and dropped the phone back into her bag. For a long time she stared around her room, stared without seeing anything.

Wesley…a girlfriend? An older woman? His father's secretary?

Wait, Nora thought. From what Wesley told her, his father worked as a trainer on a horse farm. Horse trainers had secretaries? And gorgeous young men who could have any girl they wanted dated older women for one reason only—sex.

Nora heard a knock on her door. She turned her head and saw Griffin standing in her doorway wearing nothing but well-fitting dark gray boxer briefs.

"I'm going to go check on Mick, okay?" Griffin said. Nora

vaguely remembered ordering Michael to stay in his room all day as a punishment for doing absolutely nothing wrong since arriving at Griffin's. He needed to make some mistakes or she wouldn't have an excuse to punish him.

"Fine," Nora said as she rose off the bed.

"And then I'm going to tie him up and fuck him," Griffin said, apparently deciding to press his luck.

"Fine," Nora said again as she wandered around the room.

"Groovy." Griffin started to leave but she stopped him when she remembered something.

"Yes, mistress?" he asked, smiling.

"This house. This place was a horse farm once, right?"

"Yeah," Griffin said. "When my grandfather was younger, they raised Thoroughbreds here. I sold all the horses when I got the place. Horse racing can be pretty gruesome."

"The horse trainers, did they have secretaries?"

Griffin furrowed his handsome brow at her.

"No. Not that I know of. Just my grandfather, but he owned the place."

Nora nodded and Griffin left her doorway. She saw him heading toward the nursery wing. Shaking her head, she tried to dislodge the dark thoughts that fluttered around her mind like angry bats. She couldn't dwell on Wesley right now. She had Michael to think of. Of course Wesley had a girlfriend now. Tall and handsome, smart and sweet, Wesley was a catch. What had she expected him to do? She had kicked him out of her house and given herself—heart, body and soul—back to Søren. Did she think Wesley would just sit around waiting for her to come back to him for the rest of his life?

No, she hadn't thought that. But she had secretly hoped it.

Nora took a deep breath. *Grief,* she told herself, naming the sensation that took over her body at the moment. Søren had taught her this trick years ago. If she could name her feelings, enumerate them, label them, she could distance herself from them, make them objects separate from her. Burning. Stinging. Aching. Bruising. Giving her agony a name gave her mastery over it. An old S&M trick for controlling pain, she used it now. *Sorrow,* she told herself. Irrational, stupid, feminine sorrow.

An image flared up in her mind, an image of her sweet, virginal Wesley naked and burying himself inside another woman, thrusting into her, coming inside her.

Jealousy, Nora named the new feeling. Raging jealousy.

Nora took another deep breath. She sucked in her pain, her misery, held it in her stomach and pushed it out of her nose. *Michael.* She repeated his name in her head. He had to be her focus tonight. As she opened her eyes, she caught a glimpse of a bundle of white paper sitting on her bedside table. Michael's checklist. Picking it up, she skimmed through Michael's answers. Underneath the section on S&M, Griffin had left her a note.

Mick's not just a sub. He's a masochist too. Can I have him when you're done with him?

A subtle line existed between submissives and masochists. Submissives enjoyed submitting even if they hated the pain part of the process. But masochists not only liked submitting to pain, they got off on it.

Good, Nora thought, putting the checklist aside. Tonight, for some reason, she felt like beating the holy living hell out of somebody.

Michael Dimir—Suzanne typed the name into her Google search bar and paused before hitting Enter.

For days now Suzanne had avoided researching the kid who'd tried to kill himself at Sacred Heart. It hurt too much to think about, hit too close to home. But she couldn't avoid it anymore. After one meeting with Father Stearns, she'd discovered he was a man to be reckoned with. Even now, sitting alone in her apartment, her body recalled the fissure of shock she'd experienced upon seeing the priest for the first time. And when they'd spoken, she'd had the distinct impression he was playing her, toying with her. He'd been expecting a reporter—that much was obvious. And he hadn't betrayed the slightest flicker of fear or nervousness around her. Even the purest innocent got a little nervous around a reporter. Who the hell was this priest?

Suzanne pressed Enter and started sorting through all the hits. She hated herself for digging up dirt on a kid. But she kept hitting a wall with Father Stearns. Maybe she'd have better luck with one of his parishioners.

Nothing came up about the suicide attempt, of course. A minor at the time, the newspapers would have withheld his name. His name—Dimir…young Michael must be of Eastern European stock, she decided. She'd known a couple of Dimirs during her two-month stint in Romania and Serbia. *That's it,* she told herself. *Keep it professional, keep it vague, keep it impersonal. Don't think about him as a person, as a kid, as a Catholic kid who loved the church and trusted his priest and who…*

With an angry swipe of her hand, Suzanne wiped tears off her face. She slammed her laptop shut before even getting one piece of information about Michael Dimir. Immediately she felt better. If Michael Dimir had attempted suicide for the reason she believed he did, then the last thing she wanted to do was violate him again. She had to keep her focus on her target, and her target's name was Father Marcus Stearns.

She stared at her closed laptop and knew opening it would be futile. Someone once defined insanity as trying the same thing over and over again while expecting different results.

No amount of internet stalking would get her anywhere closer to the truth about Father Stearns.

Although she no longer believed in God, Suzanne knew she was doing His work right now. Someone somewhere knew something about Father Stearns, something bad enough to send her an anonymous tip about him. Why her, she had no idea. A thousand investigative reporters lived in the New York area. She'd never worked as anything but a war correspondent. Perhaps whoever sent the tip knew someone brave, someone unafraid of war zones would be needed to get to the truth. And war zones she knew. She'd been in a dozen of them— Sudan, Pakistan, Afghanistan, Iraq... Bombs had exploded around her, she'd seen soldiers get ripped apart by IEDs right in front of her eyes. But never until now had she experienced the sort of real fear she'd felt when standing in front of Father Stearns. She wouldn't let herself be intimidated. Not by one man. Not when she'd walked into battle zones wearing nothing but camos and a camera. She would go back to church. She had to.

The phone rang and jarred Suzanne from her dark, determined reverie.

"Patrick," she breathed when she answered. "I'm so sorry—"

"Don't," he said sheepishly and she sagged with relief. For some reason, she'd been a wreck since her fight with Patrick. Now that they'd broken up, she stressed more about him than when they were officially together. "It's my fault. You've been back in the States for like five minutes and I'm all over you to commit. That wasn't cool of me, and I'm sorry."

"It's okay. I promise. You mean so much to me," she said, knowing the words weren't as good as "I love you," but it was all she had for him right now. "Let's forget about it."

"No, I don't want to forget about it. Let me make it up to

you. Dinner? No sex required, I promise. But if you insist," he said and laughed nervously.

Suzanne smiled, grateful beyond words for his call, his apology, for his presence in her life that kept her from succumbing to the grief that threatened to overwhelm her at times.

"Dinner sounds lovely. But actually, you can make it up to me in another way," she said, staring at her closed and useless laptop.

"Anything," he pledged.

She'd spent the past eight years in countries with bombs and guns and death all around her. If she could face enemy armies she could face one Catholic priest.

"I need to borrow your car again."

Michael adjusted his position just slightly to better capture the fading evening sun. His pencil flew over the paper as he traced a series of curving lines. He paused, looked at his work, erased one line and redrew it. As he turned closer to the window he inhaled and caught a whiff of something in the air. He breathed the scent in again—sort of spicy but also subtle and masculine. It wasn't cologne or anything that strong. Just…Michael inhaled again and closed his eyes…just mouthwatering. God, whatever it was, he wanted to smell it for the rest of his life.

"Damn," came a voice over his shoulder, making Michael jump in surprise. He turned his head and came face-to-face with Griffin, who stood next to him wearing nothing but boxer briefs. At least he knew the source of that incredible smell now. Michael stared at him in silence for a moment and took in the lack of clothes and the wet hair. Griffin had just gotten out of the shower obviously, and that incredible scent came from his skin. "You drew that?"

Griffin took Michael's sketchbook from him and sat opposite him on the bench in the bay window.

"It's not done." He reached out to grab his book back, but Griffin raised his finger at him, and Michael dropped his hands.

"Submit, submissive," Griffin said, stretching out his legs next to Michael. "I'm not your dom, but I am a dom, so behave."

Michael repressed the urge to do the Nora thing and growl at Griffin.

"It's not finished," Michael repeated, pulling his legs tight to his chest and wrapping his arms around his knees. Griffin looked at him, set the sketchbook aside and grasped Michael by the ankles.

"What the—?" Michael began as Griffin yanked Michael's legs out straight in front of him.

"You are out of control with the fetal-position thing," Griffin said with obvious exasperation. "You are allowed to take up space, Mick. Every time you get the least bit stressed out, you pull up into this tiny ball and practically disappear. An impressive feat considering how tall you are."

"Sorry," Michael said, trying to relax. "I get nervous and I…" He tried to explain further but words failed him.

"You turn into a hedgehog," Griffin said. "Self-protective measure. But you're with me right now. Put the spikes away and chill. You don't have to protect yourself. I'm not going to hurt you. Not even in the fun way, okay?"

Michael's heart contracted and then expanded hard enough he felt it at Griffin's words. He couldn't believe someone with Griffin's sheer physical presence, not to mention all his money, would treat Michael with such… Michael tried to come up with a good word for it. With such care.

Slowly Michael smiled. "Okay."

"Good. Now just sit there and look pretty while I nose through your book."

Annoyed and embarrassed, Michael started to cross his arms but Griffin glared at him. Obediently Michael relaxed his arms and legs.

Griffin leafed slowly through the pages of Michael's battered Moleskine sketchbook.

"Do you just do pencil sketches?" Griffin asked.

"Mostly. Pen and ink, pencil and pen."

"Charcoals?"

"Love charcoal but it's messy."

"So?"

"Mom gets mad when it gets on my clothes," Michael said and then cursed himself for saying something so idiotically childish.

"What's with all the wings?" That particular sketchbook had nothing in it but variations on a theme—angel wings, bird wings, insect wings. Maybe next he'd try griffin wings.

"It's my safe word Nora gave me. I've been doing wing drawings ever since."

Turning his sketchbook around, Griffin flipped to the drawing Michael had been working on all day.

"This is incredible," Griffin said, holding up the open book. "You're like John Coulthart, but softer, more emotional."

Michael's blush deepened. "You know Coulthart's stuff?" Michael asked, slightly stunned.

"I know I don't look it," Griffin said, "but I've got a geeky side. Plus I majored in art history at Brown."

"You went to Brown?"

"Yeah, but I didn't graduate. Long story," Griffin said with a note of something Michael had never observed in him before—discomfort. "But I do know art. I've got two Picassos in my bedroom, there's a Kandinsky in Nora's room and there are a handful of Delaunays around. I dig orphic cubism. And since I know art, I know talent. And you have it, Mick. I love this."

Griffin stared at the drawing Michael had been working on. Nothing very fancy, it was only a picture of slightly gothic-looking angel wings stretched out across the page. The huge hulking wings were attached to the back of a frail boy who sat on the ground with his legs pulled in tight to his chest. A personal drawing. Michael had never intended anyone to see it.

"Thanks. Nora ordered me to do something today to make myself relax before tonight. Drawing usually works."

Griffin closed the sketchbook with obvious reluctance. Michael took it back from him and walked over to the bed where he slipped the book under his pillow.

"Usually? Nervous about tonight?" Griffin stood up and started strolling around his old room.

"A little." Michael sat on the edge of the bed and tried not to stare at Griffin. Griffin cracked him up. He just walked around in his underwear as if he couldn't begin to care what people thought about him. Of course, Griffin had a crazy-good body, so why not walk around almost naked?

"When's the last time you fucked?" Griffin asked as he sat on the edge of Michael's bed and rolled onto his back. Michael shifted nervously. An almost-naked guy was lying on his bed. He should have disliked that, wanted to dislike that… couldn't quite bring himself to dislike that.

"Um," Michael began as he turned to sit cross-legged, his back to the headboard. Personal questions—he hated them. His dad always grilled him with personal questions. "Nora asked me the same thing yesterday."

Griffin raised his eyebrow at him.

"You know what that means, right?"

Michael shook his head.

"She's getting your sexual history. Means fluid bonding."

"Fluid bonding?"

"Sex without condoms."

"Wow," Michael said, his stomach tightening a little. "Is that safe?"

"She's clean. Gets tested constantly. All the 8th Circle big-wigs do, myself included. And she's got an IUD so I wouldn't worry about knocking her up."

"So do you and Nora, you know, fluid bond?"

Griffin sat back up and scooted to the top of the bed, leaning back against the headboard right next to Michael. Once again Michael breathed in Griffin's scent. Michael decided to find out what kind of soap Griffin used just so he could buy some and smell it whenever he wanted.

"Nope. I don't with anybody."

"How come?" Michael asked, genuinely curious. Guys at school were always bitching about their girlfriends making them wear condoms.

"Mick," Griffin said, turning his head to stare into his eyes. "There is nothing, and I repeat, nothing I haven't done. And I'm not talking just sexually. Every bad act on the face of the earth, minus murder and rape, I've done it. So there's this part of me that wants to hold something back just in case I'm ever actually in a real relationship with somebody. Does that sound sappy and romantic? If so, don't tell anybody. I'm supposedly *l'enfant terrible* of the Underground. I'd like to keep it that way."

Michael grinned, not entirely sure what a *l'enfant terrible* was but deciding he liked the term.

"A little sappy. But not in a bad way," Michael said, surprised that Griffin would have this sort of softer side to him. Art? Saving part of himself for a real relationship? "So you never, you know—"

"Come inside anyone?" Griffin finished for him. "No.

Never. Sex talk from Dad, age thirteen. 'Son, we have more money than God. You get a girl pregnant, and she'll take half of it. Condoms every time.' And then he gave me a box of Trojans."

Michael burst out laughing at Griffin's impression of his father's stern voice. Remembering something suddenly, Michael stopped laughing.

"Wait. Nora, she went—"

"Nora went down on me. If you stayed and watched until the end you would have seen me put on a condom before I finished up."

Mentally Michael dug a hole and crawled inside it. Griffin had seen him watching two nights ago?

"Griffin." He finally choked the words out. "I'm so sorry. I didn't mean… I was just on the way to the kitchen and heard—"

"Mick, calm down," Griffin said, smiling at him. "I'm not mad. This is me. I fuck in front of people all the time. I was only irritated you didn't come in and join us." Griffin gave him a wicked smile.

Michael's toes went a little numb.

"I think Nora might have not liked that," Michael said, not entirely sure if that was true. He'd fantasized about three-somes before. Last night in fact his mind had wandered a little too far and he'd imagined Nora dominating him while Griffin watched.

"Your mistress loves an audience. In fact, I've watched your priest fuck your mistress after King and I fucked her."

Michael felt his eyes wanting to pop out of his head.

"You've seen Father S…"

"Fucking? Yes. Back when your mistress was still just a sub like you, he'd do all sorts of shit to humiliate her at our club.

Which she totally got off on. You know why me and King and your priest all fucked her once in the same night?"

Michael shook his head. He couldn't imagine.

Griffin leaned in close as though he was about to share a secret. Every muscle in Michael's body stiffened as Griffin's tattooed, muscular shoulder pressed against his. Michael tried not to notice the drop of water sliding from Griffin's hair down his neck and coming to rest in the hollow of his collarbone.

"It was her birthday. And that's what she asked for," Griffin whispered.

"Oh, my God," Michael breathed, pulling his legs to his chest again. Not out of self-protection but to hide his sudden erection.

"I know. Awesome night." Griffin gave a little wistful sigh. "Things went to hell shortly after that though. Nora dumped your priest and then she just disappeared on us. When she came back, everything was different."

"She came back and started working as a dominatrix, right?" Michael knew a little of Nora's story. Father S had given him the basics. He'd met Nora when she was fifteen and still just Eleanor. Love at first sight. Training at eighteen. Consummation when she turned twenty. Seven blissful years together before she left him for reasons unknown. Then she came back and joined forces with Kingsley, who turned her into not just a domme, a female dominant, but a dominatrix—a female dominant who charged for her services. A lot.

Griffin lowered his voice as though he was telling a ghost story around a campfire. "When she was a sub, your priest kept her on a pretty short leash. She only ever wore white at the club. And he only let her wear her hair down in private. And almost no makeup, either. She wasn't allowed to speak unless he gave her express permission."

Michael tried and failed to picture Nora as Eleanor wearing all white, no makeup, her long, gorgeous wavy black hair pinned up and hidden away. And not talking? Nora silent? So weird.

"The first night she came to The 8th Circle as a dominatrix, I was there," Griffin said. "You can't even imagine the shock on everyone's face when they realized this smoking-hot new dominatrix wearing red leather on Kingsley's arm was Søren's ex-submissive. Once they did, it got ugly."

"Why?" Michael asked, trying to picture the scene.

"They only knew her as a submissive, and there she was all decked out like a domme, trying to be tough. Even the submissives laughed at her."

"Poor Nora," Michael said. "What did she do?"

A smile crossed Griffin's face, a smile that sent a thrill of something down Michael's spine.

"You know how they say if a guy gets sent to prison and he doesn't want to become the new bitch, he's gotta find the biggest guy in the place and beat the hell out of him?"

"Right." He'd seen movies with that plotline.

"There was this masochist at The 8th Circle named Trent. He was to masochists what Søren is to sadists. His nickname was Unbreakable. Your priest probably could have broken him, but Trent only let women top him. Anyway, Nora goes right up to him and asks him if he wants to play. He said yes and then tried to spit in her face."

"Holy shit. What happened?"

Griffin laughed, low and throaty, and Michael suddenly felt the need to excuse himself for a few minutes. Instead he grabbed a pillow and covered his lap with it.

"Nora ducked. That woman's got killer reflexes. She came up and slapped him so hard his nose bled. Then things got really interesting. She broke him. In one night. He safed out, started crying. She sent that big masochistic motherfucker to the hospital. After that, she owned The 8th Circle. No one ever questioned her dominant credentials again."

Michael looked up at the ceiling. What on earth was he getting into? He didn't know, but he suddenly couldn't wait to fall at Nora's feet and do anything and everything she told him to. Wearing bruises she gave him would be an honor.

Griffin stretched out his long tanned legs and crossed them at the ankles.

"Trent worshipped the ground she walked on after that. We all did," Griffin said and Michael saw a shadow of something cross Griffin's eyes. "Except Søren, of course. Those two were at war after that. But only because he wanted her back more than ever."

"Can you blame him?"

Griffin said nothing at first and Michael saw all the fire and fun momentarily leave Griffin's face.

"No. I can't." The spark came back in Griffin's eyes. "Anyway, the domme training you is a real, live legend. Cool, right?"

"Very cool," Michael said. "Can't wait for tonight."

"She won't get you until sunset. She's all about atmosphere and the mind-fuck. So you've got a couple hours. What do you want to do?"

Michael knew exactly what he wanted to do. He moved to the middle of the bed and faced Griffin.

"Tell me more about Nora."

Michael listened in awe as Griffin regaled him with story after story about Nora's legendary exploits as a dominatrix. He couldn't believe some of her clients were so famous, so powerful. It made him feel a little better that so many men the world looked up to were sexual submissives just like him. Time passed so quickly in Griffin's company that Michael barely noticed the room darkening as the sun sunk lower and lower in the sky. He couldn't recall ever having so much fun actually talking to somebody. He hated talking. Or thought he hated it. With Griffin, however, things he never thought he'd like—answering personal questions, showing his art off, talking—he discovered he enjoyed. Griffin was a good two or three inches taller than him, had at least forty pounds of pure muscle on him and was a dominant. So why did Michael feel so safe around him?

"So if she ever gets arrested again," Griffin concluded, "they have to call the paddywagon and get police backup since it's on her permanent record that she can get out of handcuffs so easily."

"That's amazing. Does Father S—" Michael started but a knock on the door interrupted his question. He turned around and saw Griffin's British butler standing in the doorway.

"Mister Dimir," the butler said in his perfectly snooty accent. "The mistress requires your presence."

Michael's heart leapt in his chest. Thirteen months since he'd been with Nora. Thirteen months since he'd been with anybody. And now, right now, the one and only Nora Sutherlin had summoned him.

He turned to Griffin, who flashed him such a wicked grin that Michael, not even standing, felt his knees buckle.

"Go on, Mick. It's showtime."

Once she arrived at Sacred Heart, Suzanne tried to figure out what the hell she was doing there. Her brief encounter with Father Stearns had only stoked her fascination with the man. As a reporter she had a highly sensitive internal bullshit meter. Father Stearns said he could spot a lapsed Catholic at a thousand yards. Maybe so. But she could tell the truth from a lie just by watching someone's eyes.

I haven't performed an exorcism in weeks.

Bullshit.

My office is always open, Father Stearns had said with far more sincerity.

Truth.

After dark on a Saturday night, Suzanne doubted anyone, including Father Stearns, would still be at Sacred Heart. Maybe she'd peek into his office and see if she couldn't get a little insight into the target of her investigation. She parked on the street about fifty yards from the church. As she walked toward the side entrance she studied her surroundings. A lot of

New York commuters lived in Connecticut towns like this one—they were safer, cleaner and had better schools. Wakefield seemed like a charming little suburb, the perfect place to raise a family. Small but well-appointed houses, orderly streets, historic shops and no real crime of any kind…such a perfect little town. Too perfect, Suzanne decided.

Suzanne didn't trust perfect. Adam had been perfect—perfectly happy, perfectly content, perfect life—until he'd committed suicide.

Closing her eyes, she pictured Adam's face, something she tried very hard never to do. They looked alike, really. Everyone always said that. But apart from their shared dark brown eyes, red-blond hair and oval faces, they had almost nothing in common. She was the skeptic, the cynic, the hot-tempered pistol in the family. Adam was the angel, her parents' perfect firstborn. Sweet, kind, even-tempered and so devout she didn't even tell him when she stopped believing in God, knowing how much it would break his heart. And all that time he had this horrible thing inside him that someone else put there…a darkness, a contamination, as the note he'd left behind called it. God, the note.

I'm unclean, contaminated. I can't face taking one more shower knowing that no matter how long I stay under the hot water, I'll still be dirty when I get out.

Suzanne forced the memories away. For Adam she would do this…for Adam and Michael Dimir and any other kid who'd been hurt by the Church.

She slipped through the side door into Sacred Heart and made her way past small classrooms. Even in the low light she could read the notices on the bulletin board:

Choir practice—7:00 p.m. on Tuesdays—Don't forget your sheet music, Gina.

Suzanne laughed a little through her burning tears. Poor Gina.

The Knights of Columbus wants you! Email adonovan@sacredheartct. org for more information.

Her dad had been a Knight of Columbus. Such an imposing name for a group of usually overweight fathers who didn't do much more than have charity barbecue cook-offs.

All couples planning to marry must meet with Father Stearns at least six months prior to their wedding. Make an appointment with Diane.

A celibate priest doing marriage counseling? Suzanne shook her head. What on earth would a Catholic priest know about sex or marriage or romantic relationships of any kind?

At the end of the hallway Suzanne found a closed door with an engraved nameplate on it. Father Marcus Stearns SJ, it read. SJ? She'd seen those initials before but couldn't quite remember what they stood for. Pulling her notebook out of her bag, she jotted them down. With almost shaking fingers, Suzanne reached out for the door handle. It turned. So he had been telling the truth. His office really was always open.

For safety's sake she left the lights off. From her bag she took out a small flashlight and shined it around the office. Immediately she gleaned Father Stearns was a neat freak. Nothing appeared out of place. Not a stray book or a single sheet of paper. A beautiful office really, Suzanne decided. The big rose window must cast glorious red-and-pink light into the room on sunny days. The ornately carved desk looked like old oak to her—probably weighed as much as Patrick's Saab. The books on the shelves were lined up with military precision. She studied the titles and discovered she could read very few of them. How many languages could Father Stearns read? It appeared that in addition to the usual Biblical languages—Hebrew, Greek and Latin—Father Stearns had books in French, Spanish, Italian…and a lot of books that seemed to be in a Scandinavian language. She didn't know two words of Swedish, Danish or Dutch but she could recognize the distinct characters—the *a* with a little loop on the top or the *o* with a slash through it. Suzanne picked up what appeared to be the oldest book on the shelf. From the shape and size of its worn leather cover, Suzanne guessed it to be a Bible. She opened it and saw an inscription on the front pages written in a woman's elegant hand.

Min Søren, min søn er nu en far. Jeg er så stolt. Jeg elsker dig altid. Din mor.

The only word in the inscription Suzanne recognized was the name Søren. She'd taken a few philosophy classes in college and learned of Søren Kierkegaard, the Danish philosopher and theologian. But if she remembered correctly, Kierkegaard wasn't Catholic. She pulled out her notebook again and carefully copied down the inscription inside the Bible. In addition she made a note to look up Søren Kierkegaard. Why would Father Stearns have a Bible inscribed to someone named Søren? A relative maybe? she wondered. He certainly looked as though he had Scandinavian blood. But her research had indicated he had an English father and a New England WASP mother. Another mystery.

She put the Bible back on the shelf and turned her attention to the desk. Something seemed off about it, but she couldn't quite put her finger on why. Then she realized—no computer. Well, maybe he had a laptop. Although she didn't see any computer accessories anywhere, either—no printer, no power cords, no internet router. She only saw Montblanc pens and high-quality writing paper on his desk. Father Stearns might be something of a Luddite. That would explain his lack of internet presence.

Slowly she opened the desk drawer and felt a distinct sense of disappointment as she found nothing but more pens and paper inside. A few file folders held nothing of interest—only schedules and lists of Bible verses in impeccable male hand-writing. The other desk drawers produced no shocking revelations, either. In the bottom drawer she found dozens more Montblanc pens still in boxes. Briefly she wondered if Father Stearns had some sort of ink pen fetish. Then she noticed many of the boxes still had tags on them—gift tags from parishioners bearing messages of affection and appreciation. It reminded Suzanne of her friend Emily, a kindergarten teacher at a private school. Every Christmas her students' parents inundated her with every conceivable sort of Teacher's Apple product in existence. Apparently the people of Sacred Heart had learned of their priest's fondness for high-quality writing instruments and showered him with them every year.

You bless us year after year, Father. Love in Christ, the Harpers, read one tag.

Thank you for saving our marriage, Father. Bless you, Alex and Rachel, read another.

Is it a sin to combine a priest's birthday and Christmas presents? We'll talk about it in Confession if it is. Merry Birthday, Dr. and Mrs. Dr. Keighley, read a tag on a box that held a Montblanc pen and pencil set.

Combine Christmas and birthday? With that sentence, Suzanne realized she'd been right. Father Marcus Lennox Stearns, born December 21st, 1965, was indeed the son of Marcus Augustus Stearns, the English baron who'd moved to New Hampshire and married money. Amazing. So her target had actually given up a title in the British peerage for the Catholic Church? Unbelievable. Not only did he give up his mother's wealth and his father's title, he'd given up women for the Church. Most priests she'd met in her day seemed of the "doomed to die a virgin" variety. Humorless, unattractive, socially awkward…the opposite of Father Stearns in every way.

Shaking her head, Suzanne pulled out one last box, this one red, and flipped open the card.

Meine andere Geschenk wird nicht in einer Box passen. AABYE

Good God, how many languages would she have to deal with tonight? Rolling her eyes in frustration, Suzanne pulled out her notebook and copied the words down. At least this language she could recognize—German. And for some reason the last word, *AABYE,* rang some kind of bell with her. She searched her memory for whatever it was that seemed so familiar about it but came up empty. Stuffing her notebook in her purse, she scanned the top of the desk once more with her flashlight.

On the desk Suzanne found one item of interest—a photograph. She stared at the picture for a long time. A young woman of only about seventeen or eighteen years old, she looked remarkably like Father Stearns—pale blond hair, gray eyes, strikingly attractive. Suzanne eased the photo out of the frame and flipped the picture over. *Jeg elsker dig, Onkel Søren. Kom og besøg snart, Laila,* it read. Again with the Scandinavian inscriptions. Suzanne opened her notebook again and copied every word. Briefly she wondered if she was staring at Father Stearns's daughter. Had he fathered a child at some point during his years as a priest? Could that be the reason for the anonymous fax and its mysterious "Possible conflict of interest" footnote?

Seemed unlikely. After all, if he did have a love child, she doubted someone as obviously intelligent and well educated as Father Stearns would simply keep a photo of his teenage daughter on his desk. She shook her head in frustration. She'd hoped for answers. All she had now were more questions.

As quietly as she could, Suzanne abandoned Father Stearns's office and returned to the hallway. For some reason she felt drawn to return to the sanctuary instead of her car. Patrick's information from the Wakefield sheriff indicated that Michael Dimir had made his suicide attempt in the actual Sacred Heart sanctuary. Trying to kill oneself was the ultimate cry for help. Whatever had inspired it, something in Suzanne wanted Michael Dimir to know she heard it.

Suzanne found the doors that lead from the narthex and into the sanctuary. Easing the heavy wooden door open, she slipped inside. Upon entering the sanctuary Suzanne discovered someone had left candles burning on the altar and scattered about the sanctuary. She froze as her eyes took in the candle nearest her. The burning wick had only begun to turn black. From behind her she heard the sound of approaching footsteps.

She wasn't alone.

Michael cast one last look back at Griffin before leaving the bedroom. Griffin gave Michael a little wink on his way out the door and a tiny part of him wanted to stay and keep talking. But he knew he wanted to spend the night submitting to Nora, needed it even. He just sort of wished Griffin could be there too.

For some reason, Michael had assumed he'd spend the night with Nora in her room. But Griffin's butler led him instead upstairs to the third floor and all the way to a room at the end of the hallway.

The butler paused at the door, nodded politely to Michael and walked away. Michael took a deep breath, turned the doorknob and stepped into the room and into another time.

Holy crap, he thought as his eyes tried to take in the scene around him. He'd seen a lot of Griffin's house by now. Every room matched Griffin—sleek and modern, minimalist, arty and sexy. But this room seemed as though it belonged in a medieval European castle. Plush oriental rugs covered the stone tile floors. Candles burned on every horizontal surface and a few logs simmered in a stone fireplace. In the middle of the room stood a bed, large and wrought iron, not unlike the one he'd lost his virginity in.

But where was Nora?

"Not bad for a dungeon, right?" came Nora's voice behind him. Michael tensed, not knowing what to do. Was he allowed to talk? Move? He decided to stay frozen in place and not talk until Nora told him what to do. "Griffin's dungeon at The 8th Circle is much more mod. I think he wanted a different vibe for his house up here. Like it? You're allowed to answer."

"Yes, ma'am. It's beautiful," Michael said, hearing the quiver in his own voice.

He felt Nora's presence behind him and took in a quick breath.

"So are you," she said, blowing under his ear.

Nora stepped in front of him and Michael's eyes went wide. Nora had grown…a lot. She met him almost eye to eye before stepping away and walking toward the center of the room. He glanced down and saw she wore thigh-high platform boots with killer stiletto heels. His eyes grazed her body from foot to face—red leather boots laced up the back, bare thighs, red leather skirt, red-and-black corset… Nora looked back over her bare shoulder and crooked her finger at him.

He could barely feel his feet as he walked toward her. Suddenly the room and its beauty faded into the background and all he could see was her…Nora and the swell of her breasts over her striped corset…Nora and the heavy, dramatic eyeliner that made her look like Cleopatra…Nora and her hair that curled in wild waves down her back…Nora and the black fingerless gloves just like the ones she'd worn the night she took his virginity. He couldn't wait to feel the soft supple leather against his skin again.

When he reached Nora she raised her hand to his neck and gently pulled his ponytail loose. Slowly, gently she ran her fingers through his hair.

"I read your checklist, Angel," she said as he closed his eyes. If he'd been a cat, he would have started purring. "I found it very interesting. You want pain, don't you?"

"Yes, ma'am," Michael breathed.

"Pain makes you feel better, doesn't it?" Nora asked, her voice soft and hypnotic. "It's like white noise…soothing, calming, blocks out the real pain, the bad thoughts, that other pain that you don't want. Right?"

Michael's eyes opened wide.

"Yeah. Exactly, ma'am. How did—"

"You aren't my first masochist, Angel."

Michael laughed a little. Griffin had told him Nora had hundreds of clients back when she was a dominatrix. Hundreds of clients who made her hundreds of thousands of dollars. Of course he wasn't her first masochist. Just looking at her, feeling himself falling under her spell, he could easily understand how men would mortgage their souls just to be able to kiss the toe of her boot.

Nora's fingers found that tight knot at the base of his neck, that place where he stored most of his tension. Michael tilted his head toward her, gave him better access to his stress.

"I think," Nora began in a half whisper, "that I'll beat you tonight. But I don't think I'm going to punish you or be mean to you like I did with a lot of my clients. I think you've had enough people being mean to you in your life already."

Michael's eyes clenched tight as her words burrowed a hole into his heart. Ever since the night his parents had discovered what he was, Michael had suffered nothing but insults—freak, sicko, fag—from his father and abandonment by his mother. No one touched him anymore, no one hugged him, no one ever even wanted to talk to him except for Father S, and even he had to keep his distance because of the Church. But now the most erotic woman in the world was touching him, talking to him, making him feel like the center of the world.

"Thank you, ma'am," he said in a voice he could barely hear.

Nora caressed his face with the back of her hand. Leaning in she pressed a little kiss to his lips before moving her mouth to his ear.

"Take your clothes off," she ordered.

Michael reached behind his head and yanked at his T-shirt, pulling it off with one swift motion. He unbuttoned his black plaid skateboard shorts and pushed them and his boxers off, kicking them off his ankles into the corner of the room. The night he and Nora met, he'd fumbled so nervously with his watchband that she'd had to take over and unbuckle it for him. Now he felt no such jitters. The watch and wristband that he always wore in public were off and on the floor in seconds.

"Your swiftness to obey is touching," Nora said, smiling at him. "But you have to slow down and let me enjoy watching you undress. Your priest makes me strip for him, you know."

Michael felt a coil of need begin to twist in the pit of his stomach.

"I didn't know, ma'am," he said as Nora looked his naked body up and down.

"We'll be having a lovely evening at the rectory. He'll be reading in his armchair, I'll be sitting at his feet writing, and out of nowhere he'll snap his fingers and order me to take my clothes off."

Michael said nothing.

"Sometimes," Nora said, pressing close to Michael's body, "he doesn't even look at me. He keeps reading. He orders me to do it just to humiliate me. Jealous?"

Once again Michael closed his eyes. He tried to imagine what it would be like to belong to someone, to be owned like Nora was. What would it be like to give his body to someone so completely that they could order him out of nowhere to strip naked. God, it would be so embarrassing, so humiliating, as Nora said. Degrading, almost.

"Very jealous," he admitted and Nora laughed.

"Do you ever imagine what your priest and I do when we're alone together?" she asked as she made a circuit around him. Her stiletto heels clicked against the stone floors.

A blush flared up on Michael's cheeks.

"Yes, ma'am," he said, swallowing hard.

"Tell me what you fantasize," Nora said and he heard the hard edge of the order in her voice.

His fantasies about Nora and Father S were beyond humiliating. Sometimes he saw them at church and Nora would be trying to annoy Father S. Nora would put her innocent face on and say something like, "Father Stearns, about St. Elmo…" And Father S would barely glance at her and say, "Patron saint of sailors. What about him, Eleanor?" And Nora would say, "Was he, by any chance, ticklish?" And Michael would hide in the shadows and imagine his handsome priest bending Nora over the back of a pew and brutally fucking her. That was just the PG stuff he thought of. When masturbating it got really intense—threesomes, foursomes, orgies, vicious beatings… The stuff that went on in his head freaked even him out sometimes.

"I…" he began and swallowed. His fingers clenched in nervousness.

"You can tell me," she said, her voice coming from behind him. "Trust me, I've heard worse. And even if I haven't, I've thought worse. Just say it."

Michael took a deep breath. He hated disappointing Nora.

He wanted to say it. Wanted to say everything to her. But the words turned to glue and stuck in his throat.

"I can't," he said, his voice flush with anguish.

Nora grazed his face with the back of her hand again.

"It's okay, Angel. We'll get there. If you're going to be a sub you have to learn how to talk about what you want and need. This," she said, indicating the room and then pointing at herself, "is a basic fantasy. Dominant woman, gorgeous dungeon full of S&M toys, big bed. Generic even. Start talking and tell me what you fantasize about in your most private moments, and we can change it. Do you want to see me in black instead of red? In lace instead of leather? Would you prefer scening outside at night? Do you have fantasies that take place in the kitchen? The shower?"

Michael shifted nervously from foot to foot.

"Maybe," he admitted.

"You do know what you want matters, don't you?"

Michael rubbed at his arms. "I guess, ma'am. Trying."

"I'll teach you that this summer. You've got a lot to learn. Let's get your lessons started."

Nora strolled off toward a table covered in a black cloth. Once she reached it she turned around and crooked her finger at him again, beckoning him to her side.

Naked but for his blush, Michael came to stand beside Nora. With a flourish she pulled the black cloth off the table.

"Wow," Michael said at the sight before him.

"Thank you. I packed a few of my favorites. A few are Griffin's he's letting us borrow. Griffin's very fond of you. You've made quite an impression on him."

Michael's blush deepened at the insinuating tone in Nora's voice. Did she know he'd watched her and Griffin having sex in the dining room? Did she somehow intuit that ever since

seeing Nora on her knees in front of Griffin, he'd been having trouble not imagining himself in that same position?

"He's really cool" was all Michael could get out before
clamping his lips shut. Nora only eyed him before turning
her gaze back to the table.

"Do you know what these are, Angel?"

"Some of them…but not all, ma'am."

"Let me introduce you then. This," she said as she lifted
the first object, "is a basic flogger. Six-inch handle, eighteen-
inch suede thongs. Feel?"

Michael reached out and ran his fingers over the flogger.
The suede felt so soft to the touch.

"Used lightly," Nora explained, "it will feeling like a tick-
ling sort of massage. Used with full force, however, the im-
pact on your back will knock the breath out of you. Tricky
thing. I could beat you with this until you cried and within
the hour it would appear no one had laid a finger on you."

She laid the flogger back on the table.

"And this…you know what this is, don't you?" She lifted
another object, this one similar to the flogger but more sin-
ister looking.

"A cat-o'-nine-tails, ma'am," Michael answered.

"Very good. This is a lighter variation of the kind used to
discipline sailors in the British Navy. Even this lighter version
could break your skin if I wanted it to. But if I use it on you
correctly, you'll have the loveliest freckle bruises on you tomorrow courtesy of these little knots on the ends of the cords.
Here," she said, handing it to him.

Michael accepted it with almost trembling hands. He
touched the knots, hefted its deceptively light weight.

"You know, there was an even smaller version of this that
was used on the cabin boys aboard ship," Nora said with laughter in her voice. "Guess what it was called?"

"I don't know," Michael said shrugging.

"A boy's pussy," she said, grinning wickedly. She took the cat back from him. "You didn't know you were going to get a history lesson tonight, did you?"

"No, ma'am."

"I believe in the value of a thorough education. Tawse," she said, naming the heavy leather strap that lay next to the flogger. "Used to discipline schoolchildren in the nineteenth century. It won't break the skin but it will burn like fire. And this," she said sliding one more object off the table, "is exactly what it looks like."

"A cane, ma'am."

"Exactly. Rattan cane, ten millimeters thick, seventy-six centimeters long. So painful that its use on prisoners has been condemned by the United Nations. It can not only permanently scar a person but permanently disable them as well. Even used lightly on the buttocks or thighs, the pain will be so intense that you will choke on it. Traditionally six strokes are delivered at a time; five horizontal and one diagonal. That is called barring the gate. It's sadistic enough that your own priest rarely uses it on me. Although, admittedly, sometimes I do deserve it."

Nora stepped back and with astonishing expertise twirled the cane in her fingers like a baton. He could hear the hissing sound as the reedy wood sliced through the air.

"Now..." Nora placed the cane back on the table. "Choose."

"Choose?" he asked, unable to take his eyes off the dozen or so various kinds of floggers, whips and canes on the table.

"Yes. Pick one. Whatever you pick I will use on you tonight. So think about it carefully."

Nora stepped away and left him alone at the table. He heard her opening a trunk near the bed to take out something. But he didn't dare turn around to see what it was.

Michael raised his hand and passed it over the objects on the table.

I could beat you with this until you cried.

Loveliest freckle bruises.

It will burn like fire.

You will choke on it.

"This one, ma'am," he said, picking up the cat-o'-nine-tails. He turned around and Nora gestured for him to bring it to her. She was standing at the foot of the bed. She took it from him. His pulse quickened as she twined the lashes through her fingers.

"Angel," she said as she gripped the thongs and pulled them taut. "This will hurt you. Badly."

"Yes, ma'am."

Nora raised her eyebrow at him.

"One for you. And one for me."

She tossed the cat onto the bed and picked up the cane again. Michael swallowed hard but said nothing.

"Come," Nora said. "Stand dead center between the bedposts. Face the bed. Back to me. Take heavy, deep breaths. Focus on the heat from the fireplace. Let it seep into your muscles."

Michael obeyed as best he could. He knew he needed to relax. As he stood and breathed as instructed, Nora clamped leather bondage cuffs around his ankles. The tension in his legs started to dissipate. She grabbed his scarred wrists and yanked them behind his back. As she cuffed his wrists, the stress he carried in his arms and shoulders flowed through his veins and out of his fingertips. He inhaled sharply as she brought a black leather collar around his throat and buckled it at the base of his neck.

"Now, Angel," Nora whispered in his ear as she ran her

hand over the one part of his body that remained tense, "let's spread your wings."

She raised his left arm and bound it to a leather cord at the top of the bedpost. With his right arm she did the same. His arms stretched out into a full, wide wingspan.

"Breathe the heat of the fire into your arms," Nora said as she strapped a two-foot spreader bar to his ankles. "Feel them getting longer with each breath."

Michael pulled on his bonds and found he couldn't move. They had no give at all. He couldn't run away, couldn't escape. Trapped, imprisoned, helpless…

Nora picked up the flogger from the bed.

There was nowhere else in the world he wanted to be.

"What's your safe word?" Nora asked.

"Wings." Michael answered.

"You'll say that word if you want me to stop, yes?"

"Yes, ma'am."

"Good boy. Now take one more breath. This will only hurt a little bit. Oh, wait," she said, laughing. "No, it won't. It'll hurt a lot."

With that one last taunt, Nora took a step back and landed a hard blow right in the center of Michael's back. He gasped from the shock of the pain. He had the time to inhale and exhale only once before the second blow hit. The third one struck his left flank, the fourth his right. Nora painted crosses across his back with the flogger and each slash left him crying out.

Fire…she'd lit his back on fire. When the blows finally ceased, Michael could do nothing but drop his head to his chest and pant. His heart raced, his blood burned. He'd never felt calmer in his life.

"Here," Nora said as she brought a small glass of water to his lips. "Drink."

She tilted the glass and he drank the water with a grateful gulp.

"You did very well," Nora said. "You took a lot of pain for a beginner and didn't even beg me to stop. Think you can take more?"

Could he take more? Did he want to take more? His entire back smoldered from neck to hip.

"Yes, ma'am."

"God, I love masochists," Nora said, setting the glass aside. "Such gluttons for punishment."

Nora slid the cane off the bed and Michael's body stiffened in fear.

"Six-bar gate," she said. "Just one. Upper thighs. Then we're done. Ready?"

He couldn't bring himself to say yes. But he swallowed air again and nodded. Behind him he heard that hissing whistle again.

"You know, Angel, some people say it's the sound of the cane that's the worst part. Personally, I think that's bullshit. What do you think?"

At that, he experienced a pain so excruciating that it would have dropped him to his knees had he not been tied up.

The second strike came before he could recover from the first.

"You see why it's used for interrogations?"

"Yes—" he cried out as the third blow fell. The pain stabbed into his legs and shot through to his stomach. The agony was so acute, the pain so precise he could feel exactly where Nora placed each blow. Perfectly spaced, one inch apart.

The third felt like a knife on his skin instead of a cane.

The fourth and fifth he couldn't even feel.

But the sixth landed diagonally across all five and the sound that escaped his lips sounded foreign to him, strange, like the cry of a wounded animal instead of a person.

Michael sagged in his bonds, barely aware of his surroundings. When Nora untied his arms, they dropped like dead weight to his sides. She unshackled his ankles and he hardly noticed.

Nora pressed her body into his burning back.

"Good boy," she whispered. "I'm very proud of you."

Proud of him? When was the last time anyone said they were proud of him? If Nora said she wanted to cane him again, he would have said, "Yes, ma'am."

She stepped away and sat in a large leather armchair. She snapped her fingers and pointed to the floor by her feet.

Michael floated to her more than walked. A pleasant lightheadedness gripped him. The sharp pains in his back and thighs had turned into a gentle throbbing. When he knelt at the floor by Nora's feet, he half hoped she'd let him curl up in her lap and sleep.

"You did such a good job, Angel, that I'm going to give you a reward. Well, both of us a reward really."

Nora's shifted in the chair and draped one leg over each chair arm. Underneath her short, tight skirt she wore absolutely nothing.

"Do I need to tell you what to do?" Nora asked.

Michael licked his suddenly dry lips.

"Good start," she said.

Heart pounding, Michael laid his hands on her inner thighs and brought his mouth to her. He'd dreamed of doing this to Nora, servicing her sexually. And now he could feel her swollen clitoris against his tongue. He took the little silver ring that pierced her hood between his lips as he brought his fingers up and slid two of them inside her. He had no idea what he was doing. Apart from a few awkward preteen kisses and gropings, he'd never been sexual with anyone other than Nora. He had zero experience with oral sex and nothing going for him but enthusiasm. From the sound of her ragged breathing, the enthusiasm seemed to be doing the trick.

She felt so wet and warm on his fingers, tasted so sweet and tart on his lips. How did Father S get anything done with this woman waiting for him back at the rectory?

Michael pushed his tongue far into her and her hips rose off the chair.

"Stop," she ordered and Michael pulled away, wiping his lips off with the back of his hand. "On the bed. Now."

He remembered Nora's instructions and moved slowly, not hurrying too much to do her bidding. Kneeling on the bed, he waited as Nora came to him and shoved him onto his back. She grabbed his arms and pushed them over his head. Using a snap hook to connect his wrist cuffs, she secured his hands to the bars of the bed.

"Knees up," she said. "Spread your legs."

Just then he noticed the tube of lubricant in her hand.

"Forgive me," Nora said. "I'm just a little a curious about something. Some men love this. Some hate it. Some are indifferent. I don't care either way. Your order is to be honest and tell me if you like it or not. Say 'yes, ma'am' if you understand."

"Yes, ma'am," Michael said, his hands going numb with nervousness. He wasn't quite sure what she was going to do to him. But if it involved lube he had a fairly good idea.

She rubbed the liquid over two fingers on her right hand, and with her left hand, moved his knees farther apart.

"Shallow breaths, close your eyes," Nora said. "This won't hurt but it will feel weird at first."

Michael nodded and obediently closed his eyes. He felt Nora's fingers on him. If he had any shame or pride left he would have been mortified by how ridiculously aroused he was. He inhaled sharply as he felt Nora's cold, wet fingers on him. Gently, so gently he sighed, she slid one finger inside him.

"Okay?" she asked.

"Yes, ma'am."

She pushed in deep and went deeper. Michael fought the urge to tense, to push her out.

"Now you know what women go through every time we get penetrated," Nora said. "Like it?"

"It's...intense."

"Good word for it. It's about to get more intense. Ready?" Michael nodded.

Nora slid in deeper and Michael felt her fingertip against what felt like a tight knot of tissue deep inside him. Gently she rubbed and Michael's back arched off the bed as a lightning bolt of pleasure shot through him.

"Oh, God," he thought he said but he wasn't sure if he spoke any actual words.

"I'll take that as a yes, you do like it. Yes?"

Michael swallowed and gasped.

"Yes, ma'am."

The sensation of her finger on that spot inside him caused every muscle in his back to knot up. His heels dug into the bed and he panted as if he'd just run a mile.

Vaguely and in the distance he heard Nora laughing as she continued to knead him.

"Born to be a bottom," she sighed. "Can't wait to torture Griffin with this news."

At the mention of Griffin's name, Michael squeezed his eyes tighter. Nora had said Griffin was bisexual. He'd been with men...sexually. Even maybe done this to other guys. Maybe even more. And without warning an image came unbidden into Michael's mind. Griffin over him with his eyes half-closed with desire, bracing his strong, muscular body over Michael's slighter frame…Michael's leg over Griffin's back, Griffin's hand in Michael's hair, Griffin's lips on Michael's throat, and Griffin's…Griffin inside him. And not just his fingers.

"Come, Angel," he heard Nora order before she brought her mouth down onto him. Once more Michael arched, pushed his feet into the bed, and came with desperate shuddering gasps that left his chest heaving and the muscles of his arms straining.

Nora pulled her fingers out of him. Slowly Michael opened his eyes and saw his bound wrists, the leather of the cuffs dark against his pale skin. If only he could stay here forever, cuffed and safe, he would never have to see the scars on his wrists again.

As Michael came back to himself, he felt Nora beginning to stroke him again. So soon after coming, her touch felt almost painful. But a good pain, a pain that set his nerves on edge again.

Raising his head he met Nora's eyes. She leaned forward and kissed him. The kiss turned into a bite that broke the skin of his bottom lip. In one kiss he tasted the copper of his blood, the sweetness of her body, the salt of his semen. Nora moved over him, straddling his hips with her thighs.

"Is it really safe?" he asked nervously as she took his bare penis in her hand and started to guide him inside her.

"Don't worry," she said, caressing his chest, his shoulders with her lips. "I'm on the world's best birth control."

"Okay," he sighed. More than okay. Her body burned like fire around him and he groaned as her heat enveloped him. She moved and he moved with her, into her. "If you're sure, ma'am."

"Very sure," she said, moving against him. "Learned that the hard way."

★ ★ ★

Slowly Suzanne turned around and found herself face-to-face with Father Stearns. He stood there looking at her with barely concealed amusement.

"Ms. Kanter, how nice to see you again."

It took Suzanne a good three seconds to regain her composure enough to even speak.

"Father Stearns…I'm sorry. I just wanted to check out the sanctuary."

"At ten o'clock on Saturday night?" He raised an eyebrow at her.

Suzanne racked her brain trying to find the perfect lie. But nothing came to her. And something told her that no matter what she told him, he'd see right through it. So she decided to take a risk, a big risk, and tell him the truth.

"I'm investigating you," she confessed.

"Yes, I know."

"That doesn't bother you? Doesn't surprise you?"

"Neither."

She raised her chin and stared into his steel-gray eyes. Steel, the perfect color to describe them. She'd never seen harder eyes in her life.

"They say you can tell an innocent man from a guilty one by arresting him. An innocent man panics and paces his jail cell. The guilty one relaxes. He's caught. He's done."

She saw his eyes soften with a hint of amusement.

He stepped forward. As he brushed past her he dipped his head and whispered in her ear, "I'm not afraid of you."

Suzanne shivered. For some reason nearness of his mouth to her ear and his fearless defiance did something to her stomach, something not entirely unpleasant. She spun on her heel and followed him down the center aisle of the sanctuary.

"I got a tip about you. A fax with your name and the names

of the two other priests up for bishop. Next to your name someone put an asterisk."

"A terrifying piece of punctuation to be sure."

"It is when it indicates a footnote. And that footnote said 'Possible conflict of interest.' Can you tell me what that conflict of interest is?"

Father Stearns stopped at a brass plaque with a roman numeral *I* above it. She stood a few feet away from him. As tall as he was, the distance made it easier to meet his eyes.

"I'm quite familiar with all of my interests, and I assure you none of them are conflicted."

"Being a priest and having an interest in children is a conflict of interest. Wouldn't you agree?"

"I would agree if it's an unhealthy interest in children. Something I don't have. If you doubt me, you are welcome to talk to every parent at this parish."

Suzanne's certainty that Father Stearns was a sexual predator wavered slightly at his calm conviction. But she pressed on, determined to find some sort of chink in his armor.

"What about Michael Dimir? Do you have an unhealthy interest in him?"

"I cannot and will not discuss Michael with you. I am his confessor."

"Are you Nora Sutherlin's confessor too?" she asked, putting suspicious emphasis on the word *confessor*.

Finally she seemed to get a reaction from him. He sighed heavily and turned to face her again. Once more she felt overpowered by his incredible handsomeness. Why would any man that attractive choose the celibate life of the priesthood when he could have any woman on the face of the earth?

"I am."

"Are you sleeping with her?"

"Not since last Monday."

Now it was Suzanne's turn to sigh heavily.

"I can't get a straight answer out of you to save my life. It's not helping your case any."

He crossed his arms over his chest and looked at her intently.

"If you asked me an actual question instead of simply making accusations, you might receive an actual answer. You've never met Eleanor Schreiber, the woman you know of as Nora Sutherlin, have you?"

"No."

"Do you make it a common practice to pry into the personal lives of women you've never met before, women who've never done you any harm?"

Suzanne rolled her eyes.

"God, you Catholic priests. Masters of the guilt trip."

"I'm very good at my job," he said, mirth shining in his eyes. What kind of man could find a conversation like this funny? This priest had balls of steel to go along with his eyes. "I'm still waiting on a question, Ms. Kanter. If you can ask it without including an accusation, I might consider answering it."

"Okay. Here's one. Why are you a priest?"

"I'm glad you started with such a simple question."

Suzanne couldn't help but laugh a little.

"It was simple to ask." She smiled despite herself.

He paused and seemed to mull his words over.

"I was not raised Catholic. I didn't encounter Catholics until I was sent to a Jesuit school in Northern Maine at age eleven."

Suzanne inwardly winced. She couldn't imagine a child so young being sent away to a school in the middle of nowhere.

"The Jesuits priests, my teachers, were the best men I've ever known. Their erudition coupled with their kindness and dedication to their work humbled me. I felt called to join their ranks. I converted at age fourteen and at age nineteen I went to Rome and started my training."

"That's it?"

"I apologize for not having a Road to Damascus story to tell you."

"You were only nineteen when you started seminary. You never wanted to get married? Date? Have kids? Have…" Her voice trailed off.

"Have sex?" he finished for her. "I'll tell you something shocking if you promise not to share it with anyone."

"Okay," she answered nervously. "I can deal with 'off the record' unless you confess to a crime. What?"

He gave her a smile that if she saw it on the face of any man but a priest she would call it seductive.

"I'm not a virgin."

His words and the gleam in his eyes left Suzanne's hands trembling.

"You aren't?" Now they were getting somewhere. Now maybe she could get something out of him.

"I wasn't born a priest, Ms. Kanter. Any more than you were born an atheist war correspondent with a burning hatred of the Catholic Church."

Suzanne's spine stiffened.

"You've been investigating me, I see," she said.

"Your opinions on the church and faith are matters of public record," he said as he strolled toward her. "And I believe you may intrigue me nearly as much as I intrigue you. Since I answered your question, might I ask you one?"

"Ask." She made no promise to answer it.

"You are an atheist. God is truth. Without God, all is chaos, all is relative and truth is meaningless. And yet you became a journalist who's dedicated her life to seeking out the truth amidst the chaos, a truth you don't believe exists. Why?"

"Diogenes traveled the world with a lantern by day looking for an honest man. I'm just Diogenes out with my lamp trying to shed a little light where I can."

"Diogenes also slept in a barrel and masturbated in public. How deep does your metaphor run?" he asked, raising his eyebrow at her.

She opened her mouth and shut it again.

"You're not a normal priest, are you?"

At that, Father Stearns laughed. A warm, open laugh, intoxicating and masculine. She wanted to hear it more, hear it again. It seemed so incongruous.

"What?" she asked.

"Eleanor asked me the very same question the day we met almost twenty years ago."

"And what did you say to her when she asked that?"

"Exactly what I'll say to you now—my God, I hope not."

Now Suzanne laughed. Laughing with a Catholic priest… the last thing on earth she ever dreamed she'd do. Suzanne abruptly stopped laughing when she remembered her job, when she remembered Adam. Father Stearns seemed smart enough that he could manipulate anyone he wanted to. She couldn't let herself get sucked in just because of his appearance and sense of humor.

"You speak of her very fondly. You two are close?"

His smiled disappeared and once again he gave her a steely glare.

"I could be a thief. Or the bastard son of the pope. Both would qualify as conflicts of interest. Why are you so certain the reason for my asterisk is sexual?"

Suzanne thought about lying then had the feeling he'd see right through it.

"I suppose it's because you're so incredibly attractive."

He laughed again, this time far more subtly.

"Finding me attractive hardly qualifies as evidence, Ms. Kanter. Wishful thinking possibly, but not evidence."

Suzanne flushed, suddenly remembering the last time she'd had sex and how for one brief moment it was this priest, this man, on top of her and inside her and not Patrick.

"I find you attractive as well," Father Stearns continued. "But I shan't accuse you of pedophilia and ephebophilia simply because I do."

Suzanne swallowed.

"You find me attractive?"

"Very much so."

"But you're a priest."

"Priests are required to be chaste. Not blind. I had planned on praying the Stations of the Cross tonight. I may pray the Lord's Prayer instead."

"Why?"

"'Lead us not into temptation.'"

Suzanne's breath caught in her throat. She couldn't deny that she too felt led into temptation. Leaving…leaving would be good. Now.

"Then I should leave you alone and let you pray." She took a step back.

"Will I see you again?" he asked, his voice perfectly composed. She detected no flirtation, no temptation at all in his tone. Only curiosity.

"You'll see me every week until I find out what you're hiding behind that collar of yours."

He raised his eyebrow at her.

"I'm hiding nothing but my throat."

"Saturday night. Empty church. Do you really wear the collar all the time?"

"Not all the time. I do sleep and shower." The words, although plainly spoken, still conjured images in her head, images she didn't want. What did he look like under his severe black clericals? What did his body look like dripping with water? What did his skin look like against white sheets?

"Right...of course. Only time I take off my collar too. Good night, Father Stearns. You'll be seeing me again."

Suzanne turned to leave.

"I look forward to it."

Suzanne's steps nearly faltered, but she kept walking.

"Ms. Kanter?"

Pausing, she slowly turned back to face him. God, had she ever seen a more beautiful man in her life?

"My collar...would you like to see me without it on?"

12

Michael rolled onto his back, moaned in pain and rolled immediately back onto his stomach. Somewhere in this massive mansion there had to be Advil or something like it. If he could just stand up, he'd be golden.

From the door to his room he heard chuckling.

"Don't laugh at me." Michael buried his face into the pillow. "It's rude to laugh at a dying man."

"Poor little subby." Griffin entered Michael's bedroom, grabbed a chair and sat next to the bed. "She nearly kill you last night?"

Michael unburied his face from the pillow and turned it to Griffin. Bad idea. Griffin sat shirtless and slightly sweating. He'd obviously just come in from a run as he had on nothing but running shorts, fuck, a good tan and his fucking sexy tattoos.

Raising his hand Michael held up five fingers.

"Five times?" Griffin asked. "I'm impressed. God, to be seventeen again."

"Why do I hurt in places she didn't hit?" Michael asked, trying to rise up but collapsing back on the pillows again.

"That's from the bondage. Gotta relax when you're tied up or you'll pull muscles."

"You don't have any drugs in this house do you? Preferably ones that will knock me unconscious?"

Michael saw a shadow cross Griffin's face, but the smile came back quickly.

"Nope. No drugs. But I have something better. Just a sec."

Griffin walked over to the wall and pushed a button on the intercom.

"Alfred, I need ice and that vitamin K goop. To the nursery. Stat."

Michael heard the crackle of static.

"I loathe you, Master Griffin," came a British accent over the intercom.

"Thanks, Alfred," Griffin answered and came back to the bed.

"Is your butler's name really Alfred?"

"No. It's Jamison, I think. Can't remember. I changed it to Alfred years ago. My first crush on a dude was Batman. Anyway, I know how to deal with pain without using drugs. I survived this," he said, pointing to the slight crook in his nose, "without taking a single painkiller."

"Awesome," Michael said, studying Griffin's face. The break in his nose made him even more handsome, not less. "How'd you get it?"

"It's embarrassing. I've been in probably five or six bar fights in my life, and it's a hundred-ten-pound girl named Rainbow Smite who breaks my nose. Accident. I think."

"Rainbow Smite?"

"Yeah, she's on my roller derby team, the Bronx Zoom."

"You have your own roller derby team?"

"I sponsor them. Sometimes even ref for the other league. Can't ref for my own obviously."

"You skate?"

"Can't ref if you can't skate. What?"

Michael stretched out his arm and pointed to the floor.

"Under the bed," he said sheepishly.

Griffin raised his eyebrow and bent over. From under the bed he pulled out Michael's skateboard.

"Zoo York. Nice," Griffin said, running his hands over Michael's board. "But your back trucks are too tight."

"I know. Turns for shit right now. The king pin's stuck. I'm going to have to get a drill—"

"Where's your skate key?"

"In the drawer." Griffin opened the bedside drawer and pulled out the key. Michael watched as Griffin used his impressive arm strength to dig in the tool and pop the stuck king pin. Carefully he adjusted both trucks.

"This good?" Griffin asked. Michael sat up and turned the trucks.

"Perfect. Thank you." Michael met Griffin's eyes and smiled. Griffin didn't say anything at first.

"You could come with me, if you want. To a bout. My team's awesome. Roller derby's like BDSM on wheels."

Michael nervously bit the inside of his cheek. For some reason he felt as though he'd just been asked out on a date.

"Can I come watch you ref sometime?" Michael pictured Griffin in tough referee gear and really liked the image.

"Of course. But when I ref you have to call me Patriarchy. That's my derby name."

"I'm there."

"I'll even let you blow my whistle," Griffin said as he handed Michael his skateboard.

Michael laughed and blushed as he flipped the board to inspect the deck.

"Jesus Christ," Griffin said and grabbed Michael's arm. "What the hell happened?"

Michael's blood turned to ice. He'd been so relaxed talking with Griffin he'd forgotten to cover his scars. Michael tried to pull his arm back but Griffin didn't let go.

"It's nothing," Michael said, holding his other arm to his stomach.

"That is not nothing. Tell me what happened to you."

A knot formed in Michael's throat. "Um, I had a bad day a few years ago."

"Bad day?"

"I slit my wrists in the sanctuary of my church. Father S saved my life."

"Saved your life? You almost died?" Griffin's eyes went wide with horror.

Slowly Michael nodded.

"Goddammit. I really like hating your priest. Now I can't anymore," Griffin said, finally letting Michael's arm go.

Michael laughed a little as he crossed his arms over his chest. "I'm sorry."

Griffin shook his head. When he looked at Michael again, it was with new eyes. Something glowed in them, burned in them, something he'd never seen before. Whatever it was, Michael liked it.

"You're okay now, right? No more bad days?"

Michael nodded, relieved Griffin didn't ask him a bunch of questions about that day or why he'd done it, the way some people did.

"Yeah, I'm okay. I promise. One day at a time, right?" He put his skateboard back down on the floor. "Plus Father S said if I ever hurt myself again, he'd kill me."

Griffin gave him a little half smile and shook his head.

"Seriously. I loved hating him. Fuck."

"Why do you hate Father S so much?" Michael asked as he lay back down again.

Griffin started to answer but Jamison appeared in the doorway with a cooler.

"Thank you, Alfred," Griffin said, taking the supplies. "There's a thousand dollars in the cookie jar. Go buy yourself something pretty."

"I will purchase a firearm and shoot you with it," Griffin's butler said, bowing elegantly. "Master Griffin."

He left the room and Griffin opened the cooler.

"Shirt off. On your stomach. Show me the damage," Griffin ordered.

Michael pulled off his shirt and tossed it on the floor. Griffin whistled at the sight of Michael's naked back. Michael knew what he saw—his entire back covered in small round red-and-brown bruises.

"Gets better," Michael said. "Thighs."

Griffin reached out and pulled the sheet down his legs. On the back of Michael's legs from the edge of his boxers to the bottom of his thigh were bright red parallel welts.

"That sadistic bitch caned you?"

Michael nodded.

"Badass. Well, we know where the ice goes then." Griffin opened the cooler and carefully placed two ice packs on the back of each of Michael's thighs. Michael sighed with relief as the ice immediately silenced the screaming heat of the welts. "And for the back bruises, liquid vitamin K. Top-secret bruise-fighting goo. Ask any woman whose ever had plastic surgery, i.e. my mother."

Michael grinned as Griffin poured out some of the white lotion onto his hands.

"I'm going to rub this in," Griffin warned, "and it's going to hurt but you'll heal a lot faster, okay?"

"Okay," Michael said, tensing as Griffin shifted from his chair to the bed and sat right next to Michael. Michael didn't fear more pain. Pain was fine by him. He tensed for other reasons, namely having Griffin's body so close to his. Michael had on nothing but plaid boxer shorts, and Griffin wasn't just on his bed, he was in his bed about to touch him.

Griffin laid his hands gently on the center of Michael's back and slowly kneaded. Michael sighed with bliss as Griffin's touch sent subtle thrills throughout his back and shoulders. His bruises ached but the pleasure of Griffin's hands on him trumped any pain. With long, even strokes, Griffin rubbed the vitamin K over Michael's sides, up his spine all the way to his neck and down to the small of his back again.

"Feel okay?" Griffin trailed his fingers across the arch of Michael's rib cage.

"Amazing actually," Michael admitted and wondered if Griffin's chest pressed to his back would feel this good.

"Good," Griffin said in a low voice. "I want you to feel good."

"So are you going to tell me why you hate my priest so much?" Michael asked, needing to talk about something, anything, to keep his mind from going where it wanted to go.

Griffin sighed heavily as he poured more lotion into his hands and began rubbing the tops of Michael's shoulders and upper arms. God, had anything in history ever felt as good as Griffin's large, strong hands on his arms?

"You can't tell the mistress. I love her, and she's really important to me so I don't want things getting weird between us."

"I won't tell," Michael said, even though Nora had promised him sexual favors in return for telling her if he found out.

"A long time ago…I fell in love with Nora."

Michael swallowed hard. For some reason, it bugged him hearing Griffin declare his love for somebody.

"You did?"

"Yeah, after she came back out of hiding. She'd been Søren's perfect little sub for years. Then she disappeared and came back this whole different person. But she was still the same Nora to me. I'd always called her Nora, by the way. Even when she was still Eleanor. Anyway, I knew she wasn't a true dominant, just a switch. I thought for sure there was a part of her that still wanted to submit to a man. The thought of this amazing, beautiful, brilliant dominatrix being my secret personal property? God, I thought I'd die if I didn't have her. But you don't do anything in the Underground without getting your priest's okay. I went to him and asked permission to talk to her about it, to tell her I loved her and that I wanted us to try being together. We'd fucked before, of course. But that year she was gone, you can't believe how much I missed her."

"What did Father S say?"

"After spending a good twenty minutes telling me what an obnoxious child I was who didn't deserve to kiss Nora's shoes, he said he'd entertain the idea under one condition."

Michael tensed again as Griffin's fingers lingered near the bottom of his back right at the waistband of his boxers.

"What was the condition?"

"Søren doesn't think any dominant should ever beat someone without first knowing how it feels to be on the receiving end of pain. He told me," Griffin said, running his hands back up to Michael's shoulders, "that if I submitted to a beating administered by him, he'd think about it."

"Oh, shit," Michael said. "What did you do?"

"Not my proudest moment. I pussed out. Couldn't do it. Not even for Nora."

"Don't blame you. I love Father S and owe him everything. But he scares the shit out of me too. Nora's the only person I know not scared of him."

"He's terrifying. And he knows it. And he loves reminding people of how scared they are of him. Part of that sadist mind-fuck shit he pulls. Anyway, it's for the best. I don't feel that way anymore. Nora and I definitely would have failed as a couple."

"Why?"

Griffin took his hands off Michael's back and removed the ice packs from his thighs. Slowly Michael rolled onto his back without nearly as much pain as he'd felt earlier. He looked up at Griffin looking down at him. Inhaling, Michael smelled Griffin's scent again, that spicy masculine smell that lingered under the other clean smell of sweat and deodorant.

"Nora's the strongest, smartest, toughest person I know. She rebuilt her life, re-created herself. She's like her own sun, and we all just revolve around her. That's why the Pope loves her so much. Topping someone that dominant has got to be a turn-on for a sadist like him. But me? If I'm going to be in a relationship with someone, I want that person to need me. I want someone to take care of, to spoil, to protect. Nora takes care of herself. I'd be useless to her."

Griffin ran a hand through his dark hair before laying it casually on Michael's stomach.

"I don't think you're useless," Michael said, his voice coming out in a whisper for some reason. Griffin looked down at him and didn't speak. "I think you're awesome. Anybody would be lucky to be with you."

"They'd be luckier to be with you." Griffin lowered his hand and let it rest lightly on Michael's hip.

Michael shook his head.

"Anybody in their right mind would run the second they

saw these." Michael held out his scarred wrists. "They're hideous."

Griffin's other hand reached out and brushed a stray lock of hair off Michael's forehead.

"Mick," Griffin began in a low voice, "there's nothing, absolutely nothing about you that's hideous."

"Who's hideous?" Nora asked as she swept into the room, catching both Michael and Griffin off guard.

Griffin winked at Michael as he moved from the bed back to the chair.

"Søren is." Griffin grabbed Nora and pulled her into his lap.

"I know. He's gross," she said. "How're you feeling, Angel?"

Nora wiggled off Griffin's lap and slid into bed next to Michael. Michael laughed as she wrapped herself around him and bit his neck.

"Sore. Happy," he said, flashing back to last night and the incredible ways she gave him both pleasure and pain and then more pleasure.

"Both are perfectly normal. Unlike the three of us." Nora tossed her bare leg over his calf. She too wore only boxer shorts and a T-shirt that read *University of Kentucky*. Weird. He thought she'd gone to NYU.

"Normal never got me laid." Griffin sat back in the chair and kicked his shoes off. He put his feet on the bed and crossed his legs at the ankles. Griffin had really big feet, Michael noticed.

"Speaking of getting laid," Nora began as she sat up and looked at them both.

"Great way to start any conversation," Griffin said.

"Søren called," she continued.

"A horrible way to start any conversation."

Nora reached out and swatted the bottom of Griffin's feet. He flinched and pouted at her.

"What's up with Father S?" Michael rolled up and pulled his T-shirt on. He caught Griffin watching his every move.

"That reporter bitch came by the church last night and interrogated him," Nora began. "She asked him point-blank if he and I were sleeping together."

"Shit." Michael pulled a pillow to his stomach in nervousness. "That's bad."

"She's smart and she's hot on our trail. We need to get her off our trail."

"Suggestions?" Griffin asked.

"We need a diversion. Let her see me with you. Make her think we're together."

"I like it. Could work." Griffin shrugged. "Just don't drag me to a Broadway premiere," he said with such disgust Michael laughed.

Nora looked at Michael and smiled. Nora looked at Griffin and smiled. Griffin looked at Michael, and Michael looked at Griffin. Neither of them smiled.

"Let's go to Sin Tax."

Griffin whistled, sounding both dubious and impressed.

"I don't know, Nora. We're in Kingsley's circle. Will they let us in?"

"Of course they'll let us in. Well, they'll let me in, and I'll bring you with me." Nora breathed on her fingernails and playfully buffed them on her T-shirt. "I have a friend there."

"Wait, what's Sin Tax?" Michael asked, utterly lost in Griffin and Nora's shorthand yet again.

"It's the one BDSM club in the city that Kingsley doesn't have his fingers in," Nora explained. "It's more public than King's clubs. Sin Tax is where celebs go if they want to look dark and cool. The famous people who go to Kingsley's clubs actually are dark and cool."

"Like us." Griffin winked at him. "So we go, get some attention, get some pics taken, show up on Page Six, reporter thinks you and I are together. That's the plan?"

"That's the plan."

"What about Bruised over here?" Griffin glanced at Michael with a grin.

"Oh, don't worry about Michael," Nora said as she crawled out of bed and headed to the door. "We're taking him with us."

"And Søren will be okay with us going out in public together?" Griffin called out after her.

Nora called back in a voice dangerous with feigned innocence.

"Who?"

13

Wednesday evening at five, he'd said. Mary Queen Junior High, two blocks from Sacred Heart. If Suzanne showed up she would see Father Stearns without his collar on. And although she knew this was a really bad idea, Suzanne couldn't stop herself from going.

Parking in the main lot, she wandered around the outside of the school. He hadn't given her any specific information, no doubt wanting her imagination to do all the work. As she neared the rear of the school—all too similar to the Catholic schools of her youth, with its careworn exterior and chipped Mary statues everywhere—Suzanne heard shouting followed by clapping.

Okay. She'd been right. This was a really bad idea. Out on the soccer field, two dozen teenagers and twentysome-things and one tall blond man in his forties played a hard-core game of soccer. Although older than the other players by a couple decades, Father Stearns wasn't only keeping up, he seemed to be wiping the floor with them. He wore a fitted black T-shirt that showed off his miraculously toned biceps and broad chest and black track pants that no doubt hid equally toned hips and legs.

She stood at the edge of the field and watched the game. No, not the game. She watched only Father Stearns—his blond hair like a halo in the evening sun, his eyes hidden behind black wraparound sunglasses, the slightest hint of sweat staining the shirt around his neck and lower back.

"Holy shit," she breathed. She'd seen naked men less visually arresting than this one soccer-playing priest.

"None of that," came a voice from a few feet away from her. A young man with sun-streaked hair sat on the sidelines with an ice pack on his thigh. "Don't even think about it."

Blushing, Suzanne sat next to the young man and put on her own sunglasses.

"Think about what?" she asked.

"Him. Father S. My priest. I'm Harrison, by the way. And you're…"

"Suzanne."

"Suzanne, lovely to meet you. You're that reporter chick, right? He warned us you might be stopping by."

"That's me. Just working on a story."

"For *Playgirl?*"

Suzanne laughed a little as Harrison adjusted his ice pack.

"You okay?" she asked.

"Strained a groin muscle."

"Poor you. Rough game?"

"Wasn't during the game." He wagged his eyebrows at her.

"You're flirting. And I'm ten years older than you."

"He's twenty years older than you and that's not stopping you from throwing the bedroom eyes at him. Best priest on the planet, and I have to tell my own damn girlfriend to stop drooling all over him."

Suzanne caught Father Stearns looking in her direction during a pause in the play. She gave him a quick wave, which he returned before heading down the pitch with remarkable grace and speed. The ball careened toward the goal and he intercepted it with a hard kick that sent the ball halfway down the field.

"Best priest on the planet? That's high praise." Suzanne wished she'd brought her notebook with her. A flirtatious teenage boy could be a wellspring of information. Reluctantly she pulled her eyes away from Father Stearns and cast them on Harrison. She remembered guys like him from high school— cocky, gregarious, always the center of attention.

"It's true. He speaks like twenty languages, has two or three PhDs…and kicks ass on our church league team. So don't go after him because you're pretty enough to tempt even him."

Suzanne shook her head.

"A teenage boy defending the unsullied virtue of his Catholic priest—interesting," she noted. "Do all the kids like Father Stearns?"

"Yeah, of course. He's really laid-back."

Suzanne's eyes widened. Father Stearns, the couple of times she'd talked to him, seemed intimidating and rigid.

"Laid-back?"

"Doesn't lecture, doesn't bitch at us for swearing, treats us like people. It's nice. Blake over there—" Harrison pointed to Father Stearns's goalkeeper "—goes to St. Mark's. His dad's a deacon there. Hates it. They've been through three priests in three years. One went to rehab for booze. The other got transferred for 'reasons,'" Harrison said, putting the word *reasons* in scare quotes. "And the new guy is sixty going on one hundred and sixty. Father Stearns rocks. So if you put the moves on him, you and I will have words."

"Have words? That's cute."

"I'm cute. And I'm not a priest."

Suzanne turned back to the game for a second. Father Stearns and his goalie seemed to be plotting. The goalie had a water bottle in his hand. He took a swig before pouring some into Father Stearns's hands. He took the water and swept it through his hair, slicking it back. At that moment Suzanne realized she'd never been so attracted to someone in her entire life. Need pooled in her stomach like a simmering fire. Priest or not, enemy or not, asterisk or not...she wanted him.

Adam, she whispered to herself. *Remember Adam.*

"So no rehab trips for Father Stearns? No weirdness?"

"Only weird thing is what's he doing here with us in the suburbs? He should be pope."

Suzanne leaned back on her elbows and crossed her legs at the ankles. She wished she'd worn shorts or a skirt, something to show off her legs to Harrison.

"Maybe he's got a reason for sticking around here." She looked at Harrison out of the corner of her eye.

"Like what?"

Suzanne shrugged. "I don't know—Nora Sutherlin?"

Harrison clamped his hand to his chest.

"God, Nora. Be still my heart. Be still my groin."

"That hot, is she?"

Harrison turned wide eyes at her and slowly nodded.

"You're a fan?" Suzanne asked.

Again he nodded.

"Father Stearns also a fan?"

Harrison rolled his eyes.

"He's male and straight. I'd worry if he wasn't a fan."

Suzanne pulled a dandelion from the grass and caressed her bottom lip with it. Flirting with a teenager to get answers? How low could she go?

"Think they're together?"

Harrison shook his head. "No way. Why would he still be a priest getting paid peanuts, putting up with us losers, if he had her waiting for him at home? Besides," Harrison said, dropping his voice to a whisper. Out on the pitch, Father Stearns blocked yet another attempt at a goal. The teenagers on the team looked tired and thirsty. He'd barely broken a sweat.

"Besides what?"

"I think Nora has a thing for younger men."

Suzanne raised her eyebrow at him.

"Got any evidence? Or just wishful thinking?" God, now she sounded like Father Stearns.

"Now I'm not one to tell tales out of school," Harrison began. "But there's this guy at church—Suicide Mike."

Suzanne's hands went cold at the mention of suicide. But she kept her face neutral.

"Suicide Mike?"

"I know. It's horrible. I never call him that," he said although he just had. "Michael Dimir."

"The boy who tried to commit suicide in the sanctuary?"

"The same," he said, nodding. "Here's the thing about Suic...about Michael. Michael, he's glass, breakable. Kid is scared of his own shadow. Barely talks. You say hi to him and it takes a year off his life."

Suzanne's stomach dropped in sympathy. Withdrawn? Anxious? Constantly on the alert? Michael sounded like a classic abuse victim to her. But where had the abuse come from? Home? Or church?

"So?" Suzanne prompted, not wanting but needing to know more.

"So Nora's a little on the intimidating side. Famous, rich, beautiful...you'd think if she said hi to him, he'd die on the spot. But no. I'm sitting there two weeks ago, Sunday morning, staring at Nora like usual. And she looks at Michael and

winks at him. I thought, 'Oh, shit, call 9-1-1—Mike's going
to have a heart attack.' But no, guess what he does?"

"What?"

"He stuck his tongue out at her like they were old buddies
or something. She stuck her tongue out back at him, and the
temperature in the sanctuary shot up twenty degrees from the
heat of those two eye-fucking each other."

Suzanne didn't say anything at first. Father Stearns seemed
rather defensive about both her and Michael Dimir. If he
acted as confessor to both of them, then no doubt he knew
the thirtysomething author was having an affair with a teenage boy. Together she and Harrison watched the game for a
few minutes in silence. Or almost silence. Despite being side-
lined, Harrison couldn't seem to stop yelling advice and encouragements at his own team.

She didn't know much about soccer, but she could tell
that Father Stearns owned the field. His team responded to
his every quiet command like well-trained soldiers. And he
seemed indefatigable, running up and down the field with the
fearsome long-legged agility of a jaguar.

"God, he's good," she said, as he weaved in between two
players and scored a goal from the center line.

"Of course he's good," Harrison said, taking off the ice and
rubbing his inner thigh. "He's one hundred and fifty percent
pure European. Got the soccer gene on both sides."

"How can somebody be one hundred and fifty percent European?" Suzanne asked, recalling what little she'd discovered
about the priest's past.

"His father's British, was British. Dead now. His mother's
Danish. And he went to seminary in Italy."

Danish mother? That would explain the hair and eyes.
And the inscriptions in the books and on the photo—must
be Danish.

"Thought his mother was from New Hampshire."

Harrison scoffed.

"Does that," he said, pointing at Father Stearns, "look American to you?"

"No," she admitted. He looked spectacular to her—masculine and handsome and so incredibly attractive. But not particularly American. "European genes—guess that's why he's your best player."

"Second best."

"Second? Let me guess—you're the best."

Harrison shook his head.

"No. Father Stearns's brother-in-law comes and practices with us sometimes. He's even better. But don't tell Father S I said that. They're really competitive."

Suzanne furrowed her brow. She knew Father Stearns had a sister, but the older sister, Elizabeth, didn't live in Connecticut.

"Brother-in-law? One of his sisters is married—"

Harrison shook his head.

"Father S was married."

Her heart shuddered a little in her chest.

"Father Stearns was married?"

"Yeah, when he was my age—eighteen. Legal adult," he reminded her. "Apparently didn't last long. She died. Some kind of accident. If I was an eighteen-year-old widower, I'd probably join the priesthood too."

Suzanne could barely speak.

"Married…" *I'm not a virgin…I wasn't born a priest…* "Eighteen…that would have been a long time ago. He and the brother are still friends?"

"They're either best friends or they want to kill each other. Hard to tell sometimes. They constantly swear at each other in French."

"French?"

"Yeah. Brother-in-law's French."

Harrison said something else but Suzanne had stopped listening. She looked out across the field and saw the practice coming to an end. Father Stearns's team had won 2–1. Standing up, Suzanne brushed the grass off her jeans and walked toward him.

As she came to him, he pushed his sunglasses up on his head.

"Good game," she said. "You were married?"

Father Stearns looked over her shoulder and shot Harrison a death stare. Harrison blew a kiss at Suzanne.

"Every Thursday I devote to praying for vocations for the church," Father Stearns said. "I pray Harrison will be called to become a Cistercian."

"Cistercian?"

"They take vows of silence. This prayer has not been answered yet."

Suzanne laughed and fell into step beside Father Stearns. She had to lengthen her already long strides to keep up with him.

"Yes, I was married," he finally said. She realized with the church so close by, he likely had just walked here. She decided to walk with him until he shooed her off. "Very briefly. She died shortly after we wed."

"Can I ask how or is that too personal?"

"Not personal," he said as they hit the sidewalk. "Merely painful. Marie-Laure fell to her death while out in the woods. I was a mile away, lest you think my asterisk refers to a murder."

"Beautiful name. She was French?"

"She was. A ballet dancer."

Suzanne experienced an odd sensation then. Something like jealousy. She pictured a beautiful French ballerina and her handsome young husband. What passion they must have had for each other.

From the street they turned onto a path shrouded in darkness. A canopy of trees lined the walkway. Ahead of them she spied a small two-story Gothic cottage.

"And your mother was Danish? I thought she was from New Hampshire?"

At the gate, they paused. Suzanne stood looking at him, waiting for him to say something, do something.

"My parentage…it's quite a long story," he said, his gray eyes as shadowed as the path they'd just walked.

Suzanne swallowed. She should not be doing this, should not be alone with him. Not here. Not in his house.

"I've got time."

A helicopter. They flew to the city in a freaking helicopter.

The entire way there, Michael sat at the window staring at the ground below, the clouds above and the horizon beyond… He couldn't believe Griffin could conjure up a helicopter as easily as one called a cab. Griffin…Griffin must think he's crazy. During the trip, as Michael nearly drooled over the view, Griffin only watched him with unconcealed amusement. Michael didn't care if Griffin thought he was nuts—he couldn't look away from the beauty of the evening at eight thousand feet.

"I've got my camera." Griffin tapped Michael on the knee to get his attention. Michael loved the way Griffin looked in his aviator sunglasses with the helicopter's headset on. "Want to take pics to send your friends?"

Michael shook his head and turned his eyes back to the vista below. After all, he didn't have any friends to show any pictures to.

The helicopter set down on the landing pad of some building in Hell's Kitchen as the sun finally sunk over the horizon. Michael followed Nora and Griffin as they headed for the roof door. In his plain cotton pants, white shirt and black jacket, he felt terribly undressed compared to Griffin in his black leather pants and black silk shirt. Nora wore a black suit too—fedora, suspenders, red shirt, black tie…the whole nine yards.

As they descended the stairs, Nora looked back and grinned at him.

"I'm going to keep you outta the papers, kid. Don't worry. I've got a private room set up for us already. You'll go there first while Griff and I cause a ruckus."

"I love a good hard ruck…us," Griffin said, grinning back as he took off his sunglasses and shoved them in his pocket. Michael blinked and forced his eyes away. He really needed to figure out how to stop staring at Griffin all the time.

They reached the bottom of the staircase and Michael heard the first strains of music. Nora went up to the door and knocked hard—three quick taps followed by two heavy ones.

"Secret code?" Michael asked in a whisper.

"Morse code for S&M."

Michael's eyes widened. "Really?"

Griffin shrugged and winked at him. "I have no idea."

The door opened and a man stepped out into the hallway. Michael looked up at him and kept looking up. And up.

"Boys, say hello to my friend Brad Wolfe," Nora said with an elegant and obviously facetious nod at the only man Michael had even been this close to who was taller than Father S. "Otherwise known as—"

"The Big Brad Wolfe," Griffin completed, stepping forward and extending his hand. "You're a legend."

The man, who Michael guessed was about six foot six with as much muscle to him as height, took Griffin's hand and shook it. He looked about forty years old and handsome in a way somebody like Nora would describe as "roguish." He thought Griffin was the height of male perfection. But women seemed to like Brad's look—chest hair and beard stubble. Nora obviously did from the way she smiled up at him.

"How's my Big Brad Wolfe?" she asked.

He raised a dark eyebrow at her.

"Little Red Riding Crop, what are you doing in my neck of the woods?"

"Causing trouble. Care to help?"

"I don't know. You still with…" Brad's voice trailed off and he glanced meaningfully at Michael and Griffin.

"With my priest?" she finished for him. "Yeah, still together. Don't take it personally. You're still the second-best sadist in the city."

"Damned with faint praise," Brad said, chucking Nora under the chin. "But I can never say no to you, green eyes. What do you need?"

"I reserved a booth for the show. Can you get Junior to it without anyone seeing him?"

Brad looked at Michael, who squirmed slightly in place.

"Nora…how old is he?"

"He's legal," she said without batting an eyelash.

"Legal for what?"

Michael coughed.

"I can drive."

"Good God," Brad said, laughing and rolling his eyes. "You might actually be more corrupt than Kingsley is, Nor."

Nora batted her eyelashes.

"You flatter me. Let's go."

Nora grabbed Griffin by the sleeve and the two of them disappeared down another flight of stairs.

"Come with me, little boy," Brad said with a voice that suddenly seemed even deeper than before. Michael swallowed.

"Yes, sir."

They entered the club through the back door. Michael kept his head down and his eyes on the back of Brad's shoes. But he couldn't help but get an eyeful of the craziness going on inside the club. Everywhere he looked he saw celebrities, or at least wannabe celebrities, dressed in costumes. Well, they were dressed like kinky people—or at least how he imagined non-kinky people thought kinky people dressed. He saw lots of latex catsuits on the too-skinny women and the guys wore leather vests and harnesses. It looked more like a super-fancy Halloween party for too-rich teenagers than a sex club to him.

"You work here?" Michael asked as Brad led him to a cordoned-off booth surrounded by a red curtain.

"Someone has to lend an air of authenticity." Brad closed the curtain and lit a smattering of candles. "I've got my own dungeon—the real thing. Ask your mistress about it sometime. I funnel the few real masochists who come here into my place."

Michael started to ask a question but Nora and Griffin burst into the booth, laughing riotously.

"How did it go?" Michael asked as Nora and Griffin collapsed into the booth.

"Perfect. I hid my face behind my hat," Nora said, flipping her fedora up her arm and perching it at a rakish angle on her head. "That got their attention. They probably thought I was way more famous than I really am. Then Griffin threatened to punch a photog."

"You did?" Michael turned to Griffin. "Can't you get arrested for that?"

Griffin shrugged. "They love getting threatened. Gives them street cred. Plus I paid him two grand to make sure we hit Page Six."

"Mission accomplished." Nora took a glass of red wine from

a leather-clad waitress. "Showtime," she said with a wicked glint in her eye.

At the opposite side of the club was a stage. As the club lights dimmed and faded, the stage lights went up. Four shirtless young men carried a beautiful olive-skinned Amazonian woman out to center stage on a divan. The club erupted into applause.

"Wow," Michael said. "She's…tall."

"She's a dude." Griffin winked at him. "Mistress Nyx."

"Seriously?" Apart from the height Michael couldn't make out any male features on the Amazon.

"Seriously," Nora said. "There are some hot male dominatrixes out there. Men can hit harder. Something to be said for that. Don't tell though. Nyx keeps that on the DL."

Michael nodded. Nyx now had one of the young men by the throat. She bodily forced him against an X-shaped cross and the other young men of her harem strapped him to it.

"St. Andrew's Cross." Nora leaned over the table to whisper loudly at Michael. "You know St. Andrew?"

"Um…a martyr?" Michael hazarded a guess. He might be Catholic but there were more saints out there than stars in the sky.

"Exactly," Nora said with an approving smile. "According to legend he requested that he die on an X-shaped crossed instead of T-shaped as he did not feel worthy to die like his savior. And he was bound and not nailed."

"Poor guy. Should have gotten nailed before he died," Griffin said and Nora swatted him on the arm.

"That's so weird," Michael said, laughing at the story. "Poor St. Andrew."

They watched the show in silence for a few minutes. Nyx had a cat-o'-nine-tails, which she used to flog the bound young man, who writhed and screamed on the cross.

"She's pulling her punches," Nora said with a knowing look. "She's barely hurting him at all."

"You can tell that?" Michael asked, suitably impressed.

She nodded. "First of all, she's hitting him all for show. Going too slow and hitting him with the flat of the tails and not the tip."

"But she's hitting him pretty hard, it looks." Michael narrowed his eyes at the scene on the stage.

"The tip of the whip is the business end," Nora said and reached her arm out and touched Griffin's face. "It's the difference between this…" She ran the full flat of her hand over Griffin's cheek. Griffin sighed. "And this." She turned her hand and flicked Griffin's ear with the tip of her fingers. Griffin flinched and grimaced.

"Ow, Nor. I'd say my safe word but I forgot it."

"It was *platypus*. So yeah, she's putting on a good show but not hurting him at all." Nora pointed at the stage, where the young man on the cross continued to cry out dramatically. "We can go to Brad's dungeon Dark Forest for some decent S&M after. It's RACK-rules there."

"Rack?" Michael asked. "Like a real rack?"

"Not a rack-rack. RACK stands for 'risk-aware consensual kink,'" Nora explained. "As opposed to SSC rules."

"Safe, sane and consensual," Griffin said, rolling his eyes as Nora yawned. "Exactly. SSC is tamer. It's for the moms and dads in the suburbs with the furry handcuffs under the bed."

"RACK is for people more like us," Nora said. "People who do the rougher stuff, edge-play, no safe words, et cetera."

"You and Søren ever play without safe words?" Griffin leaned back and rested his elbows on the back of the booth. Michael's temperature rose at the sight of the black silk of Griffin's shirt stretching across his broad chest.

Nora shook her head.

"I said I like the hard stuff. I didn't say I had a death wish."

In front of them on the stage, Nyx allowed her harem to free the young man from the cross. He crawled on all fours to her and kissed her booted feet.

"Aah…" Nora sighed. "The good old days. I miss foot worship. Nothing sexier than a male sub doing homage."

"Can't disagree with that," Griffin said, nodding.

"Are there a lot of male subs?" Michael asked as the young man kissed his way from Nyx's toe to her knee.

"A lot more than people want to admit," Nora said. "Men especially. You, Angel, are something special but you are not unique. There's probably as many male subs out there as male doms."

"Really?"

"Yeah, Mick," Griffin chimed in. "And not just in the gay kink scene, either."

"The number-one sexual fantasy reported by straight men is having sex with a beautiful woman." Nora took a deep drink of her wine. "But number two?"

Griffin grinned and held up two fingers. "Number two," he said, "is being tied up by a beautiful woman and then fucked by her. Even I was fine with that."

"More than fine, if I remember correctly…" Nora sighed wistfully and winked at Griffin.

"If there's so many of us," Michael asked, "then why—"

"Why do you feel so alone?" Nora gave him a long look. Michael nodded silently.

"You aren't alone," she said and Griffin reached out and gave his knee a friendly squeeze. Unfortunately that friendly squeeze caused a very more-than-friendly reaction inside Michael's boxers.

"Male subs paid for my house, Angel," Nora continued. "They bought my cars. They made me a very wealthy woman.

I had every walk of life in my dungeon—poets and artists, priests and rabbis, cops and robbers."

"Cops?"

"Oh, yeah. The bigger and tougher they pretend to be, the more likely they are to want a woman to call them a slut and put her foot on the back of their neck."

"Or another guy." Griffin glanced at Michael as he said the words.

"Hey, hush, boys, act two is starting."

Nyx had led her harem offstage. Within minutes they returned, but this time Nyx wore the robes of a Roman goddess. And she rode in on a chariot being pulled by her young men. They had bridles in their mouths and harnesses on their chests.

"Oh, my, pony play. How adorable. I love a pony." Nora leaned forward and rested her chin on her hand. "They are fun to ride."

"Whatever." Griffin rolled his eyes. "Like you've ever been on a horse in your life."

Nora sat up straighter. "I'll have you know, Master Fiske, that I've been horseback riding on multiple occasions. Well, like three occasions. My old intern, Wes, was from Kentucky. Apparently everyone in Kentucky rides horses."

Griffin shrugged. "Not exactly. Mostly just the Central Kentucky blue bloods. Horses are very expensive pets."

Nora grinned. "Wes Railey? A blue blood? Kid couldn't even afford a decent car. Drove a Bug. Poor thing."

Michael looked at Nora, who was smiling. But her smile seemed strange, forced even. Nothing like her usual smiles.

"Railey?" Griffin cocked his head and stared at Nora. "Like the Kentucky Raileys?"

"Well, he's a Railey and he's from Kentucky," Nora said.

"Know his parents' names?" Griffin turned away from the

pony show onstage and gave Nora his full attention. Nora seemed suddenly uncomfortable.

"Well, his mom's name is Caroline. I used it in my book that just came out. And his dad's name is—"

"Jackson." Griffin finished the sentence for her. "Jackson Railey?"

Nora's eyes widened.

"Griffin…how did you know that?"

Griffin chuckled and the chuckle turned into a laugh.

"Griffin…" Nora's voice dropped to menacing levels. "Why are you laughing?"

With a heavy exhale, Griffin dug his iPhone out of his pocket, made some quick taps on it and then smiled at whatever it was he'd pulled up on-screen. He handed his phone over to Nora without a word.

"Son of a bitch," she breathed. Slowly she handed the phone back to Griffin. Then she quickly got up from the table.

"Where are you going?" Griffin demanded.

"Make sure Michael gets home safe. I'll meet you back at the house later. Gotta check on something."

Nora disappeared into the crowd, and Michael found himself suddenly alone with Griffin. He didn't like how much he liked that.

"Griffin?" Michael whispered. "What did you show Nora?"

Griffin slid Michael his phone. Michael picked it up and studied the screen. It took a minute to wrap his mind around what he was looking at.

Michael breathed one word in response.

"Fuck."

14

Suzanne wandered around Father Stearns's living room while he excused himself to change. Such a beautiful home…a stone fireplace, hundreds of leather-bound books and the most beautiful grand piano she'd ever seen. On top of the piano sat a book of John Donne poetry. Opening the book to a page marked by an ancient embroidered bookmark, she read:

Enter these armes, for since thou thoughtst it best,
Not to dreame all my dreame, let's do the rest.

"I'm allowed to read John Donne," came Father Stearns's voice from behind her. "He was a priest."

"An Anglican priest who wrote anti-Catholic screeds," she reminded him.

"I don't take it personally."

Suzanne smiled nervously as Father Stearns took the book from her and sat it back on top of the piano. He'd showered, obviously—his blond hair looked darker wet—and wore his clericals once more. Damn. She really liked looking at his throat.

"You play?" She pointed at the piano.

"I could play piano before I even learned English. My mother taught me. "

"Your Danish mother?"

Father Stearns gestured to an armchair and he took one opposite her. The sun had set and only one small lamp cast its low light around the room.

"My mother was eighteen years old when she came to the United States. A music scholarship to a conservatory in New Hampshire. The scholarship only covered tuition. So she took a position as a nanny in my father's house. His wife had just given birth to a daughter."

"Your sister Elizabeth, right?"

"Yes. My father's wife had a difficult pregnancy, a difficult birth. After Elizabeth, she could have no more children. During her recovery, my mother became a mother to Elizabeth."

"And caught your father's eye?" Suzanne asked, smiling. She could see where this was going.

"Unfortunately, yes." Father Stearns did not smile.

Suzanne's smile died as the subtle inflection on the word *unfortunately* told her all.

"Oh, my God," she whispered.

"My father was a monster. I don't use the word lightly. His anger over his wife's inability to give him more children… he took it out on my mother. He raped her repeatedly until she conceived. She lived as a hostage as he threatened to hurt Elizabeth if she told anyone or ran away."

Suzanne covered her mouth with her hand.

"I was born ten months after she came to live with my father. The doctor who delivered me told me years later he'd never seen anything like it…a young woman in agony giving birth in utter silence. She didn't want to scream. My father would have enjoyed that too much."

"He was a sadist?"

Slowly Father Stearns nodded.

"I was born shortly after midnight on December 21st. She named me Søren after her grandfather. The doctor wrote that on the original birth certificate that he hid from my father. The official birth certificate reads Marcus Lennox Stearns. Marcus was my father's name. That is why I far prefer to be called anything but that."

Suzanne said nothing at first.

"December 21st," she repeated. "The longest night of the year."

"It was the longest night of my mother's life, she once confessed to me. Although I was a child of rape, she loved me. She remained in the home of her rapist to care for me. My father wanted to raise me as his child, his and his wife's. He might never have another son to inherit the family name and wealth. When he deemed me old enough, he sent me to school in England. She returned to Denmark and spent years trying to find me. My father had amassed incredible wealth and power by then. She told no one of what happened to her."

Suzanne stood up and walked over to the cold fireplace. *Told no one…*

"My brother Adam," she began and took a deep breath. "He loved the Church. Altar boy at age ten…he'd already decided he wanted to be a priest."

She turned back and met Father Stearns's eyes. He said nothing, only nodded for her to go on.

"We found out after he shot himself in the head at age twenty-eight…the note said he'd been raped by our priest. Repeatedly, for years. The Catholic Church had amassed such wealth and power…" she quoted Father Stearns. "He told no one, either."

Father Stearns came to her. He laid his hand gently on her face and she saw her tear trickle over his fingers.

"Because he committed suicide, the church denied him Catholic burial. Fucking Catholic Church," she said, swallowing what felt like a rock.

"Suzanne, I'm so sorry." Father Stearns gently stroked her cheek with his thumb.

"You just called me Suzanne, not Ms. Kanter."

He smiled.

"I did."

"What do I call you then?"

"The children at church have called me Father S for years. Less intimidating than Father Stearns, I suppose. Those closest to me, those who truly know me, call me Søren."

"I'd like to know you…Søren."

"You're starting to," he said, moving away and sitting in the chair again.

"Can I ask what Nora Sutherlin calls you?" She sat back down and pulled her legs in. She stared at him from over her knee.

"Eleanor calls me every name in the book," he said and they both laughed. "But mostly Søren. She says my name is appropriately pretentious."

"I can't believe she said that to you. Seriously, I've met four-star generals and they've got nothing on you for intimidation."

"Eleanor is a fearless woman, always has been."

"You speak of her very fondly. Don't tell me you're not close."

"We are close. She had a nasty run-in with the law at age fifteen. The judge had me supervise her community service.

Her parents had little to do with her after that. I suppose you could say I had to become her father."

"Are you proud of the way she's turned out?" Suzanne asked, certain of the answer. Erotica writer, dominatrix… all-around bad girl.

"I couldn't begin to be more proud of her. Her joie de vivre, her intelligence, her strength…we should all turn out as well as she."

"Strong, is she?" Suzanne had seen pictures of Nora Sutherlin—little slip of a thing.

"Strong enough even I can be weak around her."

Suzanne grinned.

"You weak? I think I'd like to see that."

Søren turned his eyes to her and gave her the coldest, hardest, steeliest stare she'd ever seen. Her blood went cold, her hands went numb, her heart fluttered.

"I assure you," he said with quiet menace, "you would not."

Suzanne wanted to flinch, to hide, to turn away, to run… but something held her there, something kept her from running. Yes, he intimidated the hell out of her. But beyond that stone wall that was Father Stearns, she caught a glimpse of something else, someone else that lived behind that pristine collar. She had to see him, had to know him.

"Tell me more about Eleanor," she said, somehow intuiting that to know her would be to know him. "Nothing secret. Nothing personal. Just about her. What's she like?"

"What is Eleanor like?" He nearly laughed the question. "You might as well ask me what God is like. She's not God, but she's nearly as difficult to explain. It could take all night."

Suzanne sat back in the chair and studied him…his aquiline nose, his strong masculine jaw, those strangely sculpted lips. Her eyes moved to his hands. A pianist's hands, graceful, agile, precise. What would they feel like on her…in her?

She did want to see him weak. She wanted to see him any way she could.

"I have all night."

Outside of Sin Tax, Nora grabbed a cab and gave the driver an address in Manhattan.

"You sure about that?" the driver asked. "That's no—"

"Just go," Nora ordered and the driver promptly shut up. In a few minutes they pulled up to a black-and-white three-story town house. Nora threw money into the front of the cab and got out without a word. She raced up the front steps and through the doors. At once four rottweilers charged at her. "Shh...down, kids."

All four dogs whimpered and sat on their hind legs at her words. Usually she took the time to play with the dogs, who had a fearsome reputation but a deep love of affection. Nora headed up to the third floor and down the hallway. At the end of the hall she opened the door to Kingsley's private office.

Files...she needed files. Nora scanned the office. So many filing cabinets. She hardly knew where to begin.

She opened the top drawer of the first cabinet and found rows of files neatly labeled with names—last name, comma, first name and a number. In the third cabinet in the second drawer from the bottom, she found *Railey, Wesley (John), 1312.* Nora flipped the folder open.

"God fucking dammit." She closed the folder, slammed the drawer and leaned against the heavy ebony wood of the cabinet. She'd forgotten Kingsley encoded all his files. No, she corrected, Kingsley and Juliette encoded his files. And Juliette, Kingsley's beautiful Haitian secretary, loved doing anything she could to piss her boss off. That would certainly include helping Nora decode one of the files. Flipping open the file again, Nora counted the pages—four. Surely Juliette could...

"*Chérie?* What are you doing here?"

Nora didn't even glance up.

"It's midnight, King. Isn't Juliette going to get cold without you on top of her?"

"She'll survive a few moments without me. And you haven't answered my question."

"Needed some light reading." She flipped again through the file, hoping to make some sense of it. "How did you know I was here?"

"I alarmed the office."

Nora looked up sharply at Kingsley. Alarm? Kingsley never even locked the doors at the town house, much less alarmed it. He loved flaunting his sense of security. All of New York, at least the criminal element, knew better than to cross Kingsley Edge.

"Whoever stole my file...you're scared of him, aren't you?" Nora asked.

"*Oui.* And that means you should be scared too. That means you shouldn't be in town without your master's permission."

Kingsley stood directly in front of Nora. Over the top of the file she saw Kingsley's bare chest—olive-skinned, handsomely muscled and riddled with old wounds, inside and out. Kingsley took the file from her hands, and Nora reluctantly met his eyes.

"Why are you here?" Kingsley asked, his voice soft but not unthreatening.

Nora said nothing at first.

"Answer me," Kingsley said. Nora glared at him. She took orders from Søren these days and no one else. "What are you doing here? You're supposed to be upstate with Griffin. Not in my office in the middle of the night."

Nora said nothing. Kingsley, wearing nothing but dark

gray trousers and an unbuttoned white shirt, glanced down at the label.

"Ah," he said, nodding. "I see. Your pet…you miss him."

"Wesley was my best friend and my roommate and my intern. Not my pet. And tonight we saw a pony show and I started talking about horses and Wesley and Kentucky and Griffin—"

"And Griffin knows. And now you do too."

"Tell me who my intern is," Nora demanded. "Griffin showed me a picture of him. He was at the Kentucky Derby talking to Prince Harry. The Prince Harry. And the caption on the photo said—"

"'The Prince of Kentucky compares racing forms with a Prince of England,'" Kingsley finished for her as he flipped open the file to the last page and showed her that very photograph. "I'm quite familiar with it."

"Goddammit. You knew. You knew who he was and you didn't tell me. How could you do that?"

"He never told you. It was his choice. It was not my place to tell."

"It is now. Tell me who my intern is."

Kingsley walked to the desk and sat at the edge.

"First, tell me why you want to know. You sent him away. He's gone."

Nora laid her hand against her chest over her heart.

"Not here. He's not gone here."

"He deserves better than this, *le prêtre* does."

Nora couldn't argue with that. "I know. I know he does. You wanted me back with Søren."

"I wanted *le prêtre* happy again. For some reason, you make him happy. But this…" He raised the file. "This will not make anyone happy."

Nora sighed. She walked to Kingsley's desk and collapsed into a chair across from him.

"I was going to go back to him, to Søren." She stared at Kingsley's bare feet. So strange to see him not in his signature knee-high riding boots. Only sex got him out of those boots. Somewhere in the town house, Nora knew Juliette was wondering where her master was. But Juliette would have to wait.

Kingsley laughed deeply. "How much have you had to drink tonight, *maîtresse?* You did go back to him."

Nora smiled to herself.

"No…I mean I was going to go back to Søren a year and half before I did. It was a Wednesday in September. That whole week…I don't know why, but for that entire week I could hardly breathe for how much I missed Søren. I had good days and bad days without him. That day started out bad. Bad enough I decided I'd give it up, humble myself, grovel at Søren's feet until he took me back. But I didn't. You know why?"

Kingsley didn't speak at first. After the space of ten heartbeats he finally answered.

"Pourquoi?"

"Because that was the first day I taught that stupid writing class at Yorke, and I went into that classroom and saw these beautiful big brown eyes that looked at me as though they'd never seen anything like me before. I met Wesley. And I just forgot. I forgot I meant to go back to Søren." Nora swallowed the tears in her throat. "Oops."

"I will pretend I never heard that."

Nora laughed miserably.

"I came to you that night. Do you remember, King?" Nora met his eyes and let her mind and body burn up with the memory—racing to Manhattan, running up the stairs… almost like tonight. "You were sound asleep in your bed, and I crawled in, and took you by the wrists while you were sleeping...."

Kingsley inhaled sharply and looked away. They had a rule they never spoke about that side of Kingsley.

"*Oui,* I remember."

"I was burning," she confessed. "For that kid in my class at Yorke. For Wesley. I couldn't take my frustration out on him obviously. I took it out on you." Nora met Kingsley's dark eyes. "That night might have been the first night we ever spent together that you and I weren't fantasizing about the same person."

Kingsley didn't speak. And Nora said nothing else.

"I've wondered a time or two if I love *le prêtre* more than you do, *chérie.* Now I know I do."

"Kingsley..." Nora closed her eyes tight but one mutinous tear escaped. "I know you know how it feels to love someone so much and not have him. Please...it's me doing the begging tonight."

"If you use any of this information to hurt *le prêtre*..." Kingsley's voice trailed off and the threat was left unsaid. He didn't have to say it. She and Kingsley were not friends, and never had been. They had been Jacob and Esau to Søren. At least in Kingsley's mind. And now if she hurt Søren...it wouldn't be a rivalry between them anymore. It would be war.

So be it.

Kingsley gave her one last look. He picked up a pair of elegant wire-framed glasses off his desk, put them on and opened the file.

He read. Nora listened. And by dawn she knew one thing.

Wesley had lied.

15

Michael and Griffin didn't linger long at Sin Tax after Nora ran off to do whatever it was she did—Michael still wasn't quite sure. Together he and Griffin watched the rest of the pony show. When it ended, Michael leaned forward in anticipation of the next act but froze when he felt fingers on the back of his neck.

Every muscle in his body tensed, every nerve tingled as Michael slowly turned his head to face Griffin, who watched him with hooded eyes.

"Let's go." Griffin gave Michael's neck a gentle squeeze and Michael had to concentrate extremely hard not to enjoy it as much as his body wanted to. "Our bird's here."

Michael nodded slowly, not wanting to dislodge Griffin's hand. But sadly Griffin left the booth and took his hand with him. Michael followed closely behind as they made their way through the crowded club toward the back exit. So intent on watching Griffin walk, Michael didn't notice the foot in his path until he'd accidentally kicked it.

Spinning around to apologize, Michael came face-to-face with a pale and handsome man in his mid-twenties with curling blond hair and smiling, empty eyes.

"I'm sorry," Michael stammered as the man took a step forward.

"I'm not." The man looked Michael up and down. "What's your name?"

"Um…" Michael looked around for Griffin but had seemingly lost him in the crowd. "Michael. I need—"

"Here, Michael," the man said, pulling a chair out with his foot. "You kicked my leg and scuffed my shoe. The least you can do to make it up to me is to sit down and have a drink with me. Then we'll talk about the most you can do to make it up to me."

Michael's heart raced. Where the hell had Griffin gone?

"I can't. I have to find—"

"You can. You should." The man smiled. "You will."

"He won't."

Michael heaved a sigh of relief as Griffin appeared at his shoulder.

The young man's eyes lit up in recognition.

"Griffin Fiske…what the hell are you doing here?" the blond man said, giving Griffin a wide and obviously fake smile. "Shouldn't you be sucking Kingsley Edge's cock?"

"I get Friday nights off," Griffin said.

"I get every night off. No, wait. I get off every night. That was it. So you're sort of interrupting here, Griff. I was making a new friend."

"Your new friend is my old friend, Jackal." Griffin edged in closer to Michael.

"Can't we all be friends?"

Griffin smiled. "No. We're leaving."

"You're leaving. He's staying. He's my date." Jackal grinned and reached out as if to pat Michael's face. Griffin's hand snaked out and grasped Jackal's wrist with such a display of lightning speed that Michael flinched.

"Don't touch my property, Jack. Not with any part of you that you wanna keep."

Michael could only stare at Jackal's fingers hanging impotently in the air inches from his face, Griffin's hand clasped around his wrist in a viselike grip. Even in the low light of the club Michael could discern the barely concealed pain on Jackal's face and the color draining from his hand.

Jackal's jaw clenched.

"Sorry, Griff. Didn't know he was yours."

Griffin raised his chin and stared Jackal down. "Well, he is."

"Honest mistake."

Nodding, Griffin let Jackal's hand go. "Of course. Could happen to anyone. Ready, Mick?"

Michael looked at Griffin. Out of the corner of his eye he noticed half the club now watching them. With such attention, Michael knew he should have felt humiliated. But to be publicly called the property of Griffin Fiske, even as a lie, made his heart, and another part of him, swell with pride.

"Yes, sir."

At the "sir," Griffin's eyes widened slightly before he quickly recovered. With an air of casual dominance, Griffin put his hand on Michael's lower back and steered him away from Jackal toward the back exit.

"Who is that guy?" Michael whispered when they got to the exit.

"Jack Albrect."

"Ex-friend?"

Griffin didn't meet his eyes as he opened the back door. "Ex-dealer. Not a fan of me now that I'm not his best customer anymore."

"Oh." Michael couldn't think of anything else to say to that. They took the stairs to the roof, and Michael already missed Griffin's hand on his lower back. "Well, thanks for getting me away from him. You know...pretending we were together. I mean, we're together but we're not...I'm not..."

Griffin turned around and looked at him. He started to say something but the helicopter blades drowned out all sound. In silence, they flew all the way back to Griffin's estate. Now night, Michael couldn't see much below them so he merely stared into the darkness and remembered the burning look of fury in Griffin's eyes when Jackal had tried to touch him and the incredibly comforting sensation of Griffin's fingers on his back guiding him through the crowd. *Don't touch my property, Jack....* Even Nora's books and the erotic orders she whispered in his ears at night hadn't aroused him as much as those five words of Griffin's had. *My property.*

If only.

In silence they walked back into the house. Michael wanted to say something more to Griffin but once more couldn't find the words. Or maybe he had the words but didn't have the balls to say them.

At the top of the steps they started to go their separate ways. But Griffin stopped him with a word.

"Just a sec, Mick. I forgot I had something for you. It's in my room."

"Really? What is it?" Michael nervously followed Griffin into his massive bedroom. Michael had only peeked his head in the room once or twice but never actually crossed the threshold. It seemed like hallowed ground to him. He didn't feel quite worthy to be in the presence of the bed Griffin slept in, the sheets he fucked on.

"What is it?" Griffin repeated. "Nothing. Just a line to get you in my room."

Michael froze. Griffin laughed and grabbed him by the shoulder.

"Don't look so terrified. Everybody who comes into my bedroom leaves it smiling. Except for Alfred, but that's only because he hates being the bottom."

Michael burst into laughter as they entered Griffin's room.

"Nora says it's not for everybody," Michael said as Griffin started digging through drawers.

"Next butler I hire, I'll make sure to ask his positions preferences first. You know, it's a good thing I'll never have to get a real job. I'm a sexual-harassment lawsuit waiting to happen."

"Nora said she put 'being sexually harassed' in her old intern's job description."

"She's a smart lady. Could have been a lawyer but wasn't enough of a sadist."

Griffin pulled a bag out from under his bed and handed it to Michael.

Michael stared at it a moment before opening the bag. From it he pulled out something square and wrapped in linen. He pulled off the linen wrap and found a large black book covered in the softest, supplest leather he'd ever touched.

"It's just a new sketchbook," Griffin said as he started to unbutton his shirt. "I saw you'd nearly filled up your other one."

Griffin tossed his shirt over the back of a chair.

So moved by the gift, Michael could barely speak. It took a few seconds to gather the words up.

"Thank you, Griffin," he whispered. "It's awesome."

He'd never had a sketchbook so obviously expensive and high quality.

Shrugging, Griffin unbuckled his belt and pulled it off. The sight of the black leather belt in Griffin's hands…Griffin shirtless, his usually perfect hair slightly mussed from the flight…

Michael suddenly found it nearly impossible to take a full breath. He kept inhaling and forgetting to exhale.

Griffin stood right in front of him. If a bomb had gone off out in the hallway, Michael still wouldn't have been able to wrench his eyes away from the flat plane of Griffin's hard stomach.

"I liked 'sir' better." Griffin tilted his head, raised his eyebrow and looked at Michael.

Michael could only blush.

"You're welcome, Mick." Griffin stepped away and sat on the edge of his bed, the belt still in his hands.

"It's really nice. I'll go, um…draw." Michael started to back toward the door.

"Have fun…drawing." Griffin gazed at him without smiling, without irony, without even the hint of amusement on his face or sculpted lips. In a gesture that seemed both mindless and calculated, Griffin pulled the belt taut between his hands.

"Okay…good night, Griff. Thanks again. You know, for everything."

Griffin finally smiled but the smile didn't quite reach his eyes.

"'Night, Mick."

Michael turned around and headed for the door. He could do this. He could leave. He was going to leave and go to bed. He was going to keep his mouth shut and not say anything because he always kept his mouth shut and he never said anything. He never asked for what he wanted, never confessed what he needed. That's how it was and how it would always be.

On the threshold of Griffin's bedroom, Michael stopped as if he'd run into an invisible wall. Slowly he turned back around.

Griffin still sat on the end of his bed, leather belt in hand, watching him.

"Um…Griffin?"

Suzanne stirred and sat up straight. What the hell? She rubbed her face and looked around. Dammit, she'd fallen asleep in Father Stearns's rectory. Søren's rectory, she reminded herself. If her father had been a rapist, she wouldn't want any part of his name, either.

Raising her wrist into a patch of moonlight she checked the time—3:53 a.m. Søren hadn't been kidding when he'd said explaining what Nora Sutherlin was like would take all night. He'd regaled her with story after story of her youth at Sacred Heart…how she'd once asked a nun if she wore holy underwear; how she'd sprained her ankle on a hiking trip after a boy shoved her after she called him a cocksucker for kicking his little sister; how the community service the judge imposed on her for stealing cars changed her from an angry little monster of a teenage girl into a compassionate young woman who wept in his arms when her favorite homeless-shelter resident died of a drug overdose.

"I think I'd like her," Suzanne had said, smiling into the empty fireplace. "Wonder if she'd like me."

"Knowing Eleanor and considering you're investigating me, she'd likely make a pass at you in the first five minutes after meeting you and threaten your life in the next."

After all their talking, Suzanne came to one single conclusion about Father Stearns—he wasn't the enemy. She still didn't know what the possible conflict of interest was and it did concern her. But no way was he a sexual predator. She felt the truth of that in her heart.

Even this stupid situation she found herself in testified to his inherent decency. She'd fallen asleep after hours of talking and one very potent glass of red wine. She'd woken up on his sofa with a blanket over her with her clothes on and her shoes off.

Overhead she heard the squeak of hardwood. She needed to go home, would go home—right now. But she couldn't just leave without telling him goodbye and thanking him for the blanket. He'd admitted he sometimes had trouble sleeping and usually worked in his upstairs office until dawn. Suzanne folded the blanket, slipped on her shoes and nervously made her way up the narrow staircase to the second floor. At the end of the hallway she saw a pale light spilling onto the floor from an open door. Walking loudly to alert him of her presence, Suzanne came to the end of the hall and inhaled sharply.

Not his office…his bedroom. Next to his four-poster bed, dressed in pristine white linens, Søren stood with his back to her. She saw his Roman collar on the table next to the bed. Watching him, Suzanne froze, unable to move, unable to look away as he slowly unbuttoned his cuffs and let his shirt slide off his arms.

Never in her life had she seen a man with a more exquisite body…every inch of his back rippled with lean muscle, his biceps were ridged with sinewy veins. The long line of his spine was a canyon she wanted to traverse with her lips again and again. She could live and die happy in that broad expanse of smooth skin between his arching shoulder blades. Her hands itched to trace the curve of his rib cage, her tongue ached to taste the nape of his neck. Her fingers tingled, her nipples tightened and liquid heat gathered deep in her stomach.

"Suzanne, are you planning on standing in the hallway all night staring at me? Or are you coming in?"

Part II

Six Weeks Later

16

If he kept his eyes closed and she didn't talk, he could probably go through with it. His hand slid under her silk blouse and stroked the soft skin of her stomach. His lips moved from her mouth to her neck while her hands roamed down his chest. With his eyes shut tight, his body started to respond to the press of her hips against his and the warmth of her curves. She released an amorous sigh as he started to push her skirt up.

"This might be more comfortable in my bed, Wesley."

Wesley exhaled and opened his eyes. One sentence from her and the moment shattered. He shouldn't have stopped kissing her mouth. Then she wouldn't have been able to talk.

Sitting up in the backseat of his car, he ran his hands through his hair, and rubbed his forehead.

"What's wrong?" Bridget asked as she tugged her skirt back down. "You didn't have to stop. Just saying we should probably finish somewhere other than in the car."

"I'm sorry. I'm just..." Wesley didn't finish the sentence

as he could think of no true words that wouldn't hurt her feelings.

"Just what?"

He heard the edge in her voice and sighed.

"Just…not ready."

As he knew they would, the words *not ready* inspired an eye roll and an unhappy crossing of her arms over her chest.

"Wes, we've been going out for two months. Two *months*. My last boyfriend and I had sex our second date. You and me? Two months and you won't even let me touch you."

"I like taking things slow. I'm…" He stopped and considered telling her the whole truth. But the whole truth would involve talking about certain things—and one certain person—he had zero desire to talk about. "Old-fashioned."

"Old-fashioned. All right. I can accept that. Maybe. Can you at least give me an idea when an old-fashioned type like you would be ready to have sex with his girlfriend?"

He turned his head and gazed at Bridget. Such a beautiful woman—dark hair with blond highlights, tall and slender, a stunner, as his dad would say; a stunner seven years older than him.

"You're Dad's secretary. I think it's a bad idea for us to be involved." A lame excuse. His Dad had been thrilled to see him and Bridget flirting. He'd practically ordered Wesley to ask her out.

"If that's what it is, then break up with me and get it over with. Stop screwing around with my feelings."

Break up? For some reason those two words that he should have dreaded sounded not like a death knell to him but like freedom. Break up—maybe they should.

"Okay," he said, nodding.

"Okay what?"

"Okay, we'll break up. You're right. I'm an ass for being

like this. It's complicated and I don't really want to go into it. But you're totally right."

Bridget's brown eyes widened.

"I didn't say I wanted us to break up. I only meant—"

"Then why—"

"Why are you being like this?" she demanded. "We're good together. At least I thought we were."

"But you complain the entire time about us not moving fast enough. Obviously you don't think we're good together."

"I think we could be. Wes…" She held up her empty hands.

His stomach clenched into a tight fist of guilt. If Bridget felt even a fraction of the misery he felt that day that Nora—

No. He wasn't going to think about Nora. He'd gone all day without thinking of Nora and he wasn't about to let her creep back into his thoughts. He and Bridget and their problems had nothing to do with Nora or what he felt for her. Felt—past tense.

"Can we—" he began and stopped. He'd meant to say, *Can we talk about this tomorrow?* But he knew he had to go through with it, get it over with. Bridget at least deserved the truth. Not the truth that he was still a virgin. That wasn't why he couldn't go through with it with her. That might even be the least of all the reasons.

"Can we what?"

Wesley took a deep, steadying breath and met Bridget's eyes through the dark.

"I'm in love with someone else. And I can't have sex with you because I'll be thinking about her the entire time, and you don't deserve that."

For a long time Bridget said nothing. She didn't even look at him.

"Who?" She finally spoke.

Wesley laughed then, a miserable, tired laugh.

"Ever heard of Nora Sutherlin?"

Bridget's jaw dropped. "That crazy writer?"

Wesley nodded. She stared at him a long moment before shaking her head and throwing open the car door.

"Dump me if you want to dump me." She grabbed her purse from the front seat. "But at least be man enough to tell me the truth."

Bridget's high heels clicked across the concrete the short distance from her driveway to her house. He heard her screen door open and fling itself shut. Wesley crawled from the backseat into the front of his father's spacious Cadillac and turned the car on. Taking Versailles Road he headed out toward the farm. He hated this drive at night. Too long, too dull, too easy to let his mind wander places it didn't need to go. The small castle some weirdo had built his wife twenty years ago constituted about the only thing of interest on this stretch of road. Wes glanced at the castle on the right. Yeah, still there. He kept driving.

The entire way home Wesley berated himself for how badly the evening turned out. Bridget…she was great. Smart, beautiful, older—he liked that. A year and three months living with a woman in her early thirties had made Wesley nearly allergic to girls his age—their drunk texting, their obnoxious Facebooking, their Ugg boots and their wide-eyed flirting. Nora didn't wear Ugg boots. Or play on Facebook. Or drunk text. She wore black leather boots with straps and zippers. She swore like a sailor, drank like a fish, fought like a man—literally. He'd watched her box once and she KO'd her sparring partner—a retired featherweight boxer named Bruce—in three rounds.

And Nora didn't flirt with anybody. "Flirting's for people who don't mean it, Wes," Nora had once said. "I seduce."

Dammit…he'd just broken up with Bridget and here he

was thinking of Nora. Again. As always. As he had every single day since moving back to Kentucky. He'd never told his parents about Nora—just said he'd decided he missed the farm too much. His mom had bought it. His dad had been more suspicious. Of course, he'd been something of a zombie those horrible weeks after Nora kicked him out of their house. He'd finished out the semester in a daze, crashing on his friend Josh's couch and staring at his cell phone waiting for Nora to call and say she'd made a mistake, that she wanted him home with her again.

But the phone never rang. And even when he called her, she never answered. And now thirteen months later, he still hadn't heard a word from her. Was she happy? Safe? Was she with Søren right now? Was that bastard hurting her? Wesley's heart clenched at the very thought of them together. Only his hatred of Søren burned hotter and stronger than his lingering love for Nora.

But just barely.

Wesley turned into the drive and paused to punch in the security code. The iron gates yawned open and he drove through. He checked the time—11:53 p.m. Mom and Dad had been in bed for hours, thank God. No one would bother him with questions if he ran into the main house for a few minutes.

He killed the headlights as he pulled into the circular drive. Ever since coming back home, he'd lived in the guesthouse way out back. But all the mail went to the big house. He'd applied to Tulane—great pre-med program—but wasn't quite sure he could handle NOLA weather. Kentucky summers were bad enough.

Wesley stood in the foyer and flipped on the lamp by the big entryway mirror. Glancing at himself he still didn't quite recognize the person reflected back. For months he'd put off a much-needed haircut. When he lived with Nora she would pounce on him about his hair when it got too long, sometimes literally. Once he'd been lying on the couch reading when he felt a weight on his chest. His book went flying and he found Nora straddling his hips with her knees; she had both hands on his chest and a pair of scissors clenched between her teeth like some kind of guerrilla hairstylist.

"What are you doing?" Wesley had demanded as Nora held him down with one hand while her right hand wielded the scissors.

"Cutting your hair. You have the most beautiful brown eyes of any guy on earth and you let your damn hair hide them. Now don't move unless you want me to blind you."

The scissors inched closer and he'd tunneled his head into the couch cushions as far as he could. Nora only backed off when he swore on the grave of Anaïs Nin—her personal hero—he'd get his hair professionally cut that week. Now his hair almost reached his shoulders. His mom gave him hell for his hair, but her complaining didn't make him nearly as happy as Nora's haircut ambushes. Secretly he thought of his long hair as a source of strength, like Samson. He hadn't cut it just to spite Nora. She couldn't see it, couldn't care less. But he knew if she saw him, she'd hate how long it was. And that gave him a little dark measure of satisfaction. Stupid really. She didn't care about him, didn't love him, didn't miss him. Why bother?

Wesley flipped through the mail and found nothing of interest. Nothing from Tulane yet. Still too soon probably. Only sent his stuff in two weeks ago. He dropped the mail back on the side table and noticed a large padded envelope addressed to him.

He read the return address and saw it came from somewhere in New York. Had one of his old Yorke friends sent him something? Wesley tore the envelope open.

For at least a full minute Wesley stared at the cover of the hardbound book.

The Consolation Prize by Nora Sutherlin.

With shaking fingers Wesley slowly opened the cover. He turned one blank page…then another. On the title page he found a note in familiar handwriting.

Turn the page, Wes.

Wesley took a shallow breath. His heart raced wildly in his chest. Thirteen months of nothing but the silent treatment and now…

On the next page he found the dedication.

Wesley leaned his weight against the front door. He needed something to keep him standing. The door didn't work, and he slid to the floor. He remembered…Nora in her bed, her hair still wet, her face devoid of any makeup. And she'd never looked so beautiful. The next day was her anniversary with Søren and as usual she intended to go see him. Finally Wesley had realized the simply horrible fact of the matter.

"You still love him, don't you?" he'd asked her.

She'd run her hands through her wet hair and let the water droplets fall to the floor.

"Many waters," she'd said.

Many waters cannot quench love, Nor will rivers overflow it. Song of Solomon 8:7.

In other words, yes, she still loved Søren.

Wesley stared at the dedication until his eyes watered.

To W.R. Many waters.

She'd dedicated the book to him. Not to Søren, as she had all her other books. Many waters… She still loved him too.

Underneath the dedication Nora had written him another note.

Wesley, you twerp, you could have told me.

Could have told her? Could have told her what?

Wesley looked up. Hanging from the ceiling in the entryway to his home was a chandelier that had once hung in Versailles—the French palace, not the town in Kentucky. And the book had come straight to this address, not his old school one and then forwarded.

"Shit..." Wesley breathed. She knew who he was now. How had she found out? Well, not that hard really. She must have looked him up on Google or something. He should return the favor. The address on the envelope wasn't anything he recognized. Maybe she'd left Connecticut, left New York City, left Søren.

Grabbing the book and the envelope, he raced through the big house and out the back door. At the guesthouse, his house, he could barely get the key in the lock. Once inside he slapped on a light, grabbed his laptop and went to Google. He typed in *Nora Sutherlin* and the city *Guilford*.

The very first hit took him to a New York City gossip site. Scanning the article he discovered Nora had gone to some S&M club as the date of a guy named Griffin Fiske. At first Wesley's heart swelled with happiness that Nora had gone anywhere in the presence of any guy who wasn't Søren. Maybe they'd broken up. Wesley quickly Googled Griffin Fiske and had the unpleasant shock of discovering he already knew him. Or at least knew of him. He'd seen Griffin's name in Nora's cell phone once and he'd casually asked her who he was.

"My personal trainer," Nora had answered without batting an eyelash. Nora's "personal trainer" was also the obscenely rich son of the chairman of the New York Stock Exchange, a former drug addict who'd had a couple stints in rehab, the grandson of the owners of Raeburn Farm, and kind of obnoxiously good-looking in a tanned and muscley sort of way. God, he looked like one of those guys in Calvin Klein ads in *Vanity Fair*. Not Nora's usual type. She went for guys like her editor Zach Easton—handsome in a distinguished sort of way, overeducated and usually older than her. Wesley had never seen Søren, not even a picture of him, but he guessed that's what he looked like too. They'd spoken on the phone once and even Søren's voice sounded well manicured. Yet another reason to hate the man.

Wesley took a long, slow, deep breath and ran through the facts in his mind.

Nora didn't seem to be with Søren anymore.

Nora did seem to be keeping bad company, however.

Nora had dedicated her book to him with the words *Many waters...*

Wesley got up and started packing.

Suzanne stared at the ceiling and tried to become one with her sofa. Emptying her mind, she slowed her breathing and focused only on the beating of her heart. It pounded hard, almost audibly. She breathed deep again but the pounding only grew louder. Groaning she raised a hand to forehead and called out, "Go away, Patrick."

"Open the damn door, Suz," he called back. "I'm not leaving until you let me in or the cops come for me." Once more he beat on the door. How the hell was anyone supposed to meditate under these conditions?

She stood up, walked to the door and threw it open.

"Fine. Come in." Suzanne threw herself back down on the couch and closed her eyes.

"What the hell is wrong with you? Where have you been?" Patrick demanded. She didn't have to open her eyes to know he stood next to the couch glaring at her.

"I've been busy. I started writing a book about my time in Afghanistan. Been living at the library."

A long silence followed her words.

"A book…about Afghanistan. That's why you haven't called me back or emailed me or answered the door or anything for six fucking weeks?"

"I'm very busy. Can't you see?"

She'd hoped the bitchiness would send Patrick running. Instead he sat down on the couch right next to her stomach.

"Suz."

She shut her eyes tight.

"Suzanne."

Slowly she opened them.

"What happened?" Patrick asked, brushing a lock of hair off her face. The tone of his voice was so gentle, the concern so intimate that tears sprang to her eyes. "Something happened. Tell me."

She swallowed hard and covered her eyes with her hands.

"I don't want to talk about it," she said, her voice no more than a whisper. "I can't…"

"That priest you were investigating…did something happen? Did he threaten you? Hurt you?"

Suzanne laughed miserably.

Hurt her? Well, she did have bruises the day after. Suzanne's whole body tingled from the memory of that night a month and a half ago. She'd been such an idiot going to the rectory. Looking back she saw that she'd started to fall for Father Stearns. Maybe not fall for him. Maybe it wasn't love. But lust definitely. Lust as she'd never experienced before in her life—blazing hot, unbearable, like a fist in her stomach and a splinter in her mind.

Suzanne, are you planning on standing in the hallway all night staring at me? Or are you coming in?

She'd come in. And he'd turned to her. And she'd reached out and laid her hands on his chest. Underneath her hand she'd felt his heart beating slow and steady. He hadn't been afraid

or nervous. Only her. In an instant his mouth had crashed
onto hers and she'd thrown herself into the kiss, body and
soul. Her nails dug into his back, her breasts pressed into his
chest. Nothing would have stopped her from having him that
night. Not the Church or the state or her better judgment or
her job or even her memories of Adam. She reached between
their bodies to unbutton his pants, and a pair of hands with
a viselike grip clamped down on her wrists. She found herself backed to the wall, her arms pinned above her head, and
Søren's face by hers, his eyes closed, the slightest grimace of
pain on his face.

"I can't…" he'd whispered and his hands had dug deeper
into her soft skin.

And she should have left at that. But she couldn't. In her
twenty-eight years, she'd had sex, she'd liked sex, she'd enjoyed sex…but not until that moment had she needed it,
needed it more than the air her lungs demanded of her.

"Please." She'd said please once and she should have stopped
there. But it came out again. "Please, Søren…please…" and
over and over again. She begged for him, begged for it. Even
now, six weeks later, she couldn't think of how much she'd
pleaded with him without blushing with utter shame. She
would have sold her soul to feel him inside her.

Instead he'd covered her mouth with his hand to stop her
words.

"Forgive me, Suzanne," he'd said and she heard her own
need echoed in his voice. "I do not belong to myself."

And slowly he'd let her go. And once free of his shockingly
strong hands, she'd run hard and fast from the rectory, back
to her car, back to the city and away from him.

The next day she couldn't stop staring at her own skin.
Søren had purpled her arms from elbow to wrist. And looking at those bruises brought back such waves of desire that

she'd lain in bed giving herself the pleasure he'd denied her and crying during every orgasm.

"I fucked up, Patrick," she said finally. "I fucked up the whole investigation. I killed my credibility."

"What did you do?"

Suzanne pulled her hands from her face.

"I kissed him."

A half-truth seemed better than a lie.

"You kissed him?"

She nodded miserably.

"And it doesn't matter. Because he kissed me back. And I know he wanted me and he didn't do anything. Just stuck to his vows. He's a good priest. I wasted his time and my time and your time… It's pointless. You were right. I shouldn't have pursued it."

Patrick shook his head.

"No. You were right. There is something weird about him. There's no way some stranger would send you an anonymous tip about him if he was the saint everyone says he is."

"I dug, Patrick. And I can't find anything. The kids at church love him and trust him. The parents love him and trust him. What else is there? I don't care if he's cheating on his taxes as long as he's never hurt a child. I wanted to believe he was a monster just because he's a priest. Look." She pointed at a box on the floor by her desk. "There's all my notes on him. There's nothing. He's a saint."

With a groan, Patrick got up, grabbed the box and sat back down on the couch. He flipped through her notes.

"Nice to see you made sure to write down how hot he is," Patrick said, reading her steno pad.

"It's ungodly how gorgeous he is, Pat. You'd turn gay for this guy."

"Don't think so. I like young, buxom redheads only." He

winked at her, and for the first time in six weeks she started to feel human again.

"I'll try to find you one then."

Suzanne sat up and stared down at the box of notes. She pulled out a newspaper. "Oh, and look at this. We thought something funky was going on with Father Stearns and Nora Sutherlin? Check this out. That guy look familiar?"

Patrick squinted at the Page Six photograph.

"That's Nora Sutherlin," Suzanne supplied. "And that gorgeous male-model clone is—"

"Griffin Fiske." Patrick shook his head. "Yeah, covered his rampages a time or two. Fucking trust fund babies. They get all the girls."

"They get Nora Sutherlin apparently. Seems she prefers rich boys over poor priests."

Patrick took the newspaper and tossed it aside before grabbing her notebook from the box.

"What's this? *'Min Søren, Min søn er nu en far. Jeg er så stolt. Jeg elsker dig altid. Din mor.'*"

"I think you just murdered the Danish language." Suzanne sat up.

"Danish?"

"Yeah, it means, 'My Søren, my son I am so proud. Your mother.'"

"The priest is Danish?"

"Half Danish, half English. Mother was an au pair for this wealthy family in New Hampshire. The wife had a hysterectomy after baby Elizabeth was born. Daddy raped the pretty blond nanny who then gave him the son he wanted."

"Jesus…" Patrick breathed. "That's fucking awful."

"Yeah. I can't imagine what that does to someone knowing your father's a rapist. She must have been an amazing woman to love her son so much considering how he came into the world."

"Søren…I thought his name was Marcus."

"It's both. Marcus is what the dad named him. Søren is what the mom named him. He says only the people closest to him, who know his past, call him Søren."

"Søren…I guess that's a good name for a priest. Like Søren Kierkegaard, right? The theologian?"

"I don't think Kierkegaard was Catholic."

"You sure?" Patrick grabbed his laptop and opened it. As long as she'd known him, Patrick would never take her word on anything. He'd been a reporter too long and had to fact-check everything. "Yup. You're right. Søren Aabye Kierkegaard—Lutheran. You two have the same initials, Suzanne Angela Kanter. Anyone ever call you Suzangela?"

"Only Adam until I punched him in the face for it." Suzanne glanced over Patrick's shoulder at the screen. Søren… Aabye…Kierkegaard. Why did that look so familiar to her?

She grabbed her steno pad, flipped through a few pages, and found the words *Meine andere Geschenk wird nicht in einer Box passen. AABYE.*

My other present will not fit in a box. AABYE.

Aabye.

Suzanne's eyes bored into the word as if demanding it to tell her what it meant. And it did mean something. She knew it meant something. From Patrick's computer she turned her gaze to her bookshelf and a book with a bloodred cover written by Nora Sutherlin. In an instant she left the couch and snatched the book off the shelf. There it was, right on the dedication page. The answer had been sitting on her bookshelf the entire time.

Søren's words from their almost night together rang in her mind.

We are close. She had a nasty run-in with the law at age fifteen. The judge had me supervise her community service. Her parents had little to do with her after that. I suppose you could say I had to become her father.

"Suz?" Patrick asked, turning his face to hers.

"Goddamn you," Suzanne said to herself. "You were her priest, her father…"

"What?"

"Do you have your car?"

"Yeah, why? What's wrong?"

"I need it. Don't wait up. I've got a priest I need to crucify."

"Suzanne, stop right now and tell me what's going on. It's almost midnight."

She grabbed her copy of Nora Sutherlin's book *The Red* off the shelf and shoved her feet into her sandals. In the doorway, Suzanne paused only long enough to recite five words to Patrick.

"'As Always, Beloved, Your Eleanor.'"

17

Michael stared down at the note in his hand and wished somehow he hadn't found it. Nora had a habit of leaving notes for him in funny places; notes that contained his orders for the day.

Angel, come to my bedroom at ten o'clock…on your knees. Bring your favorite flogger.

He'd found that note in the shower.

Angel, high noon, the swimming pool. Be prepared to skinny-dip.

That note she'd taped to his watch while he was napping.

All her notes so far amused him and aroused him. But this latest note flat-out terrified him.

Angel, you aren't a real kinkster until you have a threesome. Meet me and Griffin in his bedroom at midnight.

Threesome? With Nora and Griffin? Michael came dangerously close to puking as he walked at a sloth's pace down the hall. For six weeks now he'd been unable to think of anything or anyone other than Griffin. That night at Sin Tax…it hadn't been real, he kept telling himself. Griffin didn't really mean

Michael was his property. He'd just said that to scare Jackal off. But then the sketchbook…and the way Griffin looked at him while he held his leather belt taut in his hands…and Michael had wanted to tell him something, had tried to tell him something. He had the words. He wanted to say, "Griffin, I'm falling in love with you, and it's the scariest fucking thing ever. My dad will kill me dead if he finds out, but right now, I couldn't care less, because being in bed with you even for one night would be worth dying for."

But Michael hadn't said that. All he'd managed to say was, "Thanks for the sketchbook. Good night."

Thanks again.

Good night.

Good thing he was over his suicidal tendencies. Otherwise he might have slit his wrists again for blowing maybe his only chance with the most amazing person he'd ever met in his life. Because ever since that night, Griffin had pulled back and stopped flirting with him. They'd been buddies since that night. Nothing but friends.

Michael wanted a lot of stuff from Griffin—his heart, his body… His friendship wasn't even in the top five.

And now Michael had to watch Griffin have sex with Nora, which right now sounded about as sadistic as inviting a starving kid to a buffet and not letting him eat.

He came to the end of the hall and slowly pushed the bedroom door open. At least this thing would happen in Nora's room, not Griffin's. It would be fine, he told himself. They'd probably just take turns with Nora. That's all. No big deal. In the past six weeks he'd done kinky shit he'd barely even let himself dream about. Having sex while someone watched would be a breeze.

All thoughts of breezes evaporated when he saw Nora lounging on her bed in black panties, a black push-up bra and black thigh-high boots. A dozen black candles burned on the bedside tables. And Griffin was nowhere to be seen.

"Come here, Angel." Nora crooked her finger, beckoning him to the bed. Michael stifled a whimper, took a deep breath and nervously crawled across the sheets to her. Swinging her booted leg out, she hooked it around his waist and playfully kicked him toward her. She wrapped both legs around his back as she held him to her.

"My Angel. Can't fly away now," she teased as she took him in her arms. "My scared, shaking Angel."

Her voice dropped to a whisper and Michael buried his head in the crook of her neck.

"Terrified," he confessed.

"Want to tell me why?" Nora kissed him on the cheek, the forehead, and he sighed from the simple gesture of affection.

Michael gave a low, rueful laugh.

"Not really."

Nora nodded as if she understood everything he wasn't telling her. Knowing Nora, she probably did.

"That bad, huh?" she asked, brushing his hair off his face as he slowly pushed up on his hands and looked down at her.

Their eyes met and in that look he saw knowledge in her gaze, deep knowledge and sympathy.

"Worse."

"Believe it or not, this might help." She traced his lips with her fingertips.

"Help what?" Michael inhaled as Griffin's voice came from behind them. Nora unwrapped her legs from around his back and Michael rolled onto his side and sat up. Griffin stood in the doorway of her bedroom wearing nothing but black silk pajama pants and a slight smile on his sculpted lips.

"Help me get over my wicked need to have two incredibly gorgeous guys in bed with me tonight," Nora said as she sat back on her hands. Out of the corner of her eye she winked at Michael and something told him that somehow Nora knew about his feelings for Griffin. "Think you can help with that, Mr. Fiske?"

"Mr. Fiske is my dad. But if you want to fuck him, I think you could probably talk him into it."

Griffin came over to the bed and sat down next to Nora.

Nora stuck out her leg and rested her booted ankle on Griffin's shoulder. Griffin turned his head and nipped at the leather, a move that made Michael's stomach knot up from envy and desire.

"What are we doing tonight, boys? I'm open for anything."

"This was your idea." Griffin slid his hand from her knee up her inner thigh.

"I have wonderful ideas." She grinned at them both. "And terrible ideas. And terribly wonderful ideas. Hand me that book in the nightstand, Griff. I just had another terribly wonderful idea."

Griffin opened the nightstand and handed her a large coffee-table-size book. Nora didn't even look at it, merely passed it to Michael.

"Let's let our Angel decide where we're doing tonight. Go for it," she ordered, nodding at the book in his hands. "Pick."

Glancing down at the cover, Michael's eyes went wide. *The Joy of Sex.*

"Pick?" he repeated.

"Yup. Any position. Griffin and I will put on a little show for you. But you have to tell us what you want to see. So pick."

Michael's hands turned to ice. He could hardly feel the book in his hands.

"I think you scared him, Nora," Griffin said, giving Michael a searching look. Michael could barely meet Griffin's eyes.

"Good," she said. "I'm not the world's scariest dominatrix,

but I have my moments of evil genius. I'm horny, Michael, and Griffin's half-hard already." She reached out and cupped Griffin between the legs. Michael's groin twitched with his own hunger and need. What he wouldn't give to touch Griffin like that.... "So let's get on with it. Pick a position. Trust me, no matter how acrobatic it is, we can do it."

"No wall sex though, please," Griffin requested as Nora continued to massage him through his pants. "Nora's a lot heavier than she looks."

"Is that something you really want to say to a woman who has your balls in her hands?" Nora batted her eyelashes at him.

"Good point. You're as light as air." Griffin smiled at Michael, a friendly smile but nothing else. "Pick, Mick, before I lose any more blood from my brain."

Michael exhaled heavily and opened the book at a random page. He was fairly certain he didn't want to see Nora and Griffin having sex in any position so he'd simply let fate decide.

Fate decided on doggy style.

The book lay open on his lap and Michael barely looked at the picture. But that didn't stop Nora from grabbing the book and brandishing it in Griffin's face.

"Woof," Griffin said as he grabbed Nora by the ankle and started to drag her to him. "Wait. Anal or vaginal?"

Nora shrugged. "Pick an orifice. Any orifice. Angel?"

"What?" Michael pulled his legs into his chest.

"You decide." Nora smiled at him over her shoulder.

"Oh, God..." Michael took a heavy breath. "I don't... Vaginal."

It might be easier to watch if it was the one act he and Griffin couldn't do.

"Fantastic." Griffin grabbed Nora by the wrists and turned

her onto her stomach. Taking her hips in his hands, he brought her up to her hands and knees. "Foreplay, Nora?"

"Don't bother," she said, waving her hand dismissively. "This entire conversation has been all the foreplay I need. Go for it."

"Weirdest. Woman. Ever." Griffin shook his head as he came up on his knees behind her. "Come here, Mick. Time for some advanced instruction."

Michael almost threw up on Nora's sheets. He swallowed hard and tentatively crawled over to where Griffin knelt behind Nora. Griffin slid Nora's panties off her hips and down her thighs but left them on her at her knees.

"Makeshift restraint," Griffin explained. "Wide legs are good for deep penetration. If she keeps them closer together, however, it's a tighter fit. Little tip there. Panties around knees equals poor man's thigh stocks."

"Should I be writing this down?" Michael asked.

Griffin laughed. "And don't listen to the woman. No foreplay? Ridiculous." Griffin gave Nora a good, hard slap on her shapely bottom. Nora yelped but made no other protest. "She might not need it, but I do. Give me your hand."

Michael slowly raised his hand and gave it to Griffin.

"How are you doing, Nora?" Griffin asked as he bent Michael's fingers down until only his index and middle finger of his right hand were extended.

"I am fine. Impatient but fine. Is there any fucking coming anytime soon? I ask out of mere curiosity. I could work on the edits Zach just sent me while you two chitchat."

"Hush. I'll fuck you soon enough. Now, Mick." Griffin turned to him. "Science is divided on the existence of the G-spot. Some scientists say it exists. Some scientists don't. Those scientists that don't—" Griffin took Michael's hand and guided it inside Nora "—are fucking idiots. See?"

Griffin led Michael's fingertips to a spot a little over an inch inside Nora.

"Push down and in," Griffin said. "Hard."

Almost two months under Nora's tutelage had made it nearly impossible for Michael to disobey any order. He pushed down as instructed. Hard.

Nora gasped and her inner muscles clenched around Michael's fingers.

"Oh, God…" she panted.

"Love that G-spot," Griffin said, pulling Michael's fingers from Nora. "Don't you?"

Before he could answer, Griffin lifted Michael's fingers to his mouth and slowly, seductively licked the wetness off. Michael almost died the moment Griffin's tongue touched his trembling fingertips. Michael's fingers…inside Griffin's mouth…

"Now excuse me." Griffin let Michael's hand go. "I need to fuck your mistress."

"About damn time."

Griffin whacked Nora one more time on her bottom and she let loose another yelp followed by a lusty giggle. Michael couldn't look away as Griffin pulled his pajama pants down and rolled a condom onto his erection.

Slowly Griffin slid into Nora, who moaned as Griffin pushed deep with a sigh. As Griffin thrust forward, Nora pushed back against him. The sight of Nora's and Griffin's bodies joined together sent a thousand different feelings rushing through Michael's body. He'd never been so turned on in his life watching Griffin's hips moving in hard but graceful undulations, the muscles of his thighs and stomach thrown into high relief in the candlelight. But underneath the desire lurked longing and anguish, need and sorrow. He wanted this, wanted to be the one on his hands and knees with Griffin behind him and inside him. But he couldn't have that. Not now. Not ever. Not with his father ready and willing to kill him for even thinking such thoughts. And Michael knew Griffin deserved better than him—than a stupid kid with no money, no fame, no nothing special about him. And Griffin deserved a hell of a lot better than somebody too pussy to even tell him how he felt.

So Michael merely watched in silent envy as Nora came hard and loud with Griffin's hands on her waist. A few more thrusts and Griffin came with a soft gasp. Michael closed his eyes and tried to imprint the sound of Griffin's orgasm forever into his mind. He might never hear it again and that little sigh that caught in Griffin's throat for the barest second was easily the most beautiful and erotic sound Michael had ever heard in his life. He could hear it every day for the rest of his life and never get tired of it.

Griffin pulled out of Nora and she rolled onto her back. Reaching out she took Michael's hand.

Michael didn't have to ask. As he straddled Nora's hips, she reached into his boxer shorts and guided him inside her. She felt so warm inside, so wet. Once deep in her, Nora twined her legs around his back and gently rolled herself until Michael lay flat on his back with Nora on top and over him. He closed his eyes and let himself get lost in the incredible heat of her. Her lips caressed his neck, his cheek.

"Tell him, Michael," she whispered, the halo of her hair hiding her words from Griffin's ears. "Just tell him."

Michael shook his head.

"I can't," he whispered back.

Nora continued to move on him, taking him deep into her before sliding out to the tip and back down again. Michael groaned with physical pleasure even as a knife of agony cut into his chest.

Something brushed Michael's hand and his eyes flew open. Turning his head, he saw Griffin stretched out on his side next to him and Nora. Griffin had taken Michael's hand in his and twined their fingers together. Griffin said nothing. Michael said nothing. They only stared at each other until Michael had to close his eyes again as he came hard inside Nora.

Even as he shuddered in silence, Griffin held on to his hand so tightly it almost hurt.

And even in the middle of the climax that racked his entire body, Michael didn't let go.

Suzanne arrived at the rectory at a few minutes before midnight. First she checked the church and found it locked tight and abandoned but for the small chapel of perpetual adoration that stayed open all hours of the day and night. But she didn't find Father Stearns there. She walked the short distance to the rectory with her heart pounding so hard it felt as if it was outside her chest. In her career she'd confronted lying politicians powerful enough to destroy her and her family, foreign generals with firearms strapped to their sides. But never before had she experienced fear like this. She remembered her reaction to Father Stearns, to Søren, that night at the rectory when she'd begged for his body, begged to be with him.

But now she wanted to make him beg. And she would show him the same mercy he showed her. None.

She found the rectory dark and silent. She heard no footsteps inside, saw no lights burning through any windows. Where would he be if not at home at this time of night? Once she'd asked herself the question, she knew the answer. He could be anywhere. This priest did not play by the rules the Church imposed upon him. He could be with a prostitute right now, with a lover. Or worse, with another fifteen-year-old girl he'd seduced until she grew up and loved him enough to dedicate every last one of her books to him.

Just in case he was home and asleep with all the lights off, Suzanne knocked on the door. No answer. Then she pounded on it with the tip of her shoe. A minute passed. Still nothing. The rage welled within her. Father Stearns had no respect for the law obviously. Not if he'd slept with a teenage Eleanor Schreiber. Why show him any respect?

Suzanne turned the doorknob and found the rectory unlocked.

She stepped inside and called out a tentative, "Hello." With every minute that passed, her blood throbbed heavier and harder in her veins. If she didn't calm down, she'd pass out. What if he was here? Watching her? Waiting for her?

Calling upon all the instincts she'd learned working in war zones, Suzanne took slow, deep breaths and willed her heart to calm itself. She let the little bit of light from the moon flood her senses. She walked carefully, trying to avoid the creaking of the ancient hardwood beneath her feet.

If she was to find any evidence of his proclivities, she knew they'd most likely be in his bedroom. Her stomach recoiled at the thought of returning to that place, that room where she'd shamed herself so completely. Of course he'd turned her down, turned her away that night. She was a grown woman, not a fifteen-year-old girl. Not his type at all.

Up the stairs she crept, closing her eyes to allow her ears to hear without the distractions of sight. At the end of the hall she came to his bedroom and rested her hand on the doorknob. For the first time in what felt like a thousand years she said a prayer, a real prayer.

Please, God. Don't let him be inside.

God answered the prayer.

Suzanne found the room empty and the bed neatly made.

Cursing herself for not bringing a flashlight, she reached out
and turned on the small antique lamp on the table. Soft yellow light infused the room. Really Father Stearns's bedroom
was a thing of beauty—elegant and simple, clean and unas-
suming. And yet everything in it—the bed, the furniture, the
white linens—spoke of refinement and taste. But she'd learned
long ago how looks could be deceiving.

Making a circuit of the room, Suzanne eyed every possible hiding place. She had no idea what she was looking for.
Young Eleanor Schreiber had grown up long ago and become a notorious erotica writer—famous for her prose, infamous for her personal life. She didn't just write it. She lived
it. But did she do it here? In this bedroom? Suzanne had read
all the books. The kind of BDSM Nora Sutherlin practiced,
or at least her characters, involved equipment and lots of it.
Suzanne spied a trunk at the end of Father Stearns's bed. An
old-fashioned steamer trunk, it looked large enough to hold
a body. Kneeling in front of it, Suzanne examined the lock.
She had no idea how to pick it. She'd have to break it open.
Maybe she could find something in Patrick's car. A practical
sort, Patrick would surely have a toolbox or something in his
trunk. As she stood up she noticed a small box on the table
next to the bed. No larger than a Bible, the box appeared to
be rosewood. She held it in her hands and turned it over and
over, tracing the intricately carved cross on the surface.

This box too was locked, but with such a small lock she
knew she could break it open with her fingers. She took a
deep breath, dug her nails under the edge of the lock and
began to pull.

From behind her she heard the creak of hardwood.

"Shall I get that for you, *ma chérie?*"

18

Nora woke up in the dark in her bed at Griffin's. Stretching out under the covers, she massaged an ache in her lower back. Taking turns with Griffin and Michael had been both erotic and exhausting. Of course, her two boys had nothing on Søren and Kingsley. Together those two had given her some of the most intense sexual experiences of her life. Tonight's little play hadn't really been about sex, however. She'd enjoyed it. Who wouldn't? But for six weeks now she'd watched Griffin staring at Michael when Michael wasn't looking and Michael staring back at Griffin the second Griffin looked away. All the angst-ridden pining had started to get to her. Those two needed to get their shit together, man up and admit what they wanted, and get the fuck on with it.

With a sigh, Nora sat up and rubbed her forehead. She found Griffin sitting next to her in bed with his chin resting on his knee. Next to Griffin, Michael lay sound asleep on his stomach with the covers tucked up under his chin.

Nora rested her head against Griffin's strong bicep. He

reached out and laid a hand on her leg in a gesture of pure and simple friendship.

"That bad, huh?" she whispered. Griffin's eyes were trained on Michael and didn't glance away even to look at her.

Slowly Griffin nodded.

"Yeah...that bad."

For a moment she said nothing, merely watched Griffin watching Michael.

"It's weird," Griffin said. "Did you notice he's clinging to the sheets like his life depended on it?"

Nora grinned. Michael always bunched his fingers into the sheets when sleeping.

"I know. I teased him about it." Nora raised her hand and ran her fingers through Griffin's hair. His darks eyes glanced her way once before looking again at Michael. "He said he thought his subconscious worried that gravity would be revoked in the middle of the night. He wanted to be prepared."

Griffin covered his mouth to stifle a laugh. But the laugh quickly faded and Nora saw no mirth in his eyes anymore.

"I can't have him." Griffin stretched out his hand and let his fingers hover an inch or two above Michael's bare shoulder blade before pulling his hand back and leaving Michael untouched. "Søren—"

"Søren is protective of Michael. But he's not some kind of monster you can't reason with. Go talk to him."

Griffin finally turned and met her eyes full-on.

"Talk to Søren? Yes, as if that ever worked for me before. He'll say no, and even if he didn't, Mick's dad...his dad would kill him if he got involved with another guy. The stuff he's told me about his father... Nora, that bastard actually hit Mick. Hit him. God, it makes me..."

Griffin's jaw tightened and his hand curled into a fist. Nora knew in his mind Griffin was exacting beautiful revenge on

Michael's conservative homophobic asshole of a father. She, like Søren, didn't condone any kind of violence except of the consensual bedroom variety. But somebody would eventually have to teach Michael's father a lesson or two about how to treat a kid like Michael. Preferably a lesson that didn't land Michael's father in the hospital and Griffin in jail.

"I know. I understand, Griff. I do. But—"

"But nothing. I want him so much it hurts. Like physically hurts, Nora. And not just sex. It isn't that. I can't explain what it is but I just…"

"Wesley," Nora said and stopped. Where had that come from? Griffin looked at her.

"Wesley?"

She smiled but the smile didn't reach her eyes or touch her heart.

"Wesley…he has this problem. Type 1 diabetic. Scared the shit out of me, that kid did with his needles and his blood-testing. Every single night, I'd have to look in on him when he was sleeping. I can barely sleep at my own house anymore because he's not there to keep me up at night. Which makes no sense at all."

"No," Griffin said. "It makes perfect sense." He glanced up at Nora again. "Does this ever go away?"

Something wet and warm ran down her face, and she swiped it off with her forearm.

"No," she whispered. "Never."

Suzanne gasped and spun around. Standing in the doorway of Father Stearns's bedroom was a man she'd never seen before. Tall and frighteningly handsome, he had shoulder-length dark brown hair, near-black eyes and a Mediterranean complexion.

"Who are you?" she demanded, stepping back but finding her way of escape barred by the bed.

"I suppose I should ask you that. After all, I am allowed to be here. I'm not certain you could say the same. *Oui? Non?*"

He spoke in beautiful English tinged with an unmistakable French accent. He stepped across the threshold and for the first time she noticed his clothes. He wore black trousers and a black vest embroidered with some sort of beautiful swirling silver pattern, a white shirt with the sleeves rolled up to reveal muscular forearms, and knee-high riding boots.

"I'm…" she began. "I was…"

"You are Suzanne Kanter, the reporter who has been dogging my dear friend's steps for two months now. Twenty-eight years old. A freelance journalist who usually spends her days in war zones. I don't see any wars anywhere."

"Then you aren't looking hard enough," she countered.

"Congratulations on graduating cum laude from your journalism school. A wonderful phrase—cum laude. I've always thought it should refer to something else."

"How do you know so much about me?"

The man smiled, a roguish, dangerous smile that set every nerve in her body on end.

"My name is Kingsley Edge."

Suzanne gasped and tried to take another step back and nearly fell onto the bed in the process.

"From your reaction," he said, coming closer, "I will assume you've heard of me."

"I'm a reporter. Of course I've heard of you. You destroyed a friend of mine. Gwendolyn Black? Remember that name? You put a sex tape on repeat on every computer in her son's school. She's been in therapy for two years because of what you pulled."

Kingsley shrugged.

"*Pas moi.* I was in Tahiti at the time. Although I did hear about that unfortunate incident. Pity. But still…she was attempting to make a name for herself by exposing the private life of a man who'd never hurt a fly, a human-rights lawyer who'd saved thousands of lives and put dozens of murderers behind bars. Your friend thought his interest in alternative sexual experiences meant he did not deserve his privacy. I disagree. And so did someone else apparently."

"Someone else who worked for you."

Kingsley Edge only grinned.

"Perhaps."

Suzanne stared at him in silence as she tried to formulate an escape plan, or an attack plan if that failed. So much time in war zones had taught her how to defend herself. But she had no weapons on her, and Kingsley Edge, despite his relaxed posture and elegant attire, definitely had a dangerous air. She'd seen generals in their dress uniforms at cocktail parties who looked more deadly than infantrymen in their desert BDUs. Kingsley Edge had that look about him too. Something in the eyes. Something glinting and fearless. He looked like a man who'd seen so much blood he had the Grim Reaper on speed dial.

"You're afraid of me," he finally said as he took another step into the room. "You don't have to be, Suzanne."

"Everyone's afraid of you. Everyone in my world."

He grinned and the smile overtook his face and rendered him so handsome she could scarcely breathe.

"Then come into my world for a little while and you won't have to be afraid."

"What…" She looked around. "What are you doing in Father Stearns's bedroom? Hell, in his house?"

"He was called away. One of his parishioners is dying. The family needs him. He might not return for a day or more."

"So what? You're here to water the plants?"

He laughed, a deep, warm, rich laugh. A fearless laugh.

"I like to get away from the city sometimes. From the phone

that won't stop ringing. The endless decisions I have to make. The senator's son wants to bottom tonight but his favorite dominatrix is with the famous lead singer. My tailor is out of the country, and I need a new suit for the slave auction. And I've been so busy I haven't had time to properly violate my lovely Juliette in days."

"Juliette?"

"My secretary." He sighed luxuriously with a put-upon air.

"Poor you."

He nodded.

"My life is *difficile*. I come here for some silence."

"You just like breaking into the houses of priests?"

"I was invited. I am family, after all."

Suzanne's eyes went wide with shock.

"Harrison…" The pieces started to fall into place. "You?" She nearly shouted the question. "You're the French brother-in-law?"

"*Oui*. That box that fascinated you." He nodded at the carved rosewood box. "You wish to open it?"

"I do. But it's locked. Can you open it?"

Exhaling heavily, Kingsley reached out and took the box from her hands. He pulled a small set of keys from a pocket in his vest, stuck one in the lock and turned.

"You women…all of you are Pandora. You cannot leave well enough alone, can you? Here." Kingsley gave her the now unlocked box back. "There's the answer to your mystery."

With shaking fingers she opened the lid. Inside on a bed of bloodred velvet lay two golden bands, one large, one small.

She pulled the smaller one out.

"Wedding rings?" she asked.

He nodded.

"That was my sister's, my Marie-Laure. The other one was his."

Suzanne touched the larger band but didn't take it from its bed of velvet.

"I still can't believe he was married before he was a priest. He must have been so young."

Crossing his arms, Kingsley leaned against the bedpost and gazed out the dormer window.

"Neither can I sometimes. We were just children playing foolish children's games. We were at school together, *le prêtre* and I. Marie-Laure and I were separated after our parents died—I was only fourteen and sent to stay with my American grandparents. She came to visit…I was then seventeen, he was eighteen. She barely twenty-one. I couldn't stand to lose her again, but she did not have dual citizenship as I did. He married her to keep her here. He married her for me."

"He didn't love her?"

"He tried. For her sake. When she realized that he would never feel for her what she felt for him…"

"I know she died. I'm sorry."

"She didn't die," he said, meeting her eyes again. "She killed herself."

Suzanne nearly dropped the box.

But she held on to it despite her shaking hands.

"I'm…I'm so sorry, Mr.—"

"You may call me Kingsley. Or sir. Or monsieur. But please do not call me Mr. Edge." He rolled his eyes and laughed again. The reaction seemed so incongruous to their topic that she laughed too out of sheer confusion.

"Okay, Kingsley. I'm sorry about your sister. My brother, he—"

"I know." Kingsley said the words softly, kindly, and with a look of the profoundest sympathy in his eyes.

"Right. Of course you know…. So you and Father Stearns… you're related."

"By a long-gone marriage only. But we've remained friends all these years. I daresay I know him better than anyone."

"Better than Nora Sutherlin?"

Kingsley raised his eyebrow and took the box from her hand. Carefully he arranged the two wedding bands back on the velvet before closing and locking the lid once more.

"He said she knows him better than anyone."

Something in Kingsley's eyes went cold and deadly at her words, and Suzanne immediately regretted them.

"What he says and what is the truth are not always the same thing. He may seem omniscient but where she is concerned… well, have you ever heard the phrase *willful ignorance?*"

"They're lovers, aren't they?" Suzanne asked, hoping to shock him into answering.

Kingsley only laughed.

"Ah…Pandora never learns. Does it matter if they are? Really?"

"Of course it matters," Suzanne said, rage welling up inside her. "He's her priest. Has been her priest since she was fifteen. If he's been sleeping with her, or was when she was a kid? Hell yes, it matters. Only a monster would do that. A sexual predator. A—"

Kingsley raised his hand and shook his head.

"You have no idea who he is, Suzanne. If you judge him by his actions, you will never know him."

She narrowed her eyes at him.

"That makes no sense. There's no way to judge any man except by his actions."

"You see only a sliver of the truth. And a lie can tell you more than a partial truth."

Suzanne took a deep breath.

"Then tell me all. You say you know him better than anyone. I want to know him too."

Kingsley set the box back down on the bedside table and stepped toward her until he stood so close a whisper couldn't even slip between them.

"You don't know what you're asking." He raised his hand to her face and caressed the arch of her cheekbone with his fingertips. "Trying to know him is like wrestling with God. You remember what happened to Jacob, no? He grappled with God and limped away the next morning."

Suzanne nodded slowly.

"I've been limping since the day Adam died. Please...I know you can help me."

Gently Kingsley pressed a kiss on her face right by her ear.

"I can help you. But I give nothing away. If you want to cross the river Styx, you must pay your coin to Charon."

"I don't have a lot of money. Just a reporter."

"I have more money than I know what to do with. It isn't your money I desire." Kingsley's hand dropped to her neck. He pressed his thumb lightly into the hollow of her throat. "But if you are willing to pay, I am willing to answer."

Suzanne swallowed and felt the pressure of his thumb on her neck.

Was she willing to pay? She had no doubt in her mind what form of currency he traded in. Apart from Father Stearns, from Søren, she'd never seen a more alluring man in her life. Everything about him...his clothes, his sensual mouth, his voice and that accent...in truth, it wasn't such a terrible price to pay. Even without the promise of answers, she would be tempted....

"I wanted to believe there was one good priest in this world," she whispered. "But if he—"

"He is a good priest. And a good man. And I can supply the proof you need of it. If that is what you wish."

Finally Suzanne nodded.

"Yes, it is."

"Then come with me."

Kingsley held out his hand and Suzanne took it with more fear than she'd ever felt on a battlefield. He started off and took her out of the bedroom and down the hall.

"Where are we going?" She'd thought he'd take her in Father Stearns's bed or even on the floor, but they seemed to be leaving the house.

"Manhattan. I have something to give you…if you earn it."

They left the house and he guided her around the back where a Rolls Royce waited. A beautiful young woman in a chauffeur's uniform hopped out of the car and with a sprightly step opened the back door for them. Kingsley entered first and Suzanne followed, already regretting it.

"But I've got my car. Well, Patrick's car."

"I'll have it returned to Patrick. He's still in the Village, *oui?*"

"Jesus, you do know everything about me."

Kingsley smiled again as the car started and pulled out onto the road.

"Not quite." He cupped the side of her face and brushed her lips with his thumb. "I don't know what sounds you make when you come. Let's find that out, shall we?"

Before she could answer, Kingsley leaned forward and pressed his mouth to hers. He did nothing at first, merely waited on her. Suzanne told herself she was doing this for Adam…before slowly parting her lips. Closing her eyes, she let Kingsley take over the kiss. His hand twined in her hair. He held her neck firmly as if to remind her she belonged to him now and could not escape. As his tongue touched the tip of hers, her desire to escape died and the need to surrender was born. And she wasn't doing this for Adam or Father Stearns. She wanted Kingsley. She would do this for her.

"Tell me, Suzanne, have you ever had sex in the back of a Rolls Royce?"

Kingsley didn't wait for her to answer. He pushed her onto her back as he pulled her legs apart and rested his hips hard against hers. *Oh, God,* she thought, *this is really happening.* With deft fingers, he unbuttoned her blouse and opened it. He kissed his way from her neck to her navel and up again.

She closed her eyes and let the sensation of a stranger's hands on her body wash over her. Not just any stranger, she reminded herself. This was Kingsley Edge, the bogeyman who kept even the most hardened of investigative reporters up at night. And now she was one of them. One of the reporters Kingsley Edge kept up all night.

"Don't pretend you aren't enjoying this," Kingsley whispered in her ear. "I know you're trying not to enjoy this."

"I'm doing this for information, not pleasure."

"Liar."

Suzanne blushed at the truth in his accusation.

Kingsley nipped at her ear, her shoulder. His teeth on her skin sent shock waves of pleasure into her stomach.

"Even when I'm bending my secretary over my desk, I make sure she enjoys it. I'll see that you enjoy it too, whether you want to or not."

Before Suzanne could make another protest, Kingsley pulled up and away from her. She started to ask what he was doing but then she saw. He left the luxurious leather of the bench seat in the Rolls Royce and knelt on the floorboard. He snapped his fingers and gestured her to sit in front of him.

Suzanne slid to the center of the seat. Kingsley reached under her skirt, grasped her panties and dragged them roughly down her legs. She wanted to tell him to stop but the promise of so much information about Father Stearns kept her quiet even as Kingsley opened his pants.

He pushed her legs wide and shoved two fingers into her. Wincing, she fought the urge to close her legs.

"Breathe, *chérie*. I promise you will like this if you let yourself." He took his fingers out of her and gazed up at her. In the dark of the night, she could barely see him except when the car passed a streetlamp.

With one pull he brought her hips to the very edge of the seat. Again with his fingers he parted her outer and inner lips. He brought his mouth down on her and sucked lightly on her clitoris. Suzanne dug her fingers into the supple leather of the seat as her head fell back.

Up and down the length of her vagina he licked her, teased her with his tongue and lips. Suzanne quickly found herself opening her legs a little wider and pushing her hips forward. His tongue delved deeper until she felt he sought the very core of her. His hands gripped her thighs and Suzanne twined her hand into his hair. Underneath her the car vibrated from the roar of the heavy engine. Her entire body vibrated from what Kingsley was doing to her. The pressure built in her lower back. She leaned back into the seat, grabbed the headrest behind her and came with a low, almost pained grunt.

Before she could even catch her breath, she heard the unmistakable sound of a condom wrapper opening.

"Wait," she panted but Kingsley only pulled her down off the seat and onto him, impaling her. He'd made her so wet that she took every inch of him inside her in one stroke.

"God—" she gasped as her body strained to accept all of him.

"I said you could call me Kingsley," he whispered into her ear.

Suzanne couldn't help but laugh.

"You must be the most arrogant man alive." She wrapped

her arms around his back for stability as he grasped her by the hips and started slowly thrusting up and into her.

"Only the second. You've met the first."

She shook her head and started to speak. But Kingsley found her clitoris with the tips of his fingers and rendered her momentarily speechless.

As he nibbled at her lips, her neck and shoulders, Suzanne could only hold one thought in her addled mind. She was being fucked by Kingsley Edge. The one and only Kingsley Edge.

And she was enjoying the hell out of it.

Kneeling on his lap, she moved her hips forward and back in time with his precision movements. Everything he did sent currents of heat and electricity surging through her whole body. She came close to another climax but Kingsley stopped her with a kiss.

"Turn around," he said into her ear as his left hand did marvelous things to her right nipple.

Nodding, Suzanne lifted herself up and turned her back to him. He pressed in close to her back and bit her shoulder hard enough she winced.

"How much do you want to know about *le prêtre?*" He pushed three fingers into her from behind and Suzanne inhaled sharply at the sudden shock of pleasure.

"Everything." She parted her thighs even more and pushed back into his hand. A fourth finger joined the others. She'd never felt so open before. God, the man knew what he was doing.

"You will never know everything about him. Not if you searched the world until the end of time." He pulled his hand out and slowly penetrated her again. He sunk in deep and Suzanne moaned audibly from the incredible sensation of him filling her so completely. "But I can only tell you what I know if you tell me one thing, *ma chérie*…"

He started to thrust again, hard this time, viciously hard. Suzanne grabbed the door, the seat, anything to hold her steady as he used her body so thoroughly. She couldn't believe how much she loved this, loved being taken like this…. Kingsley found her clitoris again and as he pushed into her she came again with a loud cry as pain-sharp pleasure exploded in her back and hips. Kingsley thrust a few more times before coming with a shudder that shook them both.

Kingsley lingered inside her a moment as they both caught their breath.

"What?" she panted. "What do I have to tell you before you'll tell me about him?"

Kingsley kissed her hair, the tip of her ear as he continued to pulse inside her. She could get used to erotic attention like this.

"Tell me—" he pushed into her once more "—why you want to know."

"I…" Why did she want to know? Was it still about Adam? Would Adam be happy she was doing this? Proud? For one moment she was glad he was gone so he couldn't see what kind of person she'd become, what she'd do in pursuit of a story. "I don't know," she confessed. "I just have to know. I have to. If he's hurting children—"

Kingsley pulled out of her so quickly she winced. He straightened his clothes and threw himself across the length of the bench seat and crossed his feet at the ankles. Suzanne felt suddenly embarrassed and ashamed of her half-naked state. In the dark she found her panties, buttoned her blouse and sat gingerly on the seat across from him.

"He does not hurt children," Kingsley said in a voice as cold as winter, as sharp as a knife. "Eleanor Schreiber was never his victim. And for the record, she was never really a child. I've known her almost as long as he has."

"So what? She was a flirt as a teenager? So she deserved to be seduced by an older man? By her priest?"

"Nora Sutherlin, Eleanor Schreiber, whatever you call her or however you know her…you must know one and only thing about her. She seduces. She does not get seduced."

Suzanne took a deep breath and met his eyes in the dark.

"I don't know why I need to know. But I have to. He…" She stopped speaking and searched for the words, any words, to explain what she felt, what she wanted. "I believed in him like I once believed in God. I don't want to believe in either of them…unless I should."

Kingsley exhaled heavily as he pulled a booted leg into his chest and draped his arm over it casually.

"To believe or not to believe…only you can answer that question for yourself," he said as the Rolls pulled in front of an elegant black-and-white town house. "But I can help you on your quest. I can point you in the right direction at least. Come."

The door opened and Kingsley left the car. She smoothed her blouse and skirt and followed him through a wrought-iron gate and up the stairs.

As they hit the third floor, the most stunningly beautiful woman Suzanne had ever seen in her life appeared with a cup of tea in her hand and a smile on her face. Almost as tall as Kingsley with ebony skin, charcoal eyes and a playful smile on her full lips, the woman seemed both graceful and severe to Suzanne.

"Aah…my Jules. I've missed you," Kingsley said as he saluted the woman on each cheek with a kiss. "This is Suzanne Kanter, a reporter friend of mine."

"Bonjour, mademoiselle. Tea?" the woman who Suzanne

surmised must be Juliette, Kingsley's private secretary, asked. Like Kingsley, she too spoke with a rich accent. But Juliette's sounded different, more Caribbean. She must be from Haiti, Suzanne decided, recognizing the accent. A black Haitian woman working for a rich, white, French man…. Kingsley really was the most arrogant man alive.

"She can't stay." Kingsley took a sip of his own tea. "She's merely here for a file."

"Which one, monsieur?" Juliette asked. "I'll fetch it."

"The mistress…her medical file."

Juliette's dark eyes went wide for the barest hint of a second before she composed her face once more into the mask of the perfect submissive secretary.

"*Oui,* monsieur."

While Juliette disappeared into a room, Suzanne looked around. So strange. Kingsley's headquarters seemed as if they'd been transported from another place, another time. She saw huge black rotary phones on the large art deco desks. Wooden filing cabinets, Tiffany lamps…and no computers in sight.

"Such a Luddite," Suzanne said, taking it all in.

"I'm simply old-fashioned," Kingsley said with a wicked glint in his eyes.

Juliette returned with a thick black file folder fastened with a burgundy ribbon. Kingsley held it out and Suzanne reached for it, but he pulled it back to his chest.

"For you and you only, mademoiselle, I had a dear friend of mine send this to me. You will be allowed to keep this file for one day. It must be returned to me by this time tomorrow night. Nothing in this file can be recorded or photocopied in any way. No one but you may look at it. I will know if you have disobeyed any of these conditions. The consequences for disobedience will be severe. Do you understand me?"

Kingsley said the words with a conversational air but the threat in them was unmistakable.

"Yes, sir," she said. *"Je comprends."*

Kingsley raised his eyebrow at her before passing her the file.

"Now I'll have my driver take you home."

Suzanne headed down the stairs and Kingsley followed. Not twenty minutes ago, he'd been buried inside her body. Now he barely spoke to her, although she saw him watching her out of the corner of her eyes. On the first-floor landing he stopped and gestured for her to go on without him.

"Good night," she said, clutching the file to her chest. "I'll drop this off tomorrow, I promise."

"Bon." He nodded.

Apparently good-night kisses wouldn't be forthcoming. Suzanne nodded back and headed toward the front door where Kingsley's chauffeur waited in silence.

The chauffeur opened the door.

"Mademoiselle?" Kingsley called out and Suzanne turned around and looked up at him. "One more piece of advice on your quest."

"Yes, please? What?"

"Go see the sister. Talk to her."

Suzanne blinked.

"Sister? Like a nun? Which nun?"

Kingsley laughed then—an amused, arrogant, infuriatingly French laugh.

"No, Suzanne. His sister."

"That's right," she said, a memory clicking into place. "He has three sisters, doesn't he? Which one?"

"The one you don't want to see."

"I don't want to see any—"

"And one final thing," Kingsley said, all mirth and seduction gone from his face and his tone. "About the file in your hands…"

"Yes?"

"It was mine."

"What was—"

"*Au revoir,* Suzanne."

Before Suzanne could ask another question, Kingsley turned on his heel and headed up the stairs.

Suzanne watched him until she could see him no longer.

Holding the file to her chest, Suzanne followed the driver back to the Rolls Royce.

"It's all right," Suzanne said, making a sudden decision. "I'll walk home."

The chauffeur only looked at her before curtsying and heading back into the house.

Once alone Suzanne headed down the street until she found what she needed—a bench under a streetlamp.

She opened Nora Sutherlin's medical file, and began to read. An hour later she knew what Kingsley meant when he'd said, "It was mine."

19

Wesley drove through the night until he couldn't keep his eyes open any longer and had to stop. Thanks to two years at Yorke, he had friends everywhere between Maryland and Maine. He crashed at his old roommate's house and had a quick breakfast with him before heading on to Connecticut. By late afternoon he arrived in Westport. For nearly a day now, he'd been running on pure adrenaline, on the need to see Nora face-to-face. As he drove, two words echoed in his mind like the most melodic refrain.

Many waters…many waters…many waters…

Now back in the city he used to call home, he slowed down and had to ask himself exactly what he would do, what he would say when he saw her. His whole body tingled with nervousness as he turned into Nora's quiet suburb with all the New York City commuters who tolerated their semifamous erotica-writing neighbor with wary amusement. By the time he pulled in front of their house—her house, Wesley corrected, not their house anymore—he could hardly breathe. He didn't see her car anywhere and his heart plummeted. All he wanted was to look in her face again, into her eyes.

He walked up to the front door and knocked. When he heard no answer he knocked louder. Stuffing his hands in his pockets, he felt his car keys scraping his knuckles.

His keys…

Wesley pulled his keys out and looked at them. Surely Nora would have changed the locks after he moved out. Wouldn't she?

He found the key that he used to call his house key and slipped it into the front-door lock. Pausing, he took a quick breath and turned the key.

The door opened like nothing, as though those thirteen months of hell without Nora had been a dream he'd had when he'd fallen asleep at the school library studying, and now that he'd woken up, he could go home again.

Stepping into the living room, Wesley inhaled stale air. The house smelled abandoned, as if no one had been in it for months. He saw no piles of mail by the door. Were things that serious with her and Griffin Fiske that she'd have her mail forwarded? Griffin Fiske—New York City trust fund baby playboy with a whole lot of bad behavior in his past…and yet Wesley would almost rather find out Nora and Griffin were together than Nora and Søren. Griffin he didn't like, didn't know and certainly didn't trust. But Søren…Søren he hated.

As Wesley wandered the house, memories came back to him. Memories he thought he'd buried…but they rose up with each step, all too easily resurrected. He'd loved studying on the couch in the living room. Nora had to walk through the living room to get to the kitchen, her favorite destination. And she'd always touch him as she walked by. Maybe just a tap on the forehead, a tweak of his nose, a squeeze of his knee or his favorite—a kiss on his cheek. The bookshelves needed

a good dusting. Big and brown and carved with weird sym-
bols, the bookshelves had been an estate-sale find of Nora's.

"I think these bookcases belonged to druids," Nora had
said, running her small hands over the carvings.

"I think the druids existed prior to, you know, bookcases,"
Wesley reminded her.

Nora pretended not to hear him, her usual MO when he
attempted to bring reason and rationality into her flights of
fancy.

"Virgins have probably been ritually sacrificed on these
bookshelves."

"Wouldn't that be kind of awkward?"

"We'll figure it out. Here, hop on the top shelf, Purity
Ring. I'll get the butter knife."

God, what a weird woman he'd lived with. Weird and hi-
larious and beautiful and amazing... He missed her so much
his stomach hurt to even think her name.

They'd been so good together in this house. So happy.
Looking back he still couldn't quite believe that Nora had
asked him to move in with her. What was it about him? For
days after she'd suggested he live with her and work as her
intern, all he could do was stumble through his days asking
himself, "But why me?" He'd been a nervous wreck when
he'd moved in over that bitterly cold New Year's Day of his
freshman year at Yorke. The reality started to set in as he unpacked his clothes and rearranged the furniture in the room
Nora had given him.

He'd wanted to put some posters on the wall but couldn't
bring himself to hammer any nails without asking Nora for
permission. That night he'd wandered the house just as he
wandered it now. Nora wasn't in her bedroom, the living
room, the kitchen. Finally he'd found her standing on the

back porch in her heavy coat and boots. He put on his coat and joined her out in the cold.

For a moment he'd merely watched her in silence as she stood with her eyes closed and her face turned to the bright white moon. Inhaling slowly through her nose, she held her breath before releasing the air out of her mouth in a cloud of steam.

"Aren't you freezing?" Wesley asked.

"Freezing my ass off. I'm coming in soon." She opened her eyes and smiled at him.

"What are you doing out here?"

"I thought you might like to get settled in without me hovering over your shoulder."

Wesley had to laugh at that.

"You remember I'm six feet tall, right? More like hovering at my knees, munchkin."

Munchkin? He'd actually called the infamous Nora Sutherlin *munchkin?*

"I could do that if you want." She flashed him a wicked grin.

Wesley pursed his lips at her.

"You're terrible. You know that, right?"

"Actually, I'm pretty damn good at it. Just ask Søren." She gave him a meaningful wink.

"I wish you wouldn't talk about him."

Nora blinked at him. Even illuminated only by moonlight, he could read every little expression on her face. Such a beautiful face…he wished then he knew how to draw or paint or anything so he could do some justice to that face, those big green-black eyes of hers.

"How come? You've never met Søren. He's a very good person. Best man I've ever known."

"You told me about him. Good men don't hit women."

"Good men only hit the women who want to be hit."

"Women shouldn't want to be hit."

"Then it's her problem, not his, right?" She batted her eye-lashes up at him.

"Nora, you're nuts. Come inside. My face is about to freeze off."

"Can't have that. Too handsome a face. Just a sec. I need one more."

At that she paused and inhaled deeply through her nose again. She held the breath for a long time before releasing it almost reluctantly.

"Sorry," she said. "I love that smell. A winter's night… Does anything in the world smell better than a winter's night?"

Wesley closed his eyes and inhaled the scent of winter—so crisp and clean and cold. In the distance someone's fireplace burned and a trace of the heady wood smoke spiced the air. He could smell the memory of Christmas and the stark fresh-ness of the New Year.

"It does smell amazing," he'd agreed.

"This…" Nora inhaled again and her eyes narrowed. "This is what Søren's skin smells like. Just like this. Even in summer this is what I breathe in when I'm near him. At night before I'd fall asleep, I would lay my face on his back between his shoulder blades and breathe in and in until I'd almost pass out. And he would laugh at me. Amazing, isn't it? That someone's natural smell could be like this?"

"If he bottled it and sold it, he'd make a fortune." Wes-ley glanced at Nora's small backyard. He wondered what she would say if she saw his backyard at home in Kentucky—all one thousand acres of it.

"God, I miss that smell. I love winter. It's the only time I can smell him again without having to be around him."

Wesley turned his eyes from the snow-shrouded lawn and

back at Nora. A tear had formed in the corner of her eye and crystallized like a tiny diamond.

"You were crazy about this guy, weren't you?" he asked, not sure he wanted the answer.

Nora nodded. "Crazy would be a good word for it."

"Why did you leave him?"

The sigh that was Nora's first answer billowed out in front of her in a cloud of white.

"Winter," she finally said, "can be so beautiful and so cruel. Cruel and cold. And if you live in the presence of winter you never have summer." Nora stepped close to him and put her nose at his cheek. "You smell like summer. Like clean laundry hanging out in the sun. That's an amazing smell too."

Wesley blushed at her nearness. Her hair brushed his lips. He never dreamed someone smelling his skin could feel so intimate.

"We should go inside," Wesley whispered. If he stayed out here with her another second, he'd warm them both up by kissing her. And that would be bad. "It's too cold out here."

Nora had reached up and laid her hands on his face, warming his skin with hers.

"It's okay. It'll be summer soon."

Wesley walked in from the back porch and into the kitchen. He'd cooked a thousand meals for Nora in here. For food alone he could get her away from her computer during her writing binges. He walked up the stairs to the second floor and stood in the doorway to his old bedroom.

"Nora…" Wesley breathed as he stepped into his room. When he'd moved in, this had been a rather decadent-looking guest bedroom done up in, as Nora called it, "French bordello style." He'd quickly made it his own in what he'd called "Not a French bordello anymore style." And now it remained the same. He'd stripped the walls of his posters, taken his things out…but the same sheets covered the bed, the same pillows. The furniture still remained in the order he'd arranged it.

Had someone been staying in his room? Was that why Nora hadn't bothered to revert it back to her taste? The bed definitely looked rumpled and recently slept in. A current of anger surged through him. He'd had the most beautiful, erotic, intimate moment of his life in that bed with Nora that night she couldn't sleep, crawled into bed with him and touched him with her hand. He hated the thought of anyone but him or Nora on those sheets.

Backing out before the conflicting emotions of loneliness, anger and desire overwhelmed him, Wesley walked to Nora's room. Maybe he could find some clue in there about where she'd gone and for how long.

Inside Nora's bedroom, Wesley forced all memories back and out of the way. The last thing he needed was to recall the day he and Nora had nearly made love on her bed. He'd wanted to give her his virginity so much…and yet she hadn't been able to take it. To this day he still didn't understand why. But it was for the best now, he supposed. She hadn't really wanted him. If she'd loved him, why had she sent him away?

Wesley stared at the bed and noticed something strange about the covers. Light streamed in through the window and revealed a thick layer of dust on the coverlet of her perfectly made bed.

And the truth shocked Wesley like snow falling in the middle of summer. The bitter, beautiful truth.

"Oh, my God…" Wesley breathed out loud, hope welling high and hard in his chest. His rumpled sheets. Nora's dusty covers. "Nora's been sleeping in my bed."

"Actually, Wesley," came a voice from behind him, a voice as cold and cruel as winter, "she's been sleeping in mine."

* * *

Michael woke up at midmorning to the sound of hoot-ing. Actually, not quite hooting but his mind couldn't think of a better word for it. This hooting seemed to originate from a Griffin and not an owl. And this Griffin apparently was perched on the roof above Michael's room. Michael had crawled from Nora's bed and back into his own at about five that morning. After their threesome last night, after Griffin had actually watched him having sex with Nora, Michael worried he wouldn't be able to look him in the eye for a few days. But Griffin didn't seem to be nearly so concerned with morning-after awkwardness. He also didn't seem particularly concerned with gravity.

"Griffin?" Michael called up to the roof, where Griffin stood shirtless in the sunlight hooting and hollering in some sort of celebration. "What are you doing?"

"Six years, Mick!" Griffin called back. "Tell me I'm awe-some."

"You're awesome," Michael said without reservation. Awe-some and amazing and smart and funny and sexy. But he kept all those adjectives on the inside. "What's six years?"

Griffin strolled forward on the roof casually, as if gravity didn't apply to him. Bending over, Griffin grasped the edge of the roof and lowered himself through the window and into Michael's bedroom.

"Six years today, Mick." Griffin grinned so broadly his smile eclipsed the sun. "Six years today I have been clean and sober. Not a drop of alcohol. No drugs. Nothing."

Michael couldn't help but smile just as broadly back. He threw his arms around Griffin in a spontaneous hug but as soon as he felt Griffin's warm body against his, his heart raced and blood started going places he didn't want blood going. Michael pulled back immediately and took two big steps back.

"That's incredible. I'm so happy for you. You should celebrate," Michael said quickly, trying to cover his nervousness.

"I am. Always do."

"How?"

Griffin grinned. "New tattoo. I add on to my ink every year."

"Awesome. So you're going into town?" Michael hoped Griffin would invite them into the city with him. Six years clean and sober—Griffin shouldn't celebrate that alone.

Griffin shook his head. "Nah. Spike—she does my ink— she's coming here tonight. Tattoo party. And guess who else is invited?" Michael shook his head. "You are, Mick."

"That's fantastic. I can't wait to watch." Michael knew he was grinning like an idiot, but he couldn't stop himself.

"Watch?" Griffin stepped past him and into the doorway of Michael's room. He leaned against the door frame and gave Michael a long, meaningful look. Michael couldn't quite make out what the meaning of the look was, but he sort of wished Griffin would look at him like that forever. "You're not just watching, Mick. You're getting one too."

Griffin winked at him and left the room, still hooting in unabashed joy, a sound that lifted Michael's heart so high that he almost didn't hear what Griffin had said.

Once alone, he remembered.

Michael raced to the hallway. "Wait! Griffin? I'm what?"

20

On the subway, Suzanne found a safe spot on an empty seat and pulled Nora Sutherlin's medical file out of her messenger bag. She'd read it last night outside Kingsley Edge's house. She'd read it again at her apartment. After two readings she still didn't know what to make of it.

The file began with Eleanor Schreiber's results from a physical she'd taken before starting her freshman year at NYU. A basic physical for insurance purposes, all it revealed was a healthy eighteen-year-old girl with low cholesterol, low blood pressure and some mild hay fever. The only note of interest was that young Eleanor had refused a pelvic exam. The little scribbled note had raised Suzanne's hackles. Why would she refuse a basic pelvic? Suzanne had immediately assumed the worst: STI…pregnancy. Maybe even evidence of an abortion. But a few pages later she'd found something that blew all her dark theories out of the water. At age nineteen, Eleanor Schreiber had apparently partied too hard one night and passed out drunk. She'd woken up with a frat boy on top of her.

The file contained notes from a rape crisis counselor who'd been brought in to talk to Eleanor before, during and after the exam. Apparently the counselor hadn't gotten to perform her duties that night, as a note on the chart testified:

> Patient said she doubts the young man sexually assaulted her. Claims she vomited on him during the rape attempt. Dismissed by the patient once her priest, Father Marcus Stearns, arrived. Patient clearly suffering from severe denial.

But young Eleanor hadn't been in denial. The doctor's report not only showed no presence of trauma or fluids, but an intact hymen as well. At nineteen years old, Eleanor Schreiber was still a virgin. Suzanne knew she should have stopped reading there. To read another woman's medical file seemed such a gross invasion of privacy it turned her stomach to even have it in her hands. And yet she couldn't stop, even after learning that teenage Nora was not lover to Father Stearns, or anyone for that matter.

After Eleanor turned twenty, things got even more interesting. For some reason, instead of seeing a GP or an ob-gyn on a regular basis, Eleanor Schreiber went to a Dr. Jonas for all her all her medical issues. Dr. William Jonas, an internist at Central in Connecticut. And for a young woman who didn't participate in organized sports, Eleanor seemed to acquire a shocking number of minor injuries—a sprained wrist, a bruised rib, even vaginal tearing. To Suzanne they seemed to be clear signs that Eleanor Schreiber had been in a physically abusive relationship in her twenties. And yet Dr. Jonas merely treated his patient, took the most perfunctory of notes and sent her on her way without ever calling the police or an abuse counselor. It seemed a shocking oversight on his part.

Suzanne turned another page in the file. Her hands shook as she read. To herself she whispered, "Nora Sutherlin...you bad Catholic..."

Age twenty-seven, Eleanor Schreiber had gotten pregnant. And Catholic or not, the pregnancy ended quickly with a prescription for RU-486. After that, the medical file ended. No more injuries, no more visits to Dr. Jonas. Nothing.

Nothing...which is what Suzanne had on Father Stearns.

Kingsley Edge said go visit the sister—the one she didn't want to see. She knew Father Stearns had a sister in Denmark. He'd told her that night at the rectory. Surely Kingsley didn't mean her—that would be one hell of a research trip. So that left Claire or Elizabeth.

She'd researched Claire last night. Lovely woman about Nora Sutherlin's age—a rich Manhattan socialite, no husband, no kids, no scandals. As a war correspondent, Suzanne did really hate talking to socialites. Maybe that's what Kingsley meant. But then she'd looked into Elizabeth. Her very first Google hit on Elizabeth Stearns revealed one vital and terrifying fact. Despite also being exceedingly well-off, Elizabeth Stearns had a real job. She worked as a therapist for victims of childhood sexual abuse.

The very phrase created aching knots in Suzanne's stomach and a thousand memories of Adam came crashing to the forefront of her mind. After his suicide, the revelation of the abuse he'd suffered from their priest had tainted every memory of him. Every recollection of him from after the age of nine—Adam's goofy grin in his graduation photo, the day he pushed her in the pool on her twentieth birthday, the pride in his voice when she'd come home from her first assignment in the Middle East, alive and triumphant—was blighted by the knowledge that every grin had been a fake, every laugh a

mask. The last thing she wanted to do was spend the day with
a woman who worked with victims of sex abuse.

Suzanne closed the file as she reached her stop. In ten minutes she had her rental car. In fifteen minutes she was on the
road to New Hampshire.

In four hours, she was there.

After a huge dinner in the dining room on Griffin's anal
table, the three of them—Griffin, Nora and Michael—
adjourned to the living room. Nora threw confetti everywhere in honor of Griffin's six years clean and sober while
Michael sat in near silence on the leather sofa and watched
Griffin and Nora do some ridiculous dirty dancing on top of
the coffee table. Michael wanted to join in the celebration,
would have joined in, but Griffin's threat from earlier that Michael too would be getting tattooed that night had put him
into hardcore freak-out mode. His sexuality he could hide
more or less. At least he could keep the submission and the
attraction to guys a secret from his mom. But a tattoo? That's
not something one could keep in the bedroom.

A little after five, the doorbell rang and Griffin commanded
Jamison to answer it, which he did only after calling Griffin
a "well-arranged waste of molecules."

Griffin's butler returned with a leggy, purpled-haired
woman at his side who had elaborate tattoos running up and
down both her muscular arms. Dark green vine tattoos ran
across her ample cleavage and climbed up her neck—the tip
of the top vine ended in the hollow behind her multi-pierced
ears.

"Griffin Fiske, you dirty whore. One more year again?"
she asked in a Scottish accent.

"Spike…don't pretend you didn't miss me."

"Don't have to pretend." She slapped Griffin hard on the

biceps, hard enough Michael flinched in sympathy. But Griffin only grinned.

"Nora, Michael. This is Spike. She does my ink for me. Best in the business."

"Lovely to meet you," Nora said, shaking Spike's hand. "You do gorgeous work."

"And you have gorgeous skin," Spike said, making a circuit around Nora. "Would look better with ink on it."

Nora sat on the couch and picked up the edits on her books she'd been working on all day.

"I would love a tattoo. Big-ass Jabberwocky all over my back. But my priest doesn't allow me to get anything weird done to my body."

Griffin rolled his eyes while he stripped out of his shirt and sat two chairs side by side.

"Nora, you have your clit hood pierced," Griffin reminded her.

"Yes," she agreed. "But who do you think did that?" She put on her glasses, pulled her hair into a bun that she secured with a pen, instantly transforming herself into Writing Nora, the only version of Nora Michael found sexier than Dominatrix Nora.

"Father S did your piercing?" Michael's mouth went suddenly dry.

Nora only shrugged as she turned a page in her notes.

"You celebrate Valentine's Day in your way and we'll celebrate it in ours. Carry on."

Nora waved her hand dismissively while Spike and Griffin got settled in. Spike plugged in her electric needle, mixed her ink and cleaned Griffin's arm with alcohol.

"Anything fancy, mate?" she asked as she adjusted Griffin's arm.

"Not this year. Just add another band to the bottom."

It took less than fifteen minutes to finish Griffin's tattoo—a black vine around the bottom of his right bicep. Michael could only watch in fascination as blood pooled and dripped. Griffin barely even winced as the needle pushed ink deep into his skin. For the entire time Spike worked on Griffin's arm, Michael studied his face. He had such a handsome profile. And even in obvious pain, he couldn't stop laughing or smiling every few seconds. Where did all that happiness come from? Michael didn't really care. He just wanted to be a part of it.

Once finished, Spike cleaned Griffin off and took a photo of the tattoo.

"When are we getting that griffin on your back we've been talking about?" she asked.

"Think we'll save that for next year and lucky anniversary number seven." Griffin turned to Michael. "Spike specializes in big work. Did big black angel wings all over the back of some guy in Scotland."

"My best work," she said with pride. "I love wings. They're my favorite to do. Speaking of…" She gave Griffin a meaningful look.

Griffin looked at Michael.

"Come here, Mick. Got a present for you."

Michael stood up and walked over to Griffin. Nora put her notes away, shoved her glasses on her head and watched them both.

"Griffin, I don't think I should get a tattoo. My mom might kill me. And I don't know what to get or where."

Griffin reached out and took Michael by the forearm. He lifted Michael's hand and placed it on the center of his bare chest. Every nerve in Michael's body came alive at the contact of his fingers on Griffin's skin.

Griffin started to unbuckled Michael's watch.

304   TIFFANY REISZ

"Wait. Stop," Michael said. Griffin clapped a hand onto his arm and held Michael in place.

"It's okay, Mick," Griffin whispered. "You can trust me here. Please."

Swallowing, Michael nodded. "Okay."

Griffin removed Michael's watch and set it aside as carefully as if it was Griffin's three-hundred-thousand-dollar Audemars Piguet and not Michael's twenty-three-dollar eBay special.

After removing the watch, Griffin took off Michael's black wristband. He turned Michael's arms over and showed the scarred wrists to Spike.

"Can you do it?" Griffin asked.

Spike narrowed her eyes at the scars, and Michael inwardly writhed in mortification.

"I've covered worse. Much worse," Spike said as she ran her fingers over Michael's wrist scars. "Yeah, I can do it. 'Course I can."

"This is what I was thinking, Mick." Griffin pulled a folded piece of paper out of the back pocket of his pants. He opened it up and showed Michael. "I stole your sketchbook while you were with Nora and sent some of your drawings to Spike. This is what we came up with."

Griffin gave a drawing to Michael, who could only stare at it in speechless wonder.

"I thought we could cover the scars," Griffin whispered. He tucked a loose strand of Michael's hair behind his ear, and Michael shivered at the intimacy of the gesture. Watching Griffin have sex with Nora didn't feel as private as Griffin absentmindedly taming Michael's hair. "You won't have to hide them anymore. Your wrists will look like that."

"Like this?" In his hand Michael held a drawing of angel wings—open and unfurled and almost solid black. One wing would be tattooed on each wrist.

"You'll be able to do this," Griffin said, holding both wrists out and together, "and you'll have a full wingspan. Want to do it? My treat, okay?"

Michael swallowed a throatful of tears. No more hideous scars on his wrists he'd have to cover up… Just beautiful ink that Griffin had bought and paid for. Getting this tattoo would be like being marked by Griffin.

"Yes." He looked up at Griffin with eyes that never wanted to look away again. "Let's do it."

Griffin clapped his hands loudly and grabbed Michael by the shoulders.

"You won't regret this, Mick. Ink doesn't get into your skin. It gets into your soul. Changes you. And this will change you in the good way."

"You sure you want to do this, Angel?" Nora asked, her eyes full of concern but no judgment.

"Yeah, definitely. It's okay, right?" he asked.

"This decision is all yours to make. If you want it, do it."

"I want it."

"Good," Spike said. "I hope you mean that because inking scar tissue is a bitch. We'll do the basics tonight and get some decent coverage. I'll need you back in six weeks for touch-ups."

Michael sat down while Griffin brought a table over and placed it front of the chair.

"Griff," Spike said, giving him a stern glare. "You'll have to hold him steady. This won't be easy going."

Griffin looked at Michael, and Michael gazed back at Griffin without blinking or looking away. That strange feeling he always experienced when about to start a scene with Nora came over him. He started to sink into that weird Zen place that Nora and Griffin called subspace.

Michael extended his left hand and Spike started to swab his wrist with alcohol.

"Hold him down, mate," Spike ordered Griffin. "Don't let him move a muscle."

Griffin took Michael's hand in his and held his fingers and forearm hard against the table.

"I won't even let him flinch." Griffin and Michael's eyes still remained locked on each other. Michael felt blood surging through his body. The buzz of the electric needle started up.

"Won't lie to you, kid," Spike said, making a final adjustment on her needle. "Skin on the wrist is thin and sensitive. Getting ink on your cock would hurt less than this will."

Michael took a deep breath in and slowly let it out of his nose the way Nora had taught him.

"It's okay," Michael said and knew he'd never been so calm or certain in his life. He had Griffin's hands on him holding him down. No fear, no agony, nothing in the world could penetrate the armor of his happiness. "I can take pain."

Slowly Wesley turned around. Standing in the doorway to Nora's bedroom was a man well over six feet tall, with perfect pale blond hair, penetrating steel-gray eyes and a face too handsome to be human. He wore jeans and a black T-shirt that revealed impressively taut biceps, and in his right hand he held a motorcycle helmet.

"So Søren rides a motorcycle," Wesley said, not knowing why that was the first thing that came out. "For some reason, I'm not surprised."

Søren's eyes narrowed and the corner of his mouth twitched with amusement. He tossed the helmet onto a chair and crossed his arms over his broad chest.

"Hello, Wesley," Søren said and spoke no other words.

"I'm not going to say hello to you." Wesley took a deep

breath and took a few steps closer. "We're not friends. This isn't going to be a friendly conversation."

Søren stared at him a moment and Wesley felt himself being weighed in the priest's eyes. For more than two years, Wesley had wondered about Søren—what did he look like, how did he act, what the hell did Nora see in him? Now the man himself stood in front of him. And that's what Wesley saw. A man—mortal, very handsome, but still only a man.

"We aren't friends, no." Søren said the words with a magnanimous air. "But must we be enemies?"

Wesley summoned all his courage.

"You hit Nora. You hit her often. You've sprained her wrists. You've bruised her ribs. You've done stuff to her she wouldn't even tell me about. Yeah, Søren, I think we'll be enemies."

Søren didn't seem the least surprised or intimidated by Wesley's words. In fact, he seemed almost pleased.

"I am a pacifist, Wesley. I have no interest in getting into any kind of fight with you. I think Eleanor would never recover from the laughing fit that would induce if she discovered we'd scuffled over her."

"Where is Nora anyway?" Wesley demanded. "I came to see her, not talk to you. You're about the last person in the world I want to talk to."

The insult didn't seem to register. The man was a wall nothing could penetrate.

"She's upstate with two friends for the summer. I won't bore you with the details of why, but she's quite content, I assure you. Do you care to tell me what you're doing in Eleanor's home?"

Wesley didn't answer at first. He turned his back to Søren and weighed how much to tell the man.

"She's not," Wesley finally said.

"Pardon?"

Wesley turned back around and glared at Søren.

"She is not content. I don't believe that, and something tells me you don't, either."

"You didn't answer my question. What are you doing here?"

"I live here." Wesley pulled his keys from his pocket. "I still have a key. This was my home with Nora. What are you doing here?"

"Kingsley had the house alarmed when she went upstate. Silent alarm. You tripped it when you entered. I was nearby and came to investigate."

Wesley's stomach knotted up.

"Alarm? This is a really safe neighborhood. Why would you alarm Nora's house when she's not even here?"

Søren didn't answer and the silence scared him more than any explanation.

"Things are happening," Søren finally said.

Wesley gave a short, empty laugh.

"Well, that explains everything. Thanks for that, Father Stearns."

"Her file was stolen from Kingsley's office. That file contained everything there is to know about her. We don't know who stole it. We don't know why anyone would take such a risk."

Wesley's anger turned to fear.

"You assholes—you and Kingsley both. You keep her safe or you'll answer to me. And I know that doesn't scare you, but I'll make it scare you if I have to. Now I guess I'll go. Gotta run upstate to find Nora and make sure she's okay." Wesley headed for the door, knowing he'd have to barrel past Søren to get through. In his mood, he rather relished the idea. "Somebody's got to and obviously you don't give a damn about her."

Wesley headed for the gap between Søren's body and the

door frame, a gap just wide enough for him to fit through. But Søren's arm suddenly clapped down against the frame and barred Wesley's way.

An icy bolt of fear raced into the pit of Wesley's stomach as Søren turned brutally cold eyes onto him.

"Wesley…" Søren said his name with the unmistakable hint of menace in his voice. "I said I didn't want us to be enemies. For your own sake, I'd highly suggest adjusting your tone."

Wesley couldn't meet his eyes, wouldn't meet them. He stared past Søren and out into the hallway. Out there he could see the ghostly outline of Nora padding down that hall in her penguin pajamas with her wet hair up in a bun and a cup of cocoa in her hand. His Nora…his best friend…the woman he would have given everything to. Once he'd offered her every penny he had and she'd turned it down. Maybe he'd offer again and this time he'd tell her exactly how many millions of pennies he had. And then it would be him and her and cocoa and penguin pajamas and Battleship games and stupid jokes about druids for the rest of their lives.

"I love her," Wesley whispered. "I love her more than my own life, and you…" He finally met Søren's eyes. "You hurt her."

Søren nodded.

"I do."

"You beat her. You do stuff to her that turns my stomach."

"I know it does, Wesley." Søren spoke the words with such sympathy that Wesley's throat tightened.

Wesley took a step back.

"What? You aren't going to defend yourself? Justify it? Tell me it's what Nora likes? What she wants?"

Søren shook his head. "Of course not. I don't have to, after all. You know as well as I do that she loves being with me, loves what I can give. Even more, she needs it."

Wesley pulled himself to his full height of six feet and yet Søren still dwarfed him. But what he lacked in height he made up for in youth and rage.

"Needs it? She doesn't need getting beaten. No one needs that. You've trained her, messed with her mind, made her think that's what sex is supposed to be like."

"So you, a virgin, are going teach Eleanor what sex should be like?"

The five fingers on Wesley's right hand slowly balled themselves into a tight fist. What he wouldn't give to be able to break that beautiful face that stared at him with such arrogance, such hauteur....

"I'd do a lot better than a sick sadistic Catholic priest who can't even hold her hand in public."

Something in Søren's eyes flinched...just a little, just enough Wesley could see that he'd finally struck home.

Wesley waited. Søren said nothing else.

"I helped her paint this room, you know?" Wesley nodded at the walls. "Moved the furniture, put down the drop cloths... We painted all day. Took three coats to get the walls as red as she wanted. That print over the bed? I hung it for her. She spent a solid hour trying to figure out exactly where she wanted it. We rearranged the furniture in here until after midnight. Then we ate pizza at one in the morning. And you know what she said after all that? Do you?"

Søren stared at him.

"No."

"She said, 'Wes, I don't know what I'd do without you. I hope I never have to find out.'" Wesley smiled at Søren. "Took four months but we repainted every room in this damn house. Repainted, rearranged the furniture... This was our house. Mine and hers. I know she'd sneak over to the rectory every once in a while and let you wail on her for a night. But I got her the rest of the time. I cooked her breakfast. I answered her fan mail. I put her to bed when she fell asleep at her desk writing. I rubbed her back when she was sore from overworking herself. And when she got all wrought up over you, it was me she cried on. No, she and I never had sex. That's true. But we had love, real love that didn't take anything out of us, that didn't bruise us or break us. I loved her without hurting her. You asked me if I, a virgin, could teach her what sex should be? No, course not. Hell no. But at least I can teach her what love should be like. And she knows it too."

"Does she now?"

Wesley smiled.

"Seen her new book yet? Read the dedication page. Then you'll see why I say she's not quite as content as you want to pretend she is."

Wesley raised his chin and gave Søren the longest, coldest look he could summon. Søren only stared back, his gaze a second longer and one degree colder. Sighing, Wesley gave up and gave in.

"Whatever," he said. "Like you care. I'm gone. Have a nice motorcycle ride back to your church where you can have fun pretending to be some kind of saint we all know you aren't."

This time when Wesley pushed through the gap, Søren let him pass. Wesley made it five paces down the hall when he heard his name.

"What?" Wesley asked, spinning around.

"Wesley..." Søren gave him a look that terrified Wesley more than any of the dark, cold glares Søren had already thrown at him. This look was almost—Wesley searched for the right word—humble. "Please, Wesley. I need to ask a favor of you."

21

Money greeted Suzanne as she turned onto the tree-lined driveway that led to a grand, three-story Federal-style mansion. She parked her car, walked to the front door and rang the bell. A boy of about ten years old with wide violet eyes opened it.

"Hello?" Suzanne said, not knowing what else to say.

The boy turned his head back into the house. "Mom!" he called out and ran up the stairs, leaving the front door wide-open. A woman came down the hall with a towel in her hand. She wore a white men's-style shirt and jeans. Black streaks covered the shirt. Her red hair was pulled back in a ponytail and a dark smudge of dirt adorned her cheek like a bruise.

"Andrew obviously doesn't have a future as a doorman," the woman said, smiling at Suzanne.

"He's got good lungs though. Maybe an announcer?"

"Possibly. How can I help you?" the woman asked.

Suzanne exhaled heavily and searched for the words. She decided to simply go with the truth and see where it got her.

"My name is Suzanne Kanter. I'm a reporter. And I'm investigating your brother. Will you answer some questions?"

Elizabeth's hands tightened on the towel. According to Suzanne's records, Elizabeth was a mere forty-eight, although her face looked far younger, the veins in her hands aged her far beyond those years.

"Come to the greenhouse," Elizabeth finally said. "The boys never go in there. We'll be able to talk in private."

Once inside the greenhouse, Elizabeth handed Suzanne a trowel and together they planted tiny seedlings in large clay pots.

"Investigating my brother?" Elizabeth asked. "Do I even want to know why?"

"He's up for bishop of the diocese. The youngest priest by ten years on the short list."

Elizabeth only snorted a laugh as she stabbed her trowel into the black dirt.

"I got an anonymous tip about him," Suzanne continued. "The list of names for the priests on the short list. His name had an asterisk beside it and a note that said there was possible conflict of interest. It's not much, I know. But I get the feeling he's got secrets. Maybe dangerous ones."

"My brother has secrets on top of secrets. He has secrets he might not even know he has." Elizabeth picked up a seedling, peeled off a few leaves and set it in a hole in the dirt. "Why do you think I would know them?"

"Kingsley Edge…he told me to ask you if I wanted to know about Father Stearns. I thought about talking to Claire. She seems interesting."

Elizabeth rolled her eyes. "You won't get anything from Claire. She's in love with our brother. Has been all our life. He absolutely hung the moon to her. When she pictures God, he looks like our brother."

"That sounds…unhealthy."

"Not unhealthy. Just excessive. She didn't grow up with him the way I did. I'm not saying he's a bad person. He's not. He's almost as worthy of her adoration as she thinks he is."

"But only almost?" Suzanne prompted.

Elizabeth exhaled and sat her trowel aside.

"Ms. Kanter—"

"You can call me Suzanne."

"Suzanne…when you tell me you're investigating my brother, a Catholic priest, I have to assume you're looking for evidence of sexual abuse. Yes?"

Suzanne didn't demur. "Yes. It's really the only thing that concerns me."

"Hits close to home, does it?"

Opening her mouth, Suzanne paused before closing it again. "Yes. My brother was a victim. He killed himself a few years ago. I think that's why whoever sent that tip picked me. They knew I wouldn't stop looking until I found the truth."

"Oh, God, the truth. There's nothing in the world more misleading than the truth. The truth, Ms. Kanter—Suzanne— is that I know my brother. I know who he is. I know what he is. And I told him years ago that if he ever followed in our father's footsteps, if he ever harmed a child, if he ever took advantage of anyone in his congregation…well, I would make sure he shared our father's fate. And I wouldn't lose a wink of sleep over it."

Elizabeth picked up the trowel again and stabbed it deep into the dirt far harder the necessary.

Staring, Suzanne couldn't quite believe what she'd heard. Did Elizabeth Stearns just confess to murdering her father? No…surely not. She must not have meant it quite like that. Suzanne swallowed as she picked up another seedling and carefully cleaned the roots.

Elizabeth looked up at Suzanne. A silence hung high and heavy between them. Both women waited... Elizabeth broke first.

"I was eight years old when our father came to my room the first time."

Suzanne inhaled sharply and covered her mouth with her dirt-blackened hand.

"I'm so..."

"Sorry, yes. I know. Everyone's sorry. Especially my late father currently burning in hell. He's very sorry now."

"You were only eight years old. Did your brother know about it?"

Elizabeth shook her head.

"No. Father sent him away to some boarding school in England. Wanted his only son to have a proper British education like the one he'd had. Thankfully my brother got kicked out of his proper English boarding school and sent back to us. Otherwise my father's attentions to me would have gone on for years longer than they did."

"Kicked out? What happened?"

Elizabeth laughed a cold, mirthless laugh.

"When you met my brother the first time, were you afraid of him?"

"The first time?" Suzanne laughed coldly. "I'm still afraid of him."

"Yes, well, he's always been like that. Always. As a boy at this school... I don't know. I've only heard snippets of the story. English boarding schools were notorious back then. The older boys, the prefects or whatever they were called, would use the younger boys."

From the way Elizabeth pronounced the word *use,* Suzanne didn't have to ask her to clarify.

"What happened?"

"One of these prefects apparently made the mistake of taking an interest in my brother when he was only about ten. He was asleep in his dormitory bed when the older boy came for him. But my brother was expecting him. Light sleeper. The older boy spent six weeks in the hospital before dying of an infection brought on by his injuries."

Suzanne gasped and nearly dropped the seedling in her hands.

"Father Stearns killed a boy?"

"Boy? I suppose. The older boy was fifteen. And had a reputation for being the worst of the offenders at the school. The school knew that. No one pressed charges against my brother. They covered it all up and sent him back home to us."

Suzanne walked away from the table, from the dark earth and the tender seedlings. Father Stearns as a boy of only ten had beaten and subsequently killed a fifteen-year-old boy at his school….

"I remember overhearing our father telling my mother the story. That monster was proud of my brother. Ten years old and my brother beats into a coma a boy five years older and fifty pounds heavier. Proud. My father the rapist, proud of his son for killing a pedophile. Oh, the irony. I'll tell you more if you promise you can handle it, if you promise it's off the record. I have two sons. I don't want this nightmare to touch another generation."

Suzanne turned back around although she instantly regretted it.

"There's more?"

Elizabeth raised her chin in a kind of defiance, nearly daring Suzanne to tell her to stop or to walk away. And she would have…should have. But she couldn't.

"Tell me," Suzanne said.

Elizabeth picked up the watering can, refilled it and started making a circuit of the greenhouse.

"I was hiding outside my father's office when I heard him tell my mother that story, the story of my brother the light sleeper, my brother who'd nearly killed a boy with his bare hands. And then my brother came home. I hadn't seen him in two years."

"What was it like? Seeing him again after all that time?"

"Strange. Awkward. He didn't seem like my brother to me. He was only eleven, a year younger than me, but seemed so much older. He was such a beautiful bastard even then. And so quiet, unapproachable. He scared the hell out of me. I thought he could kill me the way he did that boy. In fact—" Elizabeth paused for a breath "—I hoped he would."

The August evening heat in the greenhouse was so oppressive Suzanne thought she might faint from it. But when Elizabeth spoke those last four words, she felt cold chills run through her body.

"What did you do?" Suzanne asked. Something told her that was the right question to ask. Not "What happened?" or "What do you mean?" For clearly Elizabeth had done something.

Elizabeth lifted the watering can and sprinkled a large white rose.

"For days after my brother returned from England, I had my father's words ringing in my ears…his son Marcus…light sleeper…nearly killed the boy who'd touched him…"

Suzanne's stomach started to plummet.

"I…" Elizabeth's voice faltered for the first time. "Mother and Father were gone. Away on some business trip of his. I went into my brother's bedroom at night. He was sleeping. I pulled the covers back…."

Suzanne watched as Elizabeth's eyes went blank and empty

as if her mind had left the present and traveled far back into the past.

"Beautiful bastard," Elizabeth said again. "I think that was the first time in my life I remember feeling attracted to someone. I couldn't stop myself from touching his face. Well, you've met him. You must know what it's like to be around him, to be drawn to him...."

"What did you do?" Suzanne repeated the question.

Elizabeth sighed, almost wistfully. When she spoke again it was in a hollow, faraway voice. The sun had started to set and shadows crept into the greenhouse.

"I wonder..." Elizabeth began and paused. "I wonder what it was like for my brother to wake up and find himself inside his own sister."

"Oh, God." Suzanne blurted out the words as she shoved both her hands hard into her stomach to steady herself.

"I kept waiting..." Elizabeth continued. "I thought any minute he'd turn on me, beat me, kill me like he had that boy at his school. But that's not what happened. That wasn't it at all."

A wave of nausea passed through Suzanne. She gripped the table and breathed through her nose, praying the sickness would pass. Father Stearns...at age eleven...had been raped by his own older sister.

"I wanted him to kill me as he had that boy in England. That's why it happened the first night."

Suzanne stood up straight again.

"The first night? It happened more than once?"

Elizabeth slowly nodded. "I told you, Mother and Father were gone. We had the house to ourselves. No supervision. We'd both been so badly damaged we didn't even realize what we were doing was wrong."

Something in Elizabeth's voice betrayed the awful truth

that she hadn't even come close to the end of the story. Suzanne wanted to turn her head and vomit, wanted to take everything she'd heard, everything she now pictured in her head, and retch until every horrible image—the young boy's body responding in his sleep, the sister's desperate gambit to find peace in death, the realization that they'd gone too far to go back—burned itself out of her mind. But Suzanne knew as long as she lived she would have Elizabeth's words emblazoned into her memory forever.

She could never go back. So she had to go on.

"What happened next?" Suzanne asked, not wanting but needing to know. "How did it end?"

"Father, of course. Mother and Father were gone for a month in Europe on his business affairs. I think he'd wanted to take me with them, but Mother…she must have started to catch on to his interest in me. She insisted they go alone. A second honeymoon. Meanwhile my brother and I engaged in acts so depraved that I can't even remember participating in them. I see them happening—" Elizabeth closed her eyes and raised her hand "—out there. As if someone else did them, and I merely watched. You should know I was as guilty as he. More so, really. I started it. He was the virgin until me. But even at that young age, he did have an impressive imagination."

Suzanne swallowed the bile in the back of her throat as Elizabeth opened her eyes and lowered her hand.

"We were together in father's library. One of our favorite spots. Mother and Father came home from their trip a day earlier than we'd expected. Mother went straight to bed in exhaustion. Father went to his office to work. He found us… together."

Elizabeth stopped talking for a moment. Gazing through the glass walls of the greenhouse, she studied the sinking sun. Suzanne couldn't begin to guess at her thoughts, and prayed she'd never know what Father Stearns's sister saw in her memory.

"I've never seen such fury," Elizabeth finally spoke. "Such rage. Father didn't even look human. My brother and I call him a monster. We don't do so lightly. He became a bestial thing that day. He pulled my brother off of me and threw him into the wall. I'll never forget the blood on the wallpaper—red on yellow. And he pushed me to the floor onto my stomach. He was speaking, but for the life of me I can't remember what he said. I don't want to remember."

"I'm glad you don't," Suzanne whispered.

"He started to rape me, to re-mark his territory I suppose. I think he thought he'd knocked my brother unconscious. But then I heard a thud. Most beautiful sound I'd ever heard in my life."

"What was it?"

"My brother hitting my father with a fireplace poker. Didn't knock him out, unfortunately. But it did stop him long enough for me to pull myself out from underneath him. Father's rage then went even beyond what I'd seen before. He grabbed my brother and threw him to the ground. With the poker he broke my brother's forearm. I heard it snap."

Suzanne covered her face with a hand. She found a lone bench and sat on it, unable to stand anymore.

"Father grabbed my brother by his broken arm and dragged him up into a sitting position. Tied him to a chair. My brother's arm…it just dangled…so lifelessly. I remember thinking—it's stupid—but I actually thought, 'Oh, no. He'll never play piano again.' Madness, the things that come to mind in moments like that. Never play piano again? Father was going to kill him."

"Kill him?" Suzanne knew she sounded like an idiot, parroting questions back at Elizabeth. But the shock and sickness had taken away her powers of speech, rendering her nearly mute with horror.

"I remember him saying that. 'You're dead, Marcus. You're dead…' Once he had my brother tied to the chair, he came after me again. Wanted my brother to watch while he raped me. But I couldn't let that happen. The rape, fine. Of course. Happened before. But I couldn't let him kill my brother. I loved him. In a sick, damaged, broken way…I did love him. We were all we each other had. So I picked up the fireplace poker, and with everything in me, I slammed it into my father's head. And, my God, he went down hard. So hard and so fast, I laughed. I think it was the laugh that got my mother's attention. I just couldn't stop laughing…."

"Your mother, she found you?"

Elizabeth nodded. "She burst into the library, saw her daughter nearly naked and bleeding, my brother barely breathing and tied to a chair, and Father a pile of bloody monster on the floor. She couldn't deny anymore what had been going on under her nose. She got me and my brother out of the house. Took him to the hospital and dropped him off—"

"Dropped him off? She just dropped him off?"

"He wasn't her son. She'd always hated him a little. She could have turned a blind eye to an affair, even one that produced a bastard. But to force her to treat him like a son? She never forgave Father for that. If only that had been the worst of his sins."

"If only…"

"So she dropped off my brother at the hospital and fled with me. She divorced Father after. That was the sixties. She couldn't bear to let our dirty laundry out in public. So no charges were pressed and they divided the assets up equally. And the assets were and are considerable. Even after dividing everything in half, they both were extremely wealthy people."

"What happened to your brother?" Suzanne asked, although she knew part of the answer. "He was sent to school, right?"

Elizabeth nodded. "I suppose once Father came to, he remembered my brother was his only son and heir. But he refused to have my brother around, so it was off to school. St. Ignatius Academy, I think it was called. Some Jesuit boarding school for boys up in Maine. Middle of nowhere. Barely accessible even in good weather."

"Sounds like a prison."

"Something like that. I think Father was afraid of my brother, afraid of possible retribution. He was wrong to be, of course. My brother is no murderer. My father feared the wrong child."

Suzanne heard a smile of satisfaction in Elizabeth's voice.

She didn't speak. Although young, Suzanne had been a journalist long enough to know that she often got the truth only when she stopped asking questions.

"I'm glad he went to St. Ignatius," Elizabeth continued. "He was happy there, apparently. Converted to Catholicism. Learned a dozen or more languages from all the priests who taught there. Met that Kingsley."

Suzanne smiled because she knew Elizabeth expected her to.

"And Kingsley's sister, right?" Suzanne prompted.

"Oh, yes. My brother's wife. Never met her. I found out about the marriage only after the girl had died. He did it for the money, of course."

"The money?"

"The trust fund. My brother and I had trust funds set up by our parents. We received a huge sum at age twenty-five or sooner if…"

"If you got married."

Elizabeth nodded.

"I think my brother just wanted to help Kingsley and his sister stay together in the States. They were both penniless, really. Didn't end well, as you know. Which I suppose is for the best. My brother was destined for the priesthood."

"He does seem to have found his calling."

"It's a lovely thing, having a priest for a brother. It's quite nice to have someone in the family who can absolve all your sins and is bound to keep your secrets even from the laws of man. My brother…he has had to absolve me for so much."

Elizabeth turned her violet eyes on Suzanne. In them Suzanne saw the truth, heard the truth, finally understood the truth.

Elizabeth Stearns had killed her father. And her brother knew it.

And to Suzanne, a priest who had absolved his own sister of the sin of murder and kept her confession secret even from the police…

"That sounds like a conflict of interest to me," Suzanne said. "A brother hearing his sister's confession."

"I suppose it is. But perhaps you have your answer now."

"Perhaps I do." Suzanne rose off the bench on unsteady feet. She had to get out of there now. She knew what she had to do, who she had to see, what she had to say. And she needed to do it tonight. "I need to go. Thank you for your time."

"Of course. Anything for my brother. I hope you understand him a bit better now. If you're looking for a sex-offender priest, you won't find him at Sacred Heart. My brother knows better than that. He'd have to answer to me."

Suzanne gave Elizabeth a tight smile.

"No, I'm sure you're right. After what happened to my brother, I can certainly sympathize with what you feel and with what—" Suzanne choose her words carefully "—with what you did. I'm glad your brother absolved you. If it makes you feel any better, I would have absolved you too. If I believed in that."

Elizabeth picked up her trowel again and started digging once more in the dirt, this time with a much gentler touch.

"I'll show myself out. I promise all of this was off the record."

"Thank you, Ms. Kanter. Please have a safe trip home."

Suzanne started for the door but paused before she touched the knob.

"You don't call him Marcus?" Suzanne asked. "Your brother I mean. That's what you call him—my brother. Why is that?"

"He hates the name Marcus. It's our father's name."

"Thank you. I was just curious. Good night."

Suzanne reached once more for the doorknob and stopped.

"I think I understand something you don't," Suzanne said as she remembered something Elizabeth had said earlier. "About your brother not waking up the way you thought he would."

Elizabeth only stared at her and said nothing.

"You wanted him to wake up that night and kill you as he did that boy who attacked him in his sleep at school. But he didn't. Because he was sleeping heavily. And he was sleeping heavily because he was home. And he thought he was safe."

Even in the low light Suzanne could see Elizabeth's eyes harden like two glinting amethysts.

"He should have known better than that. No one is ever safe."

22

Michael had never felt so safe in his life. A strange sensation considering the agony he'd been in the last two hours as Spike, the purple-haired tattoo artist, pierced black ink deep into his damaged skin. But the pain centered him, calmed him the way pain always did. But even more than the pain, Griffin's strong hands on him, holding him steady, brought Michael into a haven inside himself he'd never gone to before. Nora sat on the couch working on her edits. Spike dug into his wrists with her buzzing needle. But no one in the world existed but him and Griffin.

Every few minutes Spike would pause and reink her needle. Griffin would loosen his grip on Michael's forearms and offer him a drink of water or ask if he needed a break. The pain hit its peak and sweat would drip down Michael's forehead. Griffin would call for a break, wipe Michael's face and let him breathe for a few minutes before Spike started up again. At no point did Griffin ask him if he needed or wanted to stop.

TIFFANY REISZ

And for some reason Griffin's faith in his ability to take the pain meant more to him than anything.

"That's it, mate," Spike said, leaning back in her chair and stretching her back. "Done as much as we can do tonight. Let it heal. Six weeks, we'll do touch-ups."

Michael turned his eyes from Griffin's to his own wrists. During the entire ordeal he'd kept his gaze on Griffin's face and not on Spike's needle. He hated seeing his own scars, hated the memory of that moment of despair and idiocy that had led to them. And he'd yet to find anything or anyone in the world he'd rather look at than Griffin. But now he looked at his wrists and inhaled at the sight of them—and not with disgust as he had every day for the past three years, but with awe.

"Wow…" he breathed. "Spike, it's—"

"Motherfucking beautiful," Griffin said, gently touching the skin around the edges of the raw and still-bleeding tattoos.

They were beautiful, his black wings that covered the insides of both wrists. Somehow Spike had managed to create the illusion of delicate feathered edges out of flesh and ink. And the scars…they were gone. The body of each tattoo completely covered the angry, raised remnants of Michael's suicide attempt.

Griffin took both of Michael's hands in his and pushed his freshly tattooed wrists together side by side, creating a wingspan.

"Gorgeous, Mick. They're gorgeous." Griffin squeezed Michael's fingers. "Just like you."

The pain from the two-hour tattoo session had already pulled Michael to the very edge of arousal. And Griffin's hands on him, the hungry tone of his voice made Michael painfully aware of the one part of his body that ached more than his bleeding wrists.

"I'll be right back," Michael said and yanked his hands away from Griffin. He nearly ran from the room and into the bathroom down the hall. Standing at the sink he bent over, turned the taps on and splashed water on his fevered face.

He couldn't do this anymore. For two months now, his lust for Griffin had been like the scars on his wrists—something he hid, something that shamed him, something he was afraid to look at. But tonight on that table, it wasn't only the scars on his wrists that had been transformed.

Michael loved Griffin. He knew that now. And he had no fucking idea what to do about it.

"Angel?" The door to the bathroom opened and Nora stood staring at him with concerned eyes.

"Nora..." Michael stood up and raised his hands in a kind of surrender. "Nora...I..."

"I know, Angel," she said. "I know."

She shut the door behind her and reached for him, pulling him close. He nearly groaned at the human contact, the touch of her hand on his face, her lips on his cheek. She reached between them and unzipped his jeans as Michael raised her skirt.

He pulled her panties down and pushed inside her. Never before had he been this aggressive with Nora. But this wasn't about sex or scening or S&M. This was survival. He thrust roughly as she gently ran her hands through his hair and down his back.

Michael came quick and hard, shuddering against Nora with his face buried in the crook of her neck.

"I don't know what to do, Nora," he whispered as he pulled out of her. "I don't know what to say. He'll kill me. My father will kill me. And my mom, she'll never look at me again. I don't know..."

"You have to tell Griffin," Nora said. "You have to talk, Michael. You have to speak."

"I can't, I can't." Michael's whole body seized up in the

agony of his need and his love. His knees buckled and together he and Nora sunk to the floor of the bathroom.

"You can, Angel. You've been so brave this summer. You've faced so many demons. And I'm so proud of who you are and who you're becoming… Just say it. Tell me what you want to tell Griffin. Just get it out. No one will hear but me. But you've got to say it to somebody. Just talk, Angel. Speak. What do you want? Tell me."

"I…" Michael began and stopped. Even to Nora it seemed a Herculean task to say what he felt, what he wanted.

"Michael, this is an order from your mistress. Tell me what you want. Now."

"I want Griffin." The words came out immediately. She had trained him too well. "I want Griffin so much it hurts. I love him, Nora. I have never felt anything like this before. And it's absolutely stupid because he's rich and he's perfect and amazing and I'm a nobody. I'm a nobody, and I'm in love with someone I can't be with. He's so beautiful. I can't stop looking at him, I can't stop thinking about him. I dream about him at night. And he's the first thing I think about when I wake up. And I want to touch him so much. I want to touch his face and that fucking perfect hair of his. And his lips and his chest and his arms—and I think about those arms around me, and it's humiliating how much I want that. And, God, I want to live in his bed. I want to spend the rest of my life underneath him. I want to feel him on top of me and inside me. And I want submit to him. I want to go down on my knees in front of him. I want to call him sir and wear his collar and kiss his fucking feet if he told me to. And I want to walk down the busiest street in New York with him holding hands so the entire world can see us together and know that I belong to him. I love Griffin, Nora. I'm in love with him. And I can't be with him. But that's…that's it." Michael turned his head and buried it a little deeper into the cleft of Nora's neck and shoulder. He wanted to stay there so he wouldn't have to look her or anyone in the eyes ever again. "You won't tell him, will you?"

"She doesn't have to."

Griffin's voice came from the doorway to the bathroom. Michael gasped and looked up. Nora pulled away enough to turn her head.

"Shit," Michael breathed, his heart freezing, his stomach dropping, his whole body turning to ice.

"You meant all of that, didn't you?" Griffin asked, looking down at where Michael sat in a pile of misery on the floor.

"Griffin, I'm sorry." Michael pulled his knees tight to his chest. "I'm so sorry. Forget I said all that. I'm just—"

"Stand up," Griffin said with the unmistakable tone of an order.

Michael came immediately to his feet.

"I'm so—" Michael began but Griffin didn't let him finish the apology.

Griffin reached out and cupped Michael's neck and pulled him hard against himself. Before Michael even knew what was happening, Griffin's mouth was on his.

The kiss was everything Michael had dreamed about—powerful, possessive, unyielding. Griffin held Michael's face in his hands, allowing Michael no chance for escape. But as Griffin's tongue sought his, as their lips found each other, Michael knew he never wanted to escape.

Slowly Griffin pulled back.

"I've wanted to do that since the second I saw you," Griffin breathed, pressing his forehead to Michael's. "I've never wanted anyone the way I want you, Mick."

Michael couldn't believe the words.

"No…no way. I've been here two months. If you wanted me—"

"Your fucking priest told me if I laid a hand on you, he'd never let me see Nora again."

Michael whirled around to face Nora, who watched them both with the tiniest hint of amusement on her lips.

"Nora? Father S said—"

"He has his reasons," Nora said. "And yes, he told Griffin he'd revoke his 8th Circle privileges and kick him out of the community if he tried anything with you. And he wouldn't let us see each other again. But I told you before, Griffin. Søren's not a monster. You can talk to him. Call him. Explain—"

"Fuck calling him. And fuck the explanations. He thinks he's God making all our decisions for us. What happens with me and Mick is none of his business. And I'm going to go tell him that. Right now."

Griffin grabbed Michael one more time and gave him a kiss that left Michael panting and aching. But it ended all too quickly as Griffin wrenched himself away and left the bathroom.

"Griffin!" Nora called out. Both she and Michael nearly had to run to keep up with Griffin's long, determined strides. "It's about to storm. Can't you wait until tomorrow? Just use the damn phone."

"That won't be good enough for Søren, and you know it, Nora. When I went to him six years ago and told him I was in love with you, talking wasn't good enough. I had to prove myself. I was too pussy to do so then. And I didn't love you enough to man up. For Mick, I will. If only to show that self-righteous, pretentious asshole priest of yours that he's not the only dom with balls around."

Michael looked at Nora in abject terror.

"Griffin's not going to fight Father S, is he?"

Nora shook her head.

"No. Søren's a pacifist."

Michael sagged with relief. As strong and tough and young as Griffin was, he had a feeling Father S could wipe the floor with anybody on the planet.

"Thank God."

"No, Søren doesn't want to fight Griffin. He wants to break him."

"Oh…" Michael watched Griffin disappear down the hall. "Fuck."

Nora nodded. "My sentiments exactly."

Michael waited for Griffin to reappear from wherever he'd gone. Maybe he could talk some sense into Griffin. He remembered the story Griffin had told him that morning after his first night with Nora—Griffin had gone to Father S to ask permission to be with Nora. Father S said not until Griffin was willing to submit to real pain, real dominance. Griffin couldn't go through with it back then, not for Nora. But him…for him…

"I can't let him do it. It's stupid. We'll figure something out," Michael said, desperate to keep Griffin safe. "I'll talk to him. I'll talk to Father S. He—"

The sound of a roaring engine interrupted Michael and put an end to whatever plans he had to stop Griffin from his ridiculous idea of confronting Father S.

"What the—"

Nora sighed.

"That would be a Ducati monster peeling out of the driveway," she said. "And in high gear too. He's gonna get a shitload of speeding tickets if he's not careful."

"Nora…" Michael looked at her, his stomach a knot of pain and hope and sadness and joy in one aching, roiling mess.

She exhaled and laughed.

"Can we not have one week without some major drama around here? Come with me, Angel. I want to show you something."

Suzanne drove back to the city but didn't stop there. She kept going, kept driving and didn't stop until she'd arrived in Wakefield, Connecticut. The entire way there, she thought about Søren, Father Stearns, Elizabeth's brother… How could they all be the same person? To Claire he was the ideal older brother. To Elizabeth he was the symbol of the worst part of her life. To his congregation he was practically God incarnate. And to Nora Sutherlin he was "Beloved." But that she loved him didn't mean he loved her back, not in the same way perhaps. Suzanne knew Patrick loved her, was in love with her. But she didn't feel the same.

Or did she?

Pulling her phone out of her purse, she dialed Patrick's number. She nearly laughed at the relief in his voice when he answered.

"Suz. Goddammit. Where have you been? Is everything okay?"

"It is. I think so. Better anyway. Can you do me a favor? I'm driving and I need to look something up."

"Sure. Anything."

"Can you see if a woman named Elizabeth Stearns from New Hampshire has any kind of criminal record?"

"Google won't help much with that. Let me call my NYPD friend. He can look it up."

Suzanne hung up and waited. But she didn't have to wait long.

"So?" she said when she answered.

"Arrested on suspicion of manslaughter. Father fell to his death down several flights of stairs. He was notoriously healthy

and virile for an old geezer, so no one believed that he'd just
fallen."

"No conviction?"

"Nope. No witnesses. Spotty evidence. The only really in-
criminating thing Elizabeth Stearns did the day after Daddy's
death was head straight for Wakefield to talk to her priest-
brother."

"The cops thought she confessed the crime to him."

"They did. Tried to get him to talk. Wouldn't say a word
even though the sister's not Catholic. Apparently only baptized
Catholics are supposed to go to confession so they leaned on
him pretty heavily to spill it. Even the diocese wanted him to
spill it. He refused on theological grounds."

"And on the grounds of covering his sister's ass. Knowing
what her bastard of a father did to her, I don't blame him at
all."

Patrick exhaled and the phone buzzed in her ear from the
force of his breath. She smiled. Patrick…what would she do
without him?

"So you're done, right? This is done? You're coming home
now, right? Right?"

Suzanne grinned into the dark.

"Got one more thing to do first."

"Then you're coming home, right?"

"Right. But don't wait up. This might take a while."

"I'll wait up."

The smile lingered on Suzanne's face long after she'd hung
up. At about ten o'clock she arrived in Wakefield and Sacred Heart. A few lights still burned in the church and set
the stained-glass windows subtly glowing. How beautiful the
church looked by night…how peaceful, how sacred. She still
didn't really believe in God. Nothing would ever convince
her that some man in the sky was running the show down

here on Earth. But for once she started to believe a little in one of His believers.

She entered the church and found it empty. But surely Søren would return before long to turn off the lights and lock up. Søren… She realized all of a sudden that he'd become Søren again in her mind. But although she knew his name, knew his secrets, she didn't feel quite worthy to call him by the name only his most trusted intimates knew him by.

"Father Stearns…" she whispered aloud as she stared at the altar at the front of the church. She'd never call him Søren to his face or in her heart and mind again. Glancing around, Suzanne saw a small staircase that led to the choir loft. She climbed the stairs and stood at the edge of the balcony area and surveyed the entire sanctuary.

Sanctuary. In olden times she knew that criminals and runaways would seek real sanctuary inside the walls of churches. The church was holy ground, sanctified, and the authorities treated it as a place of real power not to be meddled with. For the first time since childhood, Suzanne felt safe in a church and safe with a priest. She used to think the only cure for the ailments of the Catholic Church was wholesale destruction. It gave her pleasure to quote Denis Diderot's words, "Man will never be free until the last king is strangled with the entrails of the last priest." She'd met both a king and priest in her investigation and had to admit that while the world might not be better off with them in it, it certainly was more interesting.

Below her she heard the door open and Father Stearns strode down the center aisle toward the altar. She watched him a moment and smiled as he crossed himself, gave a quick, elegant bow next to a pew and sat down to pray. In his hands he held rosary beads, and she had to wonder for what special intention he prayed. She started to call out a greeting to him, but she heard the door below her open again.

"Søren!" A man's angry voice echoed throughout the sanc-tuary. Suzanne took a step back from the edge of the railing and hid herself in the shadows. Father Stearns stood up and turned around.

"Griffin...how nice to see you in church."

Suzanne's inhaled in shock. She couldn't see the man's face, but from his muscular build and the photos that she'd seen, she recognized Griffin Fiske, the son of the chair of the New York Stock Exchange.

What the hell...

"None of that," Griffin said, his voice flush with fury. "Don't pull any of the bullshit mind-fuck stuff on me. You know why I'm here."

"I don't actually." Father Stearns stood in the center of the aisle and gave Griffin a placid smile. "But tell me. We can discuss whatever you like."

"Let's discuss how my love life is none of your fucking busi-ness. Let's discuss what an arrogant, pretentious asshole you are for thinking you can tell me or anyone who they can or cannot be with."

"Eleanor is very fond of you, Griffin. I've yet to discern why."

Griffin took a menacing step forward.

"Maybe because unlike you, I don't try to control her every move."

"Yes, Eleanor is utterly oppressed, isn't she?" Father Stearns's voice dripped with mockery. "Eleanor acts like a child because she's full of childlike joy. You simply are a child, Griffin. A spoiled child who has never had a real relationship in his life. I've watched you use people up and discard them over and over again. If you think for one moment I would allow you to use up and discard someone I love—"

"Me?" Griffin laughed bitterly. "Me? I use people up and

discard them? Are you blind? Are you deaf? Your precious Eleanor uses men like fucking tissues. One good hard blow and she tosses them out. Her editor? Her intern? Her thousand ex-lovers? Jesus Christ, Søren, even—"

Whatever name Griffin Fiske started to name went unuttered. And it all happened so quickly Suzanne couldn't even reconstruct in her mind the series of motions she'd witnessed. She knew it began with Griffin pointing his finger at Father Stearns's chest and ended with Griffin on the floor of the church with his arm pinned behind his back. Father Stearns had moved with such brutal force and efficiency Suzanne could only cover her mouth in shock.

"Griffin…" Father Stearns spoke the name with cold, calculating, utterly terrifying calm. "You are in God's House. And Eleanor is His Child. And when you dare speak of her in my presence or in His, you will do so with the utmost respect. Are we understood?"

Suzanne could only stare at the scene. It appeared that if Father Stearns pulled on Griffin's arm any harder, he would dislocate the shoulder. Griffin grimaced and took a pained breath.

"Yes, sir," he finally said.

"Good." Father Stearns released Griffin's arm and stood up. Griffin quickly came to his feet. "Now shall we continue brawling like schoolboys? Or should we discuss this somewhere like gentleman?"

Griffin nodded. "The Circle?"

Father Stearns sighed heavily.

"If you insist."

"I do. This ends tonight. You know what I want and who I want."

"I do, in fact. Are you prepared to earn what you want?"

Griffin's back straightened.

"I'll do whatever it takes. Last thing I want is to cause that kid any more pain. Not the bad kind of pain, anyway."

The kid? Suzanne thought that was an odd way to refer to Nora Sutherlin. From what little she knew of the infamous Griffin Fiske, he was slightly younger than Nora. And what the hell did he mean by the bad kind of pain? Was there a good kind of pain?

"Nor I. Which is why I set the conditions I do."

"Fine. Let's get this over with. I'm not going to waste another night sleeping alone if I don't have to."

Suzanne saw Father Stearns's eyes narrow as Griffin stormed out of the church. However pure his feelings for Nora Sutherlin were, surely he didn't want to hear about her in bed with some other guy. Obviously Father Stearns had considerable sway over her if Griffin Fiske had to come fighting her priest to be with her. That night at the rectory when he'd dropped his guard and talked about how he'd had to rescue Eleanor Schreiber from herself as a teenager, how he'd practically had to raise her after her home life imploded…maybe Father Stearns was to her exactly what he'd said he was—a father.

Father Stearns left the church and Suzanne collapsed into a pew, her heart still racing from the strange scene she'd witnessed. Father Stearns had nearly gotten into a fistfight with New York's biggest trust fund baby over Nora Sutherlin. Bizarre… Suzanne had so many questions, but she apparently wouldn't get to ask them that night. Why didn't Father Stearns want Griffin Fiske and Nora Sutherlin together? Why did Griffin call her "the kid"?

And what the hell was The Circle?

Nora took Michael up to his bedroom and sat him down in the window seat. She ordered him to stay while she went

TIFFANY REISZ

to her room to retrieve something. When she came back, she found him up and pacing.

"So you've just given up following any of my orders, I see," she teased as she sat on the bench in the window. "Hopefully Griffin will be able to train you better than I have."

Michael blushed and collapsed miserably onto the bench across from Nora.

"Oh, God, I'm in love with a guy..." he groaned. "This sucks."

"It also blows."

Michael groaned again and Nora could only laugh at him.

"Aah...teenagers," she said, reaching out for Michael and dragging him to her. He curled up in her lap with his head on her thigh. "Everything is life-and-death when you're seventeen. Especially love."

"It isn't life-and-death?"

Nora closed her eyes and leaned her head back against the wall.

"No, it is actually. Life and death are less life-and-death than love is. When I fell in love with your priest, I felt as though I had this open wound. I was so raw, so tender. And it hurt. But I didn't care. Love is the open wound that you hope never heals."

"Love will hurt a shit metric ton if my dad finds out about this."

"Your father is an asshole, Angel," Nora reminded him. "Why do you care what he thinks?"

Michael shook his head.

"He makes Mom miserable about me. Anything I do, he turns on her. He dumped us, divorced her, and he still comes around and gives her shit for every single thing he hates about me. And that's a lot of shit."

"Your father has terrible taste in sons." Nora ran her hands

THE ANGEL   339

through Michael's long hair and brushed it off his forehead. "I'd be thrilled if I'd ended up with a kid like you."

Nora gazed out at the manicured lawn and the empty driveway. Griffin probably wouldn't be home until morning. God only knew what Søren would put him through tonight. Nothing truly terrible, of course. Nothing he hadn't done to Nora a time or two. Just some mind-fucking and probably a hefty dose of pain. It would do Griffin good, actually. There was something to be said for fighting for the one you loved. Especially if the one you loved was a seventeen-year-old boy who didn't think he deserved that love.

"What happened to the kid?" Michael whispered and Nora pulled her eyes away from the evening sky.

"What kid?"

Michael raised his head off her lap and simply stared at her. Nora sighed heavily.

"Oh, that kid."

"I don't talk much, but I do listen."

"Too damn well apparently," Nora said, laughing without joy or mirth. God, this was about the last thing she ever wanted to talk about. "You really want to know?"

Michael nodded.

"Maybe it'll distract me from worrying about Griffin." Michael sat up and pulled his knees tight into his chest.

Poor thing...love shouldn't have to hurt this much, Nora thought before realizing what blasphemy such a sentiment was in their world. Would she ever know what love without pain felt like? Did such a thing even exist?

"I was twenty-seven," she began, turning her eyes back to the setting sun. "And so in love with your priest I couldn't see straight. But for a long time, I'd felt...incomplete, I guess is the best word for it. I hung out at Kingsley's a lot in my twenties—it was the only place your priest and I could really be ourselves together. You remember that hot French guy who came on to you in the Rolls Royce?"

Michael grinned. "Won't ever forget that guy."

"That guy owns New York. At least the Underground parts of it. He's got the hottest submissives, doms and dominatrixes in the world on his payroll. They're in and out of his town house all the time. And I would watch the dominatrixes and just stare at them. They were so beautiful, so powerful. Even the male dominants gave them a wide berth. You expect men to be tough and strong and in charge. But when you meet a woman like that? It's mind-blowing. I ached for what they had. Don't get me wrong, I love submitting to your priest. It fulfilled me like nothing else. But it never fulfilled me completely."

"I can't imagine," Michael said with a shrug. "I guess I don't have a dominant bone in my body."

"You don't. I'm sure of it. And that's fine. I envy you. Being a switch is no party. The doms don't quite trust you. The subs don't quite get you. Just being one thing or the other would be so simple… It's like being bisexual. Best of both worlds. Worst of both worlds."

"Tell me about it."

Nora squeezed Michael's knee.

"You know your priest has not one but two PhDs."

Michael blinked. "Really? In what?"

"Got his first one in his twenties in theology, of course. But when I was twenty-six, twenty-seven, he was working on PhD number two in Canon Law. Søren is, to say the least, a nerd."

Michael's eyes went wide just before he burst into laughter. What a wonderful sound, hearing Michael laugh like that—so loud, so boisterous, so open. At the very least, the summer at Griffin's had made him learn to speak up a little.

"So your sexy nerd priest went to Rome to finish his dissertation at the Gregorianum. He never left me alone when he went away for his trips. He'd always leave me with another dominant to keep an eye on me. I didn't really understand that then. First time he did I was only twenty-three years old and he drops me off as this mansion in butt-fucking nowhere New England with this brutally hot widowed librarian."

"Seriously?"

Nora rolled her eyes. "Seriously. Søren told me he knew I'd be good for this guy, Daniel. And I was. And he was good for me too. Being with him that week made me realize how much I truly loved your priest and that being with him was worth the sacrifices. And that was the plan. Every time Søren left me, it was a test. Would I still be there when he came back?"

"So what happened when you were twenty-seven?"

"He left me with Kingsley for three months." Nora closed her eyes and let her mind wander back to that time. She remembered the hot tears on her face as Søren had kissed her goodbye and warned her to be a good girl and do whatever Kingsley said. He promised her a hundred presents from Rome, a letter every week… She couldn't bear being apart from him for so long. Her stomach ached at the very thought of it and continued to ache for weeks. Well, she thought it was his absence that caused the pain in her lower stomach. "I was sick," she said, opening her eyes. "Kidney infection. Two-week course of very strong antibiotics. Didn't think anything of it. Sort of forgot that birth control pills and antibiotics don't mix."

Michael didn't speak and Nora didn't want to. But she took a breath and carried on.

"It was just a few days before your priest was supposed to return from Rome. I woke up in Kingsley's bed sick as a damn dog. I barely made it to the bathroom in time. Puked so hard I thought my ribs would splinter."

Michael winced so dramatically Nora almost laughed.

"Yeah, pregnancy isn't the glorious and beautiful thing the movies make it out to be. It's gross and painful and miserable. And no one in their right mind would ever do it on purpose. So I did it for all of...well, about one day."

"What did you do?"

Nora would never forget rolling onto the floor and curling up in the fetal position after throwing up for a solid ten minutes. The cool tiles felt like heaven on her fevered clammy skin.

Slowly her eyes fluttered open and she found Kingsley staring at her with his dark, knowing eyes.

"*Chérie...*" he'd whispered, whipping a swath of sweat-soaked hair off her forehead. "What have we done?"

"I think we know," she'd whispered in reply, her voice hoarse from the force of her retching. She didn't need any tests, any doctor's visits. She simply knew. And so did Kingsley.

"I'll call *le prêtre*." Kingsley started to rise off the floor.

Nora pulled her mind out of the past.

"I can't begin to tell you how hard it was to pull myself off that floor, Michael," Nora said. "I was so sick and so tired... every muscle in my body was shaking. But I did. I stood up and looked Kingsley in the eye and I told him..."

Nora exhaled and the past reached out and took her in its arms against her will.

"Don't, King. Don't call him."

Kingsley lifted his proud chin. "I must and you know it, Elle."

"If you call him...if you tell him, then he'll decide. Yes or no, it'll be on him. I can't do that to him. I can't make him make this decision."

She remembered the cold, hard certainty that she'd felt at that moment, the certainty that letting Søren decide would be a mistake. If he told her to keep it, it would ruin their life together. Twenty-seven years old…a job in a bookstore that paid almost nothing, and she was the mistress of a Catholic priest. Not ideal conditions for raising a child. But if he said to end it…a Catholic priest…she couldn't let him make that decision. She had to do it. She had to do it alone. Not for her sake, but for his.

"You ever heard of the Fortunate Fall, Angel?" Nora asked, coming to the present yet again.

Michael shook his head.

"It's a theological concept that Adam and Eve in the Garden were supposed to eat the fruit. That they were supposed to fall. That it was God's plan all along. Søren thinks it's bullshit. I'm inclined to disagree. That day when I had to make that decision without him… You have to understand, Angel, your priest made all my decisions for me and had for almost ten years. He owned me. He owned my body. I didn't cut my hair without getting his permission."

Michael whistled. "That's intense."

"Welcome to the world of being owned. You'll like it. Until you hate it," she said and winked at him. "Søren…I loved him too much to force him to make this decision for me. Either choice would break his heart. So for the first time in years, I made my own decision. I didn't want to lose Søren and what we had. I couldn't for one second imagine bringing up a child in the world I lived in—threesomes with Søren and Kingsley, parties at S&M clubs, slave auctions. Not a family-friendly atmosphere in our world. I went to the doctor, got the magic pills and took them. And the second I took them, it was like the Fortunate Fall. I had tasted the fruit of knowledge…but not of good and evil. The knowledge of freedom, of making my own decisions. And it tasted so sweet it scared me. I went to the rectory and waited for Søren. He came home and found

TIFFANY REISZ

me on his bathroom floor in absolute agony. I spent a lot of time on bathroom floors that week."

"Did it hurt?"

Nora wiped at her cheek with the back of her hand.

"Yes, Angel, it hurt like fuck. And in the midst of a horrible cramp, your priest found me. I told him everything immediately. It all came out in one big rush. The antibiotics and the pregnancy and Kingsley and how I loved him too much to make him decide. Oh, my God, I'll never forget the look on his face when I told him what I'd done, told him why I was in a ball of agony on his bathroom floor."

"What? Was he angry?"

Nora reached out and took Michael's hand in hers.

"No...he looked at me and..." She stopped to take a breath. "He said, 'Little one, I'm so sorry...' And he'd never looked at me before with such love or such compassion. He wasn't angry at all. The opposite really. Goddammit, he's a good priest, isn't he?"

Michael bit his bottom lip and nodded. "Yeah. He really is. The best."

"He wrapped me up in those crazy-strong arms of his and held me close to his chest. And then he gave me the one order he's ever given me that I couldn't obey."

"What?"

Nora smiled.

"He ordered me to marry him."

Michael actually gasped and Nora laughed at his shock.

"Yes. Romantic, isn't he? Well, we kinksters can never do anything the normal way. I think he thought that's what I needed—more supervision, more time with him. He said he would leave the priesthood and we would get married. Nothing like this would ever happen again. I would never have to go through anything like this alone ever again."

"And you said no?"

"I said no. And then he got angry. I wasn't afraid of him. I've never in my life been afraid of him. But I couldn't stay, not a minute longer. What he offered, I wanted it so much I could taste it. But I had that other taste on my tongue, the taste of freedom. So I got up and walked out. And when I couldn't walk anymore, I crawled. And your priest didn't see me again for over a year."

"A year?" Michael repeated in shock.

"A year. I found a place to hide out. A place he couldn't follow. And believe me, he tried. And after a year there I went back to the city and back to Kingsley. And we buried Eleanor Schreiber in the past, and Nora Sutherlin was born to take her place."

Michael smiled. "But Eleanor didn't die."

"Shh…" Nora covered his mouth with her finger. "Don't tell."

For a few moments they both sat in silence. The sun had set and the lawn had come to life with a thousand yellow fireflies.

"Do your regret it?" Michael asked, his voice no louder than the lightning bugs.

"What? Not having Junior Kingsley or not marrying Søren?"

"Both?"

Nora sighed heavily and shook her head. Leaning forward she pressed her lips to Michael's and gave him a deep, long, slow kiss. He moaned into her mouth and Nora smiled as she pulled back.

"Neither," she whispered.

Michael gave a rueful laugh.

"So you don't even wonder?"

"Sometimes," she admitted, possibly for the first time ever

out loud. "Junior Kingsley would be about seven years old now."

"That's how old Owen is."

Nora ran a hand through her hair and tucked it behind her ear. Owen Perry—wavy black hair like hers, smart, weird—every time she saw him, she remembered.

"Yes, it is, isn't it? But like I said, no regrets. Life's too short for regrets."

"Do you regret anything?" Michael asked and Nora's stomach tightened.

Turning her head she saw Wesley standing before her, his big brown eyes rimmed with unshed tears as she told him goodbye.

"Nothing," she lied.

She stood up and patted Michael on top of his head. "But that's not what we were supposed to be talking about. Didn't bring you up here to talk about all the gruesome shit in my past."

"Better than talking about all the gruesome shit in my future when my father finds out about Griffin. Nora, if Father S doesn't want me and another guy together, then maybe—"

"Angel, Father S has no problem with you being with a guy. He's worried that Griffin won't take care of you the way he thinks dominants should take care of their subs. Griffin's a well-trained partier, an ex-drug addict. He put the play in playboy. And he and Søren hate each other for no reason either of them will tell me...."

Michael looked at her with guilty eyes.

"Michael...you know, don't you?"

He didn't answer. Nora cupped his chin and forced him to look at her.

"Angel, tell me. This is an order from your mistress."

"It's not fair that you can do that."

Nora grinned at him. "I know."

"Griffin…" Michael began and stopped. "He…and you…"

"Oh, Lord Almighty," Nora groaned. Michael didn't have to say another word. So Griffin had actually been in love once upon a time. With her of all people. Maybe one of these days she'd figure out why every man in her life had such terrible taste in women. "Griffin went to Søren about me, didn't he? I should have known. Søren and Kingsley don't believe any dominant should lay a hand on a submissive until he or she has experienced pain. And apart from bar fights, tattoos and hangovers, Griffin hasn't. I guess that's about to change tonight."

"Father S is going to hurt Griffin?"

"Don't worry. He loves you. He can take it."

"You think Griffin loves me?"

Nora cupped his face and caressed his bottom lip with her thumb.

"I'm certain of it. After tomorrow, I think you will be too."

Michael blushed crimson. "Oh, God. Me and Griffin… We're going to be…" He couldn't even finish the sentence.

"He's going to fuck you blind the second he gets a chance. Hope you're okay with that." Nora grinned fiendishly.

Groaning, Michael collapsed down onto the window seat. Nora could only laugh at him.

"Don't pretend you aren't dying for it," Nora said. She picked up her laptop bag and pulled a folder out of it, a folder that contained the single most beautiful photograph she'd ever seen in her life. No matter where she went, she always took the photo with her. She'd been given a copy with the express orders to show it to no one ever. And she'd followed those orders to the letter…until now.

"Nora…me and Griffin? Seriously? I want it…I do. I want it so much it hurts. But I just can't. Father S—"

Nora opened the folder that contained the photograph and

held it out in front of Michael's face without a word. Silently Michael stared at the image in front of him. Watching his eyes, Nora saw his expression change from curiosity to understanding.

Michael finally wrenched his eyes from the photograph and looked at Nora, who stood subtly smiling at him.

"Feel better now?" she asked.

Michael nodded wide-eyed at her.

"Much."

23

The sound of falling water roused Michael from his sleep. Rain pelted the roof above him and the window next to him. Usually he loved the sound of rain, especially a morning rain in the summer. But now his first thought upon waking was of Griffin on his motorcycle, wet roads and screeching tires.

So this is love, he decided. Love was fucking terrifying.

Even awake Michael kept his eyes closed, not wanting to face the morning yet. He'd spent all night asleep in the bay window seat curled up in Nora's lap like a kid. Last night he'd been certain he'd never fall asleep, but Nora had started running her fingers through his hair and humming softly, humming the quietest of lullabies. The song and her soothing touch had calmed his racing mind and finally allowed him some rest.

He heard footsteps in the hall, familiar footsteps, and his heart soared at the sound. But he kept his eyes closed, kept pretending to sleep.

"Welcome home," Nora whispered. "You survive the night?"

Michael felt a new hand on his back, larger than Nora's.

"Barely," came Griffin's voice, also in a whisper. "Your priest... I have no words."

"Did he kick your ass? No, don't tell me. I'll be too jealous if he did."

"He didn't," Griffin said, and Michael heard the surprise in his voice, the grudging respect. "We talked."

"A talk with Søren? I think I'd rather take a beating."

"It hurt worse than a beating. But I think I needed it."

"So what's the verdict with you and my Angel?"

"The verdict is..."

Michael felt Griffin's hand slide from his lower back to his neck. Griffin's fingers dug gently into his skin.

"Enough faking, Mick. Let's go." The gentleness of Griffin's touch gave way to force, and Michael found himself being hauled to his feet.

"Griffin, it's seven in the damn morning," Nora said, yawning luxuriously.

"Good. We'll need all day to make up for lost time." Griffin's fingers dug into Michael's skin. "Excuse us."

Michael's heart raced, his hands went numb and every drop of blood in his body made a beeline for his hips.

"Excused." Nora waved them off as Griffin hauled Michael toward the door.

"Oh, message from Søren, Nora," Griffin said, pausing in the doorway.

"Good Lord, what?" she asked.

"He said you're in trouble for going to the party in the city. Told you to stay upstate and out of trouble. So he's punishing you."

Nora rolled her eyes.

"Goddammit." Nora sounded horrified at the prospect of punishment. "Whatever. I'll do it. What is it?"

"He said…" Griffin paused and Michael winced. Griffin seemed genuinely afraid to tell her. Michael hoped the pause would last forever. He had no idea what was about to happen between him and Griffin but something told him whatever it was, his life would never be the same again after.

"What?" Nora demanded, her voice edged with anger.

"Don't shoot the messenger, okay?"

Michael suddenly feared Nora's punishment more than whatever Griffin had planned for him.

"Griffin…just tell me." Nora gave him a cold, hard stare.

Griffin exhaled heavily.

"Søren said you have to visit your mother."

Michael almost laughed out loud with sheer relief. But Nora's face fell and she raised her hand to her forehead.

"Goddamn motherfucking sadist."

"Good luck," Griffin said as he beat a swift retreat, dragging Michael with him by the back of his T-shirt.

"What's wrong with Nora's mom?" Michael asked as they neared Griffin's bedroom.

"They don't like each other."

"But why do—"

Michael's question died on his lips as Griffin grabbed Michael by the shoulders and pushed him firmly but gently into his bedroom door. Digging his hands in Michael's hair, Griffin forced Michael to meet his eyes.

"Do not speak again until I give you permission."

Michael opened his mouth in an automatic "Yes, sir" but remembered himself and stayed silent.

"Good boy. Now go. In my bed. Right now."

Without a moment's hesitation, Michael threw open the

doors to Griffin's bedroom, pulled the covers back and slid into the bed. He did nothing else.

Griffin yanked off his leather motorcycle jacket, stripped down to his boxer briefs and threw himself into bed next to Michael.

Rolling onto his back, Griffin grabbed Michael and pulled him hard to his chest.

"Now go to sleep," Griffin ordered. Michael raised his head and stared at him. Griffin met his eyes and then burst into laughter.

"Seriously?" Michael asked, breaking the no-talking rule.

"I'm exhausted. Haven't slept all night. I love you too much to lay a hand on you like this. Now shut up, sub, and go to sleep."

Michael nodded and laid his head down on the center of Griffin's chest. He'd only slept an hour or two himself last night. But something Griffin said forced Michael's head back up again.

"You love me?" he asked, his voice hardly more than a whisper.

Griffin brought his mouth to Michael's. For what felt like a year but probably lasted no more than a minute, Michael was subjected to the softest yet deepest, most intimate kiss of his life. With the most expert touches of his tongue, Griffin managed to set every nerve in Michael's body firing with only his mouth on Michael's mouth.

"Yes," Griffin said, finally ending the kiss with the most erotic smile Michael had ever seen in his life. "Now go to sleep."

Michael pressed his entire body to Griffin's and luxuriated in the warmth of his chest through the soft fabric of his white T-shirt. Right before falling asleep, Michael whispered the two words he'd been waiting to say since the moment he'd met Griffin.

"Yes, sir."

Nora stared at herself in the mirror and cursed at her reflection. She hadn't seen her mother in over six years and here she was trying to decide if her mother would approve of her outfit. Last thing she wanted was to provoke a fight by showing up in any clothes that even remotely hinted at the woman Nora had become. She'd left her mother's protection and returned to the city, returned to the world her mother had prayed her daughter would one day leave behind.

Jeans. Basic jeans. A white blouse buttoned up to a respectable level. Boots with a low heel. Hair in a ponytail. Almost no makeup. Surely that would be good enough, tame enough, vanilla enough for her mother.

Nora got into her BMW and headed out at near-breakneck speed. She wanted to get this punishment over with as soon as possible. Being here in Guilford so close to where her mother had moved had been a mistake. She should have known at some point Søren would order her to visit her mother. They'd been friends once—Søren and her mom. When Nora was merely a troubled teenager everyone called Elle or Ellie, the sainted Father Stearns and her mother had worked together a time to two trying to tame her wild side. Of course, Søren's methods had proven far more effective than her mother's hectoring and disdain. Nora knew her mother always thought her daughter had far too much of her reprobate father in her. It had been a miracle her mother had taken her in at all that day Nora had shown up at the front door still cramping from the drugs she'd taken, shaking from the shock of running from the only man she'd ever loved.

But her mother had taken her in, sheltered her, fought to

keep her there when the others questioned whether Nora belonged there or not.

"She left her lover," her mother told the others who wanted her out. "He won't come for her here. He can't. He abused her. Physically."

Although it turned Nora's stomach to hear her mother tell the lie, she'd kept quiet, praying that the others would take pity on her and let her stay. And finally they had. Nora had been given her own room, chores to do, and orders to keep her head down and cause no trouble. She'd caused trouble, of course. Couldn't be helped. It was her nature. In her loneliness there at the house, she started to write a story about a girl running away from a man. Nora could see the girl in her mind's eye, see her racing through trees, turning her head back every few seconds to see who followed her. And Nora had whispered to the girl in her mind, "Don't run. He's the only one you don't have to be afraid of…." And with that one sentence, that one idea, she'd written her first book, *The Runaway*.

For that book alone, the book that changed her life, she'd be forever grateful for her year of limbo in that house with her mother. Søren once said that book had been her way of writing herself out of hell. But it hadn't been hell in the house. Hell was leaving Søren. Hell was staying away from him. Behind the gates that Nora drove through…that was mere purgatory. And it was to purgatory she now returned.

Hell punished sin. Purgatory burned it away. She'd like to keep her sins, thank you very much. No matter how much they hurt.

Nora parked the car and headed for the main house. Finding the bell at the wrought-iron gate, Nora rang it and waited.

"Yes, child?" came a weak voice from an ancient face behind the gate.

"My name is Eleanor Schreiber." Nora waited to see if the woman remembered her.

The old woman smiled and nodded.

"I'll find her for you."

"Thank you," Nora said, entirely without gratitude.

She heard the sound of cloth scraping the ground as the woman shuffled down a hall. A few minutes later younger footsteps approached. A door at the side of the gate opened and two women stepped through—one in her eighties and one in her fifties.

"Sister Mary John, this is your visitor."

The woman in her fifties heaved a deep sigh.

"Elle? What are you doing here?"

"Hi, Mom."

When Michael awoke, the morning rain had dissipated completely and warm white sunlight filled Griffin's bedroom. He guessed he'd slept to about noon or later, slept deeper and better than he ever had in his life. Griffin's chest made the best pillow in the world.

Michael laid his hand on Griffin's rib cage and felt his heart beating steadily against his hand. How had this happened? What had he done to deserve the right to be in Griffin Fiske's bed with his hand over Griffin's heart? It seemed the most ridiculous thing in the world. Like a gift. Like a grace. And entirely without meaning to, Michael leaned up and dropped the smallest of kisses on Griffin's lips.

The touch of their mouths caused Griffin to stir in his sleep. His dark eyelashes fluttered and opened. Michael froze.

"Sorry, sir," he said in a panic.

"Never be sorry for kissing me, Mick. That's an order."

Michael grinned.

"Your orders are really easy to follow, sir."

"Take your clothes off," Griffin said without blinking or missing a beat.

Michael's hands went numb.

"Okay, I take it back."

Rolling up, Griffin cupped the side of Michael's face. With his thumb he caressed the arch of Michael's cheekbone. With his fingertips Griffin kneaded the soft skin underneath Michael's ear.

"I'll help."

Reaching out, Griffin gathered the fabric of Michael's T-shirt in his hands and pulled it up. Michael hesitated before lifting his arms to help the process along.

"I'm so fucking skinny and you're so—"

Griffin clamped his hand over Michael's mouth as he sent the T-shirt flying across the room.

"I have the most beautiful sub in the world in my bed. If you insult him, the punishment will be swift and severe." Griffin gave Michael a stern glare. "Understand me?"

"Yes, sir." Michael nodded in penitence even as his heart soared at Griffin's words.

"I have wanted to do this for weeks." Griffin ran his hands through Michael's hair, down his neck and back, over his arms and down his chest and stomach. "Icing you up after your first night with Nora, I thought it would kill me. I'd never needed to touch someone or kiss someone so much in my life."

"Really?" Michael's mind boggled at the confession. He couldn't believe the entire time he'd been aching for Griffin, Griffin had been equally pining for him.

"Really. Swear to God, Mick, it's nearly killed me not to touch you for so long. Like this…" Griffin pressed his thumb into the hollow of Michael's throat. "And this…" Griffin ran his hand down the center of Michael's back from the nape of his neck to the small of his back. "And this…" Griffin pressed his hand between Michael's legs and cupped his testicles. Michael inhaled and closed his eyes.

"We don't…" Griffin began and stopped. "It's a big deal, letting a guy inside you. We don't have to do that yet. We can wait as long as you need or want. I don't mind. There's a lot of other stuff we can do. And I'm a little on the big side so I don't want to hurt you. We can wait. We should wait."

Michael opened his eyes and looked at Griffin.

"I want you inside me," he said simply. He reached out and dug his fingers into Griffin's biceps. "I will beg you for it if you order me to. And I'll beg you for it even if you don't."

Griffin looked at Michael with an expression on his face he'd never seen before. No, he corrected. He had seen it. Often. On Father S's face during prayer. It was love mingled with reverence. Reverence…for him?

The reverence quickly morphed to unabashed, unadulterated lust as Griffin gripped Michael's shoulders and pushed him down hard onto his back. Their mouths met, their tongues intermingled…Griffin's hips pushed into Michael's. Michael trembled as he felt the full force of Griffin's hunger for him pressed against his stomach. But he wanted this, needed this. All summer long he'd waited for this. He wouldn't let fear stop him. He'd worry about what his father thought tomorrow, what the world would say. Today all that mattered was Griffin.

"Stay here," Griffin said as he pulled himself up and off of Michael. Michael nodded and lay perfectly still on his back, panting. He didn't watch Griffin, merely stared at the ceiling. He could definitely get used to staring at Griffin's ceiling.

Griffin returned to the bed with rope cuffs in his hand and a smile on his face.

"Up," Griffin ordered and Michael came to his feet.

He stood in front of Griffin and inhaled with pleasure as Griffin took Michael's forearms in his hands and bound them with the rope cuffs behind his back. Michael wondered why his forearms at first and not his wrists. Then he remembered his fresh tattoos. He'd almost forgotten about them. But Griffin hadn't.

"Now…" Griffin said with a sensual smile. "Down."

Michael hit his knees without hesitation or a word of protest. Ever since witnessing Nora doing this to Griffin six weeks ago, he'd dreamed of going down on his knees like this. Griffin pulled off his boxer briefs and tossed them aside. Yes… Michael took a deep breath. Just like this.

Griffin slid into Michael's mouth. Michael discerned the subtle hint of salt on his tongue and relished finally knowing what Griffin tasted like. He took as much of Griffin into his mouth as he could. Nora had done this to him several times this summer, but he still didn't have much of a clue what he was doing.

"It's okay, Mick. Go easy on yourself," Griffin said, twining his hands in Michael's hair. "It feels amazing."

The slight catch in Griffin's voice stoked Michael on. Somehow Michael had managed to do something right. Right enough that Griffin had to call a stop to it.

"Yeah, that was as amazing as I dreamed about. Too amazing," Griffin said, pulling out of Michael's mouth. "Don't want to end this before it begins."

Griffin reached down, grabbed Michael by the arm and hauled him to his feet. As Griffin reached behind him and pulled off the rope cuffs, Michael pressed a kiss onto Griffin's muscular shoulder.

Griffin stopped moving but Michael kept kissing.

"Is this okay?" he whispered as his mouth moved from Griffin's shoulder to his neck.

"God, yes, it's okay." Griffin tilted his head to the side to give Michael better access to his throat. "Mick…I want to do something if you're okay with it."

"Anything, sir."

Griffin gave a low, throaty laugh.

"Let me tell you what it is before you say yes to it."

"Okay, sir." Michael bit lightly at Griffin's earlobe and was rewarded with a sharp intake of air. Biting…Griffin liked biting. Awesome.

"I want to go bare with you. You can say no."

Michael stopped in the midst of a protracted kiss of Griffin's collarbone.

"You mean…?"

Griffin nodded. Michael hadn't forgotten their conversation from weeks ago when Griffin revealed he'd never in his life had had sex without using a condom. He'd said it was the one thing he held back so he'd have something to give if he was ever in a real relationship with someone.

And Griffin wanted to give that part of himself to Michael.

"Yes. Yes, definitely, sir. Absolutely, yes."

"Mick, what are you trying to say?"

Michael laughed and leaned into Griffin, who wrapped his arms around him.

"Yes, sir!" Michael shouted the words and laughed as Griffin gave him a wide-eyed look of shock.

"That's the first time I've ever heard you raise your voice at all."

"Yeah…" Michael shrugged. "I didn't know I could do that."

Griffin cupped Michael's neck with both hands.

"I like it. I like hearing you. I always want to hear you," Griffin said and dropped a quick but sensual kiss on Michael's lips. "I want to hear you talk." He dipped his head and kissed Michael's throat. "And I want to hear you shout." He bit Michael's earlobe. "And I want to hear you beg." Griffin reached between their bodies, slipped his hand into Michael's boxers and took him in his hand. "And I want to hear you come."

Michael shivered at Griffin's words. Closing his eyes he lowered his head and leaned against Griffin.

"And…" Griffin said, running his hands up Michael's back. "I want to hear you laugh."

With one shove, Griffin pushed Michael and sent him sprawling across the bed. Michael laughed riotously as Griffin crawled on top of him and pinned him hard to the mattress.

"Good boy. Now don't move. I'm going to fuck you in a few minutes."

Griffin moved away again and Michael tried to do his slow deep breathing that Nora had taught him. But nothing could get him to anything remotely resembling a place of peace or Zen. He'd never wanted anything so much in his life like he wanted Griffin inside him. Fuck Zen.

Michael watched as Griffin came to the side of the bed with two black silk sashes and some gauze.

"Tying you up is going to be a lot easier when the damn tats heal," Griffin said, grinning as he gently placed gauze pads over Michael's wrists. "I've got leather cuffs, handcuffs, rope cuffs…and I plan on using every last one of them on you. For the next month though, we better stick to gauze and silk."

"I'm not going anywhere," Michael said as he let Griffin bind his wrists. "You don't have to tie me up."

Griffin grinned. "Of course I don't have to. I want to. And you want me to. Don't you?"

Michael blushed but couldn't deny the truth.

"Desperately."

"Desperately, huh?" Griffin repeated as he tied the silk sashes around one of the bedposts. Michael had to turn onto his side to get into a comfortable position. On his side…okay, so this was how it was going to happen. "You've been spending too much time with Nora and her damn adverbs. Comfortable?"

"Yes, sir," Michael said, looking up at Griffin, who laid his hand briefly on Michael's face.

"You'll be okay. We'll stop if it hurts. You talk to me the entire time. That's an order."

Michael's heart clenched at Griffin's tender concern for him. So this is what being loved felt like? Like somebody out there cared more about what he wanted and needed than what they wanted and needed… Weird.

Griffin climbed into bed again and sat at Michael's hip. Slowly Griffin eased Michael's boxers down his legs. As Griffin stripped him completely naked, Michael stared off into the corner of the room. Even the night of their threesome, Michael had kept his boxers on during the sex. Griffin had never seen him naked before.

Michael winced at his boxers hit the floor by the side of the bed. But Griffin made no comment. Instead he kissed the side of Michael's thigh and worked his way up to Michael's hips.

The featherlight kisses on never-before-kissed parts of his body sent Michael trembling on the edge of orgasm.

"I want you to come first," Griffin said, taking Michael in his hand again and lightly stroking. "You'll be more relaxed. Relaxed is what we want."

Griffin's hand did amazing things to him. Nora knew how to touch a guy. He had no complaints where her technique was concerned. But Griffin was so strong and yet the way he touched Michael so gentle…. Griffin's other hand gripped the back of Michael's neck. Griffin put his mouth on Michael's shoulder and bit down hard. The mix of pleasure and pain did Michael in. With a gasp he came in Griffin's hand with an orgasm that seemed to go on forever.

"Oh, God." Michael leaned forward and breathed into the sheets.

"I plan on practicing that until I'm making you scream when you come."

"From the orgasm or the biting?" Michael asked.

"Both."

Griffin lay down next to Michael and pressed his chest into Michael's back. For a few minutes they did nothing but lie silently spooned together as Griffin ran his hand over Michael's body. The rhythm of Griffin's touch lulled Michael into an almost hypnotic trance. Every muscle in his body started to unknot. Every ounce of anxiety seeped out of his skin and into the sheets.

When Griffin opened the bottle of lube, Michael barely heard it. Nothing registered except Griffin's touch, his nearness.

"Just fingers first," Griffin said. "I'm sure you did this with Nora."

"Yeah. I'm good there," Michael said, lifting his leg to his chest as the cold liquid met his warm skin. Almost torturously slowly, Griffin's fingers slid inside Michael. "Very good."

Griffin laughed as he nuzzled the back of Michael's neck with kisses.

"Glad you like it. Anything feel bad? Feel weird? I want you to tell me."

"Feels amazing."

"Amazing is what we're going for. This will be even better when you're healed up completely and I've beaten the hell out of you first. Sex after S&M is a new kind of amazing. Well, I guess you know that after all this time with Nora."

"I do," Michael said. "But I don't how it is with you. And I can't wait."

"Me neither. Okay, three fingers? Good? Bad?"

"Good. More than good." Michael felt open and relaxed. The orgasm had helped with some of the tension but really it was Griffin, just Griffin, who could make all the stress go away. Michael loved Nora and adored her. But she had a wildness to her, an unpredictable side that fascinated him, but scared him too. With Griffin though…with Griffin he felt safe.

"More than good," Griffin said. "That's an understatement. God, Mick. I can't believe how good you feel. I have to be inside you. I don't think I can wait any longer."

Michael pulled against the sashes on his wrists as Griffin pushed up deeper into him.

"Then don't wait."

Griffin slid his fingers out and Michael heard the sound of the lube bottle again. More of the cold liquid covered him and Michael opened his eyes and stared at his bound hands. Whenever he'd fantasized about this moment with Griffin, he'd always imagined the fear and how he would have to fight to overcome it. But now he felt no fear at all. Nothing but hunger, passion, need.

And love.

"Here's a little trick," Griffin said as he set the bottle aside and pushed even closer to Michael. "If you kind of bear down first—"

"I know. Bear down first. Then release. It'll fit better," Michael said, quoting Nora from the day she'd scandalized the crazy old bats at church.

"Nora. Right." Griffin laughed in Michael's ear. "I'm glad you had such a good teacher."

"I feel like I have a lot to learn still," Michael said as Griffin kissed his neck.

"I will teach you everything you need to know. Lesson one. When I go in, you breathe out. Cool?"

Michael gave one practice exhale. "Cool."

Again Michael stared off into the nothing at the corner of Griffin's bedroom and tried not to think about what was happening to him. He didn't want to stress or tense up. He'd learned that from Nora.

So when Griffin started to push inside him, Michael did nothing but what he'd been ordered to do. He breathed out, hard and slow, and only after his second long exhale did he let himself focus on what he was feeling.

Michael buried his face in his arm and groaned.

"Fuck."

Griffin dug his fingers into Michael's hips.

"Good?" he asked, his voice tense and breathless.

Michael nodded. "Good. Very good."

For a few minutes Griffin barely moved except to run his hand up and down Michael's arms and back and side. Michael couldn't begin to imagine the self-control it took for Griffin to be inside him without thrusting. But it worked. Gradually Michael relaxed enough that Griffin could push a little deeper inside him. And then deeper. Michael turned his head back for a kiss just as Griffin began to slowly move in and out of him.

"There's something wrong with your back," Griffin breathed into Michael's lips.

"There is?"

Griffin grinned at him. "My welts aren't on it."

Michael laughed but the laugh turned to a gasp as Griffin hit a spot inside him that made every nerve in his body sing. He'd never dreamed it would feel this good. Arching his back, he took Griffin in even deeper. He tossed his leg back over Griffin's thigh. His hands formed fists and the pain in his wrists made the pleasure all the more potent.

He let go completely, let his ego die, his fears fade…. With Griffin inside him, he couldn't begin to care what his father thought, what anyone thought. No way was this wrong. And no one would ever convince him of that.

Griffin pushed his hand hard into Michael's lower stomach as his thrusts grew faster and harder.

"God, Mick…" Griffin rasped into his ear. "It's never felt like this before. And it's not…"

Not the condom thing, Michael knew Griffin meant. But he didn't have to say it. Griffin's body said it, his hands that held Michael like the world was about to end, his lips that couldn't stop kissing his neck and shoulders, his desperate breaths that matched Michael's.

Michael felt the muscles in Griffin's thigh going taut as steel. He pushed one, twice, and with a final thrust, Griffin came hard, his mouth at Michael's ear. Michael grunted in shocked pleasure as he felt Griffin pouring into him.

For a few minutes or a few hours—Michael was too spent to notice the time—Griffin stayed inside him after catching his breath. Michael felt the first stirring of awkwardness. What did they do now? What was he supposed to say? Would things be weird now that they'd had sex? What happened now?

Griffin wrapped a strong arm over Michael's chest and held him close.

"I want to own you," Griffin whispered into Michael's ear.

Michael smiled, and for the first time in his life knew exactly what to say and how to say it.

"You already do."

"Ellie? What on earth are you doing here?" Nora's mother, Sister Mary John, stepped forward and pulled Nora into an embrace, an embrace Nora returned quickly and perfunctorily before taking an awkward step back.

"Long story. How are you, Mom?"

Nora felt her mother's eyes on her face, studying her intently. Nora kept her expression neutral as she returned the gaze. The years were being kind to her mother. At fifty-two, the woman looked barely forty-two. Of course cloistered nuns were notoriously healthy. Their lives were so regimented and cut off from the stresses of the world that many of her mother's sisters in the order lived well into their nineties and remained active during even their final years.

"I'm well. Very well. Come, let's walk, shall we?"

"Sure." Nora followed her mother through the gate and into the motherhouse. A sign warning that all men were barred from entering the enclosure greeted them as they passed into the recesses of the house. No men…not even priests. It was for that reason Nora fled to her mother's abbey when she left Søren. As much as he'd wanted her back, he would never have stepped foot inside this place. At night sometimes she'd wake up in the tiny cell she'd been given and imagine him waiting outside the gates of the abbey for her. She'd sworn she'd heard the unique roar of his motorcycle engine more than once. All that time they'd been apart, he'd known exactly where she hid.

"How have you been, Ellie?" her mother asked as they passed through the back door and onto the lawns.

"Great. Amazing. I started working with a new editor last year, a new publisher. The new book hit all the big lists."

"That's wonderful for you."

Nora cringed at the placid tone in her mother's voice. Won-derful *for you*. Not wonderful. Just wonderful for her. Her mother disapproved of her books, her erotic writing. Always had. Always would.

"You might like the new book. Almost no sex in it. Well, compared to my other stuff."

"That's quite a change for you. What brought that on?"

Nora shrugged and said nothing as they stepped onto one of the winding paths. Out of the corner of her eye, Nora studied her mother. She hated how much they looked alike—the same small straight nose, the same changing eyes, the same pale complexion.

"Nothing. Just playing around, trying to write something different. Expanding my horizons…" Nora cringed. God, she sounded like she was giving an interview with her trite answers.

"You look well. In one piece at least." A slight smile played across her mother's lips.

"Is that your way of asking if we're back together?"

"You can't blame me worrying about you, can you?"

Nora sighed. Classic motherly deflection. She loved how her mother could take all the aspects of Nora's life that were the most personal, the most private—her relationship with Søren, her sex life, her need to submit, her hunger to domi-nate…things that had nothing to do at all with her mother—and make them about her. Mothers must go to some sort of school to learn how to do that so well.

"We're back together. And we're happy. And I love him. And I always will. Oh, yeah, we're still kinky as hell too. In case you were also wondering that."

Her mother exhaled angrily.

"Eleanor, his is a man of God. He is a priest. Do you have any idea what seducing a priest means for your soul?"

"Seducing a priest?" Nora rolled her eyes. "Back in the day he was an abuser who'd seduced me. Now suddenly I'm the seducer here?"

"You're a grown woman now, not a child anymore. You know better now. You know you could have a life apart from him. Going back to him? That's willful disobedience."

"It's love. And I'm not disobeying anyone. Until God Him-self tells me he and I aren't allowed to be together, then we're going to be together. It hardly renders him unfit for the priesthood. Almost all Protestant ministers are married, and Jewish rabbis. We Catholics are the freaks making our ministers stay celibate. Can you get more medieval than that?"

"He chose to become a priest knowing celibacy was one of the requirements. If he cannot honor that, he should leave the priesthood."

"Yeah, let's take the best priest in New England and turn him into, I don't know, a piano teacher just because he's in love with me. And we'll let all those priests who like to rape the altar boys stay in the Church. Last time I read the Bible, I don't remember sexually assaulting children being part of doing the Lord's work."

"You were fifteen—"

"I was fifteen when I fell in love with Søren. Fifteen years old when I told God, the devil and anyone who would listen that I would sell my soul for one night with him. When will you believe, when will you understand… Mother, I seduced him."

"And that's why he doesn't belong in the Church. There are some priests who manage to keep their vows."

"Yes, the ones who haven't met me," Nora said purely out of spite.

Her mother winced and Nora suppressed a twinge of guilt. Goddammit. She had a priest for a lover and a nun for a mother. Between the two of them she had enough Catholic guilt to start her own religious order. After ten years, Nora still couldn't believe her mother had made good on her threat to have her marriage annulled and become a nun.

"I pray for you, Eleanor."

"I know you do. It won't be answered. Not with a yes anyway."

Nora knew her mother prayed for her every single day,

prayed the same prayer every day—Father, please save my daughter from that man.

But Nora never wanted to be saved.

"For the record," Nora said, breaking the awkward silence, "I'm only here because he wanted me to come see you. He wants us to get over our problems."

"How thoughtful of him. Now when is he planning on getting over his problems?"

"He doesn't have any problems. Except that he's up for bishop, a position he doesn't want."

"I'd hardly worry about that. God would never allow such a man to take a position of power."

"That's true. God's very good about making sure only saints get to rule kingdoms and countries."

"You lost your mind and your faith when you went to his bed."

"Neither actually," Nora retorted. "Just my virginity, and I sure as hell don't miss it."

"Ellie—"

"This is ridiculous. He's the one who's lost his mind if he thinks you and I are ever going to work this out. I love him. He's a good man. He's the best man I've ever known. I know you don't get what we are, but I don't care. It's not your private life, it's mine."

"I've accepted that, obviously. Otherwise I would have called the bishop on him years ago."

Nora clenched her jaw to keep quiet. The reason her mother hadn't called the bishop on Søren had nothing to do with what she did or didn't believe. The day her mother discovered the truth about her and Søren, Nora had threatened that if her mother did anything to harm Søren in any way, Nora would leave forever and her mother would never see her again. The threat worked, although only God knew why. When they did see each other, they always fought…just like this.

"Ellie…" Her mother stopped in her tracks and turned around. Nora avoided eye contact at first. She hated seeing her mother like this, swathed in a wool habit, her hair covered with a wimple, her entire body hidden in a sea of fabric.

"What, Mother?"

"Can you just try to love someone or even let someone love you who doesn't want to hurt you? Is that too much to ask?"

Nora bit her bottom lip and didn't answer. The question hit far too close to home for her.

"Nora? Will you answer me if I call you Nora?" her mother asked in a voice soft with concern. At the utterance of the name she'd chosen instead of the one her mother had given her, Nora blinked and two tears fell from her eyes and to the ground.

"I tried," Nora whispered hoarsely. The muscles in her stomach clenched and her throat tightened.

"You did?" Her mother sounded both shocked and happy. "Who was it?"

Nora swiped at her cheek.

"His name's Wesley. He worked for me. But it was more than that. He was my best friend. And…" Nora paused for a breath. "I love him so much. He got sick once and I couldn't find him. And I'd never prayed so hard for anything in my life, prayed that he would be okay."

"He loved you too?"

Nora nodded. "Like crazy. I didn't realize it for a long time. I never thought someone that sweet and pure really would ever want someone like me. But he didn't see me like that. He didn't see Nora Sutherlin who writes erotica and does kink… I was just his Nora, his crazy friend he wanted to love and be with and keep safe. I think he would have stayed with me forever if I hadn't kicked him out."

"Why…why would you kick him out of your life if you loved him so much? If he loved you?"

"Because all that kid wanted was to love me and not hurt me. And you have no idea how much that hurts someone like me. And I wanted to love him without hurting him… and I hurt him so badly. He deserved better than me. I made him go."

Nora flinched as her mother reached out and cupped her face in her hands as she had so many times when Nora was still Ellie, still a child, still needed a mother's touch.

"My Ellie… You sent him away on a fool's errand. There is no one better than you, my beautiful girl. Not in all of God's creation."

Only her years of training at Søren's feet had instilled enough self-control into Nora to keep her from collapsing into her mother's arms.

Nora crossed her arms over her chest and stared past her mother and tried to think of anything and anyone but Wesley.

"It's for the best," she finally said. "Whatever the reason we broke up, it's for the best. Wesley…he…"

"You still love him, don't you?"

Nora touched her face and came away with her fingers wet with tears. She held out her hand and let her mother see them.

"Many waters…"

Her mother took Nora's hand in hers and squeezed.

"I never saw you cry over him, that year you were here. Not one tear."

"Some hurts are too deep for tears."

Her mother shook her head.

"Or maybe not deep enough. Try, Ellie. Try for me. Just

once, try to be with someone who makes you cry like this, out of love. Not out of pain or fear. Is that too much to ask?"

Nora shrugged and shook her head.

"It's too late. It's been so long I'm sure he's moved on by now. I hope he has, anyway."

"Liar," her mother teased and Nora laughed. Laughed? Laughed with her mother while talking about a guy? So shit like this did happen in real life, not just movies. Who knew?

"I have to go," Nora said. "Things to do. People to beat. It was good to see you again."

Her mother clasped her hands in front of her in a posture of resigned piety.

"Of course. Try not to let another six years pass without coming to visit again."

"I didn't think they'd let me back in after all I pulled." Nora grinned, remembering all the trouble she'd caused back here behind the gates where no men could come.

"Are you kidding? They still talk about you. You've given us six years of dinner conversation."

"I live to serve." Nora bobbed a curtsy before heading back toward the back doors. She walked quickly, wanting to be out of this world and back into hers as soon as possible. All these celibate women freaked her out. She couldn't imagine giving up sex for a higher power. Even her Wesley had given up waiting and had surely slept with his sexy older girlfriend by now. The thought of another woman laying her hands on her Wesley put almost murderous thoughts in Nora's head, thoughts she had no right to have.

They walked through the motherhouse toward the gate. Her mother opened the door that led back to the real world, to the unconsecrated ground where Nora lived.

"I'll come visit again. Soon, I promise," Nora said. "Can

I bring you anything? Smuggle in anything? Pizza? Swedish fish? Pot? Anything?"

Her mother smiled.

"Just my daughter, happy and in one piece."

Nora indicted her body with a sweeping gesture of her hands.

"One piece," she said.

"And happy?"

"Believe it or not, yes. Maybe not by your definition, but by mine."

"Then I can live with that."

Nora paused and looked at her mother. She wanted to say something more, say something else, but she couldn't find the words. Or she knew the words but didn't have the courage to say them.

"I'll see you later, Mom."

"Oh, Ellie?"

"What, Mom?" Nora turned back to her and gasped as her mother slapped her hard and quick across the cheek.

At first Nora couldn't speak from shock alone.

"That seems to be the only way you let someone tell them they love you. So be it," her mother said, lowering her hand.

Nora stood up straight and smiled.

"That didn't feel like love to me," Nora said, stepping through the gate. "Just felt amateur. Next time I visit, we'll work on your technique."

Nora strode to her car and fought tears the entire way. She refused to believe her mother was right. She wasn't going to give up Søren simply to satisfy her mother and society's restrictive, vanilla, fucking boring definition of what love was supposed to be.

Didn't matter anyway. The only vanilla guy she'd ever loved was Wesley, and she would never see him again. Søren surely wouldn't allow it. Not if she told him the truth that her feelings for Wesley crept along inside her heart like the snake in the garden. Life with Søren was paradise, a dark, dangerous paradise but still, a perfect naked Eden.

"Almost perfect," she whispered to no one as she sat behind the wheel of her car. She stuck her key into the ignition but before she turned the car on, she heard the ominous sounds of Toccata and Fugue in D Minor.

Nora snatched her phone out of her bag.

"Søren…" she breathed with relief. "God, I've missed—"

"Tell me the truth, little one. Have you made your peace with Wesley?"

Nora exhaled. She and Wesley would never be together. And she could live with that. For this man and what they had, she would live with that.

"Yes, sir."

He then spoke the words she'd been waiting all summer to hear.

"Come home to me."

24

Nora nearly broke the sound barrier driving back to Griffin's estate. Once there she took only three seconds to listen at the door to Griffin's bedroom. She heard Michael laugh and then silence, heavy silence. She'd let the boys have their privacy. Scribbling a note, she pushed it under the door, letting them know Søren had given her the all clear to come home.

She packed fast and hit the road faster. After nearly two months apart, Nora couldn't wait another minute to see Søren. She had to touch him, kiss him, let his arms remind her that she belonged to him and him alone. Once she felt him inside her again, Nora could let go of those traitorous thoughts about Wesley and her regret that she'd let him go too easily, too soon.

When she arrived at the rectory, night had already fallen. She parked her car in the copse of trees that shielded her and the house from prying eyes.

Into the house and up the stairs she ran, her shoes clicking loudly on the hardwood. Her heart thudded against her rib cage, her blood burned in her veins. After almost twenty years, Søren could still stir her passions like no one else she had ever or would ever love.

She didn't even get all the way to his bedroom. He must have heard her shoes on the hardwood because he stepped into the hallway and met her halfway. Without any words they came to each other, arms holding, hands grasping, lips and tongues seeking and finding. She dragged her fingers through his hair. His shirt tore in her frenzy to get to his skin. Søren bit at her collarbone and gripped her thighs so furiously she cried out. Pain...of course pain. He had to hurt her before he could make love to her. Søren didn't have a vanilla side. He had to play hard to get hard, as she'd told Kingsley years ago. And she was okay with that.

Søren slammed her against the wall and wrenched her skirt up. In seconds he was deep inside her. Nora wrapped her arms around his shoulders and held on to him as if her life depended on it, and in that moment she knew it did. If she ever let Søren go again...if she ever walked away from him again, she didn't know if she'd be strong enough to come back. So she held on tight, dug her fingernails into his shoulders, gasped his name in his ear and gave herself over to the brutal thrusts that would leave her bruised, inside and out.

When she came, she breathed his name with her eyes closed. And even after he'd spent himself inside her, he still held her in his arms, pinned to the wall.

"My little one," he whispered as he kissed her cheek, her eyes.

Slowly he pulled out of her and lowered her to the floor. They straightened their clothes as their bodies disentangled. Holding her breath, Nora waited.

She didn't have to wait long.

Søren took a step backward. And then another.

"Hands and knees," he said and Nora knelt gracefully on the floor.

He'd asked her two years ago on their anniversary how she would come back to him if she ever returned to his bed.

If you come back to me, little one, will you run, or will you crawl?

I'll fly, she'd answered.

Tonight as she returned to him, she crawled.

Michael spent nearly three days in Griffin's bedroom. They came up for air only for food and showers and the occasional glimpse of sunlight before retreating back into bed. The second night together, Griffin strung Michael to the bedpost and flogged him for the first time. And Michael had thought Nora had a vicious flogging arm. Even getting his wrists tattooed hadn't hurt that much.

He loved every single second of it. Nothing scared him anymore about being with Griffin. The sex part took a little getting used to but the incredible pleasure of having Griffin inside him was worth all the work and occasional grimacing. The S&M they would figure out. The love…the love he had no complaints about. Michael basked in Griffin's love, wallowed it in, let his heart that had been so thirsty for affection drink in every drop. Every morning Griffin told him, "I love you." Every night he said the same. And all Michael had to do was come anywhere near Griffin's reach if he wanted to be pulled into the two most wicked-strong arms he'd ever encountered in his life. Ever since his suicide attempt, Michael had felt near-constant loneliness, anxiety, and a sense that while people like Father S and Nora would understand him, no one ever truly loved him. But with Griffin he finally felt loved, at peace and safe.

But on day three, Griffin did and said the one thing guaranteed to shatter Michael's bliss.

"I don't do secret relationships, Mick. If we're going to do this, I want to meet your mom. Pack up. We're out of here."

The words were said in a tone that brooked no challenge. Michael had known it was too good to be true anyway. Once Griffin saw how truly humble his origins were—the tiny house, the ten-year-old car in the driveway, the shabby furniture—he'd realize how different they were and how little Michael belonged in Griffin's world.

In tense silence Michael stared out the window of Griffin's Porsche as they drove from the estate to Wakefield. Griffin seemed to sense Michael's anxiety and left him alone with his thoughts.

When they hit Wakefield, Griffin cruised by Sacred Heart but they found the church empty. Michael guessed Father S and Nora were still in bed enjoying their reunion. He wished he could say the same for him and Griffin. Before leaving the church, Michael went to the shrine of the Virgin Mary in the corner of the narthex and lit a candle in prayer.

Mary, Mother of God, Michael prayed in his heart. *Please help my mom. Please help me and Griffin.* That was it. He had no idea what else to pray. He knew he didn't want to hurt his mother, but he didn't want her hurting Griffin, either. So many horrible scenarios ran through Michael's mind as Griffin drove them to Michael's house. His mother would lose her shit, for sure. She'd probably forbid Michael from seeing Griffin. And Michael would refuse. So what? Move out? Live with Griffin? Seemed a little early for that. Of course, there'd be no Griffin after all this shit with his family went down.

Griffin pulled onto the street and Michael swallowed a wave of nausea. The nausea worsened with every house they passed on the way to his. When they reached Michael's home the nausea turned to dread, shock and panic.

"Oh, fuck," Michael breathed as he noticed a familiar and truly unwelcome sight.

"What, Mick?" Griffin asked, grabbing Michael's knee.

"My dad's here."

Nora stretched across Søren's chest and released a blissful sigh.

"Thank you, sir," she purred, turning her head to give him a quick bite under his collarbone.

"Do I want to know what specifically you're thanking me for or should I simply say you're welcome?"

Nora moved completely on top of Søren and pressed her entire body into his as he wrapped his arms around her. She loved Søren's height. At six foot four he stood exactly one foot taller than her. She could lie on top of him, stomach to stomach, and her head could tuck right under his chin.

"Well, I lost count after the seventh orgasm. And you also did that thing I like with the thing."

"No thanks necessary. I rather enjoyed it myself."

Nora raised her head and looked Søren in the eyes.

"Just thank you…for being you," she said. "The world is a better, more interesting place with you in it."

He smiled as he dropped a kiss on top of her head.

"And the world is certainly a wilder, more beautiful place with you in it, little one."

"Really?"

"Quite."

"Say something else nice about me. I'm fishing for compliments, if you haven't noticed."

"I did notice," he said as he rolled over quickly, pinning Nora onto her back. "Fishing for compliments is against the rules. Continue and I'll have to punish you."

"I don't remember that rule, sir."

"I've just made it up."

Laughing, Nora raised her head and graced Søren's lips with a kiss.

She pulled back and batted her eyelashes at him.

"Tell me more about my eyes."

"Your eyes are…" he began before suddenly stopping and sliding out of bed.

"What? My eyes are what?"

Søren started to get dressed.

"I'll tell you after my meeting." He bent over and kissed her quick as he buttoned his shirt.

"Meeting?" Nora scrambled into a sitting position. "What meeting? I thought you said the search committee had decided on Father Peterson. No more meetings."

Søren slipped his Roman collar into place.

"They did. Thank God. This meeting isn't with any committee. I promised Suzanne one more long talk."

Nora narrowed her eyes.

"This reporter bitch is getting on my last damn nerve. Why can't she leave you alone?"

"She's not the enemy. Especially now that she no longer thinks I am the enemy."

"Well, if we've got her fooled that much," Nora began. Søren shot her a vicious look that nearly set her giggling. "Then why's she still hanging around?"

"She has a few final questions for me. After all I've put her through this summer, I feel she deserves some answers."

Søren headed to the door. Nora had a sudden thought and bolted upright in bed.

"Søren? Wait a sec. Let me go talk to her."

"Mick? You okay?" Griffin laid his hand on Michael's knee and squeezed.

Michael shook his head.

"No."

The hand on his knee moved to Michael's face.

"Look at me," Griffin said in almost a whisper. Michael reluctantly turned his head to meet Griffin's eyes. "I've got this. I won't let anything bad happen."

Something in Griffin's tone made Michael almost believe it.

"Okay."

Griffin smiled.

"Good. Let's get this over with. I want to fuck you before dinner."

With a playful swat on Michael's knee, Griffin exited the car and came around to Michael's side. With extreme reluctance, Michael opened the door and stepped out onto the sidewalk. Griffin held out his hand. Michael stared at it. They'd never been out in public before. In bed they'd held hands… and every other body part. But here? On his street? In his house? In front of his parents?

"We're in this together, Mick. I love you."

Michael started at the words. They seemed to come echoing from deep inside a canyon. Or the canyon was inside him and the words filled it and him and finally muted the voice inside him that warned he'd never be loved for who and what he was.

Without further hesitation, Michael took Griffin's hand as they walked up to the house. Michael opened the door without knocking and he and Griffin stepped inside.

He heard voices in the kitchen. Quiet, angry voices.

"They're fighting," Michael whispered. "They're always fighting."

"They're divorced," Griffin whispered back. "What do they have to fight about?"

Michael swallowed.

"Me."

They stepped into the kitchen and both Michael's mom

and dad immediately stopped talking. He mother's face was a mask of shock. His father's face wore an expression of confusion that quickly turned to fury at the sight of Michael's hand in Griffin's.

"Michael…" his father began.

"I'm Griffin Fiske, your son's boyfriend," Griffin said, smiling hugely at Michael's parents. "Nice to meet you both."

"No. No way," Michael's father said. "No way in hell is this happening. Michael, what are you—"

He rushed forward and Michael braced himself. But Griffin stepped between them and raised his chin.

"I guess you didn't hear me," Griffin repeated. "I'm Griffin Fiske. I'm your son's boyfriend. Nice to meet you."

This time he said the words without smiling and with the subtle hint of a threat in this voice. Michael had always thought of his father as the big bad dad—taller than him, more muscular—but compared to Griffin, he seemed slight and short.

"Who the hell are you?" his father demanded.

Griffin smiled dangerously while Michael eased out from behind Griffin and tried to get closer to his mother, who was still standing in stunned silence.

"I feel like I'm repeating myself. Mick, am I repeating myself?" Griffin asked.

"Mom, Dad." Michael tried speaking up. "Griffin and I—"

"Shut up, Michael," his father ordered, "or I swear to God—"

What Michael's father was about to swear the world would never know as Griffin raised a hand and snapped his fingers loudly in Michael's father's face.

The snap actually shut Michael's father up momentarily.

"Don't do that," Griffin said in a tone of casual menace.

"Don't tell him to shut up. Bad things will happen to people who don't treat Mick the way he deserves."

"Don't you dare tell me how to talk to my son. My fucked-up, sick son."

Michael flinched at his father's words. And next to him his mother also flinched.

"Ken, please," Michael's mother began. "Let's stay calm and talk about this. We've always known Michael wasn't—"

"Normal?" his father said. "Obviously not. And it's your fault, Melissa. You let him grow his hair long. You kept him out of Catholic school. You coddled him. Turned him into a goddamn fa—"

Michael and his mother again flinched in unison as Griffin quickly and efficiently put Michael's father into the wall. His shoulder hit the tile with a dull thud.

"Griffin, don't," Michael pleaded, not wanting the cops to come.

But Griffin didn't pay any heed. He put his hand in the center of Michael's father's chest and held him against the wall, pinned like an insect in a shadowbox.

"I told you bad things happen when people don't treat Mick nicely," Griffin said, stepping up to Michael's father and eyeing him menacingly. "I love your son. And I'll break you if you ever even look at him sideways again. Your 'not normal' son is the most talented untrained artist I've ever seen. He's intelligent, an amazing skater, has a great sense of humor and is the kindest, most humble person I've ever met. I'm so in love with him I can't even think straight. Which is fine since obviously I'm not straight. And neither is he. Anyway, I'm rambling. I do that sometimes. Hard to shut me up. The point is..." Griffin said, and pointed hard at Michael's father's chest, hard enough the tip of his finger would certainly leave a small round bruise. "Your opinions on...everything really, are not welcome here. Michael's fine. I'm taking care of him now. Shoo."

With both hands, Griffin made a dismissive gesture as if Michael's father were simply a fly or a feral cat hanging about.

"That is my son." Michael's father stabbed an angry finger in Michael's direction.

"He's my property."

"Your what?"

Michael cringed outwardly even as his heart fluttered inside. Being claimed as Griffin's property spoke to him on the deepest levels.

"My. Property. He belongs to me. Completely by his choice. And you are no longer relevant in this equation," Griffin continued. "You make him feel bad. Ergo you are not allowed to ever be in his presence until such a time comes as you can control your insecurities enough to keep your mouth shut around Michael."

"I've been paying to keep him in food and clothing with a roof over his head since the day he was born."

"Money?" Griffin stood up straighter. "This is about money? Money I have. How much do you want for him?"

"Excuse me?" Michael's father repeated.

"How much do you want for your son? I'll write you a check right now to buy you out of his life forever."

"Griffin, don't give him a penny." The words came out without warning. "He doesn't deserve it."

He doesn't deserve it. Had Michael actually said that out loud? Before he would have said, or at least thought, *I don't deserve it. I don't deserve you spending a penny on me.* But Griffin valued him so highly, treated him like the rarest and most precious possession…Michael started to think maybe he was.

"No, he doesn't deserve it," Griffin said, reaching into the back pocket of his jeans and pulling out his wallet. "But you deserve a life without him. Didn't you tell me he keeps a running total of the child support he's paid out on the checks? Where are we? What's the total?"

"Griffin…" Michael begged.

"Forty-two thousand, three-hundred dollars," Michael's mother said in a loud, clear voice, her eyes locked onto Griffin's. "And if I had the money, I'd give it all back to him to get rid of him too."

Michael watched as Griffin's and his mother's eyes met. Something passed between them that Michael saw but didn't understand.

"Let's round it up. Fifty thousand?" Griffin grabbed Michael's father by the shoulder and turned him around, pushing his chest into the wall. Then using his back as a flat surface, Griffin filled out his check. "I'm feeling generous. We'll make it sixty-nine thousand. I just love writing 69s. I'll even put that in the memo. For sixty-nining your beautiful son."

Griffin spun Michael's father back around, ripped out the check and stuffed it in his father's pocket.

"I'm good for it," Griffin said. "Aren't I, Mick? Didn't you say this guy here worked in a stock brokerage?"

Michael nodded. "At Hamilton's."

"Nice," Griffin said in approval. "My father is John Fiske. Heard of him?"

Michael's father didn't answer in words but his wide eyes confessed he knew exactly who Griffin's father was and just how much money Griffin was good for.

"Go, Dad," Michael said. "You don't want me to be your son any more than I want you to be my father. Now you don't have be my father anymore."

"You just got dumped." Griffin patted Michael's father on top of his head. "Sucks, I know. Oh, goodbye."

Once again, Griffin made the shooing gesture. Michael's father shot everyone in the room a look of pure hatred.

He stormed out of the kitchen and down the hall, Griffin following hard on his heels, no doubt wanting to make sure he actually left. Michael and his mother trailed behind Griffin.

Out on the front lawn, Michael's father turned around.

"It's a sin, you know that right?" Michael's father said, looking back and forth between Michael and Griffin. "Sex between two men. It's against nature and against God. It's an abomination even. You go to church, Michael. You know that."

"If it's an abomination, Dad, you're just doing it wrong. Bear down hard, then release. It'll fit better." Michael nearly shouted the words.

Michael's father shook his head in disgust as he strode to his car and drove off. Griffin looked at Michael and they both broke into unrestrained laughter.

"Do you usually yell sodomy tips on your front lawn?" Griffin asked, dragging Michael in for a quick kiss.

"What? You don't?" Michael was still laughing when he pulled out of Griffin's embrace. It was then he saw his mother standing on the porch in silence. "Mom…oh, Mom, I'm so sorry…" Michael said, his heart sinking through the ground. "I didn't even think…and the neighbors, I'm—"

Michael's mother took two steps forward and wrapped him into a hug.

He froze, unable to remember the last time his mother had held him like this.

"Mom?" Michael tentatively returned the hug.

"I missed you, kid. Long summer without you."

Michael glanced at Griffin, who only shrugged and mouthed, *Women,* at him.

His mother didn't seem ready or willing to let him go yet. So Michael leaned into the hug and closed his eyes.

"I missed you too, Mom."

Finally she pulled away and wiped a tear off her face. Turning to Griffin she held out her hand.

"It's nice to meet you, Griffin."

Griffin looked down at her hand and rolled his eyes. He took a step forward and hugged her so hard she came off the ground.

"Griffin, you should put my mom down."

Griffin put Michael's mother back down on her feet.

Michael looked at Griffin and then at his mother and back again.

"So," Michael said. "Lunch?"

25

Suzanne entered Sacred Heart's sanctuary and found it empty. She'd made one final appointment to talk to him; she had a few questions left to ask, but the questions weren't why she came. What she really wanted was to apologize for her suspicions and thank him for helping her believe, if not in God again, at least in one priest.

Wandering the perimeter of the sanctuary, she studied the plaques on the wall, images of Christ's passion with Roman numerals engraved on them. She stopped at one plaque that showed a woman kneeling in front of Jesus holding out her veil. Suzanne furrowed her brow and tried to remember the woman's name. She couldn't remember the last time she'd prayed the Stations of the Cross. Maybe she never had.

"What's your name?" she asked out loud as she started to dig out her iPhone.

"Veronica," came a voice from behind her.

Suzanne spun around and saw a woman standing at the end of a pew with her arms crossed over her chest. The woman wore a tight black skirt that hugged her shapely hips, strappy high heels, a fitted red blouse and a mysterious little grin on her stunningly lovely face. The woman looked familiar. Extremely familiar.

"Oh, God," Suzanne said, suddenly making the connection. "You're Nora Sutherlin."

The woman nodded as she uncrossed her arms and pushed a strand of wavy black hair behind her ear.

"Guilty," she said with the kind of smile that told Suzanne this was a woman who had possibly never experienced a moment's guilt in her life. "And you're Suzanne Kanter. You're even more beautiful than he said you were."

Suzanne blushed and shoved her shaking hands into the back pockets of her jeans. As intimidating as she found Father Stearns, she'd never felt half as nervous as she suddenly felt around Nora Sutherlin.

"Um…" Suzanne began and rolled her eyes at her own awkwardness. "Well, you are as beautiful as he said you were."

Nora Sutherlin, unlike her, didn't blush. She only stared at Suzanne with her darkly intelligent eyes.

"One question," Sutherlin said.

Suzanne blinked.

"One question? You have one question for me?"

Sutherlin shook her head.

"You've been hounding him all summer. Following him. Breaking into the rectory. You even went to see his sister. You're tenacious. I can appreciate that. It is, however, time for you to leave us alone. You know he's no danger to his congregation. I can only assume you're still here for other reasons. Reasons I don't have to guess at because, let's be honest, we've both seen him."

Suzanne's blush deepened but she couldn't deny the truth

of Sutherlin's words. Her attraction to Father Stearns was still too fresh a wound to bother denying.

"Yes," Suzanne admitted. "I've seen him."

Sutherlin raised her eyebrow, obviously hearing the deeper truth to the words. She smiled again, uncrossed her arms and sat on the arm of the pew.

"I said one question and that's exactly what I mean, Ms. Kanter. You can ask me one question—" Sutherlin held up a single finger "—and I'll answer it. Truthfully. Without subterfuge or disingenuousness. I will tell you the truth, the whole truth and nothing but the truth to whatever one question you ask me."

Suzanne's eyes went wide.

"Next you're going to tell me I won the lottery," she said, scarcely believing her ears.

"Only the truth lottery. But this prize comes with a price. I'll answer your question, but the answer will be off the record. And you can use nothing I tell you to hurt him. And you can take nothing that I tell you to find out more. If a single word of mine appears in print, I will have Kingsley destroy your career so thoroughly you won't even get a job as a weathergirl like your old professor suggested. Do you understand that?"

Swallowing hard, Suzanne nodded. She heard the threat in Sutherlin's voice and knew she meant every word. That she even knew about her old prof suggesting she become a weathergirl was a sign this woman's world was not one Suzanne needed to linger inside a moment longer than necessary.

"Also, once I give your answer," Sutherlin continued, "you will leave me, Kingsley and Søren alone. We will cease to exist to you. You will banish us from your thoughts, your memory, your conversation and your vocabulary. Can you accept that?"

She couldn't imagine completely banishing Father Stearns

from her memory. Her body still tingled when she thought of his hands on her arms. But she would try. For the sake of the truth, the whole truth, she would try.

"Okay. I accept. I'll be going to Iraq soon anyway. Time I moved on."

"Yes," Sutherlin said. "It is. Now ask your question, and we can all move on."

Suzanne didn't have to pause even one moment to think of her question.

"Are you and Father Stearns sleeping together?"

If she'd thought such an inquiry would faze Sutherlin, Suzanne was highly disappointed.

Sutherlin looked neither shocked nor scared at the question. She leveled her dark green eyes onto Suzanne's face.

"You really want to waste your one question on something you already know the answer to?" Sutherlin asked.

Suzanne's stomach fell a few inches. She'd hoped…believed… at least wanted to believe… But it didn't matter. Sutherlin had been a virgin even at age nineteen. Whenever she and her priest had become lovers, she'd been at least a legal adult.

"No, I suppose not." Suzanne sighed heavily. "How about this? The conflict of interest that's on that anonymous tip someone sent me—what is it? Is it his sister Elizabeth? She practically confessed to killing their father."

"She did kill their father, and she did confess to Søren. And Søren refused to reveal her confession. I overheard it at the funeral. And he's been worried for seventeen years that Elizabeth would find out I heard. But no, that's not the conflict of interest the church is worried about."

"Then what is it?"

"Søren's father was a very wealthy man when he died. He got half his wife's fortune in the divorce and with his ruthless business acumen, he'd trebled it by the time he died. And when he died, he left every single penny to his only son. Nearly half a billion dollars."

Suzanne gasped. "But…his father had sent him away after what happened with Elizabeth. Nearly killed him."

"True. But when his father had no more sons and had no relationship with either daughter, he had a change of…whatever he had in his chest in place of a heart. But the money wasn't a peace offering. It was a bribe. Priests take vows of poverty. To accept all that money, Søren would have had to leave the priesthood. For nothing and for no one will he ever leave the priesthood."

"So what did he do?"

Sutherlin grinned.

"What any good priest would do. He tithed. He gave ten percent of the money to the church. Five percent to his old Catholic school in Maine. And five percent to this diocese. The rest he split in half and gave to each sister. He kept not a single cent for himself."

Suzanne covered her mouth with her hand and turned away. In her head she quickly crunched the numbers. Five percent of five hundred million dollars was…

"Twenty-five million dollars," Suzanne breathed. She turned back around. "He gave that to this diocese?"

"He did. You know how it works. Parish priests get transferred all the time. Yet Søren's been here for almost twenty years. How does he get such an exemption? He bought it."

"I wondered why they hadn't moved him around, moved him up the ladder."

"He likes it here."

He likes his privacy, Suzanne realized.

"What would you call giving a promotion to a man who'd donated twenty-five million dollars to your corporation?" Sutherlin asked.

"A conflict of interest," Suzanne whispered. "I'd thought…
I thought he might be a predator. Or, you know, because…
with you he had…"

"Sex? You thought the conflict of interest was about sex?"
Sutherlin laughed as if that was the most ridiculous thing she'd
ever heard. "This is the Catholic Church, Ms. Kanter. And
the Catholic Church has been winking at sex for two thousand years. It's the money that makes them nervous."

Suzanne shook her head. Too many thoughts crashing about
inside it.

"He gave away it all? Every penny?"

Sutherlin nodded.

"He did. Stubborn asshole priest. When he and Marie-
Laure got married, he got access to his massive trust fund.
Once she died, he gave every penny of that away too. He
was born to be a priest. Money doesn't interest him. That's
the conflict of interest. Now if you'll excuse me, I'm going to
get on with my life without worrying about a reporter hurting Søren."

"You call him Søren?" Suzanne asked, the question coming out before she could stop it.

"Of course I do. It's his name. Why do you ask?"

"He said he only told his real name to the people closest to
him, to the people he trusted and who knew the real him."

"That's very true."

"How long have you called him Søren?"

Sutherlin's face softened as she turned her gaze away from
Suzanne to smile at the image of Veronica holding out her
veil to the fallen Christ.

After a long silence, Sutherlin looked back at Suzanne.

"Since the day we met."

Suzanne nodded and said nothing. Those five words told
Suzanne everything she needed to know. Father Stearns and

Nora Sutherlin had something, a connection, an intimacy... something deep and unexplainable, something untouchable, unreachable. The night that Suzanne had begged him to make love to her, he'd said that he did not belong to himself. She thought he'd meant he belonged to God or the Church. Now she knew he meant Nora Sutherlin.

"I'm leaving now," Sutherlin said. "And you should too."

"I'd like to at least tell him goodbye. Or am I not allowed?" Suzanne asked. The question held no sarcasm. Whatever Nora Sutherlin told her to do, she would do.

"I'll allow it. He does like you. I don't, but I'm a little biased."

"I can see that."

Sutherlin raised her chin at Suzanne's words and somehow knew she'd misspoken. Slowly Sutherlin walked toward her, her hips swaying with each step forward. She'd never been in the presence of a more immediately, viscerally sexual being in her life.

"No, you can't see that," Sutherlin said, coming to stand in front of her. "You can't see anything. Not me. Not him. Not us. We do not exist, remember? Do you know what I am?"

Suzanne shrugged her shoulders in confusion.

"You're...a writer."

"I am. I'm also one of the most famous dominatrixes in the entire world. I used to be Kingsley's number one. Did you know that?"

Suzanne swallowed again.

"I might have heard some rumors."

"Believe them," Sutherlin said. "And know they are only the tip of the iceberg. I once had a Texas cattle baron pay me fifty thousand dollars to brand him with his own branding iron. I had a Silicon Valley CEO pay me sixty thousand dollars to piss on his face. I have put the rich and the famous in the hospital. And they paid through the teeth for the privilege of it. I have a police file as thick as Kingsley's cock, and yet I've never been convicted of any crime as an adult. Why? The cops and the lawyers and the judges live in Kingsley's pocket. And one or two of them lived in mine. In the city, I can get away with murder."

Suzanne straightened her shoulders and looked Sutherlin directly in the eyes, something that took all of her courage.

"Are you threatening me, Ms. Sutherlin?"

Sutherlin only smiled.

"No. Of course not. All I'm saying is that I'll do anything to protect him. Anything at all. But there's no need to worry. I've hurt people. I've hurt them badly. I've left permanent scars on some clients. Some outer scars. Some inner. But all that pain I've inflicted…it was all consensual. I've never hurt anyone without their permission. All I'm saying, Ms. Kanter, is…" Sutherlin leaned forward and pressed the lightest, softest, most terrifying kiss onto Suzanne's lips before pulling back an inch and whispering, "There's a first time for everything."

And with that, Sutherlin took one step back. And another. Then she turned on her heel and walked out of the church.

Suzanne took a deep breath. She raised her hand and found it shaking. War zones, she reminded herself. She'd been in war zones. This woman shouldn't terrify her.

Determined to get a shred of her dignity back, Suzanne ran from the sanctuary and saw Nora Sutherlin heading toward a Porsche that had pulled up to the curb.

"Wait!" Suzanne called out and Sutherlin turned around.

"Yes?"

"Just one more question…please."

Sutherlin smirked.

"One more. But make it a good one."

Suzanne nodded.

"What's he like…you know, in bed? I have to know. I've never been so attracted to someone in my life. And I'll never get to be with him. Can you just tell me that?"

Sutherlin looked positively shocked by the question.

"In bed? Me and Søren? We aren't sleeping together," Sutherlin said.

"But…but I asked you if you were. And you said not to ask questions I already knew the answer to."

Sutherlin nodded.

"Exactly. Of course we aren't lovers." Sutherlin slid on a pair of chic black sunglasses. "He's a priest. That's gross."

Once more Sutherlin turned on her heel and walked away. This time Suzanne let her go.

She watched as Sutherlin reached the Porsche. Two men got out of the car. No, not two men. One man and one teenage boy. The man was Griffin Fiske. And the teenage boy was… Suzanne narrowed her eyes at him. A beautiful young man, whoever he was. Almost angelic in appearance. Shoulder-length black hair, eyes so brightly silver she could see them shining from ten feet away, pale skin, thin but only in that teenage boy way…even his wrists still had that teenage boy delicateness to them. Suzanne looked more closely at his wrists and saw they bore gauze bandages. Bandages? She made the connection finally. Michael Dimir—the boy who'd slit his wrists in the sanctuary—he would be seventeen now. Griffin Fiske and Nora Sutherlin gave each other a quick kiss as the boy, Michael, unwrapped the gauze from his wrists. Sutherlin gave his wrists a thumbs-up before she kissed him quickly on the lips. The boy leaned back against Griffin Fiske's chest as Fiske wrapped an arm possessively around him.

Michael Dimir…with Griffin Fiske? What the hell…

"Jesus, what kind of church is this?" Suzanne asked herself out loud.

"My church," said a familiar voice from behind her.

Suzanne only smiled as Nora Sutherlin patted the boy, Michael Dimir, on the cheek. She looked back, raised her sunglasses, gave Suzanne an arrogant wink and headed toward a BMW in the parking lot.

"Do you ever just want to beat the hell out of the woman?" Suzanne asked.

Father Stearns released a heavy, much put-upon sigh.

"Every day of my life."

Laughing, Suzanne turned around and faced him. She found him holding a small but exquisite bouquet of white roses.

"For me?" she teased.

"No." The slight smile left his face and he gave her a look of the deepest compassion. "For Adam. I think it's time you visited your brother's grave."

Suzanne fell silent. Her throat clenched. Tears welled in her eyes.

"I will go with you. You won't be alone," Father Stearns said as he handed her the flowers. Suzanne held them to her chest.

"Okay," she whispered. She looked up at him and tried to smile through her tears. "He's buried—"

"I know where he is. I also know where he's buried. We'll go now. I'll meet you there."

Suzanne couldn't even speak to thank him. She merely headed to her car and drove to the city cemetery where the family had laid her brother to rest. Public ground. Unconsecrated ground. When she made it to the graveside, Father Stearns was already there with his perfectly blond head bowed in silent prayer.

"I still hate the Church for refusing him a Catholic burial," Suzanne admitted as she laid the flowers on the grave. While on her knees she pulled some stray weeds off the tombstone.

Adam Gabriel Kanter. Born July 3, 1978, died November 1, 2006. The Lord hath given him rest from all his enemies. II Samuel 7:1

"I can't blame you," Father Stearns said. "But I can help there."

Suzanne looked up and saw Father Stearns pull a vial of water out of his pocket. He opened it and sprinkled it over the ground.

Holy water.

Suzanne added her own tears to the holy water that he poured onto the ground.

"You'll pray for him, won't you?" Suzanne asked. "I can't. I just can't believe enough to pray. But it would mean something to me if you did."

"I will pray for him and for you, Suzanne, every day."

"I'll never see you again, will I?"

Father Stearns didn't smile.

"I think our paths were meant to cross. And perhaps it's best they do not cross again. Not in this life anyway."

Suzanne took the hint.

"Thank you…for everything. For Adam. For being a good priest, a good man."

"I'm as human and as fallible as anyone. But thank you. Your faith in me is heartening. Maybe someday you'll find your faith in Him again."

"Maybe," she said. "But don't hold your breath."

Father Stearns nodded. He reached out and caressed the arch of her cheekbone.

"Goodbye, Suzanne. If you ever truly need me, you know where to find me."

"War zones," she reminded him with a smile. "I can take care of myself."

His fingers grazed her lips like the softest kiss.

"I know you can."

He dropped his hand and started to walk off. At the edge of a cemetery she saw a Rolls Royce waiting.

"Your trust fund," Suzanne called out suddenly remembering one last question. "Nora Sutherlin said you gave your trust fund away. Who did you give it to?"

Father Stearns kept walking.

"Rolls Royces don't buy themselves, do they, Suzanne?" He stopped in his tracks, turned around and winked at her before walking off again toward the Rolls.

The wink seemed so familiar. Nora Sutherlin had winked at her just like that.

Just...like...that...

And Suzanne realized she'd been had.

She stared after him, after the Catholic priest who'd single-handedly bankrolled New York's kink Underground. The story of the century walked on and walked off. With one phone call she could ruin him, ruin the diocese, bring more shame and infamy onto the Catholic Church than all the more horrible but less torrid sex scandals combined.

"Nora Sutherlin..." she sighed as she watched the erotica writer's lover get into the backseat of the Rolls. "You lucky fucking bitch."

Suzanne turned back to Adam's grave and smiled.

"I miss you, big bro," she said. She kissed her fingertips and touched the tombstone. She left it at that. Next time she came by the grave, she'd stay a little longer.

Suzanne pulled out her cell and hit the first number on her speed dial.

"Hey, you," she said when Patrick answered.

"Hey, you okay?" Patrick asked.

"I'm actually amazing. Wrapped up the whole Father Stearns story once and for all."

"Good. Done with that?"

"Completely. Wasn't even the sister. You were right. He'd donated some money that raised the church's eyebrow. He won't be bishop although he probably should be. But whatever. Want to get some dinner?"

She tensed when Patrick didn't answer immediately.

"I don't know. Is this dinner? Or is this a date?"

Suzanne returned the pause with a pause before answering. "It's a date."

Michael obediently closed his eyes and tried not to sneeze or flinch.

"This is ridiculous, Nora," he said. "I feel like I'm getting married."

Nora grinned.

"Nothing so formal or terrifying. Collaring ceremonies here at The 8th Circle are just an excuse to publicly humiliate a sub and razz a dominant for falling in love. Griffin is way overdue for much razzing."

"Is the guyliner part of the humiliation?" Michael opened his eyes when Nora finished adorning them with eyeliner.

"I know Griffin. He'll pee himself when he sees you in eyeliner. One of his weaknesses."

"Awesome." He took a quick breath. "I can't believe this is real. It is real, right?"

Nora took a step back and angled his face into the low light. She nodded approval at her own handiwork.

"Yes. Very real. And it'll feel very real when it stops being fun. The first time Griffin puts his foot down about something you don't like…the whole collared thing really sinks in. But it's worth it. You find the right dom, and it's completely worth it. Just enjoy the honeymoon period while it lasts."

Michael looked at Nora as she capped her eyeliner pencil

and put it away. She looked so weird tonight wearing all white. White skirt, white blouse, white collar around her neck. He was in all white too—white pants, no shoes, white button-down shirt untucked with the sleeves rolled up to the elbows.

"He's taking me to Key West for a week tomorrow. Speaking of honeymoons."

Nora adjusted her collar.

"Good choice for same-sex couples. Have you two figured out the school/living situation in all this excitement?"

"Yeah. He's getting a new place that'll be easy to get to by the train. I'll just be in the dorms during the week and be his on the weekends."

"You going to tell everybody at school that you're the bi-sexual collared submissive of the richest trust fund baby in New York?"

"Maybe not this semester."

Nora grinned.

"Good call. Your mom handling everything okay?"

"Yeah. Better than I thought."

"Mothers can surprise you sometimes."

Michael went over to his backpack and pulled a photo folder out.

"Here. I better give this back to you. Griffin might snoop."

"Thank you," she said, taking the photo back. She opened the burgundy folder and smiled at the picture. "God, they were sexy as hell, weren't they?"

"Seriously," Michael agreed as he looked over Nora's shoulder at the black-and-white photograph. In the picture he saw an eighteen-year-old Father S sitting casually in an armchair in a dark suit, tidy and pin neat. At his feet sat another boy, only a year younger, with longer dark hair and his Catholic school uniform artfully rumpled with the jacket abandoned, the tie loose and the collar open.

"Kingsley and Søren…I think this is the only picture ever taken of them as teenagers. Looks like they were studying, working on something. Wonder if anyone else other than us kinksters get it."

Michael had gotten it. He understood. Young Kingsley's neck bore two bruises that anyone without any kink experience would simply assume were hickeys or love bites. But Michael knew those marks, had borne them on his own skin. Lips hadn't made them, nor teeth. A thumb and index finger pressing into the skin had left those bruises. Kingsley had been pinned down by his neck during sex with a young Father S.

"We all have to start somewhere, right?" Nora asked, closing the folder and tucking the photograph away. "Søren and Kingsley have no shame at all that they were lovers when they were kids. Kingsley just doesn't want anyone to know he's a switch."

"I won't tell. I promise. Not even Griffin."

"I know," Nora said. "We better go. They're waiting."

Together they left Father S's private dungeon at The 8th Circle, the club where he, Nora, Griffin and Kingsley did their hardest playing a couple of times a week.

A few doors down was Griffin's private dungeon. Michael had already been warned he'd be spending a lot of time naked and tied up in this room. Even now as he entered it unfettered and fully clothed, he felt naked and bound. Nakedly vulnerable. Bound to Griffin.

Looking around as the entered the room, he saw Father S and Kingsley Edge talking to each other in hushed tones. Both of them wore all black apart from Father S's white collar and a white handkerchief in Kingsley's pocket. An incredibly beautiful woman with ebony skin wearing a jaw-dropping ivory dress sat on a black leather sofa. Kingsley snapped his fingers and the woman rose and came to his side. It must be Juliette.

Nora had told him about her—Kingsley's Haitian secretary who kept both Kingsley and all of his business interests in line outside the bedroom while Kingsley kept her in line inside. Juliette gave him a dazzling smile and Michael's knees nearly buckled from the force of her beauty.

Nora guided Michael to the center of the room and stood next to him. Griffin entered, wearing black pants and a black silk shirt and no shoes. He took one look at Michael and made a beeline for him. Before they could meet, Nora interposed herself between them.

"Whoa, slow down, Fiske. You don't get to kiss the sub yet. Down, boy," Nora ordered and Griffin playfully bared his teeth at her.

"Then let's get this over with. I need to kiss him. Now. Right now," Griffin said, trying to step around Nora.

"Patience is a virtue, Griffin," Father S said as they all formed a loose circle around Griffin and Michael.

"I haven't seen him all day. That's as much patience as you'll get from me," Griffin said.

"It's a start," Father S said. "Go ahead."

Nora stepped to the side and Griffin pulled a black leather collar out of his pocket, clasped it around Michael's neck, buckled it and locked it shut. Michael closed his eyes as Griffin's arms came around him.

"I love you," Griffin whispered as the tiny lock in the back of the collar clicked shut. "And you belong to me."

"Yes, sir," Michael said, smiling. He opened his eyes and Griffin kissed him deeply, passionately and without reservation.

"Gross," Nora said. "Those two guys are kissing. That's disgusting."

"It's quite unnatural," Kingsley agreed. "I shudder at the very thought."

"Is that so?" Juliette asked in her rich, melodic Haitian accent. "Then what were you doing with that young man last night?"

"Business meeting. We were discussing the ledgers at the Möbius."

"While naked?" Juliette asked, batting her eyelashes.

"It was an informal meeting," Kingsley said.

Michael had to stop kissing so he could laugh. At least here among these weirdos and perverts, he and Griffin would always find acceptance. And maybe if they were lucky, others would accept them too.

"Griffin Randolph Fiske," Father S began, "you are now the proud owner of Michael Dimir. He is like a son to me. If you hurt him in any way that he does not want, you will answer to me."

"And me," Nora said, stepping forward to give both Michael and Griffin quick kisses on the cheek.

"Et moi," said Kingsley.

"Et moi aussi," said Juliette.

Michael swallowed a lump in his throat. He knew Griffin would never do anything to harm him, but it moved him beyond words to know he had all these amazing people on his side if he did.

"Don't worry. Not going to happen," Griffin said, taking Michael by the hand. "But I would like to hurt him in the ways he likes right now. So unless you want to watch, scoot."

Griffin made the shooing gesture that had worked so well on Michael's father.

No one moved. Griffin glared at Nora.

"What?" she asked with feigned innocence. "We all want to watch."

26

Nora couldn't stop smiling. She took a sip of her white wine and set the glass back on the table. It tasted so good she wanted to chug the whole thing, but they were at The 8th Circle and the new bartender Kingsley had hired actually enforced the two-drink-maximum rule. Surely she and Søren would play later that night, so it was for the best she stay sober and alert. Søren had been acting strangely all night. He and Kingsley kept sneaking off to whisper to each other. It wasn't like either of them to keep her this out of the loop. But she trusted Søren. He'd tell her what was up when it was time. From across the room he glanced at her, and Nora smiled. He didn't smile back.

After a few minutes he made his way to her. She stood at the edge of the bar in the VIP section looking down on the horde below. Music pounded in the background, bodies writhed. She used to love to play in the pit at The Circle. Topping… subbing…didn't matter. Public kink was so humiliating, so primal. She'd experienced her worst agonies in the pit, had her strongest orgasms. But tonight, it seemed like another world to her—alien, foreign, distant.

"You're quiet tonight, little one," Søren said as he came to her and kissed her forehead.

"I'm fine, sir. My mind's been a lot of places lately."

"Has it been in Kentucky?"

Nora looked up at him sharply.

"Kentucky? No, it—"

"Eleanor." Søren covered her lips with one finger. "Tell me the truth or do not speak at all."

She nodded and he pulled his hand away.

"Yeah," she admitted. "Sometimes it wanders to Kentucky. But it always comes back here, comes back to you."

"I know it does. Being separated from you this summer… you should know I too felt my heart touched by someone else."

Nora's stomach tightened.

"That reporter was much hotter than she needed to be."

"And intelligent and damaged."

"Just your type. I'm glad she didn't, you know, get to you more than she did. Get to us. I was worried there for a while that she'd find out what we are. Things could have gotten ugly. But I guess that would have kept you from being bishop, right?"

"The fact I had a reporter digging into my past kept me from becoming bishop," Søren said, a little glint shining in his eyes. The glint told her all.

"Oh, you son of a bitch," Nora groaned. "You were the one who tipped her off, weren't you?"

"Kingsley, actually. Although it was my idea. I knew if I could tell the search committee that I had a tenacious reporter dogging my every step, they wouldn't risk making me bishop and the news of my donation to the diocese going public."

"You manipulative Machiavellian asshole, I love you." Nora burst into laughter. She should have known. She absolutely should have known Suzanne's presence in their lives had been Søren's idea all along.

"In my defense," Søren said without a hint of shame or contrition, "we did choose her because I knew I could help her."

"Yes, you're a saint. St. Søren the Bastard, Patron of Manipulation." She couldn't stop laughing. He really would do anything to protect them, to protect her.

"I'm still awaiting final approval on my canonization."

Nora rose up on her toes and kissed him.

"You can open the card now," Søren said into her lips.

"The card? Oh, the card." Nora remembered that infuriating note Søren had given her at the beginning of the summer. She'd resisted the temptation to open it for weeks. From behind the bar she grabbed her bag and dug through it. Pulling out the card, she tore it open and read the words written on it in Søren's elegant script.

You are formally invited to attend the collaring of Griffin Fiske and Michael Dimir.

Nora's jaw dropped. She looked at Søren and swatted his arm with the card.

"You knew?" Nora's eyes nearly fell out of her head.

"Of course I knew," Søren said. "I've known Griffin for years. I'm Michael's confessor. I knew they'd fall in love with each other. I knew it would be a good opportunity for Griffin to redeem himself. I'm quite happy for Michael. He needs someone as out and as effusive in his affection as Griffin."

"So you ordered Griffin to stay away from Michael because…?"

"We value the most what we must sacrifice to have. I never want Griffin taking Michael for granted. I don't think he ever will."

Nora looked at the card before tearing it into pieces and throwing it up in the air like confetti.

"I love you, you terrifyingly brilliant man." Nora threw her arms around Søren in what she thought would be a quick, playful hug. But Søren pulled her close and held her tight to him. So tight it almost scared her. He buried his face in her hair and inhaled.

"Søren? What's wrong?" she whispered. "You've been tense all night."

Søren's hand rested at her neck. She felt something, heard a click, and her white collar came off in Søren's hands. She looked down at the collar and up at Søren.

"Sir?" Nora's hands went numb. Her heart raced.

"I love you," he said. "I love you enough to take this from you for a little while. I love you enough to give you this in return."

He reached into his pocket and handed her a key with a white ribbon on it in place of a keychain. A white ribbon... the key to the White Room. She'd met Michael in that room last year and taken his virginity. Søren had given her this very key with the words *He's still a virgin... You can close your eyes and pretend it's...*

"Søren?"

"You came back to me after years apart. And it gave me such joy to have you again that I neglected to ask the most important question—why? Why did you come back to me? And were you coming to me? Or were you leaving someone else?"

"You know I was—"

"I saw your book. I saw the dedication."

Nora closed her eyes. She'd hoped Søren wouldn't notice that for the first time ever she'd dedicated a book to someone other than him.

"Many waters..." Søren said. "You still love him."

A tear fell from Nora's eye. She couldn't deny the words. But she didn't want to admit it, either.

"I love you too much to keep you against your will," Søren said. Nora looked up at him.

"Even if against my will is what I want?"

"Even then." The key felt warm on the palm of her hand. She stared at it and wondered. "Go. You know it's what you want."

Nora's fingers curled around the key. A well of hope sprung up in her heart. But she tamped it back down. No… she couldn't believe…could it be?

"I'll come back," she promised. "I'll always come back to you."

"I know," he said with cold, calm arrogance. "If I didn't believe that, I wouldn't let you go."

"Believe it. It's true." She took a step back. Then another. "Always."

"Eleanor, if you have any mercy in that dark heart of yours, when you leave right now, you will walk and not run."

She gave him a smile, a smile that told him everything she wanted to say but didn't have the words or the voice to say.

"I'd never run from you, remember? But I'll always run back."

Nora didn't kiss him or touch him anymore. If she did, she feared she wouldn't be able to stop. And she had to go, had to leave, had to see whoever waited for her behind the door of the White Room.

Turning around she walked with agonizing slowness to the door at the back of the bar. She opened the door and stepped across the threshold, shutting the door behind her.

Once alone, Nora stopped and looked down at her feet. She wore high heels. She always did these days at the club. Søren preferred them to the boots she'd always strapped on during her days as a dominatrix. More demure, high heels were. More ladylike. She could do anything in her heels if she had to. Anything but run, and she knew that was the real reason Søren made her wear them.

She kicked off her shoes and left them behind in the hall. And Nora didn't walk and she didn't crawl and she didn't fly.

She ran. Down the hall she ran as if the hounds of hell nipped at her heels. She ran as if God himself had ordered her to. She ran as if her life depended on it and in that moment she might have sworn that it did.

She didn't know why she ran. She didn't know who or what waited for her in the White Room. She only knew she had to get there as fast as she could and whoever it was, he was worth running to.

Nora's hand shook so hard when she finally reached the door to the White Room, she could barely get the key in the lock. But then it was in, and the door flew open, and she stopped running. She stopped running because for no reason, none that made sense, none that mattered, he was right there in front of her.

"Wesley..." she breathed, unable to take another step. But she didn't have to, because he was on his feet and running to her now, and he held her in his arms and she held him in hers, and she knew she'd never run again. Not from him anyway. Not from her Wesley.

"Nora...I missed you...so much..."

She pulled back to stare at him. Her Wesley—same boyishly handsome face, same big brown eyes that looked at her like he'd never seen anything like her before.

Nora took his face in her hands, still unable to really believe it was him, her Wes, right in front of her.

"My God, you need a haircut."

★ ★ ★ ★ ★